Sh ... to be…

H ... at Last

There's more than one reason to get married and it doesn't have to be for love…

Cindy Gerard** and **Shirley Rogers
welcome you to two wedding stories with a difference.

Dear Reader,

Welcome to Desire!

Kicking off this month we have **Taming Her Man**—two stories of irresistible, stubborn men, *The Taming of Jackson Cade*, a MEN OF BELLE TERRE book by BJ James, and Kristi Gold's *Cowboy for Keeps*.

There are two surprise 'packages' in store for the unsuspecting bachelors in Barbara McCauley's *Sinclair's Surprise Baby* and Kathie DeNosky's *His Baby Surprise*, coming to you in **Surprise Baby**. (Well, we couldn't call it anything else…)

Finally, in **His Bride at Last** Cindy Gerard's *The Bridal Arrangement* and *A Cowboy, a Bride & a Wedding Vow* by Shirley Rogers take us through the pitfalls and benefits of marriage to two handsome but proud hunks.

We hope you love them all!

The Editors

His Bride at Last

CINDY GERARD
SHIRLEY ROGERS

SILHOUETTE®
DESIRE™

All the characters in this book have no existence outside the imagination of the author, and have no relation whatsoever to anyone bearing the same name or names. They are not even distantly inspired by any individual known or unknown to the author, and all the incidents are pure invention.

First published in Great Britain 2002
Silhouette Books, Eton House, 18-24 Paradise Road, Richmond, Surrey TW9 1SR

ISBN 0 373 04762 2

51-0902

Printed and bound in Spain
by Litografia Rosés S.A., Barcelona

THE BRIDAL ARRANGEMENT

by
Cindy Gerard

CINDY GERARD

If asked, 'What's your idea of heaven?' Cindy Gerard would say a warm sun, a cool breeze, pan pizza and a good book. If she had to settle for one of the four, she'd opt for the book, with the pizza running a close second. Inspired by the pleasure she's received from the books she's read and her long-time love affair with her husband, Tom, Cindy now creates her own evocative and sensual love stories about compelling characters and complex relationships.

This number-one bestselling author of close to twenty books has received numerous industry awards, among them the National Readers' Choice Award, multiple *Romantic Times Magazine* nominations and two RITA Award nominations from the Romance Writers of America. Cindy loves to hear from her readers and invites them to visit her web page at www.TLT.com/authors/cgerard.httm

This book is dedicated to those who understand that courage is often silent and proud.

My thanks to Joan Marlow Golan for her vision and trust, to Carole Loveless for sharing and, as always, to Glenna McReynolds, for her brilliant insight, generosity and friendship.

One

Lee Savage felt like a man on a collision course with disaster. Guilt settled, heavy and solid as he climbed out of his pickup, thumbed back his Stetson and worked to ignore the sad condition of Shiloh Ranch. Even the dark tint of his sunglasses couldn't dim the ragged edges of neglect.

Every building and fence within eyesight needed painting or repair. A pair of black shutters, faded to a chalky gray, hung crookedly from a broken hinge on the second story of the house. And those were just surface blemishes. Still, it all registered on a peripheral level as he climbed the front porch steps and a rotted floorboard creaked beneath his booted foot.

With a resolute set of his jaw, he squared his shoulders and shut out everything but the job he'd come to do. He raised his hand, made a fist and knocked on the door of the only real home he'd ever known.

Only moments passed before small, delicate fingers brushed aside an age-yellowed lace curtain and a pair of soft violet eyes peered out at him from behind the wavy windowpane.

He knew those eyes, but he knew them as a child's eyes. At nineteen, it seemed that Ellie Shiloh was hardly more than a child now. Yet, as the door flew open and she slipped outside, he recognized both an ageless knowledge and an endless innocence in their sparkling, velvet depths.

Involuntarily he felt his mouth soften with tenderness as she tugged the door shut behind her. The scent of cinnamon and vanilla and a sweetly musky fragrance he couldn't quite identify wafted lightly in her wake, stirring rich reminders of home—along with unsettling twinges of awareness.

''Hello, Ellie,'' he managed in a rusty voice, swamped by memories of sugar cookies cooling on a baking rack, stunned by more immediate sensory impressions of silken skin and sensual, probing eyes—eyes completing a smile that was too huge and too hopeful and unreasonably happy under the circumstances.

''Mornin', Lee.'' Her voice was as pure and perfect as the Montana air. ''And what a fine morning.''

Tugging the belt of her fussy pink robe tighter around her tiny waist, she tipped her face toward the golden glow of the horizon. She drew in a deep, pleasured breath, then tilted her head, giving him a playful, assessing once-over. ''A little early for someone of your advanced years to be up and around, though, isn't it?''

She was messing with him. He'd been eighteen when he'd left Shiloh, and he'd rarely made it back in the fifteen years since. When he had, she'd always liked to tease him about being older and wiser…practically ancient in the face of her youth. Not only couldn't he smile at her gentle barb as he once might have, it took effort to keep from cringing. He notched his chin instead and stared past a truth he couldn't ignore—and beyond an unnerving notion that the laughter bubbling in her eyes was prodded as much by blissful ignorance as it was by mischief.

She had no idea. No idea at all, what she was getting in to. The fact that she found humor instead of uncertainty in the situation proved it—though it didn't change what had to be done.

He tugged off his sunglasses, folded them into the breast pocket of his shirt and transferred his attention toward his polished boot tips, only to be thrown off balance again. Damn if his heart didn't catch—just a little half hitch—at the sight of the tiny pink toes peeking out from beneath her floor-length flowing robe.

He cleared his throat. Got down to business. "So. The fourteenth will work out for you, then?"

He could sense the softness of her gaze even before he lifted his head, struggling with his bad feelings about all of this.

Her nod was quick and certain. "Oh, yes, the fourteenth is perfect. I've ordered sunshine. And a sweet breeze. It only seems right, don't you think?"

He studied her gamine features—the saucily turned-up nose, delicately winged brows, tiny fairy ears partially hidden beneath a silken fall of riotously tangled copper and gold curls that tumbled midway down her back. She looked as though she ought to be running barefoot through a sun-dappled forest, flower petals woven in her hair, hummingbirds and butterflies flitting around her head as she conjured up her sunshine and her sweet breezes.

"Would that be all right, Lee?" he heard her ask and knew he'd been so immersed in the daydream the sight of her invoked that he must have missed something.

He shook his head, glanced toward the porch overhang where the spring breeze set a glass and copper wind chime singing. On a deep breath, he met her eyes again. "I'm sorry, Ellie. Would what be all right?"

Her small hand reached out, touched his arm with gentle care, as if she was suddenly in charge of looking out for him—him, who, at six foot two and 210, towered over her by a full foot and outweighed her by a good hundred pounds.

"Are you okay?" Her too-perfect brows were knit together in studied concern.

"I'm fine," he grumbled abruptly, then made a concentrated effort to relax as he pulled away from the warm, tingling sensation that flowed along his arm where her fingers had lingered with the lightness of air.

Forcing a patience that neither fitted his dark mood nor eased his tension, he softened his tone. "I'm fine, Ellie. Now what was it that you asked me?"

"The church?" That beatific smile lit her face again. "I'd like for it to be in the church, if it...if it isn't too much trouble."

Her voice was as soft as meadow grass. Like her eyes. Like her sweet, curvy little body bundled in that fussy pink robe that he had no business thinking about. That he hadn't stopped thinking about since she'd breezed out into the morning to compete with the spring sunshine.

He made himself concentrate. She wanted a church. It was the first direct request she'd voiced since this whole sorry business started.

He gave her a clipped nod and bucked a sudden and unreasonable need to call the whole thing off. "Not a problem," he said instead, because he really had no choice. "I'll take care of it."

He didn't want to catalog the effect of yet another one of her radiant smiles. He didn't want to acknowledge how innocent, how trusting she looked. How unrelentingly bewitching.

Bewitching. Well. There was someplace he definitely didn't need to go. What he had to think about was duty. His. And a debt owed. A debt he had every intention of repaying as soon as he tidied up some unfinished business back in Texas.

"If you're sure you'll be okay, I'll be taking off then. I'll see you in two weeks."

He hadn't meant to sound so stiff and formal, but there it was, and there was nothing to be done for it now. He turned his back on those velvet eyes that pinned him with so much hope. Hope, when in fact, the situation seemed pretty hopeless at this point. Nothing to be done for that, either. Not at this late date.

He dug out his sunglasses, slipped them on and headed for his truck. He stopped abruptly, squinted against the burning ball of the morning sun and cupped the back of his neck where he swore he felt a sudden and soothing sensation of a caress.

She was watching him. He knew it. Just like he

knew it was a bad idea to turn around. He did it, anyway.

She'd walked to the edge of the porch. The bare toes of those impossibly tiny feet were curled against the morning chill; one arm hugged a porch post. With a china-doll cheek pressed against the peeling wood, she smiled with a shimmering expectancy that made his mouth go dry.

He drew in a bracing breath. "Everything's going to be fine, okay?"

She nodded, her eyes trying to make him believe it. The best thing for both of them was that he did. He didn't like the idea of leaving her on her own—even though he'd arranged for the neighbors to look in on her—and even if it was only for a couple of weeks while he tidied up those loose ends.

"I'll pick you up around ten on the fourteenth then," he croaked around the lump that had somehow found its way to his throat.

"Ten would be wonderful. Ten would be superb!" Her smile was far too buoyant for her to have yet grasped how drastically her life was about to change. "If...if it's not too much bother, that is," she added quietly.

Not too much bother? If the situation weren't dead serious, he'd laugh out loud. Hell. Picking her up and taking her to town was the least of the things that was bothering him.

For her sake he forced the requisite response. "You call now if you need anything. You've got my number, right?"

When she nodded, he headed back down the path toward his truck.

"Lee."

It took a long stride for him to stop, stiffen, react too strongly to the sound of his name on her petal-soft voice. He turned slowly—and found her shy smile touching.

"Thank you." A wealth of pride and far too much happiness colored her appreciation.

He merely nodded, knowing she was thanking him today for what would happen in two weeks that would change both of their lives forever.

In a church, he reminded himself when the sinking sensation that *he* was about to make the biggest mistake of *her* life, coupled with the realization that he still needed to pick up a wedding ring.

Ellie stood in the sun-drenched light of her east bedroom window. Excitement bubbled just beneath her skin like water dancing along a pebble-strewn brook.

She hugged her arms to her chest, bursting with feelings too big to contain. It was her wedding day. It was the day her oldest, most cherished dream was coming true.

Outside her window birdsong floated on a crisp breeze, a joyous harbinger of what was about to happen. In less than an hour Lee would be here.

He'd called her last night from the Sundown Hotel where he'd spent the night. She'd nearly melted at the sound of his voice. And she'd pictured him there—lying on the bed, his long legs crossed at the ankles, that deep frown that she found both endearing and sad creasing his brows. His dark hair would be a little mussed, his blue eyes would be crinkled with concern, with worry, and with the fatigue of his long drive from Houston—and, she hoped, with a little of the sweet anticipation she was feeling.

"And he's on his way to pick you up this very minute," she reminded herself, and felt another fluttering ripple of excitement.

She wanted to be ready. She wanted to be perfect for this perfect man that she had adored from the moment she could say his name.

She'd hurried through her morning chores—feeding the horses, gathering eggs—then given in to the luxury of a long, soaking bubble bath. And now she would get ready for her bridegroom.

Heart racing, she flew back to the full-length pedestal mirror in the corner of the room—the room she would soon share with Lee as his wife.

A flush crept from her checks to her throat and spread downward to stain the gentle round of her breasts revealed above the lacy white cups of the exquisite bra that had arrived just yesterday in the mail. She touched her fingers to sheer silk and delicate lace, blushed anew at the way her nipples hardened and pressed against the gossamer fabric.

Was she big enough to please him, she wondered with a critical frown and a tilt of her head as she turned sideways and studied her reflection in the beveled cheval mirror encased in ornately carved oak? A long, assessing look took in the matching lacy panties and thigh-high white hose that barely covered the rest of her. Was she pretty enough? Would the cobalt-blue of his piercing, thick-lashed eyes darken with desire when he saw her this way? Would his skin get all warm and tingly and his long, strong body go weak with yearning the way hers did at the mere thought of seeing him?

Or would he be disappointed?

Would she be less than he expected…or needed…or preferred?

Gaze fixed critically on her reflection, she saw a slim, slight woman with pale skin, average-size breasts and a long tumble of copper-colored hair that she'd had marginal success taming into a complicated tangle of curls on top of her head.

"It's your crowning glory, princess," her momma used to say when they would sit together in the pale evening light and Ellie had groused about the thick, unruly mass of it.

From the time she'd been a little girl, she had loved it when her mother had brushed her hair. The long steady strokes soothing her, lulling her into believing in fairy tales and happily-ever-afters.

"Someday a handsome prince will come and make me his princess, just like Sleeping Beauty, right, Momma?"

"Right, princess," her momma would agree, but with such a sad and guarded smile that Ellie had known her momma had thought there would be more frogs in her future than princes.

"Well, he came, Momma," she whispered to the empty room as the familiar ache of loss edged in to undercut her joy. "My prince came. I wish you could be here. I wish you and Daddy could be with us today."

Three years her mother had been gone. Time had eased the grief but not the sense of emptiness that had been compounded when her father died a month ago in March—and for the first time in her life, Ellie had been alone.

Turning away from the mirror and the melancholy

that threatened to overtake her, she thought, instead, of the man who would come for her in less than an hour—and she knew she wouldn't be alone any longer.

She walked to the closet and the carefully preserved wedding gown that awaited her. It was a dress made for a princess. Antique lace and virginal white satin hung in luxurious folds from a padded hanger. On the floor beneath the dress, age-softened slippers of the same pristine, shining fabric lay waiting.

"How pretty you must have looked in this dress, Momma," she murmured, and taking great care slipped it from the hanger. "How Daddy must have loved you."

Just as Lee would grow to love her.

She knew that he would. In time. Once he got to know her better. Once he understood that she was a woman, not a child. Once she showed him what she had learned from her parents about love.

And once she proved to him that she could be more than an obligation—which, she understood, was all she was to him right now.

Disappointed in that knowledge, but not defeated, she eased the dress over her head. She could make him love her. Even if she wasn't perfect.

Her gaze flashed quickly away from the mirror as she reached behind her back to fasten the many satin-covered buttons on the gown. No, she wasn't perfect, but she wasn't going to think about that. She wasn't going to let it interfere with her wedding day.

A twinge of guilt, the same one that had been niggling since Lee had explained why he was marrying her, suggested that she *should* think about it. Lee really didn't understand what he was getting into. She should have talked to him about it. But, since it was something that had never been talked about in this house, she didn't even know how to start.

In her entire life, she couldn't remember her parents ever saying the word. Doc Lundstrum had been the one to fill in the blanks for her. He'd been the one to put a name to the force that caused her to lose herself, to lose time, to lose memories and, it seemed, lose the right to live a normal life.

Epilepsy.

She closed her eyes. Swallowed.

No. It wasn't a word that had ever been spoken in this house. And it wasn't something that was easy to talk about with your prospective husband.

Yet, shouldn't he be armed with enough information to decide if he really wanted to go through with this?

He knows.

"He knows," she said aloud this time, working to convince herself as she reached for the fingertip veil crowned in baby's breath and white satin ribbon and allowed fear to trample over the guilt. Fear, prompted by an uncharacteristic selfishness and a buoyant hope, outdistanced the guilt and abetted her conviction.

"But *what* does he know?" she asked point-blank to the woman in the mirror. "What does he really know?"

Only what her momma had let him or anyone else know.

"Don't worry princess. No one saw anything."

"Saw what, Momma? What happened? What did I do?"

The answers had always been the same.

"It was just a little dream, baby. That's all that

happened. You just had a little dream and now you need to rest.''

She had no memories of life without the threat of seizures, just like she had no memory of what happened to her during one. She remembered only the aftermath, countless incidents of waking up in her bed, or other places, and the humiliation of not knowing how she had gotten there coupled with the headaches that followed and kept her down, sometimes for hours, sometimes for days.

The rush of frustration—of being totally out of control, totally vulnerable to the disease, of a loss of time and self that sometimes gave her nightmares—was far too familiar. She fought it back and settled the veil on her head.

And then she justified. Maybe it was best for now that Lee didn't know what to expect. She'd been four years old when he'd left Shiloh and Sundown, Montana, for college in Texas. As the years passed and he'd made those rare but treasured visits home, he'd never actually witnessed a seizure—at least she wasn't aware that he had. If he found out the whole of it before he got to know her for who she was...well. He'd get that look in his eye. The one she'd seen so many times before from others. The one that spoke of wariness and pity, or worse, ridicule and rejection. She would lose him before she ever had the chance to love him.

From downstairs, the grandfather clock in the hall chimed the quarter hour. Her stomach did a little flip-flop as she sat down at her dressing table and reached for a new tube of lipstick.

Less than an hour.

A lifetime of waiting and he'd be here in less than an hour.

That's all she had to think about today. Not the epilepsy, not the fact that her momma couldn't be with her, not the fact that her daddy couldn't give her away.

She brought the creamy, rose-colored gloss to her lips, surprised to see how violently her hand was shaking.

It's just nerves, she told herself, and frowned as the chimes sounded again.

She didn't think about reaching for a tissue so she was puzzled as, with a disconnected sort of awareness, she watched the unsteady motion of her hand lift one from the box and touch it to the light sheen of perspiration that had broken out across her brow.

And then she flinched when the chimes sounded again. Louder this time. Then again. Louder still.

Nausea rolled through her stomach in a heavy, arching wave.

"Why don't they stop?" she whispered, courting a shifting confusion she couldn't identify, fighting a creeping, disassembled anxiety that seemed to seep into her body from the outside in.

She tried to laugh at her bridal jitters but ended up closing her eyes to steady herself instead. When she opened them and met them in the tri-fold mirror, fear mushroomed and grew. She tried desperately to deny what she saw. A slight dilation of her pupils. A glassy mist covering eyes that looked vacant and unfocused.

She slowly looked away, and on a level she couldn't quite comprehend, watched the pretty silver tube of lipstick slip and, in slow motion, tumble end over end from her suddenly rigid fingers. It fell to her dressing table with a sharp, deafening clatter, then rolled to the sound of thunder before dropping with a booming crash to the floor.

The noise was piercing. The serrated, insistent clamor of the chimes got louder and louder until she clapped her hands to her ears and whimpered at the stab of pain the sound shot through her head.

"Oh, please," she pleaded, as the part of her brain that clung precariously to cognizant thought sounded the alert and she suddenly understood what was happening.

Seizure.

"No...oh, please, no. Not now. Not today."

But even as she prayed to a god that for whatever reason chose not to answer, a too-familiar metallic taste flowed into her mouth and she knew she was powerless against it. As she had always been powerless against it.

On shaking legs she rose to her feet just as the walls began a surreal dance that made them shrink, then swell, then close around her like a vise. She stumbled across the room, groping for the tall corner post on her four-poster bed, then gripped it with a soft cry as the noise exploded like crystal shattering against steel.

She clung to the bedpost, but her strength, like her hope, deserted her. On a level that was once distant and oh, so near, she felt the smooth, spindled wood slip through her hands like water, slide like cool rain against her cheek as she sank to the floor in a pool of white satin and crumpled lace.

A tear trailed down her temple and trickled into her hair as she lay back, stared at the ceiling and gave in to the void…defeated, defenseless, completely vulnerable in the darkness that took her.

The beauty of the day and the joy of her anticipation—gone. Her sense of self and time and hope—lost, just like her awareness of the moments that passed, of the actions of her busy hands that flitted clumsily to her throat to button buttons that did not exist, then button them all over again.

The childlike whisper that echoed through the empty room was hers. She didn't hear it. No one heard it.

No one heard the haunting loneliness, the tortured helplessness of the words she chanted over and over and over. "I'm sorry. I'm sorry. I'm sorry…."

Two

Four major rivers and at least a dozen minor tributaries snaked across the cracked plaster ceiling in room number six of Sundown, Montana's ancient and only hotel. Lee knew, because he'd been awake half the night staring at them. Staring and thinking and wishing there was a better way.

At 9:15 the next morning he still hadn't come up with one. So he'd dressed in his black suit and tie, stowed his luggage and the few belongings he'd brought with him from Houston in the back of his truck and he'd headed for Shiloh. And his bride.

A half an hour later, as he made the final turn up the narrow, rutted lane to Shiloh, a stray, two-week-old memory entered and softly settled.

I've ordered sunshine.

Despite everything that was wrong about what he was doing, one corner of his mouth edged up in a tight smile. It looked like Ellie was going to get her order filled on her wedding day.

Golden sunlight flickered through the budding aspen and shimmering evergreens flanking the high meadows, spreading warmth and the promise of summer over the slowly greening range, and gilding the vista of snow-capped peaks in the distance.

Easing back on the gas, Lee thought about the first time he'd made this trip up the mountain. He'd been ten years old. Ten going on fifty. He'd been angry, distrustful and so needy and full of fear that his gut still tightened at the memory.

Will and Clare Shiloh had changed all that. They'd saved him from the mean back streets of Denver. They'd brought him to Sundown. More specifically, they'd brought him to Shiloh Ranch. Twenty-three years later it had been Will who had brought him home again.

For what seemed like the hundredth time, he went over the string of events that had brought him back to the mountain. It always replayed the same—just like his conversation with his boss, Curt Tompkins.

"Is it more money you need, Lee? Hell, we can work something out. I don't want to lose you. And I can't believe you really want to leave Houston for some little inkspot of a town in Podunk, Montana."

Lee had hated letting Curt down. He'd been the manager of Curt's corporate spread for eight of the past ten years.

"Dave knows the ropes," Lee had said. "He'd be the one I'd look toward to take over. He can step in without missing a beat."

Curt had just shaken his head. "I don't get it."

And he never would, Lee had realized, so he'd simply stated the bottom line. "I owe Will Shiloh my life. Now I'm going to pay my debt."

He tipped his sunglasses up to the top of his head and squinted against the glare of sun bouncing off the truck's black hood. Yeah. He would pay his debt. Trouble was, Ellie was going to pay, too. It didn't help his conscience any to know that she was too young and too naive to realize what this little arrangement was going to cost her.

He knew though. Just like he knew that no amount of justifying could pit duty against guilt and balance the scales—or minimize his disappointment that Shiloh had come with strings attached.

He looked around him at everything that would officially become his in a little less than an hour. At one time owning Shiloh would have been an unreachable dream. He let go of a grim snort. "And look at me now."

He was a long way from where he'd come from. He'd like to think he was more than the boy who had cut his teeth on the bad side of the tracks. He hadn't understood it then. He hadn't cared that he'd been shuffled through an understaffed and inadequate social system by the time the Shilohs had found him. What he'd understood was hostility. What he'd understood was abuse. That had been life.

As young as he'd been, he'd known way too much about hunger. Way too much about pain. Most of all, he'd known about loss. He'd known it like a stray dog knew the hollow ache of an empty belly. And he'd known it every day of his life until Will and Clare had taken him in. Because they were kind people. And because, in their late forties, they had given up on having children of their own.

He let the truck roll to a stop at the top of the rise, eased it into park and thought about everything they had offered him—mountain wilderness, patience, hard work and endless understanding. In return he'd given them ten kinds of grief that first year. No matter what he'd done they hadn't sent him away.

"Run all you want, boy," Will had told him one midnight when he'd tracked him down near Butte. "Do your worst. You will always have a home here."

Significant. For the first time in his life he considered that he might actually be significant until, finally, he'd begun to believe that to Will and Clare, at least, he was.

Propping an elbow on the open window frame, he worried an index finger over his upper lip and stared at the house just the other side of the rise. The house where he'd known love. The house where the woman—barely a woman—waited to become his bride.

Ellie. Ellie, who he remembered as a sweet, laughing toddler. Then a shy little girl with a big bad crush on him with her guileless eyes and endless smiles. Ellie who was never supposed to be.

He remembered every moment of the day Clare had nearly died giving birth to the child she and Will had given up on the idea of ever having. He'd been fourteen—and he'd wanted to hate the wrinkled, mewling little thing that had almost killed Clare and had shaken the only firm turf he'd ever stood on. But from the first moment of her pretty pink little life, Ellie Shiloh had enchanted anyone who set eyes on her—Lee had been no exception.

Will and Clare had been amazed by her. They had sheltered this special gift that had brought a dawn sunshine into their twilight lives, moved heaven and earth to ensure that nothing would ever happen to the miracle that life had previously denied them.

It had been subtle and no way intentional, but Lee had felt the shift just the same. He was on the outside of the candy store looking in again. It had been a wake-up call. A reminder that as much stock as he placed in the Shilohs' love, he could only count on himself for the long haul. He'd also understood the deeper significance—Ellie had been born a Shiloh, and for as much as Will and Clare had given him, they had never offered him their name.

And it was only at times like these, he thought grimly—when he thought too much, brooded too much—that he let that lone fact bother him.

He drew in a deep breath of the fresh, mountain morning, adjusted his necktie, smoothed a hand down the lapels of his suit coat. And sat there, a million memories both drawing him to and keeping him from driving that final stretch into the valley.

Ellie had just had her fourth birthday when he'd gone off to college on a rodeo scholarship. She'd been eight, when at twenty-two, he'd received his degree in business management, sixteen when he'd come back to Sundown to mourn the death of the only mother he'd ever known.

And now Will was gone, too. Grief pressed down, cold and heavy. He flexed his fingers around the leather-wrapped steering wheel. It was just a month ago that Will had called him home. Just three weeks since he'd lay dying and extracted a promise Lee would give his own life to keep.

"You know she's special, our Ellie," Will had whispered as he lay in his hospital bed, shrunken and frail, the droning beep of the monitors seeming to ration out each heartbeat. "She's not strong like most folks, Lee. She's...delicate. She needs you, boy. And I need you to make sure nothing and no one ever hurts her or takes what we worked all our lives to preserve for her."

Delicate. That had been the word Clare and Will had always used in regard to Ellie's condition. On a gut-deep level, Lee had known that *delicate* didn't even begin to cover it. Admittedly, he didn't know what he should about her epilepsy. He'd never wanted to know. He wasn't very proud of that fact, but Clare and Will had never volunteered information, and frankly, that had been just fine with him. Hell. When the seizures had started, he'd been a kid himself. It was the best excuse he could come up with.

Honest truth? It scared him, what happened to her. It scared him for her. It scared him because he'd felt helpless...and excluded.

"Fever," Clare would say when a seizure would grab her, then she'd shoo him quickly out of the room. "Just a fever. Little ones have 'em all the time. She'll grow out of it."

Only she hadn't grown out of it. And he hadn't been around to see what happened to her. Once he'd made the break from Shiloh, he hadn't come home often and he'd kept the visits brief. It became easy—convenient—not to wonder or worry or feel guilty because it was happening to her and not him and that he still couldn't do anything to help.

Well. Now he was back. And now...now he would take care of her. He'd promised Will.

He hadn't thought once about saying no to Will's dying request to take over Shiloh Ranch. And, yeah, he'd figured that Ellie would come with the package—just not quite the way Will had in mind.

He'd been stunned when Will had asked the unthinkable.

"You're the only one I trust with her, son. You're the only one I can count on to do right by her."

Lee would have bled and died for Will Shiloh. For the giving man who had loved him without qualification, who had made him the man he was today. The man who was about to marry Will's pride and joy—because Will had asked him to.

He shifted in the seat, watched a curtain in a second-story window part, then fall back into place. It was going to happen. As sure as the sun came up it was going to set tonight with Ellie as his wife. He'd left the life he'd built in Texas, the friends, the women who had been a part of it.

"And you've sat here too damn long telling yourself you're doing Ellie wrong, when the fact is we're both getting everything we want," he muttered aloud, as if hearing it would make it all right.

Ellie wanted him—at least she thought she did. He wanted Shiloh, the place that had been in his blood, in his head, in his heart since the first day he'd set foot on the mountain. And Will had been right about one thing. Ellie did need someone to take care of her. It had just as well be him.

He slid his sunglasses back in place, eased the truck into gear and rolled down the last stretch home.

Home.

Where his child bride waited with trusting eyes and a hopelessly romantic soul.

Ellie was slow to answer his knock. When she finally opened the door, Lee was stunned all over again by the fragility of her beauty.

For a long moment he didn't speak—wasn't sure that he could. He just stood there, luggage in hand, flooded with foolish notions of fairy-tale princesses in shimmering satin and huge, enchanting eyes. And he wondered what the hell he was getting himself and her into.

She looked as if she'd just been kissed awake and the blush hadn't yet found its way to her pale cheeks. Beneath a delicate wreath of tiny white flowers and a shoulder-length veil, her red gold curls tumbled in an untidy fall from the top of her head, whispered in feathery ringlets along the porcelain column of her throat.

Those brilliant violet eyes were a misty shade of lavender and, he realized in a startling moment of alarm, as pale as the ashen pallor of her face—a pallor that he recognized came from pain.

"Ellie?" He set down his luggage and quickly went to her. "Are you okay?"

Her nod was slow in coming, her smile forced and breakable. Both lacked her usual exuberance. "I-I'll just get my wrap."

Her movements were calculated and careful as she reached for a shimmering white shawl of intricate lace and trailing fringe that was touchingly old-fashioned. Without asking, he took it from her unsteady hands, placed it carefully around her—too aware of the contrast of his big, work-roughened hands cupping her delicate shoulders. Acutely aware of her trembling.

He closed his eyes, let out a deep breath and accepted what was happening here. She wasn't well.

"Ellie," he said gently. "If you're not up to this—"

"I'm…fine," she insisted but without much strength in her words. "Really," she repeated, reacting to the frown of concern he knew was darkening his face.

She wasn't fine. That much was obvious. But this was new ground for him—as was the possibility that something other than illness could be responsible for that feverish look in her eyes. Maybe the reality of what was about to happen was finally hitting her. Maybe his virgin bride was simply scared to death.

And why the hell wouldn't she be? He hadn't exactly played the part of the love-struck bridegroom. Because he wasn't. And never would be. It didn't mean that he couldn't be kind, and it didn't mean that he didn't care about her. It was past time he gave her at least that much.

He smoothed a hand down her veil. "You know, we don't have to do this today. If you need more time to get used to the idea—"

"I don't…need time," she whispered, her speech uncharacteristically slow, her head down, her small hands clutched tightly together as if she had to concentrate to get the words out. "I've waited for you…all my life. I don't want to wait any longer."

The guilelessness of her admission both humbled and angered him. She deserved better than this. She deserved a white knight to sweep her away to a gilded castle in an enchanted forest. Instead, she was getting him. Her head was filled with illusions about who and what he was.

Well, he knew exactly what he was…and what he wasn't. He'd never been and would never be Lancelot material. And he would never be the man she needed him to be.

Still, this was going to happen, even though she was a total innocent—something he didn't think he'd ever been. It didn't mean, however, that he didn't have enough compassion to know she needed time.

"Ellie, there's no shame in admitting that you're…uneasy about this." He ran his hands in a gentle caress down her arms to cup her elbows.

She raised her head, her eyes beseeching. "No. Not uneasy. Excited." She smiled again, tragic and trembling. "I'm just excited."

When he shook his head, damned if she didn't try to put him at ease. "It will be all right, Lee. I'll make you happy. I promise I'll make you happy."

For a long moment he simply searched those glittering eyes that gazed up at him with such faith. He knew then that even though he couldn't give her what she wanted, he could at least give her something she needed. Whatever it took, he would earn her trust and her father's. Starting right now.

He touched his fingers to her cheek, smiled. "Let's go do this, princess. We can't let your sunshine go to waste now, can we?"

Tears glistened, at once hopeful and weary and achingly vulnerable. "No. We can't let it go to waste."

She smiled then, and a foreign and flooding warmth filled his chest. "You look beautiful, Ellie."

"So do you," she exclaimed breathlessly.

Against all odds he laughed and, prompted by instincts that mandated chivalry and grand gestures, tucked her small hand in the crook of his elbow.

"Well, now that we've got that established, your chariot awaits, m'lady."

Then he walked her to his truck and tried to ignore the unsteadiness of her gait and the unsettling notion that a thief other than anxiety had stolen the sparkle from her eyes.

For Ellie the wedding ceremony drifted by on a murky mist of excruciating pain. It was always like that after a seizure. The aftermath was a headache and a bone-deep exhaustion that often sent her to her bed for one or two days. She hated the helplessness, hated that it dictated how she could live her life.

Not today. She was not going to let it beat her today. She stood at Lee's side by sheer force of will, fighting to absorb it all, to stay on her feet, to feel the beat of her heart that assured her this was real. That she was here. She was with Lee, bathed in the blinding cylinders of sunlight refracting through the stained-glass window behind the altar. Smelling the sweet scent of the flowers he had thoughtfully placed in her hands. Watching the teary smiles of Martha Good, the pastor's wife, who stood as witness. Saying the vows she had waited her lifetime to repeat.

"By the power vested in me—" Pastor Good's lyrical voice reached through the fog and captured her full attention "—I pronounce you man and wife."

With every thread of strength in her, she fought to hold on to the day that would mark the beginning of the life she had always wanted.

"You may now kiss the bride."

She swallowed thickly, focused on Pastor Good's warm, encouraging eyes, then turned toward Lee. A gentle smile played on his beautiful mouth as he folded her in a loose embrace.

She tipped her face to his, wanting to draw it all inside—the moment, the magic, the feel of the plain gold band warming on the ring finger of her left hand and binding them together as man and wife. The burning heat in his eyes as he searched her face and drew her slowly toward him.

She fought the pain, battled to keep and cherish this moment forever. Their first kiss as husband and wife. *Their first kiss.*

She lost herself in the searching blue of his eyes, the promise of his breath, warm and mint scented against her cheek. They were so kind, those eyes, but it wasn't only kindness that she wanted from this man. She wanted always and forever. She wanted the magic that bubbled just below the surface every time she saw him. The thrill that raced along her nerve endings when he smiled. When he touched her. As he was touching her now.

As the pain touched her now.

She struggled to outdistance it. Willed away the crush of fatigue and thought only of him, of his lips brushing across hers, soft as a dream yet firm, commanding yet gentle. It was everything she'd imagined, many things she hadn't. She melted into the warmth of his mouth, loving the scent of him, the heat of him, the power inherent in his big body, the tender caress of his hands.

But, despite the magic, despite the defiance with which she clung to the moment, she finally accepted that this was a battle she could not win, a victory she could never lay claim to.

For the second time that day her body betrayed her.

That above all else she would remember about her wedding day as her world went black and she collapsed in her husband's arms.

"Ellie. Ellie-girl, it's time for you to join us again, honey."

She came around slowly. Struggled until she placed a face to the kind older voice. "Doc?"

"That's right, kiddo. Now open those pretty eyes for me so this wild man standing over my shoulder will know you're all right. There you go. That's the girl."

Even though the only light in the examining room spilled softly from the hallway of Dr. Lundstrum's office, pain exploded in her head when she opened her eyes. Pain, and a dawning realization of where she was, and where she wasn't. She wasn't at the church. She wasn't alone with her husband sharing the romantic picnic she had planned.

The physical discomfort suddenly paled in comparison to the pain in her heart. She flung an arm over her face to block the light and hide from the humiliation.

Doc's voice floated over the top of it all. "I want to give you something to take the edge off, Ellie."

"No," she whispered, defiance threaded with defeat. "No. It will make me sleep. I don't want to sleep. Not today."

A soft, affectionate chuckle followed a reassuring pat on her arm. "Now's not the time to be stubborn, little one. If we cut it today, you'll be up and around tomorrow. Otherwise, you know it could be another day or two before you're feeling better. *You* might be able to take it, but frankly, I don't think your bridegroom can.''

Bridegroom. A hot tear welled up then spilled from the corner of her eye, trailed down her temple and got lost in the thickness of her hair. She hadn't wanted Lee to see her like this. Not today. Not ever.

''Ellie, please.'' Lee's voice was gruff with worry, softly pleading. ''Let Doc give you something.''

She squeezed back another tear, shamed and helpless to deny him. ''Okay.''

Doc touched her arm lightly. ''Good girl. I want to examine you first, Ellie, just to make sure I know what we're dealing with here, then we'll take the hammer out of that headache.''

''She just fainted, right, Doc?'' Lee demanded in a hoarse and urgent whisper.

In the silence that followed, Ellie sensed Dr. Lundstrum's speculative frown. She opened her eyes, saw the questions in the pale-gray eyes behind smudged bifocal lenses, and the furrows above his bushy white brows. She gave a small, pleading shake of her head.

Doc cleared his throat, let out a deep breath. He patted his blunt-fingered hand on the round belly that his sweet tooth had netted him over the years of enjoying his wife's blue ribbon pies and smiled kindly at Lee. ''Why don't you wait outside for a minute? Let me look your lady over. Then the two of you can go home.''

Ellie watched Lee's eyes darken as he scowled from Doc to her. With grim reluctance he finally nodded, then left the room when Doc deliberately walked him to the door. She heard his footsteps echo down the hall as Doc turned back to her.

"I'm going to have to turn on the light now. I'm sorry."

She closed her eyes to the blinding glare as he flipped the switch, then shut the door behind him.

The minute they were alone she asked the question that had haunted her since she'd come to on the examining table. "Did I...did I—"

"You fainted, kiddo," Doc assured her as he lifted her limp wrist to check her pulse. His smile was gentle and indulgent. "You just fainted. Just like a blushing bride—or like someone who might be recovering from a seizure?" he suggested, then waited patiently while her silence confirmed his suspicion.

"Was it a bad one, Ellie?"

She started to shake her head. The pain slammed back full force. "No. No worse than usual."

"Long?" he prompted as he wet a cloth with cold water, laid it gently over her eyes, then reached for a blood pressure cuff.

"Two...three minutes, close as I can figure. I...I was getting ready for my wedding. I...I thought I could recover. I thought I could put it behind me...get through the ceremony and...and no one would... know."

Doc didn't say a word. He just rhythmically pumped the bulb, then watched the gauge with a practiced eye. He didn't have to say anything. He was thinking the same thing that she was. Physically it was the recovery time after a seizure that was the hardest to handle—at least it was for Ellie. The overwhelming fatigue, the unsettling sense of disorientation, the blinding headache took a toll. It had been beyond foolish to hope she could hide the residual effects from anyone. Foolish, but it hadn't stopped her from wanting to be whole for her wedding day.

With an unrevealing look, Doc removed the cuff, folded it into its sleeve on the wall and reached for a thermometer.

He squinted behind his glasses, then inserted the thermometer gently in her ear. "Have you been feeling okay otherwise?"

"Yes," she murmured, then restated, "Yes," when he leveled her a pointed look.

"Taking your meds on schedule?"

She frowned, gave a small nod, then flinched when the thermometer beeped and he checked her temp. "I hate them."

"I know." With one hand on her shoulder and one on her back, he helped her to sit up. He warmed the stethoscope in his palm, waited for her to steady herself then listened to her chest sounds.

She remained quiet throughout the rest of examination, holding the cold cloth to her eyes, knowing what was coming, ashamed of the answers she must give him.

He helped her lay back down then turned to prepare the hypodermic needle.

"This is going to bite a bit now," he soothed, swabbing alcohol on her arm. "Probably not as much as the bite your young man wanted to take out of my hide when I shooed him out of here."

She swallowed, waited.

"Lee's been gone from Sundown and Shiloh Ranch, oh, for quite a spell now, hasn't he?"

She held a breath, let it out and anticipated the questions she knew would follow.

"He does know about your epilepsy, doesn't he, Ellie?"

Another silence. "Sort of."

"Ellie—"

"I know," she preempted his gently scolding tone. "I know I should have talked to him. I know I should have let him know exactly what he was getting into. I...I just didn't want it to be today. I wanted today. I...needed today."

Doc set the syringe aside then covered the small puncture with a cotton ball and a strip of surgical tape. "He should know the details so he'll know what to expect." Folding her hand in his, he squeezed gently. "So he'll know how to react."

She couldn't stop the tears then. "Why does this...have to be a part of me?" Years of hurt and anger and a self-pity that she rarely gave in to spilled out in a broken demand. "And why...why couldn't I have had this one day without...without—"

"Sweetheart," Doc smiled, his voice wise and commanding yet soft with affection. "It's just one day. It's just one bad day in a string of good days that you know how to take one at a time."

"And I'll be stronger for it," she whispered with uncharacteristic bitterness.

"You are already strong. Stronger than anyone I know. And you'll get past this. Just like you always get past it. You and your young man will have a wonderful life together."

A wonderful life.

The words echoed, then drifted haphazardly around in her head until they tangled with everything that could get in the way of it becoming a reality.

Her reality was epilepsy. That alone was more than

enough to get in the way of Doc's prediction of a wonderful life. While her parents had done everything in their power to make it so, life, for Ellie, had never been wonderful. Life had been never knowing when or why a seizure would strike. Life had been home schooling to protect her from bold stares and whispering tongues, the cruelty of children who teased because they were afraid and didn't understand. While it would have hurt her parents greatly if they had known, life had also been isolating—both emotionally and socially.

It had been knowing that medication could lessen but not eliminate the seizures that stole her control and left her vulnerable and dependent and eroded little pieces of her spirit and her pride.

And life, quite often, had not been hers to live.

Like now.

She had a vague awareness of the drug taking a slow, slippery grasp on the pain, then a moment of simmering anger that her control had once again been stolen from her. Then even the anger drifted away with her consciousness—isolating her once again.

And then she slept—without a single dream of happily-ever-after.

''How is she?'' Lee demanded when Doc Lundstrum finally strolled out to the waiting room where he'd spent endless time flipping through magazines he hadn't wanted to read, counting the worn gray tiles on the floor, then counting them all over again.

Old Doc just smiled. ''She's fine. She's sleeping. It's what she needs right now. Take her home, let her rest and she'll be as good as new.''

''Is it always like this for her?''

Doc laid a hand on his shoulder. ''No, son. It's not always like this. You have to remember what she's been up against lately. Her daddy is gone barely a month. And now she's a wife. The excitement, the stress of being on her own, taking care of things...it took a toll. That's all. She'll be fine. You just let her rest now, and when she's up to it she'll tell you what she wants you to know.''

The Doc had kind eyes, but he was too damn tight-lipped to suit Lee. ''I want *you* to tell me.''

Doc seemed to consider it, then shook his head. ''It's not my place.''

He couldn't help it. He blurted out the question that had been lurking like a black cloud since he'd caught her limp and lifeless body in his arms at the alter. ''Is she...is this...hell.'' He scrubbed his hands roughly over his face. ''What's it doing to her? Is it slowly killing her? Is she dying?''

''No,'' Doc assured him with a quick smile. ''No. She's not dying.''

A relief so swift it damn near drove the air from his lungs burst through him. While he was still recovering, Doc cast him an assessing look.

''This is something she's dealt with for a long time now, Lee. She's better prepared to handle it than you are. That will change with time, but for today, she's as humiliated as she is hurting. Both will pass, but she'll need you to get to that point. So, just tread carefully with her, son.''

He ran a hand through his hair, still frustrated by all the unknowns, hating the thought of her in pain.

''Patience,'' Doc dictated with a slow nod. ''It's what you both need right now. After you and Ellie have a talk, then you come back and see me and I'll fill you in on what you still have questions about, okay?''

No. It wasn't okay, but it was all Doc was going to give him.

Lee lifted Ellie, drowsy and mostly asleep, carefully out of the truck and headed down the walk to the house. She was like a little bird in his arms. Satiny soft, featherlight and so vulnerable it made his chest hurt. Her thready sigh fluttered like a butterfly's wings along the hollow of his throat as he shifted her slight weight more securely against him.

An April breeze rustled the satin of her flowing gown, stirred the downy curls at her nape while the late-afternoon sunshine she'd been so determined to shine on her wedding day, shot golden fire through her hair. The delicate little snore that snuffled out would have made him smile if he hadn't felt so frustrated and helpless and still so damn uninformed.

He looked down at the woman in his arms and accepted that it would be a while before she was up to talking—or for anything else for that matter.

Until today, the *anything else* had been a concern, yes, but still, a foregone conclusion. He was no monk. Even though he'd known she was an innocent, he'd also known he wouldn't be able to leave her that way. Look at her. What man could leave her alone? He'd planned on going slowly with her, but he'd had every intention of making her his wife in every way.

Now, though, now he wondered if maybe…well, now he wondered about a lot of things. Not the least of which was this intense and unfamiliar surge of feelings that went beyond obligation and duty. Hell, they even went beyond concern, and courted an unsettling notion that maybe there was more in jeopardy here than her health—like his lifelong contention that other than a physical relationship, he had little else in him to give a woman.

Large as life and with the clarity of crystal, a six-month-old conversation came to mind. The immediacy of it startled him. So did the content.

"You don't give a damn do you?" Sara O'Brien had fired the accusation at him like a bullet when he'd broken things off between them last fall. He'd been seeing Sara for several months. She was a nice woman and he'd enjoyed her company. But she'd developed feelings for him, strong feelings, and he'd known it wasn't fair to her that he couldn't return them.

Her brown eyes had been swimming with hurt and anger that he had apparently put there, and with what he'd strongly suspected was love—an emotion he had never trusted. He'd been up-front with her from the beginning. He hadn't been looking for forever. He'd thought she'd accepted the ground rules. By the time he'd figured out he'd been wrong, it was too late to do anything but back away—like he always backed away.

"You don't give a damn that I love you." She'd shaken her head, her soft, chestnut curls dancing around her face. "You never have."

"I'm sorry, Sara. I don't know what to say. I never meant to hurt you." And he *was* sorry, even if his words had sounded hollow.

She'd laughed, a harsh sound, tempered by grim acceptance and anger. "And that's the kicker, isn't it? You really don't want to hurt me. You stand there, and even now you cannot comprehend, cannot even fathom, why it hurts so much. Because you don't understand love, do you, Lee? Don't understand it. Don't get it.''

She'd turned her back then and, squaring her shoulders, reached for her pride. ''You know what? I feel sorry for you. At least I know what it feels like to love someone. You never will. You'll never let yourself—and of the two of us, that makes you the most pathetic.''

Ellie stirred against him and dragged him away from that uncomfortable Texas memory to the woman in his arms. She tried to lift her head as he climbed the porch steps.

''Where—''

''Shush.'' He pressed his lips against her temple and concentrated on her. On what she was feeling, not on what Sara had known that he couldn't feel. Her skin was smooth and warm there, her hair as soft as silk and just as fine. ''We're home, Ellie. Just rest and I'll put you to bed.''

She looped her arms tighter around his neck as he reached for the door. ''This wasn't what I had in mind when…when I pictured you carrying me over the threshold,'' she murmured and snuggled closer.

A flood of affection filled his chest. His fairy-tale princess had been up for a fairy-tale wedding day. He wished it could have turned out that way for her. ''How about you just hold that picture and when you get to feeling better we'll do it right, okay?''

''Okay.'' Her misty response was so faint he barely heard her, yet with that one word, she gave her trust over to him completely.

Just like that. Just that sure. It rocked him, that

trust. More even than Will's entrusting him with the ranch had rocked him.

He hadn't come back to Shiloh planning to let Will down. And he wouldn't. Ellie—well, Ellie was a different matter. He didn't want to hurt her, but he pretty much figured it was a given. She had stars in her eyes. She saw him as romantic. She wanted a marriage built on love—not deathbed promises and payment of debts.

He wished, for her sake, that he could give it to her. Just like he wished he could have given something more to Sara. She'd been wrong, though. At least about one thing. He did understand love. He'd known love in this house. He'd just never learned how to give it back. He strongly suspected that it had never been a part of him in the first place—either that or it had been beaten or leached out of him long before the Shilohs had found him.

Whatever, it hadn't been a part of him then. It wasn't a part of him now. For that, for Sara and especially for Ellie, he was sorry.

Grim-faced, he climbed the stairs with her curled like a kitten in his arms. ''But we'll get by, Ellie,'' he whispered into her hair. ''We'll get by just fine.''

He would take care of her. He would give her everything that he could...and knew in his gut that it would never be as much as she deserved.

Three

It was after midnight and Lee was in her virgin's bed.

He hadn't intended to be. He'd set his mind to making her comfortable, tucking her in, then doing some serious brooding.

He'd wanted to brood about all the things that he wasn't now and could never be for her. About this feeling of helplessness. Of knowing she was in pain. Of not knowing what lay ahead for her.

But more than he'd wanted to brood, he'd hated the thought of leaving her alone. So when he'd laid her down and untangled her arms from around his neck, her softly murmured ''Don't go'' had shot his intentions all to hell.

''Shush,'' he'd whispered to those big lavender eyes that were clouded with a medicated haze and a distant-but-very-real discomfort. She'd still managed to make him see how desperately she wanted him with her. "I won't go anywhere, Ellie. I'll be right here in the chair."

"In the bed," she'd insisted, and damned if that hadn't finally made him smile.

The lady knew what she wanted. And she knew how to get it. At least she knew how to get it from him.

He'd touched his hand to her face. "All right. In the bed, but let's get you comfortable first, okay?"

With grim determination, he'd gone to work on her gown.

His hands were big. The satin-wrapped buttons were small. And there must have been a hundred of them. He hadn't been prepared for that.

He really hadn't been prepared to deal with the sweet little body he'd uncovered underneath all that billowing white satin.

"I'm too small," she'd whispered as she'd lain there, too out of it to cover herself, yet very much aware that he was watching her.

It had taken several long, deep breaths to recover as he'd stood there by the bed, his hands full of yards of wedding dress, his chest full of a heart that was hammering like a sledge.

Sweet Lord. She was so tiny. So flawlessly exquisite against pale pink sheets in her white lacy underwear and sheer, shimmering stockings. He was stunned by the delicate, porcelain perfection of his bride and tried to think of how fragile she was, how breakable.

But all he could think of was that she was his. All the heat of that pale silken skin he'd uncovered belonged to him now. The romantic heart that had tucked a dainty blue hanky beneath the lacy edge of her thigh-high hose, his. The soft fullness of her breasts covered by sheer lingerie that had been sewn in the shape of flower petals. The shadow of downy, copper curls at the apex of her slim thighs.

His.

The picture came before he could squelch it. So vivid, so immediate it hit like a sucker punch. They were naked. It was full daylight. He wanted her in the sunlight. He wanted to see all of her. He was on his back in her bed, cushioned in down, covered by her; she was poised above him, that magnificent hair spilling down her back, her breasts rosy and wet from his mouth, her nipples pearled into tight little beads as she settled down on him, took him deep.

She moaned. It was soft but full of pain, and it snapped him back to the moment like a bucket of ice water. Board stiff, he studied her face, relieved that she appeared to finally be sleeping.

On a deep breath he laid her dress over a rocker in the corner of the room. Then he cleared his mind, settled his blood, slowed his breathing. With deliberate and calculated movements, he pulled the sheet and coverlet up to her chin, then sat down on the edge of the bed with his back to her. He loosened his tie, undid a couple of buttons. Elbows propped on his thighs, he dragged his hands wearily through his hair.

The reality of what he'd just done finally hit him. Like a bare-knuckled fist, it pounded dead center into the middle of his chest.

What had he gotten himself into? Worse. What had he gotten *her* into? A marriage that she'd really had no say in choosing, that's what. Sure, she thought this was what she wanted, but she was young. Naive. She was also absolutely dependent upon him.

And he wanted her.

He buried his face in his hands.

She was ill.

A slick ball of nausea rolled over in his gut.

"Lee."

He cleared his head and turned to her with a strained smile. "I'm right here, Ellie."

"Don't leave me."

Something inside of him tightened, then gave, like a bow when the tension was released—and just that fast, everything snapped into perspective. He couldn't exactly call it relief. What he could call it was acceptance.

He owed Will. That was the bottom line.

So he was struggling now because he'd finally figured out that he owed Ellie more than what he'd come to Shiloh prepared to give her. He'd thought it had been enough that he'd left his life, his work, his plans, that he'd made a sacrifice coming back to Shiloh—even as he'd told himself Shiloh was what he'd wanted, what he deserved.

Ellie…Ellie had just been part of the package. From a distance he'd been fine with that. He'd intended to be good to her. He'd intended to take care of her. He still did. He just hadn't realized until now what that might entail.

In sickness and in health.

From Texas the actual consequences of returning to Shiloh had been abstract. Workable.

Now…now it was getting damn sticky. He hadn't counted on the extent of her dependence on him. He also hadn't planned on—was having trouble coming to terms with—this knot of desire he'd been trying to deny since he'd come back two weeks ago and made arrangements for her father's funeral and her wedding all in the space of a week.

Her wedding.

His wedding.

In a way, he supposed, he'd viewed this marriage as a solution for him of sorts. Long ago he'd tired of the singles scene, the ritual dating dances, the plastic smiles and hungry eyes of the women who hadn't understood that the most he could give them was never as much as they had ultimately wanted. Women like Sara. Who he had hurt.

So, yeah, marriage had taken him out of that loop—efficiently, effectively. Good for him.

Not good for Ellie.

She needed more. And gradually, he was realizing that she deserved more.

"Lee?"

Resigned, he slipped out of his jacket, tossed it over her gown and eased down on top of the covers beside her.

"I'm right here." He folded her carefully into his arms.

"Promise. Promise you won't leave me."

If he hadn't been lying down, the whisper of desperation in her request, whether drug-induced or real, would have brought him to his knees.

"I won't leave you." He pressed a kiss to the top of her head, tucked her closer to his side. "I won't ever leave you."

And he wouldn't.

He was here. He was committed. He would stay.

She snuggled against him, all warm curves and unquestioning trust. An ache of emotion welled up behind his eyes, as acute as it was unexpected. It blindsided him, caught him completely off guard. He squeezed his eyes tightly shut then blinked back the sting of moisture that he refused to acknowledge was actually there.

He pressed his face into the cinnamon-sweet fragrance of her hair. Then he hung on. Just hung on to her as if she was suddenly his anchor—when he was supposed to be hers.

"I won't let you down," he murmured into the silk of her hair and tried to outgun these unfamiliar emotions she wrung out of him with absolutes. She was his obligation. She was dependent on him. And he'd promised Will.

"I promise, Ellie, I won't ever let you down."

Twilight came and went, and still he held her.

The grandfather clock in the downstairs foyer chimed the midnight hour, then one. He stared into the dark, his arms full of woman, his mind rejecting thoughts that just kept twisting back around into a stunning conclusion, no matter how hard he tried to divert them.

He'd come back to Shiloh to claim what was his. And yes, he'd come back to take care of Ellie. He hadn't come back because he needed her softness in his life. He didn't need anyone—never had. He didn't need this sense of home. He didn't need it...so bad he hurt with it. Refused to acknowledge that he was afraid to trust the good of it. The goodness of her and the weakness of needing everything she represented.

She murmured in her sleep, squirmed restlessly.

With his hand in her hair, he settled her. With his eyes wide open, he stared into the night and waited for morning to come—and with it, the detachment and distance from all these feelings that he counted on daylight to bring.

When Ellie finally awoke it was raining. It was also morning. She could tell even as she lay for a moment with her eyes closed, testing the weight of her headache and finding it mostly gone. The gentle patter of a morning shower rapped at her window, hurried by a wind gust, then abated again to soft little spattering taps.

She smelled the damp-earth scent of it and thought of her garden. She smelled the rich scent of musk on her pillow—and thought of her husband.

Eyes suddenly wide open, she stared first at the ceiling, then turned her head to find him. Gone.

The disappointment of it slowed the rapid beat of her heart. She touched her hand to the indentation in the pillow where his head had been. Cold.

But his scent lingered. And her memory stirred. He'd held her in the night. Warm strength. Gentle hands. Solid muscle.

A tear welled up before she could stop it. She'd wanted to give him so much more on their wedding night. She'd wanted to give; instead she'd ended up taking, like she always ended up taking from the people she cared about.

Rolling to her side, she pulled the covers up to her chin and glanced at the clock by her bed—10:15 a.m., Sunday, April fifteenth. Her first day as a wife. She was alone in her bed. And she was still a virgin.

Her heart sank as she watched the rain bead then run like tears down the windowpane.

That's how Lee found her.

He stood in the doorway, peripherally aware of the

garden of pink roses that adorned her bedroom walls, the fussy lace curtains, the four-poster bed covered with an acre of fluffy white down coverlet.

But it was the look of his bride that held him spellbound. Her back was to him, and she didn't know he was there. Her hair trailed behind her on the pillow like a tumble of shining ribbons as she lay watching the rain. The way she'd tucked her fisted hands under her chin was childlike and vulnerable—not so the soft curves that even all that down couldn't conceal. It was a woman's body that warmed the sheets. A woman's body that had snuggled against his through the night.

And it was a man that she needed this morning. A man who knew her limits and could impose a few of his own.

He had a handle on all that now. He had a handle on what she needed from him. She needed his strength and she needed his care. Beyond that, it was up to him to keep the lines from blurring and the mix from getting too intense until she was ready for more. *If* she was ever ready for more.

''Mornin', Ellie.'' His voice felt gravelly, sounded gruff as he stepped farther into the room and set the breakfast tray he'd prepared on the table beside her bed.

He watched her carefully as she lay there, her silence telling of how uncomfortable she was. With him in her bedroom? With the memory of him in her bed?

Or are you still sick, little one, and berating yourself because of it?

He settled a hip on the mattress at her side. ''How are you feeling?''

She continued to stare out the window, avoiding his eyes. After a long moment she let out a breath that spoke as eloquently as her words. ‘‘I’m sorry I ruined our wedding day.’’

So, it was humiliation not nerves that kept her from facing him.

‘‘Ellie…you didn’t ruin anything,’’ he insisted gently. ‘‘You were sick. It wasn’t something you could help.’’

She slowly rolled to her back, then lay there, staring at the ceiling with eyes devoid of emotion. ‘‘It’s never something I can help.’’

He’d witnessed her laughter; he’d witnessed her tears. Neither had as profound an effect on him as this blank look of utter defeat. He reached out, brushed a strand of hair from her cheek, a hundred questions rattling around in his head. For starters, what could he do, what could he say that would lessen the bruised look on her face? Bruised pride. Bruised spirit.

He didn’t want to add more damage by hammering her with questions. He decided instead to let her set the pace, but he had to know one thing first. ‘‘How are you feeling…really?’’

‘‘Fine. Better,’’ she amended when he slanted her a doubting look. ‘‘Really.’’

There was little he could do but take her at her word. ‘‘Are you hungry?’’

She gave a little shrug that told him nothing and everything about her ambivalence. It also managed to expose one creamy white and very bare shoulder.

Sometime in the night she’d started fidgeting with her bra straps and he’d helped her out of it. The scrap of white lace, along with the pins that had held her hair in place, lay scattered on the floor by his feet. Both stirred his memory of a tantalizing glimpse of pale, perfect breasts, the alluring tips of berry-pink nipples bathed in moonlight.

He blocked the picture from his mind. ''I think you should try to eat something.'' He cleared his throat and, dragging his gaze to her face, tried again. ''There's enough food in the kitchen to feed threshers. Did you do all that? For me?''

She'd snaked an arm out from under the covers and, looking anywhere but at him, pinched the fabric of the comforter between her thumb and finger, pleating and repleating it. He covered her hand with his, stilling her nervous motions.

''Ellie, it's all right. I want you to stop feeling so self-conscious. When you're ready, we need to talk. But only when you're ready, okay?''

When she closed her eyes and swallowed hard, he turned her palm to his and linked their fingers together. ''I'll take care of you.''

She stared at their clasped hands. ''I'm your wife. I'm supposed to take care of you.''

He'd been taking care of himself for more years than she'd been alive, so the thought of a little slip like her looking out for him made him smile. He didn't think she'd want to hear that, though, so he suggested something he thought they could both live with. ''How about we take care of each other?''

That finally earned him a small smile. He let out a breath that seemed to have been bottled up since he'd walked into the room and found her staring so forlornly at the rain. He squeezed her hand, then nodded toward the tray.

''Those wouldn't happen to be peach muffins?'' he asked, even though he knew the answer.

Her smile blossomed and grew. He couldn't shake

the ridiculous notion that he felt as if the sun had come out.

"You baked them for me? Because they're my favorite?"

She nodded. "I remembered."

"There, see? You're already taking care of me. Nobody's made me peach muffins in..." He let the words trail off. The last time had been before Clare died. The thought turned the promise of a lighter mood back toward darkness. He could see in Ellie's eyes that her thoughts echoed his. "Well, let's just say that it's been a long time.... Now, how about you help me polish off a few?" he suggested, forcing a lightness back to his tone that brought her gaze to his. "I brought coffee, and I found some tea. Do you drink tea, Ellie?"

She smiled again, shyly this time. "We don't know much about each other, do we?"

Again he touched a hand to her hair. "We've got a lifetime to learn."

Everything in her expression told him that she liked the sound of that. Almost everything. The shadows in her eyes hid secrets that gave her pain and shut him out.

"Tea, please," she said, looking away. Clutching the comforter to her breasts, she concentrated on sitting up.

He quickly moved to help her. Gathering a trio of pillows, he propped them behind her back. She leaned into him, her weakness still obvious.

Her nakedness was also very evident as he reached around her and settled a pillow at the small of her back. The first touch was accidental, a brief brush of his fingers along the sleek line of her spine. The second touch was not. He shouldn't have done it. And yet, he couldn't stop himself. The temptation was too great. The indulgence too sweet.

His hand lingered there on the resilient warmth of her skin where the slight round of her hip met the indentation of her waist. It was like silk, that skin. It heated beneath his hand. Nothing short of her flinching could have stopped him from caressing that tender flesh, tracing the small ridges of her backbone as his hand slowly ascended.

She did not flinch. She sort of melted into him, her lips pressed to the hollow of his throat, her breath fluttering along his skin, heating his blood as her warmth filled his palm and her hair trailed like heavy lace along the backs of his fingers. He closed his eyes, savored it all, the scent of her, the supple resilience that was his virgin bride, before easing away.

Her eyes were huge and round, full of questions and wonder as they met and held his.

Are you going to kiss me?

Well. He really had no choice then. He cupped her jaw in his palm, tunneled his fingers into the hair at her nape and touched his lips to the petal softness of hers.

It was supposed to be a brush of a kiss, a hello, an invitation to trust. A promise that he would be here for her.

It turned into something more.

Her lips were warm, like her skin. Her response was instant. She opened for him, moist heat, incredibly soft and giving.

A spear of desire shot through him like fire.

He knew about practiced seduction, understood the art of guile. Neither was a part of Ellie's response. It was instinct, not practice that invited him inside. Honesty, not guile that sent lightning-swift pleasure singing through his blood.

No, she knew nothing of seduction. Yet he was being totally and thoroughly seduced. With an artless touch of her tongue, a breathless little shiver that filled his head with images and urges and hunger. The thought that she could take him to that edge so quickly only made him realize the care he had to take with her.

He was the one with the experience here.

He was the one with the control.

"I wonder..." he said, forcing himself to back away, to smile into her eyes and cater to her innocence and her needs instead of giving in to his own. "I wonder if your muffins taste as good as you do."

He'd never seen a woman blush before—at least not this prettily. It painted her cheeks a rosy-pink, then spread in a rush to color the flesh above the bedcovers, which her fisted fingers had let slip to reveal a tantalizing glimpse of high, round breasts, faintly marbled with a delicate network of translucent blue veins.

It took more than he'd thought he had in him to resist the urge to tumble her back on her pillows, slowly drag those covers to her waist and feast on the sight and then the taste of her. To take her sweet, pink nipple in his mouth, tongue it, graze it with his teeth and feel her body arch and yearn, ache and burn, slowly awaken to the woman she would become.

He gathered a necessary breath, a mandatory presence of mind.

He was way off the mark. This was not the time. This was not the direction he needed to go with her.

Not today. Maybe not for a very long time if he didn't get a handle on her illness and on her limitations.

And then there were his limits and the way she seemed to stretch them every time he was around her. He had to get a handle on that, too.

"Ellie, sweetheart, it would probably be a very fine idea if I got your robe."

Ellie blinked once, slowly, then wet her lips, trying to capture the taste of his mouth, searching to read the dark look in his eyes, longing to know him as a bride should know her husband on the morning after her wedding.

Questions. She had so many questions about what they would do together. In this bed. How he would touch her. Where he would kiss her. She had so many fantasies. Many of them were nurtured by the book she'd ordered by mail so she would know how to be a wife to him. Many more were fostered by just looking at him and knowing he could probably teach her more than she could ever learn from that book.

"In the closet," she said, instead of telling him what she wanted. Another kiss. The touch of his hand. On her bare skin. On her naked breast.

She didn't know how to tell him those things. At least, that's what she told herself. The way he'd reacted when he'd kissed her—oh, my. It seemed they'd been communicating just fine. The truth was that she was a coward. She was his wife now, but the part of her that kept her from being so many things still kept her from being his woman. Not just the physical part of her illness, but the part that affected how she felt about herself, how she felt about who she was and what she was. The part that made her different. The part that made her vulnerable to the whim of misfiring brain waves and shook her confidence.

She watched him rise and walk across the room. Watched the perfectly strong, long length of him, the breadth of his shoulders, the dark satin of his hair, the deep-blue of his eyes when he turned back with her robe, and felt a throbbing ache low and deep inside her.

In the wake of what she recognized as wanting rode a stark reminder of reality and regret. She quickly looked away. She should have told him everything. She should have prepared him. It hadn't been fair.

Even before she met his eyes again, she felt the loss a full disclosure would bring. His kiss had said he wanted her. But would he want everything that came with her?

Guilt settled like a stone.

I won't ever leave you.

That's what he'd said last night. Even through the medicated haze, she remembered. That's what she'd begged for. That's what he'd promised. She wouldn't hold him to it. She knew that now. Now that she realized she hadn't really wanted him at any price. She'd wanted him at the price of love. At the price of forever. But after yesterday and last night, she realized she did not want him at the price of her pride.

So she would tell him. Everything.

But not now.

Not naked.

She couldn't talk to him about it naked. She felt too vulnerable. And that vulnerability, like her faint but lingering headache, justified her decision to stall what was unavoidable for just a little while longer.

* * *

Ellie had been worried about her chores, so Lee had left her with orders to please stay in bed while he took care of things for her. He'd needed the distance. He'd needed the physical labor to clear his head. So he'd fed the chickens, gathered the eggs, then checked on the handful of horses stabled in the barn. The rest of the herd grazed free on the open range.

Going through the motions had been both grounding and disconcerting. It reminded him of years past, the satisfying simplicity of physical labor when it had been just him and Will and Clare. It reminded him of what his life no longer was—high tech and profit driven. Oddly, he felt equal measures of contentment and loss.

Mainstay, the corporate cattle operation he'd managed for Curt outside of Houston, had been his life for the past ten years. He'd run the bulk of the operation from behind a desk with the assistance of the Web that kept him apprised minute by minute of the markets—the high-tech software that defined to a pencil-sharp point rate of gain, profit and loss, market trends. It had been a high-pressure position that he'd competed to get, worked like a dog to keep. And while it would never erase a starving street kid's memories, it had given him what that kid had never had. Financial independence. Some shrewd investments and a knack for playing the markets had cemented his future.

"I thought you liked it here," Curt had protested in a last-ditch bid to convince him to stay.

"I don't just like it, I love it. I love the competitiveness of it. The orderliness, the cutting-edge technology. But I also hate it," he'd confessed, trying to help Curt understand. "I hate the loss of hands-on management. I miss the physical labor—it's cleansing and real...like the creak of saddle leather and the scent of horses."

He'd laughed when Curt had looked at him like he'd gone over the edge. "Okay, okay. I know it sounds sappy, but I miss the sense that I play a critical role in the day-to-day operations of a working ranch. Shiloh will give all that back to me."

And he could give to Shiloh what Will hadn't been able—or had never wanted—to give. He could make it into something other than a hang-on-by-the-skin-of-your-teeth proposition. He could ease Shiloh into the twenty-first century. In the process, he could preserve a way of life that was becoming as obscure as a working horse in an SUV age.

He looked around him at the outbuildings that hadn't seen a coat of paint in four decades, the hulking giant of a house that had been built at the turn of the twentieth century and had benefited from very few updates since. He had the capital to invest in repairs, improvements and innovations. He had the desire to keep the ranch intact. And he had the will to say no to the pressure to sell out to the moneymen who'd been sniffing around. If they had their way, they would own Shiloh, then turn it into their personal game preserve or subdivide and make millions selling little pockets of paradise and populating the mountains with Hollywood types gone country. Well, that wasn't going to happen. Not on his watch.

He stepped onto the back porch, made a note to get to work on both the front and back porch floors and tried to understand why Will had never accepted his offers to help out.

"Don't need your money, boy," he'd say in that soft, slow cadence that promoted trust and relayed pride. "We're doin' fine. Me and Mom and the girl. Sure would like to see your face, though. Know you're a busy man, but when do you think you can get home for a spell?"

He opened the kitchen door, set the bucket of eggs on the table and felt the guilt eat a little deeper. He hadn't come home often enough. He'd known it then. He knew it even more keenly now. Now that it was too late to do anything but miss them.

The house was comfortably quiet as he washed his hands, then dried them on a towel that had been looped through the handle on the refrigerator door. It was the same refrigerator that had been sitting on the same worn gray-and-white linoleum flooring twenty-three years ago when he'd come to Shiloh.

After pouring a mug of coffee, he leaned back against the counter and studied the room. It had never seemed shabby to him back then. Even though Ellie obviously worked to keep the house clean and welcoming, he couldn't get over how sadly neglected it seemed now. How neglected everything seemed.

When a floorboard creaked overhead, he realized that he'd been listening, hoping even, for some sign that Ellie was up so he'd have an excuse to go check on her. Harder to admit, despite his concentration on his chores and his plans, she hadn't been out of his mind for a moment since he'd left her in her bed. All pretty and pink and kissable.

With a disgusted breath he looked up, took another sip of coffee. Then he made an honest effort to tuck her neatly into a cubbyhole alongside the rest of duties on his list. Fix everything in sight—including both porch floors, paint the house, check the herd, take care of Ellie. Just take care of her. She was fragile, she was vulnerable, and that's what she needed from him most. His care.

He knew that. And yet, he hadn't—not for a minute—stopped thinking about her lying in her bed, her expression open with wonder, inviting him to kiss her again. Inviting him with her velvet eyes to do all the things he'd been wanting to do and more.

He didn't like it much. He didn't like it that he couldn't get her out of his head but he could—and would—handle it. Starting right now. He would do what Will had asked him to do. He'd take care of her.

Setting the mug aside, he walked slowly into the living room, determined to do just that. He hesitated for only a moment before gripping the worn oak banister and ascending the stairs.

"Ellie?" he called out softly as he rounded the corner in the upstairs hallway and walked into her room. The bed was empty.

He heard water running in the bathroom and followed the sound. It made sense that she would want to bathe. It would also make sense that if she weren't feeling up to it, she wouldn't tackle it on her own. Or would she? She would be shy about asking for his help. She would be modest. And if she'd known that he was picturing her sweet-scented and naked and wet, she'd have been running for her life.

Disgusted with himself and determined not to shock her, he walked slowly toward the bathroom door at the end of the hall—and found it mostly open. He was about to knock, about to ask if she was doing okay, when he saw a shadow of movement and she walked into his field of view.

Her back was to him. She was wrapped from neck to ankle in her pink robe when she stopped beside the deep, claw-foot tub that was slowly filling with hot water. With a grace and unconscious sensuality that made his pulse leap, she swept that riot of curling copper hair into a loose knot on top of her head and secured it with a gold clip. Then, still unaware that he was watching her, she undid the belt of her robe.

He should have left her to her privacy then. At the very least he should have let her know he was there. But he couldn't seem to move, was beyond speech as the soft chenille slid from her creamy white shoulders, slipped down her slender back, and caught low on her hips before pooling in a drift of pink at her feet.

Four

She was, in one very inadequate word, exquisite. Her skin was pale and flawless, her neck long and graceful. Her waist was small, like the rest of her—the flair of her hips woman soft, her legs sleek and supple. Twin dimples saucily winked at him from above her sweetly rounded bottom, drew his gaze, stirred his sex—as did a strawberry-shaped beauty mark riding a little left of center at the small of her back. He wanted to touch her there with his lips, stroke her there with his tongue.

Mine, he thought again, unaccustomed to the hard, swift punch of possession that swamped him.

He wasn't conceited and he wasn't blind. Women found him attractive. The women he'd taken as lovers had been sophisticated and beautiful—and they hadn't looked at him with forever in their eyes and a trust that ran river deep.

Just as none of them had never moved him as she did. None of them aroused him like she did. And none of them—not even for a moment—could make him forget who he was and who he wasn't and what he wasn't prepared to give.

He had to back away from her. Now. But then she leaned forward and turned enough in profile to show a teasing glimpse of one sweetly rounded breast. He was already semihard when the sight of that velvety pink nipple turned him to stone.

And he wasn't going anywhere.

There was nothing about her that wasn't a bewitching paradox of eroticism and innocence. And when she reached across the tub, tested the water with a slow swish of her hand, then poured a thick, creamy liquid from a clear glass bottle, he nearly groaned. Had to tell himself to breathe when she stepped over the rim and eased into the water.

She leaned back as the tub filled slowly, scenting the air with the fragrance of vanilla. Clouds of bubbles built until they reached her waist, flirted with the undersides of her pretty breasts.

As he watched, her nipples tightened.

He damn near went to her then, knelt beside her, touched her where the water didn't, and where it did.

It would embarrass her, he told himself. Just as his watching would embarrass her. He knew he should look away. He was her husband, yes, yet he felt like a voyeur, invading her privacy, breaching her trust. At least he thought he was until, with a languorous yet deliberate sigh, she turned her head and looked him straight in the eye.

His heart thumped like the recoil of a shotgun. Before he could recover, it rocked him again, slamming against his sternum, pumping blood to his head in a dizzying rush.

She blinked once, held his gaze for a long, searching moment, then slowly turned her head, draped her arms over the rim of the tub and let her eyes drift shut.

Shock held him there, right where he stood, for several long, mind-numbing seconds.

She'd known.

She'd known he was watching her.

A jolt of something closer to pleasure than surprise shot through his blood—until it occurred to him that he might have underestimated her.

Maybe he'd been a fool to think she'd come to him a virgin. She was very beautiful. And he seriously doubted that the young men of Sundown were blind or stupid. He remembered how he'd been at nineteen. He remembered what he'd wanted from a woman then.

He knew what he wanted right now.

He took a long, lingering look at all that creamy wet skin until looking was no longer enough.

Lust teamed in a diccy alliance with a hard, tight clutch of jealousy and took over, told him what he wanted to hear. The hell with being careful with her. The hell with what she needed from him. She'd invited this. She'd stripped for him, posed for him. Woman sure, seductive, inviting.

''You don't have a clue what you just invited, princess,'' he uttered under his breath.

Good intentions or no, he'd be damned if he'd feel guilty for reacting to her like a man. She wasn't Lolita, and he wasn't a lecherous old coot. He was thirty-three years old—and he wanted his wife.

He shoved the door all the way open, let it slam against the wall with a satisfying smack.

Her eyes were open now, growing wide and round as he crossed the room and loomed over her. He didn't even attempt to hide the hunger when he swept his gaze over the part of her that the bubbles covered and the part they didn't.

Mine was all he could think again, when he leaned over her and braced his hands on the tub's edge at either side of her head. Satisfaction coiled in his gut, as fierce and sharp as a whip, when she crossed her arms over her naked breasts and sank a little lower in the water.

She wasn't feeling so sure of herself now.

You play with fire, little girl, you're gonna to get burned.

Only he was the one burning. He was the one who could barely breathe, could only think of the silk of her, the heat of her, the need of her.

He followed her down as she sank deeper, caging her in. Biceps bunching, he lowered himself until his mouth hovered a breath away from hers.

"Open," he demanded, not checking the growl, not denying the need as he roughly captured her mouth. Once, a quick, primitive nip of lips and teeth. And again, to make it clear that she'd roused the beast in him—and that she'd better be prepared to deal with it.

Then he wasn't acting on his needs, but reacting to the force of them. And just like his reason, his resolve got lost somewhere in the pool of pink cloth that lay, along with her innocence, on the floor by the tub.

Desire rocked through his blood at the taste of her, shot to oblivion any concern. The silky heat of her mouth, the giving resilience and the shimmering threads of her startled breath, fed his need to an inferno.

Her strangled little gasp spoke of her inexperience as he found her tongue, stroked it then drew it into his mouth. The restlessness of her trembling sigh told of her awakening desire…and a burgeoning awareness of a woman's control over a man.

Control.

A flash of cool blue broke through the fiery-red haze clouding his eyes and his judgment. He didn't lose control. Not like this. Never like this. And he'd never given it over to a woman.

He pulled away far enough to break the contact of flesh on flesh. The warm, hurried pulse of her breath beat in short, quivering bursts against his lips.

He meant to leave her then but couldn't stop himself from looking his fill. She was drenched in color and fragrance. A dew of steamy bathwater and a dawning sensuality painted her skin, from her cheeks to her breasts, a rosy pink glow.

When her eyelids fluttered, he willed his hammering heart to settle. But she wasn't done with him yet. Her eyes opened with a slow, languid sensuality, and her tiny pink tongue slipped between kiss-swollen lips to lick and taste, savor and soothe.

Even as his heart slammed into race speed, an intense wave of tenderness swamped him and finally accomplished what that damn control he so valued hadn't been able to. It cleared his head.

He had to get out of here.

He had to do it now before he said the hell with taking care. He'd never wanted so badly. He'd never needed this much. Hell, he was still only a deep breath away from stripping off his clothes and crawling into that old claw-foot tub full of bubbles and Ellie.

Ellie. She'd made him forget who he was dealing with. She'd made him forget that he had to take care. She couldn't handle what he had in mind. He wasn't even sure that *he* could.

He made himself push away. Made himself stand, walk out of the room and away from the house and the knowledge that he'd almost taken her in that moment—without regard to her innocence or her health.

And he didn't hate himself nearly enough.

It was a long time before Ellie gathered the nerve to walk downstairs. Her headache was completely gone. The sluggish aftereffects of the pain medication had pretty much worn off. As much as she hated knuckling under, she was glad now that she'd let Doc talk her into the shot. She wasn't as sure how she felt about her behavior when she'd discovered Lee watching her prepare for her bath.

Or how she felt about that kiss.

One thing she was sure of. After she'd gotten past the fierce look on his face and the crushing surprise of his mouth on hers, she'd liked it. A lot.

Places inside her—well, she still got all warm and achy and weak just thinking about the places in her body his kiss had affected.

She felt her skin flush beneath her faded jeans and her soft white T-shirt as she gathered her hair at her nape with a wide gold clip and made her way to the kitchen that she knew was empty.

She knew it was empty because she'd heard the back door creak open, then shut right after Lee had left her a little more than an hour ago. Since then she'd caught glimpses of him outside. His face had been set in a hard, grim line as he'd gone to work on the woodpile by the garage.

Why he'd thought he needed to split wood in April when Don Ferguson, the next-door neighbor, had made sure she'd had enough to get her though any cool spring evenings was beyond her.

She couldn't say that she was sorry Lee had chosen to work himself into a glistening sweat, though. Especially after he'd taken off his shirt, then mopped his brow and his flat belly with it.

She'd watched him from her bedroom window. All that woman heat he'd set aflame when he'd kissed her in the tub had warmed up all over again. His shoulders were so broad. His chest was beautifully covered in an interesting pelt of soft brown curls. And lower, where his belt buckle met his abdomen just below his navel, his belly was taut and hard—like the corrugated roof on the machine shed. All firm and fine and…well. She hadn't been around many men in her life. Not young men, at any rate. Not any naked men.

Not that Lee was naked—although she sure had been wondering about him that way. And not that he was a young man. Not like John Tyler was young. Young and stupid and mean.

Frowning, she located her prescription bottles in the cupboard by the sink, uncapped them and tipped the appropriate doses into her palm. As she filled a glass with water and swallowed the medication, she tried not to let long-remembered hurts bother her. But they were always there. The memories. The taunting. The malicious smiles of a boy she'd wanted for a friend way back when. It had turned out that he'd only had one thought about her.

"What's the matter, Ellie?" John had asked, all sweetness and smiles when she'd finally gotten brave enough to stay put when he'd approached her one morning after church. "Cat got your tongue? Or did you bite it off throwin' one of your fits?"

Okay. So he'd only been twelve at the time. And he'd been a boy, not a man—so had his buddies who had stood by laughing like loons at her expense. It hadn't helped when his mother had made him apologize, then dragged him to the car by his ear. It hadn't helped when her own mother had held her to her breast when she'd cried.

"Ignorance, Ellie. The boy's only excuse is ignorance. Everybody's got something about themselves that they don't like. Sometimes the way they go about making themselves feel better is to make other people feel bad."

It hadn't been the first time someone had succeeded in making her feel bad about herself and mortified about how she was perceived by others. But it had been one of the few times she had made a real effort to be accepted by her peers, so it hurt all the more because she'd been foolish enough to open herself up to the attack.

She'd quit begging her mom and dad to let her go to regular school that day. And she'd quit making eye contact with anyone but the people she completely trusted.

Five years later, when John Tyler had asked her to go for a ride with him after church to get an ice cream cone and then to watch the fireworks at the Fourth of

July celebration, it had been easy to turn her back and walk away.

John and everyone like him had had all the shots at Ellie Shiloh they were going to get. She no longer cared what they said about her. Besides, she had always known who she trusted. And who she loved. She loved Lee. It had always been Lee, from her first memory of him holding her on his knee and she'd smelled horses and leather and sensed the strength that had made him a man, she had loved him.

And now she was his wife.

At least in name.

She walked to the fridge, opened the door and thought about that kiss again. Of how she'd started out feeling a little fearful, a lot exposed and ended up feeling…she wasn't sure what she'd been feeling. Wanting. Restless. Yearning for something she couldn't explain but knew would be wonderful. She hadn't wanted that kiss to end. She hadn't wanted him to leave her like that. All hot and wet and alone.

Cool refrigerated air washed against her heated checks as she thought of what she'd done to entice him.

She still couldn't believe how bold she'd been. She'd heard his footsteps on the stairs; she'd known he'd come looking for her. Her first thought had been to quickly shut the door. Her second—her second thought brought heat to her cheeks again.

Leave it open. Let him find you. Let him see you.

She'd suddenly realized that she had wanted him to come to her. And when he had, and he'd just stood there, thinking she hadn't heard him, some instinct had told her what to do. How to act to make him want her.

It had become important suddenly that he want her. It had been a necessary risk of her pride. And she'd been shameless. She'd been brazen and breathless as she'd slipped out of her robe. Knowing he was watching. Hoping he'd been wanting.

Except for Doc, no man had ever seen her naked. Even her mother hadn't seen her that way after she'd started developing. She'd felt too self-conscious.

She hadn't felt self-conscious today. She'd felt... like a woman. His kisses had told her he'd thought of her as one, too.

Until he'd walked away.

She looked at the wall clock, saw it was close to noon and gathered the cold fried chicken she'd made the day before yesterday.

He'd looked hard and angry and distant when he'd walked out of the room. That's the part that worried her most. What had he been thinking?

It didn't take much imagination to come up with some possibilities. Had he suddenly seen what everyone else saw when they looked at her? Had he thought, *What am I doing?* Worse, *What have I done? I married Ellie Shiloh. Epileptic Ellie Shiloh. What have I tied myself to for the rest of my life?*

Maybe Momma had been right, she thought, as an anger that lived deep in a forgiving soul had her hands trembling and her heart thumping at her breast like a raging fist. Like John Tyler, maybe Lee was just another frog disguised as a prince and she'd been a fool to expect he'd be any different.

Tears threatened to spill over into her fried chicken. Tears of outrage, injustice and a disappointment that sliced deep to the marrow.

"We need to talk."

She jumped at the sound of Lee's voice, startled that he'd climbed the back porch steps and was standing just the other side of the kitchen screen door. It was a measure of how lost in thought she'd been that she hadn't heard him.

But he was here. Big and beautiful, the hair at his nape and forehead spiked with sweat, the shirt he'd thrown on still hanging loose and unbuttoned. He looked hostile and dangerous. His blue eyes were as dark as a storm cloud and sent her already galloping heart into a flat-out run.

Her biggest surprise was realizing that it was anger, not fear that sent her heart racing. She had a little thunder to deal with too, thank you very much, and he was going to be on the receiving end.

''You're right, we do,'' she agreed, pleased with the startled look on his face and the fact that she'd put it there.

The phone rang before she had a chance to rattle him even more.

And Lee *was* rattled. He'd spent the better part of an hour trying to work off about a semi load of sexual frustration with an ax and an ugly attitude.

All he'd gotten was tired. And all he'd been able to think about was her.

Very wet.

Very willing.

She still didn't have a clue what she'd invited, or she'd be running like hell instead of standing there ready to face off with him in a game that she couldn't possibly win because she didn't know the rules.

And that, he'd decided as he'd whacked away, was the problem. He didn't know the rules anymore, either. She'd changed them. With her sweet little body, her vulnerability and her ability to make him feel...feel what, Savage?

He didn't know. He just knew he didn't like it. Was absolutely clueless about how to deal with her, what he felt for her, what he wanted from her.

In one day—twenty-four hours—she'd turned him inside out, flipped him upside down and spun him sideways.

He had to have some answers—about the epilepsy, about her expectations, her limitations, so he could get a handle on all this...this stuff that was rattling around in his head. Stuff he didn't understand. Stuff that made his chest hurt, made his head hurt. Stuff he'd never had to deal with before and didn't much like dealing with now.

Stuff that had made him lose it earlier. Yeah. He'd flat-out, combat-ready, lost it. His hands still shook when he thought about how he'd practically attacked her. Hell, he *had* attacked her, there was no *practically* about it. And outside, just now, he'd damn near lopped off a foot because he'd been thinking about her...about her mouth, about her breasts—

He was doing it again.

He drew a deep breath, unclenched his fists and made himself level. They would talk. He would get his answers—and then he would decide how this was going to play out.

"Shiloh Ranch," he heard her say as she snatched the receiver up on the second ring.

"Oh, hello, Pastor Good."

Lee watched her smile, then respond to whatever the good reverend was asking on the other end of the line.

He curbed his impatience and waited out the call.

"Oh, yes. Yes, I'm feeling much better today. Thank you."

She listened, smiled again, then blushed. "He's fine. Yes. He's right here. I was just putting out lunch.... Oh, no, of course you aren't interrupting.... Okay. Yes. And thanks for calling."

She hung up the phone, stared at it for a moment, then wiped her palms nervously on her jeans. "Pastor Good," she explained unnecessarily as she turned, making a vague gesture toward the black wall phone. "He wanted to know..."

She trailed off, and Lee felt compelled to prompt, "Let me guess. He wanted to know the same thing that Doc Lundstrum wanted to know when he called this morning while you were still sleeping. Then there was the call from old Mrs. Porter who had heard from Mrs. Stiller down at the library and Mrs. Waldrop over at the Christian Women's Club and, let's see, who else—Hap Callihan down at the hardware store. Lord, I thought he died a couple of years ago."

He was frowning and didn't know why. He should be grateful that people checked in on her. Instead he felt excluded. They knew things about her that he didn't. They knew how to take care of her better than he did. He didn't know a damn thing. But he was going to find out. Starting right now.

"Look, Ellie—"

Before he could finish, the phone rang again.

She started, her eyes big and round as she stared at him, waiting for him to continue as the phone rang a second time.

He stalked over, snagged the receiver off the hook and shoved it toward her. Then he dragged his hands through his hair, resigned to wait out another call.

''Um, Shiloh Ranch,'' she said after a long heartbeat. ''Oh. Hi, Buzz. Good. I'm good. Thank you... No. No, I don't have a list. No. I've got everything...actually, um, Lee should be able to pick up anything I need from now on.''

Lee frowned as he listened to her end of the conversation.

''Oh, Buzz, of course you can still come out and see me. Whenever you like. Yes. What would I do without our cribbage games? Right. Okay. I'll see you sometime soon.''

She hung up, turned to him again with another embarrassed little lift of her shoulders. ''That was Buzz.''

''Stop & Shop Grocery Store Buzz?''

She nodded.

''He has to be pushing eighty...and he's delivering groceries to Shiloh?''

She turned abruptly, showing him the view he'd been trying not to appreciate the hell out of since he'd walked into the kitchen and found her nose in the refrigerator and her sweet little butt pointed his way.

''He started when Momma got sick and Daddy was busy with foaling,'' she said reaching into the refrigerator and digging out a bowl of potato salad to go with the chicken she'd already set on the table. ''We needed groceries one day, I called and asked if anyone happened to be coming out this way and would he be willing to send out an order. Buzz ended up bringing it out, and he's been delivering groceries ever since when we needed them.''

He was about to ask why it was necessary for decrepit old Buzz to deliver their groceries when she met his eyes, looked quickly away, then started fussing with the tea towel that hung over the handle on the old gas stove.

Because she couldn't drive, that's why, he realized a split second later. He understood then, on a level that made him stop and really consider the implications, another facet of her limitations. It was pretty much common knowledge that, by law, the probability of seizures prevented many epileptics from possessing a valid driver's license. And what till now had been a tidbit of information that had never affected him or his life affected him deeply.

How would it feel, he wondered with a knot of realism tightening in his chest, to lose a basic freedom that he'd always taken for granted? How would it feel to be denied the excitement of plopping down a fee and trying to pass a driving test when you were sixteen years old? How would it feel to know you were breaking the law if you drove without a license to just get to work or to school or to the grocery store?

He studied her face, saw in her eyes both the pride she was entitled to and the shame that she had no reason to claim.

''Okay,'' she said into the silence that settled, ''you wanted to talk.''

Then she blushed from the roots of her hair to the pale flesh that disappeared beneath the round neck of her T-shirt. She'd dropped the tea towel. In fact she stood utterly still. The rise and fall of her breasts beneath her shirt was the only indication she was breathing.

He'd so been worried about how he would handle the information about her epilepsy. Well, what about her? How would talking about it make her feel? It would be hard for her. Harder than he'd ever realized.

It would hurt her. Leave her feeling exposed and vulnerable and, as she so often was, dependent on someone else's decision on how they would deal with the information. Would he reject her? Pity her? Use it against her? Worse, would he ridicule her as he was sure so many had?

Hell. He didn't want to think about it anymore. And he didn't want to talk. He wanted to hold her. He wanted to kiss her. Long and deep. Then he wanted to carry her to bed and do things to her that would guarantee she'd forget, at least for the moment, everything that put that look in her eyes.

And accomplish…what, Savage? *He'd* feel a hell of a lot better, yeah. But what about her? What kind of threat did a physical relationship pose to her health? That was the issue here. That was the only issue, he assured himself, refusing to acknowledge feelings that were as foreign as they were unthinkable.

The phone rang again.

He swore under his breath, waited out the call, then raised a brow when she finally said, ''It's okay, Dorothy, we'll be right there.''

Everything happened at warp speed then, as she disconnected then shoved food back into the refrigerator all the while giving him a hurried explanation of where they had to go and why it had to be right now.

Five

"There." As Lee's truck rolled to a stop, Ellie pointed toward a large pole building about a hundred yards west of the Fergusons' ranch house. "She'll be in that barn."

The phone call had been from their neighbor, Dorothy Ferguson. Don and Dorothy had always been good neighbors. When Ellie had lost her mom, it had been Dorothy who had sat with her in the night and held her while she cried. It had been Don who had watched over Shiloh when her dad had gotten sick and Ellie was dependent on someone to help her with chores and drive her to the hospital to see him and into town for supplies.

Now the Fergusons needed her. She would move heaven and earth to help them.

"Ellie, we're in a fix over here," Dorothy had said, her voice sounding breathless and worried over the phone lines. ‘‘Don is down in the back. Doc put him to bed this morning with some muscle relaxants and wouldn’t you know it, May Belle picked today to deliver. The fact is, darlin’, I’m just no good with birthings. Cal won’t be home for his spring break until the end of the month, so I don’t have anyone here to help me.

‘‘Gosh, honey, I hate to ask, being you’re on your honeymoon and all, but do you suppose I could borrow that beefy bridegroom of yours to help pull the foal? I’m afraid it’s comin’ breech or it would be over by now. The vet’s out of town—something about a convention and the on-call vet is tied up at Chester Gorman’s place. It may be hours before he can get here. I really hate this, honey.’’

Lee had listened to Ellie’s urgent but calmly detailed accounting of Dorothy Ferguson’s frantic call as he’d buttoned up his shirt. Then he’d snagged his truck keys from the windowsill above the kitchen sink. ‘‘I’ll be back as soon as I can,’’ he’d said, as the screen door slammed shut behind him.

As bad as he felt about the Fergusons’ dilemma, he was suddenly more than grateful for the chance to put a little distance between his libido and his bride.

What little perspective he’d gotten from his hour of slamming steel to wood had gone AWOL when he’d found Ellie in the kitchen, looking luscious and wholesome and, curiously, like she had a burr the size of Texas under her saddle. Even more curious were the violet eyes that had blurred to a cool-blue flame and suggested he might have been the one to put it there.

That had thrown him. That sweet, innocent, dependent little Ellie also had a backbone and a temper that could simmer near flash point had thrown him in spades. It had also excited him and gotten them right back where they'd started when he'd left her in the tub to let off some steam.

Dorothy's call was going to give him the distance he needed before he made another mistake. So he didn't walk, he ran to his truck at a fast jog. When he reached it and realized that Ellie was opening the passenger door at the same time he was crawling in the driver's side, he figured he'd kissed his distance—and his sanity goodbye. That didn't stop him from giving it one last try.

''You don't need to go with me, Ellie,'' he stated firmly as he jammed the key in the ignition and waited, his hand on the wheel, hoping she would climb out of the cab.

She didn't budge. She buckled herself in, looked straight ahead and said, ''Yes, I do,'' in a deceptively soft voice that fronted a quiet and set determination.

He looked at her over his extended arm, saw the stubborn set of her pixie chin and recognized not only another interesting facet to this woman, but a force to be reckoned with.

It could have been pride in her as much as surprise that sneaked in to undercut his irritation. And he might have smiled at her tenacity if the situation weren't so urgent—and if he hadn't needed some distance from her so badly.

He was supposed to be the voice of experience here. He was supposed to be the one who knew what to do, yet he'd made one mistake after another with her. The first had been in not realizing the extent of her dependence on him because of the epilepsy. The second had been in underestimating the strength of her will.

The most costly error of all, though, had been in letting her totally and completely mess with his head with that little stunt in the tub. He couldn't afford to make any more mistakes where she was concerned because she was the one who was going to suffer if he did.

But since the issue of her staying home or going along to the Fergusons' wasn't a hill he would pick to die on, he slipped the truck in gear and tore out of the drive.

Dorothy was wringing her hands when she walked out onto the porch to greet them.

"Thank goodness you're here! I can't go down there. I just can't stand to see May Belle struggle that way. Besides, it's all I can handle keeping Don in bed. He's bound and determined he's going to crawl down to the barn and help that mare."

"You go take care of Don," Lee heard Ellie say as he rounded the truck and headed for the barn at a trot. "We'll take care of things."

"Ellie, you stay with Dorothy," he ordered over his shoulder—for all the good it did. She was right behind him when he unlatched the barn door and let himself inside.

"I told you to stay with Dorothy." He leveled her his best, take-charge glare. "You don't need to be involved in this." And he didn't need her distracting him. He thought again about that close call with the ax. He'd been thinking about her, seeing her all wet and willing and naked.

It hadn't ended there. He'd just spent fifteen long minutes in his truck at breakneck speed getting over here—had almost lost control at one curve because, instead of concentrating on his driving, he'd been thinking about her. The buoyant softness of her breasts, the inviting resilience of her thighs, the downy copper curls sheltering her virginity.

And she *was* a virgin. He'd been a fool to doubt that. A jealous fool. Everything about her response to his kisses said she was untried, from the sweetness of her sighs to the tentative explorations of her tongue.

He, however, wasn't nineteen anymore, randy as an alley cat and ruled by the pulse below his waist that was raging yet again as he glared down at her. And just kept on glaring because he couldn't seem to take his eyes off her.

A desperate, high-pitched whinny brought his head around and reminded him why he was here. ''Please. Go to the house,'' he said one more time, because he really had to get away from her.

''How long has it been since you pulled a foal?'' she asked, sticking to his side as he headed for the back of the barn.

He set his jaw, drew a breath between clenched teeth and, finally resigned to the fact that she wasn't going away, kept on walking. ''A while. But I've pulled plenty of calves. It's not that different.''

''This is very different.'' She shouldered past him and unlatched the birthing stall where a big bay mare lay panting and frothed with sweat. ''It's different because this is May Belle and she's very special, aren't you girl,'' she crooned softly as she knelt by the mare's head and soothed her with tender strokes to her jaw.

Another one of those strange, fisting sensations

clutched at his chest as he looked at her there on her knees in the straw.

He made himself look away, check out the situation.

Oh, man. He scrubbed his hand over his jaw. They were in trouble. The mare had lost a lot of blood and, judging by the consistency of the fluid leakage, the umbilical sac may have broken. May Belle's eyes were wild, her breaths rapid. She knew she was in trouble, too. Fatigue and pain showed in the tension in her abdomen and her stiff-legged stretch.

He cupped his nape with a palm, shook his head. Very likely Dorothy's call had come too late.

''No.''

He shifted his gaze to Ellie's. The passion of her denial told him that she'd read his thoughts.

''Ellie—''

''We can't lose her. May Belle—May Belle is Don's foundation mare. He's built his breeding program on her babies and her babies' babies. She's Bud's momma,'' she said, referring to her own chestnut gelding. ''We cannot lose her.''

Both a child's hopes and a woman's determination fired in her eyes—and kicked an errant Lancelot gene into high gear.

With his gaze fixed on her face, he started rolling up his sleeves. ''Talk to her, Ellie. See if you can get her to relax,'' he suggested softly.

Then he went in search of a bucket of soapy water and prepared for both the physical and mental concentration required to pull, what he hoped, wasn't a dead foal.

Late-afternoon sunlight filtered into the stall. The scent of must and hay and the struggles of life emerging permeated the air and melded with a quiet that had settled over the barn.

"She's so pretty," Ellie whispered as she stood by May Belle's withers and stroked the hip of the still-wet and tentatively nursing filly.

A soft, reassuring nicker and the greedy suckling smacks of the newborn foal having her first meal brought a slow smile to her face.

For the past fifteen minutes Lee had sat quietly in the corner of the stall, watching Ellie, watching the foal, rubbing the circulation back into his right arm. And brooding. He was getting damned good at that.

A stray beam of sunlight flitted around her curls and set them afire. He wanted to wrap a fiery gold curl around his finger, fist his hand in the heavy silk of her hair, draw her to him, feel his hands on her skin, fill her as a woman can only be filled by a man.

He let out a deep breath, let his head fall back against the wall of the stall.

What are you doing to me, Ellie?

She drew feelings from him—anger, desperation, longing—that he had never let himself feel. He'd had little time for emotion in his life to this point, less need. And now…now he couldn't think for the havoc she was wreaking. He didn't like it, but he couldn't muster up enough resistance to shove it all out of the way. It was starting to wear on him.

"Your arm? Is it getting any better?"

Her soft voice brought his head up. He blinked, willed the sexual haze to lift. "The good news? The feeling's back. The bad news? The feeling's back."

She smiled. "It hurts bad, huh?"

He shook his head. "It's fine."

It wasn't fine, and he'd been stupid. They both knew it—she was just kind enough not to point it out.

He'd made a mistake. Big surprise. He'd been on his knees in the straw behind the laboring mare and reached in to try to turn the foal. It was standard operating procedure. The trick was timing. Never enter a birth canal until after a contraction. He'd been so entranced by the look of his bride as she'd sweet-talked and whispered and murmured tender encouragement to a thousand pounds of laboring horseflesh, that he'd lost sight of anything but her.

When May Belle had gone into a full contraction, he'd been in shoulder deep. Idiotic move. Painful move. Only luck had kept him from ending up with a dislocated shoulder or a broken arm. Just like it was only luck that both mare and foal had pulled through.

"They're going to be okay, aren't they?" She left the bonding pair and walked to his side, looking down on him.

He let out a deep breath, still baffled. "They shouldn't have made it. Neither one of them. But, yeah, they're going to be just fine."

He'd given them up for lost the minute he'd sized up the situation. Ellie hadn't let him get away with it. He could tell that she wanted to give him credit, but if anyone was responsible, she was—just as she was responsible for a lot of things he didn't understand and didn't want to deal with right now.

Determined not to, he rolled wearily to his hip, then his knees and started to stand.

Her hand reached down for his. He hesitated for a moment, then grasped it.

Her hand was small, but there was strength in her

grip. It shouldn't have surprised him—but then, why not. Just about everything about her did.

He let her help him to his feet—and then stood there, holding on to her hand, searching her eyes.

How did you get so strong, Ellie? he wondered. How do you stand so strong with all you have to deal with?

"Thanks," he croaked around the lump that had suddenly lodged in his throat. And then he couldn't help it. He pulled her into his arms, tucked her head under his chin and thought of a hundred things he wanted to say to her. But that would require some disclosure on his part. He wasn't even close to wanting to deal with that—or with the truths he might reveal if he did start talking.

So what came out was, "I'm a mess."

He squeezed her hard and because his overriding need was to keep her there, set her away. "Come on. Let's go tell Dorothy the good news. Then let's go home."

Home.

He drove back to Shiloh in silence, trying not to think about how quickly he'd come to associate the word with the woman who sat by his side.

A sliver of lavender, deep purple and shimmering silver was all that was left of the sunset when Ellie watched Lee walk into the kitchen, fresh from his shower.

They'd been back from the Fergusons' for a little more than an hour. She was determined to talk to him, and while he'd showered, she'd put all the words in place, lined them up like soldiers, steady, strong, direct. But then she saw him. Her mouth went bone dry and the words…the words got lost somewhere between her scattered heartbeats.

He was barefoot, his clean jeans riding low on his hips; the tails of his worn chambray shirt hung loose, the buttons were undone. The forest-green towel he held in his hands was damp. So was his hair. Thick and dark, it curled softly at his nape, even as he worked it ruthlessly with the towel, brushing it back from his forehead.

He was so handsome it made her chest hurt. And his blue eyes were so distant and closed off it made her stomach knot.

"You go ahead and shower," he'd insisted when they pulled into the drive. "I'll do chores."

So she had. She'd showered and thought and then she'd waited in the kitchen, set out their dinner that had turned into supper and rehearsed what she was going to say the minute he came downstairs.

Now here he stood, and all she could do was ache at the look of him. And feel the chill.

They'd shared something special in that barn with May Belle and her baby. Ellie couldn't name it, but she recognized the subtle difference just the same. She'd thought they had turned a corner—only now it looked as if they'd lost their way again in the lonesome silence on the drive home.

He'd been fighting mad when he'd found her in the kitchen earlier. For that matter, so had she been. She'd been ready to tell him a thing or two about frogs and princes and how she wasn't so sure she hadn't ended up with the green one of the two.

She understood now where her anger had come from. She'd been conditioned to always be on the defensive. Past experience had taught her it was the best protection from curious stares and taunting remarks. But Lee wasn't like that. He'd never been like that. He didn't see her as an oddity, and she was ashamed that she'd sold him short—even if she'd had provocation.

But now she was dealing with something else again. Something that made her want to shout, "Talk to me. Tell me what I'm doing wrong."

Instead she watched him snag a drumstick as he headed for the fridge, where he searched inside until he found the milk.

"You must be starving."

Great. All those words she'd rehearsed and that's what came out. She'd lost her courage now that she was face-to-face with him again. Her insecurities took over just like that, much stronger than she was.

What if he simply didn't want to be with her? What if there had been another woman in his life in Texas? A woman he had left because he'd promised her daddy he'd take care of her.

A woman. Not a girl with a problem.

Suddenly she didn't want to know.

So instead of facing her demons, she followed his lead and walked to the cupboard and got him a glass.

He made a humming sound around the chicken leg, which passed for appreciation that he was finally getting something in his stomach.

"Good," he managed after swallowing a healthy mouthful and washing it down with milk she'd poured for him. "Nothing better than cold fried chicken. You're a good cook, Ellie," he added after helping himself to the potato salad and a homemade bun.

"I had a good teacher."

The wave of sorrow that swamped her was as powerful as it was unexpected. So were the sudden tears she tried like crazy to blink back. She quickly turned her back to him and stared out the kitchen window.

I miss you, Momma. I miss you, Daddy. I need you. Both of you, to tell me how to be a wife. I don't know what to do. I don't know how to reach him—or if he even wants me to. If he even wants me.

"Ellie."

She felt him at her back, his heat, his strength, and because it was what she needed most, she turned into the arms that opened to her.

Then she held on. Just held on as his heart beat strong and sure beneath her cheek. "I miss them," she confessed against his shirt.

"I know, baby." His arms banded tighter around her. "I miss them, too."

She pressed her face into the warmth of his throat. "I'm sorry. I didn't mean to do this." She clutched at the soft cotton shirt that smelled of him and of soap. "Sometimes…sometimes it just sneaks up on me. And I feel so alone."

He rocked her gently back and forth. "You're not alone anymore," he whispered, and pressed a kiss to the top of her head.

"Come on." He set her gently away. "You're tired. And you need to eat as much as I do."

So they ate. In a fractured silence filled with carefully guarded smiles and little else.

He helped her do the dishes.

Then they went to bed.

At least she did.

With her heart in her throat, she waited for him to join her. But he never did.

Not that night. Or any night in the week that followed.

Each morning he would greet her with a smile, a careful distant peck on her cheek and a ''How are you?'' that was quickly followed by ''I'll see you later, then, if you're sure you're okay.'' Then he'd take off fixing this and fixing that as if there wasn't going to be a tomorrow—or as if he didn't want to spend any time alone with her.

Ellie would feed her birds. She would water her seedlings and plan her garden, cook his meals, wash his clothes and wonder what to do.

Each night in the dark, in her bed, she would close her eyes and wish that it was Lee who was with her—instead of just his words that played like an echo in her mind.

You're not alone anymore.

But she was.

She was alone and she wished with all her heart that she were woman enough to make him understand.

Every day, along with the mail, Leon Wilks brought the daily edition of the *Wall Street Journal* and the *Denver Post.*

Every night after supper Lee snagged them like they were lifelines and went out to the porch to read each one from cover to cover.

They'd developed a pattern. It was working, he told himself.

Yeah, right. That's why he averaged two hours of sleep a night on the couch because he didn't dare use one of the bedrooms upstairs that was so close to hers.

And it was why Ellie looked so lost.

He'd hurt her.

When he left her alone in her room each night, he hurt her. He knew it. He just couldn't get past it.

He told himself it was because he was giving her time. In truth, he was the one who needed the time. He really didn't know how to handle this. Any of it. Not his physical desire for her that had become a matter of pride that he control. Not his inability to figure out how to approach the subject of her epilepsy.

In that moment last Sunday when he'd held her and she'd cried for her parents, it had hit home again just how young she was. How fragile. And he'd known he had to back off until he could get a grip.

For all the good that idea had done him. He was as owly as a bear with beestings. And he was restless. As restless as she was.

From the porch he could hear her in the house, setting the kitchen right after supper, tidying up the dining room.

They couldn't go on like this. Something had to change. He just wished that he knew how or where to go from here. Folding the papers, he pulled off his reading glasses and set them both aside. Rocking forward in the ancient and creaking wicker chair, he tried to think things through—then frowned at the lane leading to Shiloh.

"What the hell?"

He stood up, walked to the end of the new porch floor just as Ellie came outside, her brows furrowed, a dish towel forgotten in her hand. She'd seen it, too—or heard it.

A long line of what—with a little fanciful imagination—looked like a ribbon of fireflies, trailed down the road. In reality it was a string of headlights cutting through the darkening dusk.

There must have been close to twenty cars and pickups, and they were all blowing their horns non-stop.

"Something's wrong," he said as he headed for the bottom step with Ellie right behind him.

They stood there, prepared for the worst, when one by one the vehicles pulled up in front of the house and killed the horns. The loudest cacophony of clanging and banging and hoots and hollers and laughter erupted then as dozens of people spilled out into the night beating on pots and pans that they carried like drums.

Lee shot Ellie a baffled look.

She just lifted her shoulders, as befuddled as he was, until the wrinkled old face of Buzz Sheppard grinned up at them from the bottom of the steps.

"Shivaree!" Buzz shouted gleefully and, pounding a wooden spoon on the bottom of a blackened old stew pot, led the laughing throng around the house in a shuffling dance that only they knew the steps to. "Shivaree! Shivaree!"

"Shiva-what?" Lee shouted above the noise, bending his head close to hers.

Ellie smiled then, and a laugh bubbled out as the howling, pan-banging parade passed by.

"Shivaree," she shouted, then clasped her hands together as warmth filled her chest. "They're giving us a shivaree."

"What the hell is a shivaree?" He placed an arm over her shoulders and drew her against his side.

"It's a noisy mock serenade to newlyweds," she

explained, tipping her head up to his so he could hear her. "It's an old Sundown custom."

A mock serenade to a mock marriage. The irony hit him where it hurt—and where he knew it must hurt Ellie.

But she was smiling, and for her sake he put on his game face.

"An old custom and a loud one," he said with a forced laugh, then waved when he recognized Pastor Good and his wife, Martha. "Does this mean I have to share your leftover pot roast with them?"

Her eyes were shining. "Something tells me they're going to be sharing a lot more with us than we are with them."

The noisy bunch rounded the house about that time and headed back for their vehicles. When they trooped back up the walk, the only noise was their laughing chatter. Buzz had traded his stew pot and spoon for a fiddle. Someone brought out a guitar. Everyone else carried covered casseroles, bowls of salad and armloads of prettily wrapped packages. There was even a wedding cake—compliments of Doc Lundstrum's wife.

Lee wanted to be annoyed. He was frustrated. He was concerned about Ellie. But when he looked down and saw her smiling face, he couldn't be anything but happy for her.

He simply stepped aside as their unexpected guests trooped inside and took over.

Six

"He watches you." Peg Lathrop lifted a forkful of wedding cake and grinned at Ellie.

Ellie blinked, then looked at the young woman who had sought her out where she'd sat in the corner of the living room surrounded by wrapping paper and the wedding gifts she and Lee had recently opened.

When Peg laughed at Ellie's look of disbelief, Ellie searched for Lee. She found him standing in the arched doorway that separated the living room from the dining room. He *was* watching her, but he quickly looked away and returned his attention to Dorothy Ferguson, who had arrived with a slow-moving Don in tow.

"Can't keep his eyes off you," Peg added knowingly when Ellie met her gaze again.

"Um," was all Ellie could manage as she looked from Peg to Lee again.

He looked so tall and lean, so confident and strong as he laughed at something Dorothy said, his white teeth flashing, the creases around his eyes and mouth deepening.

She thought about that mouth, about the way it had felt on hers the day of their wedding, the morning after in her bed and later in the tub. She thought about it when she washed dishes or when she was gathering eggs. She thought about it each night, as she lay alone in her bed.

Peg touched her arm, smiling softly. ''So I take it the feeling's mutual?''

The pair of embroidered pillowcases Martha Good had given them as a wedding gift suddenly became the focus of her attention. She wanted desperately to confide in Peg. She had always been one of Ellie's most special alliances. Peg was twenty-six and a single mom. In Sundown, Montana, population 473, that alone was a pretty big cross to bear. Ellie hadn't cared about any of that. She liked Peg, who had always made it a point to talk to Ellie when they'd run into each other at church, or at Lathrop Feed Store where Peg kept books for her dad.

Unlike most people close to her age, the epilepsy didn't bother Peg. For the most part those same people ignored her or stared with either a warped sort of fascination or a guilt-ridden pity. Peg was different. Peg accepted her for who she was. And for that alone, Peg, with her flashing brown eyes and long slim body, would always be special to Ellie.

''Well,'' Peg prompted with a gentle elbow in Ellie's ribs, ''How's it goin'?''

Ellie felt the blush all the way to her toes.

Peg laughed. ''That good, huh?'' But her smile

faded as she took a second look at Ellie's face and didn't like what she saw. ''Uh-oh. What's wrong?''

Even though Ellie was a private person, with Peg she didn't feel so guarded. The words were out before she knew it. ''I wish I knew.''

Wisely Peg didn't say anything. She simply waited.

''I'm not so sure he's all that happy about...about being saddled with me,'' Ellie finally admitted.

She ran a thumbnail along the intricately embroidered stitches that made a purple iris and a yellow crocus on the pillowslip and dodged Peg's probing gaze.

''Oh, honey.'' Peg grasped her hands, glared over at Lee, then relaxed when she saw he was watching Ellie with a quietly predatory look, and with a hunger that even Peg—who had been in dry dock for longer than she cared to admit—recognized for what it was. ''I don't think for a minute that's the problem. When he looks at you, there's enough heat in that man's eyes to fire a furnace.''

''Then why am I still a virgin almost a week after my wedding?'' Ellie blurted out in a whisper.

Peg blinked. Ellie watched her blink again before she added a quiet, ''Oh.''

Ellie spilled it all then. She'd needed someone to talk to for so long. Peg listened with quiet encouragement while Ellie told her about the seizure on her wedding day, about Lee holding her all night that night, about what had happened in the bathtub, and about every night she'd slept alone in her bed since.

''Come on,'' Peg said, after a moment. She stood and tugged Ellie out onto the porch. ''I think I know what's going on here but, just to make sure, tell me everything again. And don't leave one thing out.''

* * *

Later that night Lee sat alone in the big wicker rocker on the shadowed porch. Storm clouds had ruled the morning but had given way by midday to full sun. Now, close to 1:00 a.m.—an hour since the shivaree had ended and the last old dog had packed up his pots and pans and tottered home—thunderheads were stacking up again. An egg-shaped moon winked in and out of the clouds that scudded across the sky like a troop of slowly patrolling night watchmen.

He leaned forward, propped his elbows on his knees and stared at his loosely clasped hands as a night breeze picked up and sent Ellie's wind chimes dancing.

She had been exhausted by the time the crowd had left. Exhausted and happier than he'd been able to make her since he'd come back to Shiloh and married her.

In spite of himself he had to smile when he thought of the gathered throng. Old Doc, Buzz and a couple of dozen others. His smile faded to a frown. One person. There had been only one person in on the shivaree who was even close to Ellie's age.

It told him too much about Ellie's life that Peg Lathrop was the only young person from Sundown in the group. Where were the friends her own age?

Even as he formed the thought, he knew the answer. There weren't any. These were her parents' friends. These were the people of Sundown who cared about her. These were the ones she trusted to accept her as she was.

He leaned back again, listened to the muffled creak of the rocker and the chirp of spring's first crickets in the grass around the lattice-wrapped porch. In the far distance a low roll of thunder rumbled across the mountain ridge. In the not-so-far distance rumbled the grim reminder of how cruel kids could be.

He'd had his own mechanisms in place back then for dealing with the taunts that had labeled him everything from ''outsider'' to ''loser'' to ''welfare case.'' He'd knocked the snot out of anyone who'd even looked at him sideways. He raised a hand, rubbed a finger over the small crescent-shaped scar at the corner of his mouth. That scar, along with the slight bend in his nose that hadn't set quite right after it had been broken by a fist in the face were reminders of those angry, defensive fights he'd been quick to start and slow to walk away from. While his anger hadn't changed anyone's view of him, or for that matter, his view of himself, his choice of expressing it had shut them up. And, right or wrong, it had given him an outlet for his rage and humiliation.

You didn't have that option, did you, Ellie?

At a level that he'd hadn't let himself fully acknowledge since returning to Shiloh, he understood that he didn't hold the only advanced degree from the school of hard knocks. He'd grown up on the streets, been kicked around, left to twist in the wind and fend for himself until Will and Clare had found him.

Ellie was a graduate of that school, too, except she'd had a different set of classes to deal with. With her illness came so many limitations, so much disappointment. So many reasons not to trust and so much time alone. And so many reasons to be bitter and disillusioned and swayed to the side of defeat.

Yet look at her. She was none of those things.

He drew in a deep breath. Let it out. And wished he'd been around to slay her dragons for her.

Well, he was here to take care of her now. And he'd been right to leave her alone each night. It was for her good, not his.

Walking away from her bed each night had nothing to do with wanting her so badly it consumed him. Walking away had nothing to do with a creeping, seeping suspicion that if there was a need here, it was the one he felt to be surrounded by her goodness, to draw from her strength, to open himself up to feelings that he'd spent his entire life convincing himself didn't exist—or that he, at least, had control over.

That control went on red alert when he heard the front door open, then close.

He stiffened when she walked past him on bare feet. With her back to him, she leaned against the porch rail to watch the shifting shades of gray cloud creep across the moon and douse the light.

"You couldn't sleep, either?" Her voice was as soft as the night breeze that tugged at her hair that hung nearly to her waist. The tumble of curls looked as soft as she looked bewitching.

He swallowed hard as a break in the cloud cover flooded moonlight across his bride and the white-on-white nightgown she wore.

Where was her robe, he thought frantically? Where was her fussy pink robe that covered her from ankle to throat and only gave him glimpses and guesses at the curves that lay beneath?

Where did she get that…that whisper of a gown that left nothing and everything to the imagination? Virginal white. Long and flowing. As gossamer as sea mist, as concealing as a bridal veil. Her back was still to him, and he could see every curve and contour of her womanly body. The soft flair of her hips, the rounded firmness of her buttocks, the slim line of her legs.

He tried to look away; he couldn't. And he knew in that moment he was in very large trouble.

"I like to come out here, too, when I'm having trouble sleeping." She turned to him then and pressed her cheek to a porch post that he'd painted two days ago. When he was sane. Which he wasn't now. Which he had no hope of becoming as she hugged the post with her arm and leaned against it.

"I guess I shouldn't have had that last cup of coffee," he croaked, unable to take his eyes off her, which only got him into more trouble.

It was a honeymoon gown, he realized finally. Very sheer. Very flowing. Very—he suppressed a groan—very sexy.

The hem skimmed the floor, though the toes of her tiny bare feet peeked out beneath it. The neckline was round and low, held together between her breasts with a single delicate white satin ribbon. He could see the shadowed outline of her nipples pressing against the softly clinging fabric that the night breeze molded against her sweet, sweet breasts. Against her flat belly and the slight indentation of her navel. The downy curls at the apex of her thighs.

"You." He cleared his throat, tried again while his heart jumped into a jungle beat. "You should go back inside. You—" He swallowed as her nipples tightened then pressed like diamonds against silk. "You must be…cold."

And he was hot. Blistering hot and already imagining that with one flick of his finger he could undo the ribbon that held her gown in place. With one tug of his hand he could peel that skim of material from her breast and feel the velvet softness of her nipple against his tongue. Taste the silk of her skin. Draw her deep into his mouth.

"Do you want me to go inside, Lee?" She took a slow step toward him.

He groaned, closed his eyes…and opened them to find her kneeling at his feet…searching his face with eyes the color of summer violets…covering his thighs with small, warm hands—hands that he'd imagined touching him in places that would shock her and send him straight over the edge.

"Ellie." It was a serrated, grating whisper that begged her to leave before he forgot why he was still clinging to a desperate notion that he was saving her from whatever the hell he was so certain he needed to save her from.

He clamped his fingers around the arms of the rocker to keep from reaching for her. To keep from ravaging her. "Go to bed," he ordered gruffly.

"I've been to bed," she whispered as she rose and eased onto his lap.

He swallowed hard, dug deep and found very little to hang on to—except her. She looped one arm around his neck, pressed the palm of her other hand against his chest where his heart slammed like a jackhammer. She smelled like vanilla and cinnamon and woman.

"I've been to bed," she repeated softly. "It was lonely there. It's *been* lonely there."

It was too much. He was only human. And she was his wife. Her scent surrounded him, her slight weight, the heavy curtain of her hair, teased by the wind, fluttered across his face, snagged on his midnight stubble.

He wanted everything she offered. He craved it. And as she shifted so she could look into his eyes, and inadvertently pressed her hip against the rock-hard length of his arousal, he thought he'd die if he couldn't take it.

"Don't you want me, Lee?"

Moonlight danced across her fiery curls and cast her face in shadow.

"Don't want you?" He groaned, incredulous, and surrendered…to the night that tempered his sanity, to the eyes that begged him to love her, to the need that had grown beyond denial.

"I have wanted you…" His hands moved to span her waist and settle her hips deeper into his lap. "I have wanted you for what seems like forever."

He skated a hand up her ribs then across one sweet breast and higher, to span his fingers along her throat and tip her face to his. "Your mouth. Ellie—" he brushed his thumb across her lower lip, felt her tremble "—how I've wanted your mouth."

Ellie caught her breath, bit back a moan as a wild, delicious arc of heat shot from her breast to her belly where it pooled, then spread like liquid fire.

Peg had been right. He *did* want her. And she'd been a fool to wonder and worry and not take matters into her own hands. The problem, she realized now, was not that he saw her as different, not that he didn't want her, but that he didn't want to see her as a woman. He wanted to think of her as his charge—or thought he *should* think of her that way. That much Peg had helped her figure out. She just wasn't sure why he was so determined on the issue.

Determined or not, he was seeing her differently now.

He'd started seeing her differently, she realized, that morning when he'd kissed her in the bathtub. She wasn't sure why she knew—maybe it was that woman's intuition Momma had always talked about—but she understood now that in that moment he'd not only seen her as a woman, he'd wanted her as one. And he hadn't been very happy with himself because of it.

The *why* of it still puzzled her. The *how* of getting him past it, however, was starting to become very clear. To make him treat her like a woman, she simply had to behave like one.

"Will you kiss me, Lee? Will…will you kiss me like you did that morning in the bathtub?"

She barely got the last word out before he lowered his head and covered her mouth with his.

And kissed her. The way a man is supposed to kiss a woman, she thought, as she threw her arms around his neck and hung on, ready to go anywhere he wanted to take her.

"Oh. Oh," she murmured on a breathless sigh when he tilted his head to increase the contact, adjust the angle, heighten the pleasure. And there was pleasure. So much, so fast, her heart was racing as she turned into him, wanting, suddenly, to crawl under his skin and be a part of him from the inside out.

"Ellie…Ellie, sweetheart."

From a distance she heard him whisper her name. With a small whimper of protest she felt his mouth leave hers, only to slam back hard for a fierce, hungry kiss before he dragged his mouth away again.

"Lee."

"Shush, baby."

A warm hand cupped her cheek as he pressed his lips to her forehead and drew in a ragged breath. "I'm not going anywhere. I'm just…just slowing things down a little."

"I liked it fast."

A harsh laugh rumbled against her breast. "Oh, I know. I know you did. But…just trust me on this, okay? You're gonna like it this way, too."

"What way?" she felt dazed as she lay back in his arms and watched his face, watched his eyes go dark and hazy.

"Slow and easy," he whispered, and good to his word, eased his hand slowly down her cheek, along the column of her throat. "Very, very slow. Very, very easy."

She was breathless with anticipation as, in agonizingly slow motion, his hand stole lower to finally cup and caress her breast through her gown. Everything inside her clenched at the wondrous pleasure, at the electric thrill of his hand touching her where she had longed for him to touch her for what seemed like forever.

She closed her eyes, arched into his hand as he caressed and stroked, then circled her nipple with the tip of his thumbnail.

"Oh." Stunning sensations spiraled through her body. She wanted them to go on forever, yet she wanted more. "Lee."

"Shush. Easy, remember? Let me go slow and easy with you, Ellie. We've both waited so long."

She opened her eyes, her trust complete, her need enveloping her in a new set of feelings, a new sense of awareness.

He lifted her then, shifted her until she was no longer lying sideways in his arms but straddling his lap. Her knees pressed into the flowered cushion on either side of his hips, her gown bunched around her thighs in silky folds. Her bottom nestled on his muscled thighs and he very purposefully lifted her arms and draped them over his shoulders as her hair drifted over hers. He clasped his hands at her hips and held her there, warm against him, open against him.

It was shocking. Exciting. She'd never felt more vulnerable, or more alive.

"Kiss me, Ellie." His blue eyes were dark with promise, his voice, a velvet command. "Kiss me the way you've been wanting to kiss me."

She searched his face, then studied his mouth, the full lower lip, the lovely cupid's bow of his upper lip, the tiny scar that resembled a crescent moon. She wasn't aware that she had licked her own lips, savoring the feast to come. When his mouth curved up in an indulgent smile, she realized what she'd done and felt her face flush in the moonlight.

"It's all right." He turned his face to the inside of her forearm, bit her gently, then kissed the tender flesh in supplication. "I love how you look at me."

"How do I look at you?" Her voice sounded breathless, just the way she felt as he turned back to her, his cobalt-blue gaze drifting across her face beneath the sweep of dark thick lashes.

"Like you want to eat me up in little bites."

It was her turn to smile as a newfound confidence bolstered her. "I'd rather have a big bite, please."

He laughed, and the sound filled her with love and desire and a confidence she'd never dreamed she had in her. She leaned forward, touched her mouth softly to his.

He drew in a breath, closed his eyes. And she smiled and, still smiling, touched her mouth to his again. This time she lingered and licked and learned the shape of him, and understood that she fed his hunger when his arms banded around her and he dragged her hard against him.

She loved his tongue. The taste of it, the bold possession as it swept inside her mouth and claimed, then teased, then gentled until she was the one teasing and he was the one squirming to draw her closer, he was the one fighting for a steady breath.

"Umm." She licked her lips as she pulled away and sat back down on his thighs. "You taste like coffee. And wedding cake."

"And you taste…Ellie, you taste like heaven." His gaze on hers, he skimmed his hands up ribs and stopped, just below her breasts. Ever so softly he brushed his thumbs up and along the tips of her nipples.

She shivered and tried not to whimper.

"Can I taste you here?" he asked quietly, making it clear with the steady sweep of his thumbs where he wanted his mouth, what he wanted to do.

She'd read the book. She'd seen the pictures. She'd imagined what it would feel like to have Lee's mouth on her breasts. To feel him kiss her there. But she'd seen pictures of a man's hands on a woman's breasts, too, and she'd imagined what that would feel like. Imagination hadn't begun to compare to reality. So just thinking of Lee's mouth there, where his hands had been, sent a lush, liquid heat gushing through her body.

"Yes, oh, yes," she answered, and with flying fingers reached for the ribbon that held her gown closed.

His hands stilled hers. She looked up, watched him through a curtain of hair.

He brushed it back from her face, tucked it behind her ear. "First like this." With his hands spanning her waist, he lifted her until she was standing on her knees before him.

Her breasts were on a level with his mouth. She could feel the tips tighten just thinking about what he would do next. And what he did next made her draw in her breath and dig her fingers into his shoulders.

He urged her forward with those big, gentle hands on her waist and breathed on her. A warm breath, a gentle caress, a promise that made her shiver and burn all at the same time.

"More?" He bussed his nose around the edge of her aureole.

She did whimper then, and pressed herself against him.

"Definitely more," he murmured with a smile in his voice as he kissed the valley between her breasts, then worked his way in small, eating kisses to the peak of her left nipple.

She clutched a handful of his hair, sighed his name.

And then he surrounded her, biting her lightly through her gown, driving her wild with the wet sweep of his tongue against fabric and skin, making her moan, making her yearn. He tasted his fill, lingering over one breast, then the other until he finally pulled away and with his eyes gone slumberous and dark, gave her permission to undo her gown.

Her fingers were shaking as she untied the small ribbon. Her breath was shallow, as shimmering silk fell open, exposing a pale slice of flesh to the night and to his eyes. His hands moved slowly, first to cover her, then to caress, then to separate silk from skin. Slower still, he brushed the gown aside. Her heart was in her throat as she shrugged it off her shoulders, then lifting her arms, let it slide free to pool at her hips.

She watched him swallow, felt his fingers spread wide beneath her shoulder blades as he looked his fill, murmured his approval, then pulled her unerringly toward him.

It could have been her name she heard escape his lips, it could have been a prayer. She didn't know. Didn't care, couldn't think for the feel of his mouth on her skin. Naked lips to naked breast.

She had never imagined. Had never known about the magic, the magnitude of sensations. A man's mouth. Lee's mouth, drawing on her breast. The stubble of his cheek brushing her skin, the heat of his breath. It was more than a delicious, mind-numbing sensation, it was a deep, soul-deep communion. And she understood in that wonderful moment that she wasn't the only one who needed this physical contact. *He* needed. He needed her. She felt it with the gentleness of his touch, the endless depth of his hunger.

His eyes were deep, dark extensions of his soul as he kissed her breast one last time, then slumped back in the chair, watching her. Wanting her. His gaze never left her face as he ran his hand up and under flowing silk that drifted across her thighs. He spread his fingers wide, absorbing the resilience of her muscles beneath his palms, the warmth of her flesh.

His gaze locked on hers, he slid his hands slowly toward her center.

"Can I touch you here?" His voice was a scratchy, velvet whisper.

She shivered, felt her inner muscles clench, felt herself pulse and swell—and for the first time felt a twinge of self-consciousness. But this was Lee. This was her husband whose lap she straddled, her husband whose gaze had gone smoky and dark, her husband whose mouth had suckled her breasts and wanted to touch her intimately. This, finally, was her lover.

The night breeze lifted her hair, whispered across her breasts still wet from his loving, still tight with longing.

She leaned forward, brushed his lips with hers. "Please," she murmured into the warm, wet wonder that was his mouth as his hands moved higher up her thighs, his thumb stroking, enticing, "Please, please touch me. Touch me there."

She watched his eyes as he brushed the back of his knuckles against her curls. She breathed his name, waiting, waiting for the touch of him. For the love of him.

He touched her then.

Finally.

Gently.

Then deeply.

She heard herself moan, felt her fingers dig into his shoulders and didn't care that she was completely open, totally vulnerable. It felt so…exotic and so unexpectedly shocking. So extraordinarily good.

With a light hand he stroked her, a delicious little swirl of his finger to her core. She felt her own wetness, thought she should be embarrassed by it but was too lost in sensation to do anything but hold him tighter and wish she knew how to ask for more.

Somehow he knew. He gave more without her asking, intensifying the pressure, increasing the speed until she rocked involuntarily against his touch, begging him for something…something. She didn't know. She just wanted it to go on and on, this pleasure that was so pure and so perfect that she gave herself over to it. Lost herself in the wonder as it built to an electric, enveloping climax that eclipsed thought, vanquished control and ripped through her body like a starburst. With a shattered cry she let it take her, let it toss her, let it consume her until she collapsed against him, boneless and winded and deliriously devastated.

Lee gathered her against him, his heart pounding in tandem with hers. He wanted—more than he wanted his next breath—he wanted to free himself from his jeans and bury himself deep inside her. He was past denying that he wanted her—all she'd had to do was ask. All she'd had to do was offer, and all of his resolve had folded like a tower of precariously stacked cards.

She'd held the trump card tonight. In retrospect he realized now that she always had. He'd just been fooling himself into believing he was the one who would call the shots and make the rules.

He knotted a fist in her hair, absorbed her heat and the aftershocks that rippled through her delicate, hot little body. Her first time. He'd been amazed by her responses. He'd expected hesitation. He'd expected shyness. And yes, there had been some. It had flickered across her face just as the moonlight had flickered through the clouds, but she'd quickly denied it and leaped without fear into his arms. Into his soul, with her breathless sighs, her fearless heart.

Addiction. He'd never understood it. He thought he might have a loose handle on it now. He could get addicted to the look of her, the feel of her, the scent of her coming apart in his arms.

She shivered and snuggled closer, her breathing leveling, her heartbeat settling. She was so limp, so…wasted…he tempered his desire, dived headlong into concern—where he should have been from the moment she'd walked into the moonlight and stolen his breath and his sanity.

Too much. He'd taken too much. He'd pressed her too soon.

"Ellie? Sweetheart?"

She sighed and wrapped herself around him as if he was a bed and she wanted to cover him like a satin sheet.

He stroked a hand over her hair. And did what was essential that he do. He catered to her needs and put his on hold.

"Let's get you to bed before you catch a chill," he whispered, and, shifting her in his arms rose and carried her into the house and up the stairs, the gown that was tangled around her hips trailing them like a shadow.

She was asleep before he laid her down on her white-on-white bed, where the covers were thrown back, where the sweet indentation of her body lingered on both the sheets and her pillow. He didn't know whether to feel smug or cheated.

What he absolutely did feel was protective as he leaned over her and simply looked at her—the wild tangle of copper-gold curls trailing across the pillow, her pale, slim body languidly sated, her rose-pink nipples soft as velvet now.

She'd come apart for him. Eager and proud, curious and brave. The punch of desire hit him again. This time he was prepared for it. He'd had a week of practice. A week of holding back, holding off. He could go another night. Or as many as it took to make sure she was ready for him.

He couldn't wait to take her up again, then take her down with him. But not tonight. Not as exhausted as she was. He knew that he hadn't gotten much sleep the last week. He seriously doubted that she had, either.

So he bit back the need, curbed the desire. He looked longingly at the bed, at his beautiful sleeping wife, and knew that if he joined her there, he wouldn't be able to leave her alone.

Tomorrow, he promised himself as he headed back downstairs to his bed on the sofa. Tomorrow they would talk. Tomorrow he would know what their future held.

Tomorrow he might even come up with an explanation for this indescribable warmth that clotted his chest when he looked at her and made him want to believe that maybe he'd been wrong. Maybe Sara had been wrong.

Maybe…just maybe, he had the capability of being something more to a woman than just there.

Seven

Ellie had been awake since sunup. She'd lain in her bed and tried to make sense of why Lee wasn't with her. It had been incredible. Out on the porch, when he'd kissed her, and touched her. It had been so…wonderful.

And then he'd left her. Asleep in her bed. Alone again.

When all of her reasoning pointed back in the same direction, she swallowed her pride, got dressed for church and went downstairs.

She'd already fried the bacon and the pancake batter was ready for the griddle when she heard him walk softly into the kitchen. She tried not to stiffen. Tried not to let the hurt show. But he must have sensed it, anyway.

"Ellie?"

His voice was soft behind her. She lowered her

head, then immediately lifted her chin and reached for the bowl of batter. She would not let him see her humiliation.

''Good morning,'' she said brightly, and shot a quick smile over her shoulder.

That was a mistake. He was all sleep rumpled—pillow creases dented his stubbled cheek, and his hair was beautifully mussed. His shirt hung open; his feet were bare. Seeing him that way, still warm from his bed on the couch when he should have been warm from her bed, was a grim reminder of how much of him she didn't have, how much she might never have.

She closed her mind to the picture and its message. ''I thought you were going to sleep all morning. Church isn't for a couple of hours yet so I made pancakes. I can scramble some eggs if—''

''Ellie.'' His hand on her shoulders stopped her forced, cheery banter. ''Look at me.''

She didn't want to look at him. Didn't want to see the pity or regret or distaste or whatever it was he was feeling this morning. But she forced herself. She pasted on a smile, met his dark scowl.

And waited with her heart in her throat.

''Ellie, what's wrong?''

''Nothing. Nothing's wrong.''

''You feeling okay?''

''I feel fine.''

A long moment passed. ''But you're upset,'' he finally decided.

She drew a bracing breath. ''I'm not upset. Why would I be upset?'' She heard the bite in her reply. Was sorry she hadn't been able to curb it. Or maybe not. Maybe she didn't just want to roll over and play the I'm-fine-don't-concern-yourself-with-me game.

Maybe she wanted to hurt him, the way he had hurt her.

"Why would I be upset?" she repeated, letting loose with some of the fire that had been building in her belly. Let him see what he'd done to her. Let him deal with it.

Lee watched her warily. He'd expected that she might feel self-conscious this morning. He'd expected she might feel shy. He hadn't expected anger. And she was angry. Beyond angry.

He walked to the cupboard, snagged a mug from the shelf and poured a cup of coffee. He needed a hit of caffeine to help clear his head. He hadn't slept much last night. He glanced at her. At her fever-bright eyes that were agitated and narrowed in accusation and in complete contrast to the serene pastels of her pretty flowing dress that made him think of her flower garden of a bedroom.

He figured that he knew what this was all about. He'd made another major mistake last night. He'd known it then, was sure of it now. He should have trusted his instincts. He should have walked away from her before...well, by the looks of her, before he'd taken her somewhere she wasn't prepared to go, let alone to deal with in the cool clear light of morning.

"I'm sorry," he said finally. When she just glared at him, her eyes filled with hurt and anger and a humiliation that he'd put there, he set aside the coffee and went to her.

"Don't. Don't touch me." She threw her arms wide, bolting away from his outstretched arms. "Don't touch me like I'm something that will break."

He stopped in his tracks, suddenly confused. He

was low enough on sleep and high enough on sexual frustration that a healthy bite of anger of his own shot out before he could rein it in. ''I don't recall touching you that way last night,'' he said carefully, and felt an unwelcome twinge of satisfaction when her cheeks flamed.

''No. Oh, no. Last night…last night for a moment you forgot, didn't you? You forgot who I was and what I was, and you touched me like a woman.''

He watched her with a frown, not at all sure now where this was coming from. ''Do you want me to be sorry about that? Am I supposed to be sorry for kissing you?''

''Aren't you? Aren't you sorry? Sorry about that and about agreeing to this…this arrangement of a marriage?''

There were tears now. Big and bright and brimming and winning the battle with her pride. He didn't know what to say to her. She, however, had plenty to say.

''It's not that I expect you to…to love me. Not…not right away. But I thought…last night…I thought you at least wanted me. But you don't see me as anything but an obligation, do you? And why wouldn't you? That's all I am. That's all I've ever been.''

''Ellie—''

''Don't! Do not talk to me like I'm a child. I am a woman. And for better or worse, I am your wife!'' Violet eyes, wild with hurt and anger, glared him. Then, with a frustrated kitten's roar, she made a small, tight fist and popped him in the chest.

She roared again when he just stood there, unfazed

by the physical blow but stunned by the fury and passion that had prompted it.

"I am supposed to be your partner, not your charge! And I have epilepsy, not the plague. You can't catch it. If it scares you or repulses you, I'm sorry. I can't control what you feel. I can't control the disease. But that doesn't mean I can't be your wife if you would just give me the chance."

His head was swimming—at the depth of her anger—at the source of the pain that had prompted someone so gentle and kind to physically strike out. At the words she'd fired at him like bullets. One word in particular. She thought she repulsed him?

While he was still reeling, she tugged off her apron, threw it in his general direction and ran out the kitchen door.

Tossing the apron aside, he turned off the burners on the stove and stormed after her, wincing his way across the gravel on bare feet and followed her to the barn.

It was quiet as he shouldered through the door and eased inside. It was also dark. His eyes adjusted slowly until he found her there, a spot of spring in her pretty dress as she pressed her face against Bud's neck and let the tears flow.

He was leery of touching her so he stood by her side, one hand on the big gelding's withers. "Ellie...you don't repulse me. You *so* don't repulse me. I want you. With every breath I draw, I want you."

She didn't look at him. And only after a very long, doubtful silence, did she quietly ask, "Then why? Why did you...why did you do that to me last night?"

He watched her carefully before he finally spoke

and even then he felt totally out of sync with the workings of her mind. ‘‘I thought you liked it. I thought you liked it when I touched you.’’

‘‘I did. I…I did,’’ she finished softly, her voice muffled against Bud's neck. ‘‘But then…then you left me. Alone again. You gave me something… something that made me feel wonderful and powerful and…and strong. And then you took it away when you wouldn't let me give it back to you.’’

He closed his eyes, pressed his forehead against the hand he'd formed into a fist on Bud's broad neck as the light finally dawned. ‘‘Baby, that's not why I left. You were exhausted. It was late. I didn't want to take advantage.’’ How could he say this without making matters worse? ‘‘I didn't want to take you further than you were prepared to go.’’

‘‘So you made a decision. For my benefit.’’ The steel was back in her voice. So was the heat.

‘‘Yes,’’ he said carefully.

He knew he'd been hung by his own rope even before she quietly murmured, ‘‘Like my keeper.’’

He drew in a deep breath, let it out and bit the bullet. ‘‘Like someone who cares about you. I see now that I was wrong to take that choice away from you.

‘‘Ellie, please look at me.’’ He waited for her to do just that, and when she finally did, he saw how deep his error in judgment had cut her. ‘‘I'm on shaky ground here. I'm not doing a very good job of…’’ he trailed off, searching for the words, but before he found them, she found some for him.

‘‘Of taking care of me.’’

‘‘Yes,’’ he admitted again even though he knew it

might set her off. "Of taking care of you. It's not a bad thing. I *want* to take care of you."

"I thought we agreed to take care of each other."

Okay. So he'd sold her short on that one, too. "You're right. Again. We did agree to take care of each other. But I can't...hell." He dragged a hand roughly through his hair, felt the ground he'd gained shift, like sand, beneath his feet and settled himself down.

"I want to make love to you," he said candidly and saw her reaction through her soulful, searching eyes. "After last night I don't know how much longer I can hold out.

"But I don't want to hurt you," he added, trying to make her understand. "I don't ever want to put you in a position where I could hurt you."

She let out a deep breath, sectioned off a small handful of Bud's mane and started absently working it with her hands. "I get so tired of being a...consideration," she said at last as she began the intricate but automatic process of making a braid. "I just want to be seen as a person—not a person with a problem."

He'd hurt her again but he'd be damned if he'd apologize. "Would you rather I didn't care? Would you rather I didn't consider your health?"

Another long, weary sigh. "I'd rather this wasn't a part of me. But it is."

The long silence that followed underscored the fact that it was his wish too. That was the bottom line, and they both knew it as she forked her fingers through the braid she'd just completed and smoothed it back as it had been. Then she turned to him with those beautiful, troubled eyes.

''You can't fix me,'' she said at last. ''Even though you want to.''

He frowned. ''Ellie, no—''

''You think I don't see what you've been doing? Every day since you've been here, you've charged around like a man possessed. Fixing this. Fixing that. But you can't fix me, Lee,'' she repeated, daring him to deny the truth of her conclusion.

He had to look away. It was true. That's exactly what he'd wanted to do—and she'd figured it out before he had. He'd wanted to fix what he had control over because he had no control over what the epilepsy did to her. Suddenly he was ashamed.

''You say you don't want to hurt me? Then you need to accept me. As I am. The epilepsy is part of me. It's not going away. Ever.''

He drew in a weary breath, let it out, met her eyes. ''Then help me understand,'' he said gently. ''Help me know what you deal with.''

''So you'll know how to take care of me,'' she concluded, driving her point home with a bite that didn't quite rally what she'd lost of her pride.

''Yes,'' he said, honestly. ''But more than that. I want to know. I want to know you better. For all the reasons you just said. The epilepsy is part of you. I'm your husband. That makes it part of me.

''Help me, Ellie. Help me understand so I don't go on hurting you.''

He was asking a lot of her. He knew it; so did she.

When she turned to him, it wasn't so much with acceptance as it was with defeat. He saw in her eyes, her sad, brave eyes that she'd reconciled herself to the idea that it was the only way they could start getting past this. Reconciled, that's all.

He held out his hand, determined that she would never be sorry for anything she shared with him.

After what seemed like an eternity, she reached out, took his hand.

He didn't feel the strength in her hand today, only the reluctance that trembled through her. And the fear of rejection that she'd lived with too long and that he promised himself she would never feel again. Not from him.

He led her back to the house. Sat down with her on his lap in the big wicker chair on the front porch. And he just held her that way and rocked her until, with the spring breeze humming through her wind chimes, she slowly, and with grim determination, started telling him things she'd never told another living soul.

They were late for church. He couldn't help but smile as one of Clare's favorite platitudes came to mind.

"Timing's not as important as presence. Showing up's what counts, not being early or late, but just being."

Being, however, was different from belonging. Lee had never belonged. Every time he stepped through the double, arched doorway of the Sundown Congregational Church, he expected to hear the creak and groan of the roof giving way and falling in on his head—if for no other reason than the shock of seeing him there.

As a ten-year-old boy he'd never been inside a church until Will and Clare had dragged him here, practically kicking and screaming. He still felt that odd sense of a benevolent but judgmental presence, a supreme power, whenever he sat before the altar and the music swelled out of the ancient organ and rang out over the congregation.

Hard as Clare had tried, he still considered himself more sinner than saint. Except for attending Clare's and then Will's funeral and his own wedding ceremony last week, he'd seldom found his way inside of any church in the past several years. Even so, there were some things he hadn't forgotten—like the peace that settled over him as he walked Ellie toward the Shiloh family pew.

Beside him she was quiet, just as she'd been quiet on the ride to town. He understood why. He'd been quiet, too. He had a lot to think about. And he had a big reason to hope that Doc Lundstrum could fill in some of the blanks that Ellie had left empty.

Starting today he wanted to be more to her than he had been. Because he understood now. He understood that he wasn't the only one who felt as if they had never belonged.

He wanted to be more than her protector; he wanted to be things he still couldn't be for her, not through any failing of hers but because there were some things he still wasn't capable of. Like the fairy-tale love she wanted and deserved.

But he could be her husband. He wanted to be her husband. Not because he was bound by duty, he'd realized with no small measure of surprise. But because he wanted to be someone important to her. Because she deserved to have someone who wanted to be important to her.

And he wanted to make love to her. He wanted it to be tonight.

The sun was clear and high as they walked outside

after the service and people broke off into little pockets of conversation. Lee stood by himself, a little surprised that Peg Lathrop had practically attacked Ellie and pulled her aside. The two of them were locked in conversation at the edge of the aspen grove that flanked the church on three sides. Peg's little girl, a five-year-old tomboy with blond braids and a grass stain on the knee of her Sunday school dress, was busy playing on the swing set that was part of the city park playground adjacent to the church grounds.

Lee stood on the bottom step, a hand in the pocket of his suit pants, and squinted against the sun that was only an hour away from noon.

"How's it going, young man?"

He turned to see Doc's bushy brows pinched together in question and breathed a sign of relief. Cutting a look toward Ellie and Peg and seeing that they were still deep in conversation, he steered Doc aside.

"You got a minute?" he asked Doc, but didn't wait for confirmation as he maneuvered him toward the corner of the church where they could have some privacy.

"What's on your mind, son?" Doc asked.

"We need to have that talk now."

Doc drummed his blunt-tipped fingers over his robust belly that was covered in a crisp white dress shirt and a slim paisley print tie. "Well now. It's about time. It sure is about time."

Later that afternoon Lee sat on the ridge above the valley that overlooked Shiloh. Bud shifted beneath him, the saddle leather creaking as the old gelding resettled his weight.

Below, in the house by herself, Lee knew that Ellie

was wondering. Wondering and waiting and reading a hundred different messages into his distance and his silence.

He wished that he could have saved her that anxiety. But he'd needed some time. To absorb. To digest. To acclimatize himself to the glut of information he'd received today from both Ellie and Doc.

After church he'd taken her out to dinner at the Dusk to Dawn, Sundown's one and only restaurant, bar and youth center all rolled up into one. She had protested at first. He'd overridden her feeble excuses. He'd wanted to show her a thousand reasons why he didn't put any stock in her fears.

Afterward he'd been sorry that he'd forced the experience on her. She'd been uncomfortable, self-conscience. Miserable. While he recognized some of the faces, many, he didn't. And many had stared—or tried not to.

He needed time to deal with that, too. With what those stares did to her.

So once they'd gotten home, he'd changed into his work clothes, kissed her tenderly and saddled up Bud. Then he'd headed out to check the herd. That had been nearly three hours ago. He wasn't really needed out here. Most of the mares had dropped their foals before he'd returned to Shiloh last week, but there were a few holdouts, so it was a good excuse to see how they were making out.

But she'd known. She'd known as well as he had that he needed some room to draw conclusions, make decisions, deal with what he now knew that he'd never known before.

There were so many terms. So much information.

So much of it hard to accept. Big deal. It was hard for him; she lived it. What must it be like for her?

He dismounted, ground-reined Bud and let him graze. Then he lay down on his back in the pasture grass. Crossing his arms behind his head, he stared at wispy clouds that drifted like mare's tails across acres of blue Montana sky. He used to do this a lot when he was a kid. Laze around in the sun. Think and brood. Later in the summer this pasture would be alive with colors—the brilliant yellow of wild buttercups, the burnt orange of Indian paintbrush, the soft lavender of harebells.

Lavender, like Ellie's eyes.

Ellie.

"Partial complex seizures," Doc had said. "No, no son. Surgery's not a good option for her, although we did consider it for a time. She does well on her medication."

Anticonvulsants. Phenytoin, phenobarbital. And more. Some he couldn't pronounce or remember.

"She hates them," he'd told Doc, confiding what Ellie had confessed, trying to understand why.

"I know. She remembers when she first started on them, or the times we've had to adjust. The side effects are always more noticeable when we have to mess with her meds, but then her body settles in, the chemistry becomes more balanced and the effects aren't as severe."

Dry mouth, periods of depression, sluggishness.

The epilepsy wasn't bad enough. She had to live with the treatment, too.

"The medication has done a remarkable job managing her seizures," Doc had added. "We always have to keep that in mind."

''What causes them?''

Doc had shrugged. ''It's not always something we can pinpoint. With Ellie we suspect it was a birth trauma. And at this point it really doesn't matter. The results and the treatments are the same.''

''What happens? What, exactly, happens to her?''

Doc had frowned as he thought to formulate a response. ''There are innumerable cells in our brains, and they normally work in perfect harmony—relaying the electrical and chemical signals that allow us to tell a story or clap our hands or even to feel happy. With Ellie things work smoothly most of the time. But sometimes certain brain cells go haywire and misfire. That's when she has a seizure.''

More helplessness. More questions. ''What triggers them?''

Doc had shrugged again. ''When she was little, it was usually a fever. Any time she cut a tooth, got the flu. Puberty was especially hard on her—all the hormonal changes. Now her seizures are mostly controlled. But sometimes, if she gets too stressed or too tired...'' He'd trailed off, lifted a hand as if to say, you never know. ''Sometimes it's nothing at all. It just happens. No explanation.''

He remembered what she'd told him this morning. ''She says she hears chimes.''

''Her aura,'' Doc had said with a nod. ''With Ellie, her warning aura comes in the form of chimes. Sometimes, if she tunes in soon enough, she can actually forestall an episode, or at least diminish the severity if she can lie down in a dark, quiet room and just wait it out.''

''But not always.''

''No. Unfortunately, not always.''

The shadow of a bald eagle, its wingspread as wide as a small car, sailed overhead. Lee watched it soar, wished for that kind of freedom for Ellie.

"What do I do?" he'd asked Doc. "When she has a seizure. What do I do?"

"Just give her room. If you're around when it happens don't crowd her. And unless it lasts for more than two or three minutes, don't panic. Anything more, you get on the phone and you call me. She'll be in a form of suspended consciousness. You may think she's alert, but she's not. She may speak, but she doesn't know she's talking and what she says may not make sense to you. She may roll her wrist, or pick at things… Clare once told me that she usually has busy hands…like she's buttoning and unbuttoning nonexistent buttons. That sort of thing. She won't be violent. She won't be self-destructive. She may lie down or just sit. But if you crowd her, she might become frightened, distraught. So you just leave her be, make sure that if she's up and walking that you keep tabs on her so she doesn't hurt herself.

"And when it's over," Doc continued, "you help her cope. She won't remember it but she'll have a humdinger of a headache, and she'll be disoriented for a while. She'll also be as exhausted as if she'd run a marathon. And then she'll have to mourn the fact that she's lost a little bit of herself again. I think that's the hardest for her. Knowing that she was completely vulnerable, not knowing what she did, how she acted."

As the sun beat down, Lee remembered the way his breath had felt huge and thick in his chest as he'd listened to Doc. "How does she deal with it?" he'd asked aloud, without even knowing he'd said the words.

Doc had laid a hand on his arm. ''Son, she deals with it like a trooper. She's one of the most adjusted individuals I have the pleasure of knowing. You've probably already figured that out for yourself, though. She could be angry. She could be bitter. She could be frightened and insecure. She's none of those things. Oh, I know she has her moments, but, for the long haul, she's solid.''

Lee closed his eyes. He'd given her some of those moments with his own insecurity, his own ignorance and inability to get this out in the open. She had been so right this morning in the barn. He did want to fix things for her. He was a man of action. He felt crippled by his inability to help her, just as he was crippling her by not allowing her to be what she needed to be for him.

''Acceptance of herself, of her epilepsy are the most critical factors to help her live with it,'' Doc had added meaningfully. ''It's also critical for you to accept it if you hope to develop the kind of relationship you'll both need to see you through the tough times.''

Doc had looked at his boots, looked at the sky.

''But I reckon you've already got that part figured out, too. It's the other part of the relationship that's worrying you now.''

''I don't want to hurt her,'' he'd said quietly.

''But you want her,'' Doc had concluded.

He'd pushed out a disgusted snort. ''What does that make me?''

Lee hadn't seen anything funny but Doc had laughed. ''Why, it makes you a red-blooded American male, son. And it makes her a lucky woman. The only thing you could do to hurt her is to refuse to let her be a wife to you.

"Look, Lee, Ellie is experiencing all the feelings a bride is supposed to feel—along with some that no bride should have to contend with. She has to deal with the reality of her epilepsy—with the moments it steals from her life, the strength it saps from her psyche, with the cost to her pride. Most of all she has to deal with the differential treatment she's afraid she's going to get from you because of it."

Doc had placed a fatherly hand on his shoulder. "She needs the physical part of your relationship as much as you do. Probably more and, given the male libido, that's saying quite a lot," he added with a chuckle.

Lee's scowl must have told Doc how little humor he'd found in the situation.

"Take her home, son. Love her. Give her babies."

"Babies?" He'd looked at Doc as if he'd sprouted horns.

"You don't want babies?"

He'd cupped his nape, rolled his shoulders. "Could that be good for her?"

"There's a risk, sure, but with proper monitoring and special care, she can have babies."

Lee hadn't heard anything beyond the word *risk*. There would be no babies. He would never put her at risk and was relieved to know that one of the medications she was taking to control hormonal imbalances that could worsen her symptoms was, in essence, also a form of birth control.

So that risk, at least, was factored out—but wasn't he putting her at risk right now? As he stalled for time out here on the mountain and left her alone to wonder and worry about the conclusions he had drawn, the decisions he had made—wasn't he putting her at risk with his distance?

He sat up, propped a forearm over an upraised knee and looked toward home. Where his wife waited. For him. To make her a woman.

Not much rattled him. This did. He didn't want to let her down, was determined that he wouldn't.

He rose to his feet, walked over to Bud, snagged the reins and swung into the saddle.

The setting sun followed him home.

Home to the house where, somehow, without his being aware of it happening, everything that mattered waited along with the light that burned in the bedroom window.

Eight

Ellie sat in front of her vanity mirror. The low, wide bench was upholstered in an antique satin tapestry of ivory and pink. The triple-fold antique mirror was large, its beveled glass encased in aged, lustrous oak. She could see herself from three angles; each one revealed her uncertainty about whether she'd done the right thing today.

Maybe Lee really hadn't wanted to hear some of the things she'd told him this morning. Maybe he hadn't liked what Doc had told him, either. She'd seen their heads together after church. While Peg had pumped her for information and she'd done her best to assure her that everything was wonderful and that Peg's plan had worked, she'd worried that they had actually drifted further apart instead of closer together.

Hadn't he left her alone all afternoon? Hadn't he

ridden out with excuses about checking on the herd and then stayed away until almost sundown?

She dropped her silver-filigree brush to her lap, ran her fingers across the bristles. She didn't want to spend another night alone in her bed.

Why had she told him so much? Why had she told him that one story in particular? She stared, without seeing, at the mirror. A soft light burned by the bed, illuminating her reflection. She'd had her bath, pulled on her old pink chenille robe and sat down to brush her hair.

She wouldn't wear her honeymoon gown tonight. She figured there would be no need. If Lee hadn't wanted her before, he couldn't want her, now that he knew so many more things about her.

Some places were harder to go to than others. The day that she'd told him about this morning had been one of them. She'd never talked about it before. Not even with her mother. She'd been fifteen and she'd been scared. Why, oh, why had she told Lee?

Because he'd felt so solid and strong as she'd sat on his lap that the story had just tumbled out.

"I rode Bud up to thc north pasture one day," she'd begun, hearing her voice as if it belonged to someone else, seeing herself in the sunshine riding Bud bareback, his hide warm and solid and wide between her legs. "I was fifteen. I'd taken Daddy lunch. On the way back..." She'd stopped, swallowed, concentrated on remembering the warmth of the sun, the bear grass and fireweed dancing in the breeze, the hawk she'd spotted riding the wind currents.

"On the way back, I cut over to Mile High Pass so I could ride part of the way on the road. I'd seen a spring fawn at Miller's Creek the week before, and

I thought maybe I'd get lucky and it would be there again.''

She hadn't been able to look at him as she'd talked, and even now, all these hours later, she remembered staring at her hands that were gripped so tightly together her knuckles had turned white.

''This old truck came barreling down the road, kicking up gravel, stirring up a dust trail. It was almost on Bud and me before they saw us and slammed on the brakes. Bud bolted and dumped me in the ditch.''

Lee's big hands had stroked her back.

''I wasn't hurt. Humiliated, but not hurt. I took off walking after him but he was hell-bent on home. I was still dusting myself off when I heard them behind me.''

She stopped. Swallowed. ''I'd…I'd seen them before. Once at the feed store. Once at the Stop and Shop. They were brothers—new in Sundown—and I'd heard Momma and Dad say that they were bad news.''

Just like this morning when she'd told her story to Lee, her vision got blurry, and she felt the hot sting of tears, tasted the salt of them in the corner of her mouth.

''I…I could smell their breath when they…when they started walking beside me. They'd been drinking.''

She'd felt Lee's hard body tense beneath her. Heard him say her name.

''I was so scared. They were…they were so mean. They laughed and made fun of me. 'You're Ellie, right? Ellie Shiloh? We heard about you. You throw fits, don't ya? Crazy as loon, right? But hey—you're kinda cute so what do you say Ellie? What you got under that shirt there? How about goin' crazy with us?' "

Even now she remembered both the humiliation of that day and the contrast of Lee's arms wrapped around her this morning. For a moment all the hurt, all the shame those boys had made her feel, had eased back into the past where it belonged. Where it couldn't touch her.

"They hurt you," he'd said, his voice hard and cold and edged with something that traced a trail of fear down her spine and made her shiver.

"No. They didn't touch me. They just humiliated me. And scared me. I got so scared that I…I had a seizure. When I came…came back to myself, they were gone. They'd just left me there."

She'd swallowed, stared at her hands. "They didn't know if I would be all right or if I needed help. They just left me. Like—"

She hadn't said it. But she'd felt what she'd left unsaid many times over the years. Like she was nothing—or worse than nothing. Like she was something revolting.

She'd tried for a smile. "Guess I scared them more than they scared me, huh?"

Lee had been quiet for a long time when she'd finally looked up and met his eyes. She'd seen rage, compassion and something she hadn't understood then but thought she understood now.

He wasn't here. That was all the understanding she needed.

She heard a sound behind her—the creak of a floorboard. Her heart jumped, with something that was more surprise than hope.

She didn't turn around. For the longest time she didn't even look up. She stared at her hands, at her fingers wrapped around the silver brush handle and wished she knew what to do, what to say to the man who stood in the doorway to her bedroom.

Finally she gathered her courage, lifted her head and met his reflection in her vanity mirror.

And her heart skipped several beats.

He'd showered—evidently in the basement, because she'd never heard him in the upstairs bathroom. Like the night they'd come home from the Fergusons, his hair was still wet. She should be used to seeing him this way. Her heart shouldn't flutter so. But it did as he stood there in his bare feet and blue jeans, his shirt hanging open, the tails falling loose at his hips.

Between the open placket of his shirt, she could see the softly curling hair that covered his chest and arrowed down his hard abdomen to disappear beneath jeans that were zipped but not snapped. Her gaze was riveted there, at that spot where denim met flesh, and the slight rise and fall of that beautifully taut skin was the only indication that he was a living, breathing man, not a figment of her imagination.

She swallowed and finally raised her gaze to his. And her heart stopped. In the diluted bedroom light, in the reflection of her mirror, she saw the deep-blue of his irises, the dark intensity of his bold stare.

He watches you.

In her mind she heard Peg's words, remembered how he had looked at her the night of the shivaree.

He was watching her now…the way he had watched her last night on the porch, just before he'd kissed her.

And then she heard Lee's words, like a song that floated on the cusp of her memory.

Not want you? I have wanted you for what seems like forever.

Her reservations forgotten, her insecurities locked back in that place from which they had escaped, she held his gaze.

And smiled.

Her smile was heartbreaking, head-spinning. It was full of wonder, full of trust. Full of a love Lee was sure he didn't deserve but was determined to never betray. She had more than enough reason to feel angry and confused and insecure. And yet she sat there, with her strong, brave heart. Waiting for him. Eager for him. Smiling for him.

He wanted her so much in that moment, he thought he would explode with it. She wouldn't want to hear it, but now, more than ever, he needed to take care with her. Not just because of what he'd learned about her disease—but because of how huge his need had grown. And because she deserved the best he could give her.

And, yeah, there was more to it than that. He'd not only learned things about her today, he'd learned a few things about himself. It was still a tough pill to swallow, but if he were being utterly, brutally honest, he had to admit that it hadn't been Ellie as much as himself that he'd really been trying to protect all this time. What he felt for her…what she did to him.

It wasn't just this tightening in his chest when he looked at her, the constant craving of his physical need when he touched her. The feelings she was dragging out of him he hadn't even known were there, they'd been buried so deep, protected so well by years of building shields.

It scared the hell out of him to think about letting the barriers down. But his fears were nothing compared to the fears she had to overcome on a daily basis.

He flexed his fingers, realized his palms were sweating. And then she said his name, in welcome, in anticipation, in the wonderful way she had of making him feel like the one man, the only man, the most important man on earth.

And he quit thinking. He just felt.

Sundown had come and gone. The small bedside lamp glowed softly, casting the room and her face in gentle shadows. It made him want to see her by candlelight. It made him want to make love to her under the stars.

Her hair was loose. It spilled down her back and drifted across her shoulders like a cloud, trailed like a spool of vibrant, curling ribbons over her breasts.

He went to her. Pressed a knee onto the bench beside her hip and felt, more than heard, her sigh as she leaned back against him. Her eyes were warm and searching as she met his in the mirror; her hair was cool against his skin as it grazed his belly.

Without a word he gathered the curling mass in his hand. Heavy, like satin. Thick, like sable. He inhaled the honeyed scent of it and leaned toward her. Her breath trembled out on a sweet little catch, her fingers suddenly limp on the handle of her delicate silver brush as he eased it from her hand.

"You are so beautiful." He met her gaze in the mirror. Her violet eyes, misty with anticipation, followed the motions of his hands as he gathered her hair, draped it over her left shoulder, then began brushing with slow, long strokes.

"That...feels...wonderful," she whispered as she relaxed against him, the back of her head pressing against his bare abdomen, her shoulders nestled between his hip points. His erection pulsed, huge and hot between her shoulder blades. "*You* feel wonderful," she added, turning her head slowly from side to side, caressing him with her eyes and that slight, subtle pressure.

"Tell me what you want, Ellie," he managed, aching with need, determined to please her, then please her some more.

"I wish...I wish I'd worn my white gown," she said shyly.

With the brush still gripped in his hand, he rested his hands on her shoulders. "But you look so pretty in pink." He smiled when she blushed. "Even prettier out of it."

Very slowly he stroked the cool silver back of the brush along the curve of her jaw. She shivered, and with her eyes closed in sensory pleasure, reached back and gripped his thighs with her small hands.

"Open your eyes, Ellie," he commanded on a gruff whisper. "Look. Look how pretty you are."

With slow, pleasured languor, she obeyed. He watched her eyes fill with wonder and fascination. The picture she made—the picture they made together—equally fascinated him.

She was so pale and delicate; he was dark, muscled and rough around the edges. He was stunned by the contrast, yet it helped him get a firmer grip on the importance of making this good for her.

Torn between watching her face and the progress

of his hand, he lowered the brush and with deliberate, downward motions, caressed her slender throat with the same sensual motion. Cool silver touched warm, flushed skin and he felt another delicate little shiver eddy through her body.

He edged the brush under the robe's lapel, pushed it aside. Her breasts rose and fell sharply, straining against the fabric as he leaned forward, found the loosely knotted belt at her waist and, with a gentle tug, pulled it free. Her robe fell open to reveal a deep vee of pale, creamy flesh, wide at her shoulders, narrowing to a slender opening just below her navel.

''So pretty,'' he whispered, and, setting the brush aside, splayed his fingers wide at her throat, then over her collarbone and slowly pushed the pink chenille down her arms, baring her breasts to the night.

A slow shudder passed through his body as he watched her reflection in the mirror. Watched her eyes cloud over with a sensual haze, watched his hands, work roughened and as big as bear paws glide over her delicate flesh where they rested just above the gentle round at the top of her breasts.

He was mesmerized by the contrasts, by her heat, by the velvet softness of her nipples that tightened into stiff little peaks as he lowered his hands, covered her, then filled his palms with the soft, resilient weight of her.

She liked it—she liked him touching her this way, and he loved experiencing her reaction when he ground his palms against her, then shaped her with his fingers, lifted and flicked the tips of his thumbs over those velvety hard little beads.

When he lightly pinched, then rolled, her erect nipples between his thumb and forefinger, she clutched wildly at his thighs, then, with an urgency that thickened his pulse, raised her arms above her head, reaching for him, arching her sweet breasts deeper into his hands.

He lost it then. Caressing her breast with one hand, he dragged the other hand up her chest, bracketed her jaw in his hand and tipped her head back for a deep, searing kiss.

Touching her wasn't enough. Tasting her wasn't enough. He wanted her tongue. And he took it, then showed her with an intimate ebb and flow, a calculated stroke and withdrawal that he wanted more than his tongue inside her, more than his mouth invading her sweet, giving body.

He wanted in a way he'd never wanted anything in his life. He wanted to own her. He wanted to be owned by her. Heart. Body. Soul. He poured everything that he was into that kiss, told her with the hands that held her, the body that burned for her that she was the one, the only one he wanted or needed or desired.

Ellie's head was spinning. Her blood was flying through her veins, throbbing at her pulse points and lower, woman low. She ached there. She burned. She yearned with all that was in her to know what a wife should know about the physical love that only her husband could show her.

''Make love to me,'' she begged against his mouth, his busy, busy mouth that was devouring hers, worshiping hers, telling her with his kisses that tonight would not be like the others. Tonight he wasn't leaving her.

Strong arms banded around her and lifted her as if

she weighed no more than a feather. He carried her across the room to the bed, where he laid her down.

He stood above her, like a dark angel, like a man who saw only his woman, and roughly shrugged his shirt from his shoulders and stripped it down his arms. She hiked herself up on her elbows, not wanting to miss anything, not one move, not one single event as he reached for his zipper and drew it down.

He stopped abruptly, his thumbs hooked beneath the denim at his waistband, where his skin was pale and that arrow of silky, dark hair narrowed and disappeared out of sight.

''Do you have any idea...'' His voice sounded raspy and rough, and he swallowed as his blue gaze strafed her body then returned to her face. ''Do you have any idea how incredible you look?''

She blinked slowly, then looked down at herself. She should probably be embarrassed. The warm flush she felt spreading in tiny, tingling fingers beneath her skin told her she was, at least a little.

But the look in his eyes, oh, the look in his eyes. He made her feel achy and wanton and proud. She was completely naked. She was sprawled shamelessly on the bed. Her elbows dug into the mattress, which made her back arch and thrust her breasts forward. His gaze was fixed there, as if he couldn't get enough of looking and yet what he really wanted to do was touch.

Just like she wanted him to touch her. With his hands. With his mouth.

''Please,'' she whispered, and lay back down on the bed, lifting her arms in reckless abandon to lie, palms up, on the pillow by her head.

He peeled his jeans and briefs down his hips and

shoved them down his legs—and she couldn't stop staring.

He...he wasn't exactly like the pictures in the book that even now lay tucked between her mattress and springs at the edge of the bed. He was—he was more. He was better.

He was bigger. Much, much bigger. And for a moment, to her mortification, she felt the stinging pinch of anxiety.

What if...what if—

"Ellie."

Her gaze flashed from that part of him that was so fascinating and so male to his face as he eased a hip on the corner of the bed. He was smiling as he reached out, brushed an errant curl away from the corner of her mouth.

"Tell me what you're thinking," he demanded softly.

She swallowed, then groaned when his fingertips drifted across the round of her breast, then returned to cup her, mold her in his palm.

"That...that you're beautiful," she managed, and covered his hand with hers, riding the motion of his hand, forgetting that she'd been concerned and instead drifted on sensation.

"And?" he continued as he lowered his mouth where his hand had been.

"And, umm. Oh..." She squirmed, needing to be closer, begging him without words to keep on doing those wonderful things he was doing.

"And what, baby?"

"And...and that you're very, very big." The words spilled out on a restless sigh, and then, realizing what she'd said, she opened her eyes to see what he made of that.

He chuckled softly and lay down beside her. "We'll fit just fine," he told her, drawing her snugly against his side. "I'll make sure of it."

"You will?" She threaded her fingers through his hair as he moved from one breast to the other to sip and savor, lick and softly nip. "H-how?"

"By doing what I'm doing. Am I making you want me, Ellie?"

"Yes. Oh, yes," she exclaimed without inhibition.

"Am I making you wet?"

"Yes. I'm…sorry."

He lifted his head. "Sorry? Ellie, it's beautiful. The way you feel." His hand trailed down her abdomen, found her curls, covered her with his palm, then with the drift of a finger, delved into warm, slick flesh. "Wet," he murmured, as he brushed his open mouth over hers, catching the sigh that escaped her parted lips. "You are wonderful. And wet. Just for me."

"I…I get that way sometimes," she confessed, as her hips moved involuntarily with the slow, wondrous motion of his finger. Inside her. Stroking her. Moving her toward something she craved. Something she couldn't describe but didn't know how she'd ever lived without. "Sometimes," she tried again breathlessly, "sometimes, all I have to do is think about you. About, oh—" she shivered when he touched her deep "—about your mouth."

The mouth in question crushed down on hers. A deep growl sounded low in his throat as he moved over her, supporting his weight on his elbows, edging a powerful knee between her thighs.

She drowned in the kiss, then floated in the wonder

of it and all the feelings he'd coaxed to life with just the gentle probe of his finger, the delicious pressure and skillful strokes.

She gazed up at him, her eyes dreamy in anticipation of more.

"What?" he asked, responding to the yearning in her eyes. "What do you want? Tell me, Ellie. It's yours."

"I want your hand back," she said a little desperately. "Where it was."

"Do you now?" he murmured with a smile in his voice and dropped the most tender kisses on her cheek, then on her brow before returning to her mouth. "What else do you want?"

She swallowed, closed her eyes, hardly believing what was coming out of her mouth. "Your...your finger. Why did you take it away?"

For a moment he just stared at her, then his beautiful mouth curved up into a smile so tender, so indulgent, she forgot about being embarrassed.

"You liked that?"

She nodded and felt her cheeks flame.

"You're going to like this even better," he promised and with exquisite care, reached down between their bodies and guided that part of him—that very big part of him—to the spot where his finger had been.

She closed her eyes as he rested there, just rested with a steady, heavy pressure.

"Ellie?"

"Hmm," she sighed dreamily and because she couldn't not, lifted her hips, just a little, increasing the contact, enhancing the sensation as her body stretched, accommodated and allowed him penetration.

She caught her breath. He groaned. She opened her eyes. His were pinched tightly shut. The veins on his neck were bulging, his lips compressed like he was in pain.

"What's wrong? What's wrong?" she whispered urgently.

The sound he made fell somewhere between a groan and a laugh. "Nothing. Lord. Not one thing." He opened his eyes then. They were dark and deep and full of passion and concern.

"Are you okay? Did I hurt you?" He ran his thumb in a gentle caress along the line of her brow.

She thought about it, about the sharp, biting sting that had already settled into a distant, pulsing ache that only made her wonder and want more. She shook her head, her gaze locked on his and pressed her small hands against his hips. "More. Please."

He closed his eyes, swallowed hard. "How did I ever get so lucky to have you? In my life. In my bed."

Lucky? He was lucky? To have her? To have *her?* A rush of love so intense, so profound filled her chest—as her husband filled her body. Little by little. Inch by precious inch.

She bit her lower lip between her teeth, felt tears sting her eyes.

"I'm sorry."

"No. No. Don't...don't go," she begged, when he started to withdraw. She clutched his hips in her hands, holding him close, keeping him near. "It's...it's just so...good. Stay. Please, please stay with me."

Above her, her husband, her husband who filled her body in the most intimate, most cherished of ways, smiled. "I can make it better."

An incredulous laugh escaped her. "Better?"

"Trust me."

"I do. Oh, I do."

A look crossed his face then—a look so tender, so deeply touching—and warmed her in places that had nothing and everything to do with this physical joining that bound them together as husband and wife. She wanted to tell him...how he made her feel...how much she loved him. But he started moving inside her then. A slow, lazy withdrawal that stopped her heart—a long, deep penetration that sent it racing and stole all coherent thought.

Over and over he entered and withdrew. And he was right. It *was* better. It was...it was... "Lee..."

"I know, baby. Let it happen."

Trust. It was all about trust. She let herself fly free, let herself tumble, head over heels out of control into the fall.

Heat. Flight. Heaven. He took her there. He took her beyond, and for the first time in her life she willingly and without reservation gave in to a power that stole those most precious pieces of what made her whole. Her sense of time, her sense of place, her sense of self. She gave them over to his keeping—completely consumed, utterly lost in the shelter of her husband's loving arms.

Lee had forgotten about Montana mornings like this—where the cool was so pure you could breathe it. Where the sun was so crystalline and bright it cut through the chill as it edged over the mountain ridge and flooded the valley with light. In Texas it would already be so hot this time of day you could feel the weight of it pressing down from above even as it pushed back up from the baked earth until you felt wedged in the middle of an oven.

He stood on the front porch, drank from the mug of coffee he'd brought outside with him. And thought of his wife. All silky and warm and snuggled deeply in the covers of her bed where he'd left her sleeping. Of *their* bed, he amended with a smile and set the coffee aside. He headed for the barn, hurried through the chores, then climbed the stairs to join her there again.

He was quiet as he entered the bedroom, silently shucked his clothes and slid back beneath the covers beside the sweetest heat, the most delicate flesh.

She warmed him like a fire. But she needed to sleep. So he tried. He really tried to lie there, to let her be, to content himself with her softness snuggled against him. To let it be enough.

But it wasn't enough, and he was beginning to wonder when he would ever get enough of her. It played hell on a man's ego to realize that one tiny little woman could turn him inside out like this, and all she had to do to accomplish it was sleep.

She lay there with her hair spilling across her pillow and sunshine slanting into the room. He loved the look of her by daylight. He loved the tiny sprinkling of freckles that dusted the bridge of her nose and the soft slope of her shoulders like angel fire. He loved the snuffling little sleep sounds she made when she curled into him and pressed her face into the hollow of his throat.

He loved her.

It hit him like a velvet punch.

He loved her.

He loved.

He—Lee Savage—loved.

He waited for the denial. For the profound and pathetic panic that always edged in whenever he even skirted the perimeters of a territory he'd always considered uncharted, overromanticized and, for him, unattainable.

He tried it again. He loved her. He waited again for the thundering heartbeat, for the inconsolable urge to run. For the anger that reminded him he wasn't capable, couldn't possibly be entitled to anything this good.

Nothing.

Just peace.

Just…love. Sweet, healing love.

Man, oh, man, who'd have thought it. From the beginning he'd planned on a physical relationship. He'd counted on affection. He hadn't anticipated this emotional commitment she'd dragged out of him with her undeniable trust. Her true and honest giving.

It rocked him. And in an unexpected way it also anchored him, as he'd never felt anchored. He'd thought he could physically love her without giving too much of himself away. Hell, it had worked for him for thirty-three years. But with Ellie he'd not only dropped all of his shields, he'd walked over them, left them in the dust.

Will and Clare, for all they had given him, for all he had cared for them, they'd never gotten past his defenses. They'd never gotten this deep. Not soul deep the way she had.

He loved this woman. And he couldn't help himself

any longer. He folded back the covers, hiked himself up on an elbow and simply watched her sleep. His wife.

Her breasts were so pale, her areolas so deliciously pink and delicately pebbled around the tip of her nipples. Even as she slept, they knotted into tight little beads.

He glanced up, saw that her eyes were open, watchful.

"Good morning, Mrs. Savage." His hand moved automatically to her breast, drawn, as his gaze was drawn to her eyes.

She stretched and pressed into his hand. "Good morning, Mr. Savage."

They shared a smile then, one full of longing and memories and discoveries they'd made in this bed. He'd made love to her again after that first time. After he'd gently bathed the signs of her virginity from her thighs, he'd taken her again before he'd let her sleep. And now he wanted to do it all over again.

"I trust you slept well." He watched her face, loving the glazed look in her eyes as he played with her breast and she responded with the sweetest sigh, the most seductive little shiver.

"What time is it?"

He lowered his mouth to where his hand had been. "Close to ten."

She scrambled to sit up. "My chores—"

"Done," he informed her, and pushed her down to her back again.

"Oh. Well…but you must be hungry."

"Oh, I am. I was thinking about breakfast in bed."

She may be an innocent, but she was quick, and she was beautiful when she was coy.

"Breakfast," she said, luxuriating again in the touch of his mouth to her breast. "In bed?"

"Oh, yes, ma'am. And you don't even have to do anything."

"Nothing?"

"Just lie there," he murmured, moving over her, then moving down, nibbling, caressing, tasting as he went. The slender curve of her jaw, the delicate slope of her shoulder. The delicious tip of her breast that he couldn't seem to get enough of.

"Lee..."

"Shush. Let me. Just let me." He looked up her body, held her startled, excited gaze as his mouth cruised along her skin, to the hollow of her navel, then nipped lightly at her hip point.

He watched the fire kindle, then burst to flame as he tunneled his hands under her bottom and tilted her to his mouth.

"Let me, Ellie. Let me love you like this." He brushed his lips across her curls, feeling her tense and shiver and yearn.

He told her how beautiful she was, how perfect, as he pressed a kiss there...there where her heat was the sweetest. There where she was most sensitive, most vulnerable. There where he knew he could please her most. He wanted to take her over in a way she would never forget, in a way that would claim her absolute trust, in a way that would shatter her with pleasure.

Only he was the one who fell apart. It was a beautiful thing. The way she tasted. The way she moved. The way she moaned and cried his name when she splintered into a million fragmented pieces.

But if she was shattered by the experience, he was obliterated, bound, tied forever to the wonder of her trust, the openness of her responses. She was still coming down when he moved slowly up her body and held her while she wept softly in his arms.

And he knew. For the first time he truly understood what he was holding. In his arms he held the power to make him more than he was, more than he'd ever been. And it humbled him.

She turned in his arms then, and with her gaze intent on his, rose to her knees, took him in her hands. And destroyed him.

He bucked involuntarily against the acute, intense pleasure as she lowered her head. If he hadn't given over his heart to her before, he would have handed it to her on a platter in this moment.

"Ellie..." He dragged a hand over her tangled hair. "You don't have to."

"Oh, but I do. I have to. I want to. I need to," she whispered softly, and touched him with the tip of her tongue. "Let me. Let me..."

And he was lost.

Nine

Ellie breezed around the kitchen, hurrying to finish the dinner she'd prepared and tuck it into the oven. She wanted everything done before Lee came in from the south pasture range. She planned to feed him well. Later.

That done, the only thing on her mind was finding the bottle of wine she had ordered from the Stop and Shop for their wedding night and never had the chance to share with Lee—with her husband.

She felt the blush as it warmed her breasts, then rose to color her face before it disappeared into her hairline.

He couldn't keep his hands off her. He'd told her so. She laughed, joyful and disbelieving, and caught a glimpse of her face in the mirror that hung beside the wall phone. Hugging herself, she twirled around in a circle, remembering the way he'd looked and everything he'd said when he'd left her.

"I have to go do something," he'd said right after lunch as he'd dragged her back into his arms by the kitchen door and kissed her until she thought she'd melt from the pleasure and the pressure of his hot strong body pressed against hers.

"I have to…do…something. Just for a little while. Just long enough to check the black mare—and because I won't be able to leave you alone if I stay here."

"I'm not asking you to leave me alone," she'd assured him, then smiled when he'd pressed his forehead to hers and groaned.

"All the more reason to go." Another quick, tender kiss. "If you don't have the sense to shove me away, then I'm going to have to be the one to make the rules."

"I could go with you," she'd suggested brightly.

"No," he'd said on a deep chuckle. "You could not! Leave it be, woman. Get some rest, because I promise you, you're going to need it for what I have in mind for later tonight."

Well, she thought saucily, I've got a little something in mind for tonight, too.

She blushed again thinking about it. Then she took another long look in the mirror. She liked what she saw. She saw a woman, not a girl. She saw a wife, not an obligation.

And when Lee walked into the house an hour later and found her waiting for him, naked in the middle of their bed, the room flickering with the light of a dozen candles and a chilled bottle of wine sitting on the side table, she knew that he saw her that way, too.

"Ellie."

That's all he said. That's all he had to say. She opened her arms, opened her body and welcomed him home.

He lay panting and spent, spread eagled on his back in the middle of a wild tangle of sheets. Ellie sat beside him, her hands folded prayer-like under her chin, a grin as wide as the sky lighting her face.

"How did you...where did you... Good night, Ellie. How did you know how to *do* that?"

She laughed. "You didn't like it?"

He groaned. Then he laughed, too, huge and happy and utterly wasted. "I'm not sure. Maybe we ought to try it again."

She hit him with a pillow, then squealed when he reached for her. They were both laughing when he dragged her beneath him. "Talk. I mean it. Where did you learn about that?"

She groped for the side of the bed, tugged the book out from beneath the mattress and shoved it under his nose. "Page thirty-four."

With a frowning glance he set her carefully aside. When he opened the book, he blinked long and wide at the page in question, checked out the cover, looked at her smug little smile, then back at the page again. "*Where* did you get this book?" he asked with an amazed laugh.

She tucked her feet beneath her bare bottom and brushed her hair out of her eyes. "I sent for it."

When he just stared at her, she shrugged. "Momma belonged to a book club. She used to get books on cooking and quilting and gardening...and things. They just kept sending ads. When...when I realized we were going to get married, well, I figured...I wanted to know how to make you happy. This book caught my eye.''

He laughed again, delighted, then with a wicked grin, handed it back to her. ''So...'' He reached out, toyed with a shining ribbon of hair that curled over her left breast, ''are there any other pages in there that you found noteworthy?''

''Actually...'' Looking thoughtful, she thumbed through the pages, opened the book wide, studied a picture, tilted it sideways, studied it some more, then showed it to him. ''I was kind of thinking that this looked interesting.''

He didn't even look at the book. He just looked at this woman, this amazing, inventive, brave and sensual woman he had the good fortune to call his wife. ''I so love a resourceful woman,'' he murmured as he pulled her to him. Then he tossed the book over his shoulder and showed her a little resourcefulness of his own.

He wanted to take her somewhere. It hit him while he was out checking fences about nine o'clock one morning a couple of weeks later. She needed a honeymoon. In her entire life she'd rarely been farther than Bozeman, and she needed to go someplace special. Someplace she would love and absorb and remember. As Lee rode down the lane toward the house, he wondered why he hadn't thought of it sooner.

Because he'd been so enamored with his wife, that's why. For the past two weeks he'd been completely consumed by her vast and delightful intelligence, her charming lack of guile, her extreme enthusiasm. She was bright and funny and had a wicked spark of mischief that made him laugh and reminded him that she wasn't the only one who had been missing a vital piece of her life. He'd been missing something, too—and he wasn't altogether convinced that he deserved to wake up each morning and feel such a rich, rare and indefinable warmth fill his chest when she snuggled her warm little body up next to his in bed.

It felt so good, and sometimes he couldn't help but wonder what he'd done to deserve it. In the next thought he would try very hard not to be angry with Will and Clare. They had done what they'd thought was the best thing for her, but it was clear to him now that in the process of sheltering her from a world that they wouldn't allow to corrupt or scar her, they hadn't cultivated and encouraged her boundless imagination.

She could have been so many things. He smiled, thinking about how she was making up for lost time now.

One midnight he'd awakened alone and gone looking for her. He'd found her outside. She was wearing her white gown, dancing barefoot in the starlit meadow, her fiery mop of long, tangled curls flying about her cherub face like angel hair in the moonlight. When she'd realized she'd been discovered, she'd laughed, held out her arms and damned if she hadn't had him dancing with her…and making love under the stars.

She'd coaxed him into that old claw foot tub with her more than once, too, where she'd fed him chocolate and strawberries and pressed butterfly kisses to his face with the soft flutter of her lashes.

She took him to so many places he'd never thought

he'd had in him to go. He'd discovered emotions; he'd discovered needs. He'd discovered the capacity to give in ways that stunned him; he'd discovered the ability to take and hold and trust the love she offered—and that had been the biggest surprise of all.

So, yeah, he wanted to take her somewhere, to show her how happy she made him. Because she did make him happy.

It was almost too much to digest, sometimes. He'd never figured he was entitled to this much goodness. In fact, he'd conditioned himself all of his life to live without it.

Even now, past experience raised its ugly head on a regular basis with a pat, conditioned reminder. *Something that seems too good to be true probably is. And who ever said you were entitled?*

No one. No one had ever said he was entitled to anything. And what he'd found with Ellie *did* seem too good to be true. More and more often he had to fight to outdistance the creeping sensation that not only was it too good to last, it was too rich to count on.

No sooner would he start brooding, though, and he'd see her. Like now. As he loped down the lane on Bud, he spotted her in her garden, fiery bright hair and busy hands—and a negative thought didn't have a snowball's chance in hell of denting his optimism.

She was sitting with her back to him in the middle of the freshly turned earth that he'd tilled for her just yesterday. Getting ready to plant those zinnias she'd been so anxious to get into the ground, he thought with a grin as he reined in and looped the reins over a fence post.

She was so deep in concentration that she didn't

hear him walk up behind her. With a smile of anticipation, he dropped to one knee, wrapped his arms around her and pressed a kiss to her hair.

She jumped as if he'd shot her, then tore at his arms as if he'd bound her in barbwire. Her eyes were wild, her hair flying around her face as she frantically scrambled away from him on all fours.

"No-no-no-no-no-no." A desperate, ragged whisper, a disjointed, murmured chant.

He backed off immediately, a warning shot firing through his head as she knelt there, agitated, combative, shaking her head from side to side. "No-no-no-no-no."

Seizure?

His heart rate doubled. "Ellie?"

"Sorry-sorry-sorry. I'm sorry. I'm sorry. Sorry."

He glanced quickly around, saw what he hadn't noticed before—her bucket of seed packets was scattered all over the ground like shards of colored glass. The garden hose was running, cutting a snaking river through her carefully cultivated plot.

Panicked, and afraid for her, he went to her.

She crab-walked farther away. "No-no-no-no."

He stopped abruptly as Doc's words came back to him.

Keep your distance. Don't try to restrain her. Just give her room.

He clenched his fists to his sides. It hurt. Dammit, it hurt to see her like this. Her eyes were glassy and vacant, her movements unnatural yet oddly choreographed as she sat there, hands in motion, moving her head slowly from side to side, seeing but not seeing him, speaking but not speaking to him.

"No-no-no-no-no. I'm sorry. I'm sorry. I'm sorry..."

"Ellie. Sweetheart. Can you hear me?"

"No-no-no-no-no. Don't-don't-don't-don't. Sorry-sorry. I'm s-s-sorry."

He'd never been so scared in his life. He'd never felt so helpless. But he made himself stand. Made himself stay right where he was, which was too far away.

His heart hammered as if he'd been running uphill, as a stiff breeze cooled the sweat that beaded on his brow, at the small of his back. And all he could do was stand there. Watching, worrying, agonizing over what was happening to her and pained at his utter and absolute uselessness.

He checked his watch, was debating a call to Doc when she drew in a deep breath and became utterly, disconcertingly still.

For another moment he did nothing, said nothing. And then he couldn't stand it any longer.

"Ellie?"

She sat back on her hip, lifted her hands to her face. For a long moment she just sat there and then slowly she raised her head. Her face was smudged with the dirt from her garden. Her fingers were caked with it. She looked lost. And confused. And a deep breath away from falling apart. "Lee?"

He wasn't conscious of moving, but in the next moment he was on his knees in the dirt beside her, touching a hand to her hair, soothing her with quiet words. "I'm here. I'm right here."

She swallowed several times, slowly licked her lips. "I...I..."

"Shh, baby, it's okay. I've got you. I've got you.

Let's go to the house, okay? Let's get out of the sun and get you to bed."

A tear tracked slowly down her face, cut a pale thin trail through her dust-smeared cheek.

"Lee..." With trembling hands she reached for him. His heart broke for the helplessness and hopelessness in her voice.

"I know, princess. I know."

He picked her up, cradled her in his arms and carried her to the house and up the stairs. He slowly undressed her and put her to bed. After he'd gotten a cold cloth for her head, he convinced her to take the medication that would lessen the headache that he knew would follow.

Then he pulled the curtains to darken the room, washed her face and hands, and then he just held her. He simply held her so she would know he wasn't about to let her fall apart.

Her tears were silent and hot as they fell against his throat. Her breath was irregular and ragged.

Not one word of complaint. Not one word of self-pity. Just a silence that was as heartbreaking as her tears.

Finally she slept.

He left her long enough to take care of Bud.

And then he returned, sat in the corner in the rocker and watched over her.

He thought about all the things that made her Ellie: her wonderful smiles, her buoyant enthusiasm, the little quotes she'd framed and hung here and there around the house. One in particular, by Ralph Waldo Emerson, struck a very deep cord.

"He has not learned the first lesson of life who does not every day surmount a fear."

He'd thought he'd known fear until he'd found her there. In the dirt. Lost. Alone.

He'd thought he'd known fear.

He'd been wrong.

But she knew. She surmounted fear every day of her life.

Just last night she'd confessed one of her deepest, darkest ones.

"It's the uncertainty," she'd said, snuggled in his arms after they'd made love. "It's knowing that I'll lose time that I'll never get back. I hate giving in to it. And even though, intellectually, I know I can't fight it, it still feels like a failure on my part some how."

"Ellie—"

"I know, I know. It's just hard to see past it."

She'd been quiet for a long time as she lay against his side, threading her small fingers through his chest hair.

When she spoke again, her voice had been childlike and hesitant. "I used to try to not be aware of things. Like my heartbeat. Or my breathing. Or even blinking. I was afraid that if I was too aware, I might see or feel whatever it is that's inside of me—and it would think I was inviting it. Asking it to come out.

"So I would do anything to keep from being aware. I'd sing, or talk or laugh—anything."

He hadn't known what to say. So he'd held her. And then she'd smiled up at him. "I used to be afraid. Not anymore. You gave that back to me. My self-awareness. Now I don't want to miss anything. I want to know what my body says—the way it responds to you. The way my breath catches sometimes when I see you, the way a shiver runs along my arm when you touch me, or the way my heart beats, sometimes in my throat or my ears when you kiss me. I'm not afraid of feeling those...those physical reactions anymore. And I'm not afraid of giving up control the way I have to give up control to a seizure."

She'd hiked herself up on an elbow, her eyes full of emotion and wonder. "When...when you make love to me, it's...it's like I fly, Lee. I've always been so afraid of being out of control. But with you...it's so wonderful. It's so wonderful to let go."

He'd felt the sting behind his eyes and hadn't even tried to deny the cause.

"You're wonderful," he'd whispered. "And so very brave."

"I'm not brave."

But she was. She'd grown into a woman who had yet to realize her own strengths.

He hadn't told her that. She wouldn't want to believe it, anyway. Just as he hadn't told her that he loved her. Because for him, it was still hard to believe he had the capability. Ellie had moved past her fears, but he was still struggling. If he tried not to be aware, if he tried not to overthink it, maybe, just maybe, it would happen without him spoiling the best thing that had ever happened to him.

So, no. He hadn't told her he loved her. He'd shown her instead. With soul-deep kisses and the most gentle kind of love that he knew how to give, he'd taken her to that place where she could fly and not be afraid of the fall.

That had been last night. Just last night.

In the rocker in the corner of the bedroom, he looked from his tightly clasped hands to the woman, pale and exhausted, in the bed. He hadn't been there to catch her this time. The helplessness of it ate at him.

And no, he'd never understood fear.

Not the way he understood it now.

Ellie opened her eyes slowly. The sense of lethargy, the lingering headache, the dead weight of her legs and arms—they were all too familiar to her.

It took only a few moments to understand what had happened, but as usual after a seizure, what she didn't know was when. When did it happen? Where had she been? What had she done? How had she gotten into bed?

She looked around her room, willed the clock on her bedside table into focus—11:52. Almost midnight. Almost midnight of what day? How many had she lost?

"Hi," a gruff voice said from across the room.

She turned her head and saw Lee sitting in her rocker. His face looked haggard in the pale light that leaked in from the hall. His eyes looked weary.

"Hi," she whispered. She hadn't wanted him to ever see her this way, even though she'd known it had been inevitable that he would. It still didn't make it any easier to face him, to wonder what he'd seen and how he'd reacted. Had she done something horribly embarrassing? Had it repulsed him?

She heard him cross the room. Felt his weight as he eased a hip onto the mattress.

"How are you feeling?"

Lost. Embarrassed. Angry. Confused. "Fine. I'm feeling fine."

He touched a hand to her hair. "And I'm Martha

Stewart, but, hey, if you believe me, I'll believe you. So...should we move on to the weather?''

She smiled. He made it so easy to smile. ''Dark. The weather forecast is dark.''

He smiled too. ''Well, that's a relief. Now I can plan my night.''

She snaked her hand out from under the covers. He took it in both of his, brought it to his lips.

The breath he let out wasn't at all steady. She understood then how upset he was. ''I'm sorry—''

''Don't. Don't even think it. You have nothing to be sorry for.''

But she did. She was sorry this was a part of her. His silence said he was sorry, too.

''Do you need to get up?'' he asked gruffly. ''Use the bathroom? Are you hungry?''

She shook her head on both counts.

He watched her face. ''Want some company in there?''

A wave of tenderness, of gratefulness, of love washed through her. All she could do was nod.

He was out of his clothes and burrowed next to her so fast she was hardly aware that he'd moved.

''Wow,'' she said when he'd wrapped himself around her and surrounded her with his heat.

''Yeah,'' he said, snuggling close. ''Wow.''

''You make everything good,'' she said against his throat, and felt his lifeblood beating there.

''You *are* everything good.'' He pressed a kiss to her hair.

And, wrapped in his arms, she fell asleep, less diminished and, because of his total acceptance, far more complete.

* * *

It was hard to listen to him tell her about it. But the next morning, feeling much better though not fully recovered, she asked him to tell her what her parents never would.

"What happened to me? What did I do?"

He sat with her at the table, where the morning sun cut prisms through the ancient leaded-glass window, and told her what she wanted to know.

He held her hands while he talked, slowly rubbing his thumb over the backs of her knuckles, his gaze drifting from there to her face and down again.

When he finished, she sat back with a bewildered sigh. "That's it?"

He shrugged. "That's everything."

He rose, refilled his coffee mug then poured her more tea.

She was quiet for a long moment, digesting all he had told her. No, it hadn't been pretty and, yes, it was difficult to hear, but it was also as if this huge black hole that was a part of her wasn't as huge and as black as it had been.

"You know those scary movies," she began thoughtfully, "the ones where all through the movie you want to hide your eyes behind your hands because you don't know what monster is going to jump out at you from the dark?"

His gaze was intent on hers as he sat back down at the kitchen table. "I don't hide behind my hands. Ever."

She smiled. At the wonderful way he had of giving import to what she was saying, yet turning a potentially dark conversation back toward the light.

"Okay. So a big, brave, macho guy like you doesn't hide behind his hands. But for a scaredy-cat like me who does, I'm terrified for the first three-fourths of the movie and then, when the monster finally makes his appearance, it's really not so scary anymore. It was the unknown that was frightening. It's still the unknown,'' she added softly.

She ran a thumb over the rim of her cup, thought for another long moment—thought of all her parents had given her and of this one thing they had withheld. ''I wonder why they would never tell me.''

''Maybe they thought it would upset you.''

''Not knowing upset me. Imagining the awful things I could have done upset me. But now I know and it…it sounds pretty…I don't know…uneventful, really.''

''If you don't count the fact that you scared ten years off my life.''

Again she smiled. ''Ten years? Hmm. Good thing I'm a sucker for older men.''

He snagged her wrist, pulled her carefully onto his lap. Kissed her with feeling. ''Damn good thing.''

A couple of days later, when Lee mentioned his plan for a honeymoon and had asked Ellie to think of a spot she'd like to go, she'd been thinking Bozeman. Maybe Denver. He'd been thinking bigger, and a week later he delivered. He took her to New York City.

They'd explored MOMA and the Frick. He'd taken her to Chinatown and Union Square, to Tavern on the Green and *Phantom of the Opera.* She'd cried at Ellis Island—''for those poor desperate souls''—and lost her breath at the top of the Empire State Building, gaped at the opulent extravagance of tea at the Plaza Hotel and the elegance of a candlelit dinner at the Rainbow Room.

And now they stood in the middle of Times Square with life and noise and excitement teeming around them like a wild carnival ride. It was their last night here. It was midnight and she was glowing. Tomorrow he would take her home. But first she wanted a midnight carriage ride around Central Park.

''He's from Dublin,'' she whispered dreamily as they clip-clopped by Rockefeller Center and moved on toward St. Patrick's Cathedral. ''Imagine that. Our carriage driver is from Dublin.''

Everything was a wonder to her. It showed in her eyes as she settled back and smiled, looking for all the world like Cinderella in her pumpkin coach, the night of the ball.

He'd have given her a castle if he could have worked out a deal. He'd have given her anything. And as soon as they returned to Shiloh, he did what he could to lay the world at her feet—at least a new world for her.

''But I don't know anything about computers,'' she said, when he'd finished setting up a new desktop model in her father's den.

''You don't have to know much more than this.''

He showed her how to boot up and how to log on to the Net. Then he gave her the address of a Web site dedicated to epilepsy.

''I didn't know,'' she said, when he found her still in front of the monitor almost six hours later. ''I didn't have any idea.''

''And now you do,'' he said gently.

The site was one of many that linked to others, where not only medical facts but also personal stories were posted and shared.

She rose from her chair, tears in her eyes, and

threw her arms around his neck. ''Oh, Lee. I feel like I know these people. I know what they feel. I live what they live. Thank you. I...I don't even know how to explain how this makes me feel.''

She wiped her eyes with the back of her hand, smiling and crying and laughing all at the same time. ''It's one thing to know you are one of many, but...it's not the same as actually reading someone else's story and knowing that they've been where you've been. It's...it's the difference between looking at a pie chart and eating a piece of pie,'' she exclaimed with a huge grin. ''It gives it texture and flavor and heart.''

He looked into her smiling eyes and didn't think he'd ever known anyone with more heart than she had.

''Now tell me,'' she demanded, and bounced back to the keyboard. ''Tell me how I can talk to them.''

''Tomorrow,'' he insisted with a laugh, and tugged her into his arms. ''Tomorrow will be soon enough. I've got something else in mind for you tonight.''

Ellie had never been happier in her life. She felt as if she was bouncing around in a magic bubble, insulated from old memories and past hurts. It seemed too good to be real, too sweet to be true. And then it just got better.

''Classes?'' she said, when Lee came home from a trip to Bozeman one night and tossed some brochures from the community college onto the kitchen table. ''What kind of classes?''

''Take your pick.'' He dug around for a course catalog and handed it to her. ''I thought we could both take one. I could use a refresher on Excel for some spreadsheets I want to work up on the breeding program. You could take anything you like. Something on creative writing, maybe? Poetry? They have gardening classes and some art classes. Even a class on building a Web site.''

She launched herself into his arms. Kissed him long and deep.

''What?'' he asked, grinning because she was so happy.

''You.''

''Okay.'' He sat down on a kitchen chair and lifted her onto his lap so she was straddling him. ''I'll bite. Me what?''

''You are a wonderful man.''

''Because I brought you some course catalogs?''

''Because—'' she started unbuttoning his shirt ''—because I love the idea of going to school.'' She peeled the shirt back from his chest, nibbled on a spot just below his collarbone. ''And because I love you,'' she added shyly.

When he only smiled, she started unbuttoning her own shirt. ''And because you like page fifty-three as much as I do.''

He let out a whoop of laughter. ''*You* are an insatiable little wanton.''

She bounced off his lap and headed for the stairs at a run. ''Page fifty-three,'' she reminded him with a huge grin.

He was right behind her. ''I'm too old for this.''

It was her turn to laugh. ''Come on, *old man.* I promise, I'll go easy on you.''

''The hell you will,'' he growled, and catching her on the third step, tossed her over his shoulder and took the rest of the stairs two at a time.

Ten

Lee gathered the spread sheet he'd been working on and zipped it into his briefcase. Then he slipped out of the classroom and headed across the hall to wait for Ellie's class to let out.

They'd been making the trip to Bozeman for night classes twice a week for a little over a month now. It hadn't taken but one class and he'd started struggling with some truths that had been easy to dismiss—or at least ignore—while the two of them had been fairly well isolated at Shiloh. Truths he couldn't ignore any longer.

Old man.

She'd kidded him about being an old man on more than one occasion. Her teasing words had banged around in his head more and more often as the days went by—and now the joke wasn't so funny. In fact, it was giving him a headache.

Okay, so he may not be an old man, but Ellie was definitely a young woman—a fact that he'd never been more aware of since seeing her in a college setting.

She was nineteen, for Pete's sake, and she should have been given the chance to experience some of the things nineteen-year-olds are supposed to experience.

Old man.

He'd been fooling himself. All along he'd been fooling himself into believing that he done her a favor by marrying her.

His expression grim, he looked through the textured-glass windowpane of her classroom door. She didn't know he was there. Neither did the young stud putting on the moves, when Ellie laughed at something he said and smiled prettily up at him.

The kid had the build of an athlete and the look of a ladies' man, and Lee should be used to his—and every other man's—reaction to her. She turned heads no matter where she went, and these college guys were perpetually on the make.

He looked the younger man over and couldn't shrug off the twinge of envy he'd tried to deny during the past couple of months. This guy was heartbreak material—even Lee could see that. He oozed confidence and charm and had a smile that no doubt had every coed within grinning distance drooling on their keyboards.

He couldn't have been more than twenty. Just as he couldn't have known that he wouldn't live to see twenty-one if he didn't back away from his wife.

Lee shoved open the door.

"Lee." Ellie's smile grew wider when she saw him. "We're just about done here but come look—

look what John showed me. John, this is my husband, Lee Savage.''

John should have had the sense to go about three shades of pale and the presence of mind to back off. When he did neither, but sized Lee up with a long, assessing once-over instead, Lee placed a hand on Ellie's shoulder.

It was sophomoric and proprietary, not to mention possessive and defensive, and there hadn't been a damn thing he could do to stop himself. Ellie was oblivious to his ridiculous show of staking a claim.

John, with a pointed look at Lee's hand, gave a small but reluctant nod of concession.

``Savage,'' he said, and with a murmured goodbye to Ellie, strolled back to his computer.

All the way home Lee had brooded about how he'd reacted, what he'd done, how it had made him feel. Most of all, though, he brooded about those truths that wouldn't go away.

When he'd returned to Shiloh, it had been with the conviction that Ellie had needed him to take care of her. It was obvious now, that all she'd ever needed was the chance to find out who she was and what she wanted. She hadn't needed him for that.

In fact, it was becoming more and more apparent that she really hadn't needed him for much of anything.

Their classes ended mid-June, and Ellie was anxious to go to work setting up her own Web page.

``I have so many plans,'' she told John on the last day of class. ``So many people I want to reach, so many invitations I want to extend to anyone and everyone who doesn't understand...who might feel as alone as I did and who just need a chance to share what they've been through.''

Aside from her plans for the Web page, one of the most wonderful things to have come out of her class was her friendship with John Tyler. When she'd encountered him that first session, she'd been a little nervous about having to see him on a regular basis. But they'd both grown up a lot since those hurtful years when he'd been, in his words, ''a Neanderthal idiot'' and she'd been, in her words, ''a poor pitiful Pearl.'' All those years that she'd harbored resentment toward him he'd been hating himself and trying to figure out some way to break through the stone wall she'd erected.

Well, they were friends now. They even shared a little bit of a history, and she was glad he'd made that first overture of peace. Now that class was over, she missed talking to him.

And as the days passed and she worked on her Web page, she also missed Lee. She tried to ignore the unsettling feeling that something was very wrong between them. She told herself that the reason he was a little quiet lately, the reason he seemed to be working outside longer, staying up later, was because he was busy, too. And because he was giving her room and time to work on her project.

Life was good. Life was very good. She had a new friend in John, and she and Peg made it a point to have lunch together at least once a week. She wasn't going to let her insecurities, her niggling little suspicion that suggested Lee was pulling away from her, interrupt it.

It was only her imagination that something was out of place when he seemed sort of thoughtful or preoccupied. Didn't he still make love to her with a tenderness that made her weep? She was just imagining that there was desperation when he kissed her—even though she couldn't stop wondering and worrying about what was going on in his mind.

Ellie heard the truck pull up one Saturday morning and walked out onto the front porch. When she saw who it was, she bounced down the steps to greet him and was promptly wrapped in strong arms, swung around in a circle, and given a big smacking kiss on the cheek.

''John Tyler,'' she gasped, laughing up at him as he held her and grinned his poster boy grin, ''a simple hello would have done just fine.''

''But this way is so much more fun.''

She laughed again. ''Well put me down. I can't breathe, for heaven's sake.''

''Ellie, sweet thing, you've stolen my breath for so many years now, it only seems fair that I steal a little bit of yours.''

''Is that what you've got on your mind, Tyler? Stealing?''

Ellie looked over her shoulder to see Lee standing behind them, his face grim, his voice as hard as the hammer he held in his hand that he'd been using to rebuild a box stall.

''Hello, Savage,'' John said, slowly letting Ellie go with an affectionate squeeze and another quick grin. ''How's it shakin'?''

''It's shakin' just fine,'' Lee said in a steely voice that made Ellie frown and wonder about the heat in his eyes and his rigid stance.

''So...'' Lee slung his weight onto one foot and

crossed his arms over his chest. ''You were in the neighborhood or what?''

Since Shiloh was nowhere near anyone's neighborhood, Ellie thought Lee's question a little odd, but she was so happy to see John that she let it roll on by.

''What *are* you doing way out here?'' she asked, then remembered her manners. ''Oh, wait. I don't get to play hostess very often. Come on up to the house. I'll get us all something to drink, then we can talk.''

She was halfway up the steps before she realized the men were still planted where they stood.

''Are you coming?'' she asked, puzzled by John's grin, which could only be described as challenging, and Lee's scowl, which was flat-out fierce.

''In a minute,'' Lee said, his eyes never leaving John's face. ''You go on, Ellie. I want to show John the box stall—maybe get his take on a couple of things.''

When she hesitated, unsure, John's grin just widened. ''Give us five and we'll be there.''

Then the two of them turned and headed for the barn, leaving Ellie with the distinct impression that there was much more to their conversation than box stalls.

Lee was steaming. Because Ellie was beaming at John-boy here, who didn't have the wherewithal to comprehend that he was about a hammer handle away from losing a few of the pearly whites that made his lady-killer grin so irresistible.

''You can't get your own woman, Tyler? You've got to come out here sniffing after mine?''

''Is that what she is? Yours? As in property?'' John

asked, his smile gone, his expression leaning toward combative.

Lee stared at the young man long and hard, then purposefully dropped the hammer so he wouldn't be tempted to use it. "You want to explain to me where you get off, coming to *my* home, kissing *my* wife and asking me a question like that?"

Tyler didn't have anything to say for a long moment. When he finally spoke, Lee figured the kid couldn't possibly know what kind of risk he was taking. "A long time ago I did a lousy thing to Ellie. I hurt her. Worse, I let her be hurt. I was a kid then. And I was stupid. I'm not a kid anymore," he added, just a hint of a threat in his voice. "And I don't figure that it would be right if I stood by and watched her get hurt again."

"And you figure I'm going to hurt her," Lee said, more statement than question.

"I guess that's what I came here to find out."

The anger came from deep inside. So deep he hadn't known it was there. So fierce he wasn't sure what kept him from laying John Tyler and his White-Knight attitude lower than barn dirt. "And I guess that still leaves me wondering why you think you have the right."

Something flickered in John's eyes. "Oh, no. No, man," he said, patting the air between them as if to ward off the thought. "It's nothing like that. Hell, I've never had a chance with Ellie. Not that way. Not when we were kids…not now. And even if she was interested—which she absolutely is not," he added with emphasis, "I'd never graze in another man's pasture, if you know what I mean."

"Then your point is?" Lee ground out.

"My point is, she is nuts about you. I just want to make sure the feeling's mutual."

The silence that settled would have made a lesser man head for the nearest exit. At a run. John Tyler, for all his coverboy looks, was not a lesser man. Either that or he had a death wish.

"Shiloh," John said, holding his ground. "It's a pretty high-ticket piece of property."

"Ah. So it's the profit margin you figure I'm working toward," Lee said, understanding where this was headed.

"It's crossed my mind. Quite a bit, in fact, until I ran into Ellie again at those night classes."

"And?"

"And I'd never seen her so confident. Or so happy."

Quiet filled the barn like the daylight that crept in through the door when Ellie opened it and called out to them.

They remained locked in combative silence until John broke it. "So, I came out here to make sure I was reading the situation right."

"Overlooking the fact that it's none of your business…what's your read now?"

John grinned. "It's a good read. And you're good for her. So…congratulations on your marriage. You're a lucky man."

He sobered then, looked Lee straight in the eye. "Keep her happy. She deserves to be happy. And now that I've seen for myself that you're ready to knock the block off any fool stupid enough to question your good intentions," he added, tongue in cheek, and with a quick glance at the hammer lying by Lee's feet, "I think maybe you just might be good enough for her."

Ellie had crossed the barn and had tucked herself along Lee's side before he could manage to do anything but shake his head and give up a halfhearted smile when John shot another flirting grin at his wife and invited himself up to the house for a cold one.

As Ellie stood at the kitchen sink finishing up dishes that night, she decided that she would never understand men. True, she'd had limited experience dealing with them, but the experience she'd had, well, it was baffling. Take this afternoon with John and Lee. She could have sworn that when she went looking for them in the barn she was going to find one or both of them covered with blood—though she didn't have a clue what they'd been angry about.

Instead, they were actually laughing at each other's stupid jokes by the time John had left after a supper that she hadn't had to work too hard at talking him into staying for.

Lee…Lee was still something of a puzzle. After John left, he'd withdrawn again. She was ready to admit that he'd started pulling away from her about the time they'd started taking those classes. She'd sensed then that he'd been struggling with something. She'd seen the look on his face whenever he'd come into her class to pick her up.

Sometimes he'd actually looked angry. No. It had been less than anger. It had been something else…something she had never been able to figure out. Something that had haunted her—and evidently haunted him, too.

On a deep sigh she looked hard at the picture she'd

propped on the kitchen windowsill and dried her hands on a dish towel. She'd found it when she'd been cleaning the roll-top desk this morning. It was a picture of Lee when he'd first come to Shiloh, before she'd ever been born. The look on his face—as he'd stood there by her daddy's side—made her heart break. It was a look full of hurt and distrust and defiant pride. Her daddy's hand had been on his shoulder, his touch an extension of his love, an overture of trust, a welcome that the ten-year-old boy Lee had been had only to reach out and take to his heart—yet Lee had looked as alone as she felt without him.

He looked, she realized, with tears misting her eyes, as he had looked so often during the past few weeks. Distrustful, confused. Alone.

Her heart tripped. Her breath quickened. She stared at the picture of that lost little boy who had come to Shiloh broken and abused. And with the wisdom of a woman in love, she finally understood. So many things.

''Oh, Lee,'' she whispered, taking the picture in her hand. Running her thumb over that beautiful, unsmiling, defiant face, she finally understood that of the two of them he was still the most wounded.

She went to him at dusk that night. In her flowing white gown, with the wind whipping her hair, she went out on the porch where he sat in brooding silence.

''Go inside, Ellie,'' he said after a long moment. ''It's too cool out here tonight.''

She wasn't going anywhere. Not without him. Not ever again.

''It's colder in there. Without you.''

She moved to kneel at his feet, watched the turmoil in his eyes and knew she'd been right to come to him. As she'd once before come to him, a woman determined to love her man.

Then she eased up onto his lap until he was forced to put his arms around her or let her tumble to the cold porch floor. It took no leap of faith to know he'd never let her fall.

He let out a deep breath, then surrendered and, pulling her to him, buried his face in her hair.

She hugged him to her breast, loving the feel of his hair beneath her hands, the heat of his big, strong body surrounding her.

"I love you, Lee."

His breath came out on a long and ragged shudder. He stared at her face, ran his thumb along her cheek. "You could have been anything. Anything you wanted to be."

Her heart broke as the complexities of this man's soul started to unravel around them. "That's what's been eating at you lately? You think you've taken something away from me?"

He looked away, and her heart stuttered for several beats. "Are you sorry you married me?"

He held her hard against him. "I'm sorry that I took away your choices."

"Listen to me," she said after a long breath. Framing his face in her hands, she made him look into her eyes. "Everything I am, everything I need, is right here with you. I know my own mind, Lee, and it has always been with you. Always.

"No," she insisted when he shook his head. "Just listen. For too long, I let something I couldn't control, control me. Who I was, what I did, what I thought of myself. You've opened up my world. *You,* Lee. You have shown me who I am. And the only choices I've ever had—you have given to me. Choices, Lee. About that, you're right. It's all about choices. Now please…please trust me to make them."

She caressed his face, looked deep in his eyes. "I choose Shiloh. I choose you."

Lee stared at this woman who was his wife. He listened to her words, heard the strength in them, saw the conviction in her eyes, felt the love that spilled out from her heart. She believed. She believed every word she said, that he had given her choices, not taken them away. That she was strong, not in spite of him but because of what she was and what they were together.

She believed. In them. In him. And in that moment, she finally made him a believer, too. Right or wrong, deserved or not, he was going to hold on to the belief—just as he was going to hold on to her and in the process give her the gift of every opportunity she had ever missed.

"Well," he whispered, folding her against him, feeling the heart that she had given him so freely beat, steady and strong and true. "You may have had choices but I never have. Never. Not when it comes to you."

Midnight was soft, and securely wrapped around the bed in the room with pink flowers on the wall. Shiloh slept even as husband and wife lay awake.

"I want to have your baby," Ellie whispered into the quiet.

As happy as he was in this moment, he felt his body tense involuntarily. He'd been waiting for this.

Dreading this. Wrestling with what he would say when she asked.

"Give me some time," he said into the dark. "Give me some time to get used to the idea."

In the moonlight he saw her eyes mist over with tears. He brushed the back of a knuckle across her petal-soft cheek. "And then we'll talk to Doc, okay? Just talk," he insisted, then banded his arms around her. "As much as I'd love to give you a baby…it tears me up to think of you taking that kind of risk."

She kissed him gently. "Life is a risk. The sweetest kind…. When you're ready," she murmured, settling back down in his arms, "only when you're ready, we'll talk with Doc. Then we'll make the decision together."

He was quiet for a long moment, aching for her and the disappointment that their decision might bring her. "And what if the decision is no? What if it's not safe for you to have babies?"

She was quiet, too, dealing with the possibility, mourning the potential loss. "Shiloh has a lot to offer a child," she said at last, her eyes like velvet mist in the night. "Especially a child who has never been offered much of a chance."

A child like he had been. A child who had grown into a man who had thought the exceptional woman in his arms had needed mending. Instead he'd been the one who'd been broken—and she had mended him.

So much warmth, so much wisdom, so much love. He hung on to it. He hung on to her. As he was going to hang on to her for the rest of his life.

"I love you, Ellie."

"I know," she whispered softly. "I think I've always known."

He showed her with his touch then, with the deep glide and penetration of his body, what he couldn't hope to accomplish with mere words.

He took her up, he took her over, to that place where they could both soar free, to that place where she was woman-strong and he was the best man he could ever be...and where neither one of them had to be afraid of the fall.

* * * * *

A COWBOY, A BRIDE & A WEDDING VOW

by
Shirley Rogers

SHIRLEY ROGERS

lives in Virginia with her husband, two cats and an adorable Maltese named Blanca. She has two grown children, a son and a daughter. As a child, she was known for having a vivid imagination. It wasn't until she started reading romances that she realised her true destiny was writing them! Besides reading, she enjoys travelling and going to the movies.

Shirley loves to hear from readers. Please enclose a self-addressed, stamped envelope and write to: PMB No. 189, 1920-125 Centerville Tpke., Virginia Beach, VA 23464, USA.

To my father,
Frank Steadman, Jr.
1921-2000

I miss you.

One

"I think you're my father."

Jake McCall stood stock-still and sucked in a hard breath. His heart began to pound, causing a roaring in his ears that resembled the rumbling sound of cattle being herded on his family's remote Texas ranch. As he stared back at the tall, lanky youth on his porch, Jake's face was blank. He couldn't possibly have heard right.

No way.

I think you're my father.

The words reverberated through Jake's mind, robbing him of an immediate coherent response. He fought for lucidity as he tried to make sense of what he'd just heard. His eyebrows drawn together, Jake shook his head, searched for his voice and stated quite emphatically, "I believe you're mistaken, son."

His tone was deep and firm, his eyes steady as his

gaze studied the disheveled kid. He was dressed in faded jeans that rode low on his hips and looked at least two sizes too big, as did his white T-shirt, spattered with what Jake thought must be the name of some rock group. The thick layer of road dust on the boy's Nike sneakers nearly hid their black color. His brown hair was well below his collar.

Jake met the kid's guarded expression as he shifted his backpack from his shoulder. He caught it just as it hit the porch, his hand grasping one of the thick black straps, then tightening, indicating his unease.

The brand name on the backpack was one Jake recognized, which made him realize that the boy wasn't just some displaced kid off the streets. He belonged to somebody, Jake thought, immediately alarmed.

"You're Jacob Matthew McCall, aren't you?" the boy asked. His gaze held Jake's, and though his voice held determination, his shoulders slumped a bit in defeat.

Jake nodded and waited. It seemed like forever before the boy spoke again.

"I came a long way to meet you," he stated, his green eyes cautious, as if he wasn't sure of his welcome or what to expect from his sudden visit.

Jake was sorry to see so little trust in such a young boy's eyes. Who was he, and where had he come from?

When he had answered the door and seen the boy, he'd thought he had come from the nearby town of Crockett. School had just let out for the year, and several kids had stopped by to ask for summer work—mostly teenagers who lived in town and had never set foot on a ranch.

The boy said he'd come a long way. Jake looked

behind him, but didn't see a car. "How'd you get here?" he asked.

The youngster's lips curved into the bare resemblance of a smile. "I took a bus, then hitched a couple of rides. I got a ride in Ozona with someone who was headed for Crockett. I was walking this way when a lady stopped her car and waved me over. She said her ranch was next to yours, and she gave me a lift here."

"Mary Beth Adams?" Jake asked, thinking of his neighbor.

"Yeah, that was her name," the kid replied as he nodded his head.

Jake couldn't believe this young boy had taken such risks. That aside, the secrecy of the boy's parentage must have been burning in his heart to have made him take drastic chances.

Jake knew firsthand how secrets could drive a person crazy. When he'd taken over the ranch after his parents' death, he'd learned that the woman he'd known and loved as his mother hadn't given birth to him. He'd never been able to discuss it with anyone, not even his brothers or sister. Jake shook the hurtful thoughts from his mind. This wasn't about him or the family secret he'd buried in his heart.

He looked again at the boy whose green eyes were watching him. It took a lot of guts for the kid to knock on Jake's door and confront him. Jake knew his size intimidated most people. At six-two, he towered over most men, given the exception of his brother Ryder, who was six-three. Their younger brother, Deke, wasn't far behind them at six foot. The fact that Jake was the least outgoing of the bunch sometimes made him seem unapproachable to strangers, yet this kid had faced Jake without hesitation.

The boy shrugged. ''She said you go by 'Jake' and described what you look like, so I figured I had the right person when you answered the door.''

''What's your name?'' Jake asked, studying the boy while trying to figure out where he'd gotten such an absurd notion. Oddly, he did look a tad familiar. There was something about the color of his deep-green eyes that tugged at Jake's memory.

He wished he knew why. At thirty-four, Jake wasn't ancient by any means, so at least his mind wasn't slipping. Maybe it was that he had a bit too much to think about lately. Ryder and Ashley, his wife, had brought twin daughters into their family home, which added a new, but welcome, dimension to all of their lives.

Jake quelled the flash of envy that sometimes attacked him when he thought of his two baby nieces, and reminded himself that he was happy for his brother.

''Matthew. My friends call me Matt,'' he answered, his expression guarded. As if gathering courage, he straightened and his shoulders stiffened.

Noticing that Matt didn't offer his full name, Jake didn't know what to make of the kid. A strange, not at all comfortable feeling crawled up Jake's spine. Odd that they shared the same name, though Matthew was Jake's middle name and he'd never gone by it. Jake tossed that off as pure coincidence and probably one of the reasons the kid had mistakenly knocked on Jake's door.

The one thing in his life that Jake was positive about was that there was no way he'd fathered a child. Not long after he'd returned to the ranch, Jake had been thrown from a horse he'd been training. In a fury the horse had stomped on him and left Jake unable to have children. He had been devastated when the doctor had told him, but in time he'd learned to accept it.

It wasn't until he'd met and dated Maxine that Jake realized not having children meant he would never get married. He and Maxine had been seeing each other for nearly six months when Jake had confessed he was unable to father a child. She'd been upset, but she'd told him she loved him, that it didn't make a difference.

Foolishly Jake had believed her. He'd started making plans to ask her to marry him. He'd even bought her a ring. His heart cramped with renewed pain of the memory. The night he was going to propose she'd abruptly broken off their relationship, telling him she'd thought she could live with his "condition," was what she called it, but she'd changed her mind. She wanted a *whole* man.

Hurt and disillusioned, Jake had vowed never to allow himself to be that vulnerable to a woman again. He didn't need a permanent relationship in his life. He settled for an occasional evening or two of pleasure when he desired company.

Still, it was painful when he thought about never being a father, especially when Ryder seemed intent on populating the entire county singlehandedly. With the twins, Michelle and Melissa, and another baby on the way, Ryder was walking around with a silly grin on his face nearly all the time.

Jake glanced over the boy once again, taking note that his head came to about Jake's chest. His size, Jake thought, was deceiving. Hazarding a guess, Jake figured he was around twelve, much too young to be traveling alone.

"Well, Matt," Jake began, opening the screened

door to the porch, ''why don't you come inside, and let's see if we can figure this thing out.''

Matt hoisted his backpack onto his shoulder. He stepped inside the house, and his gaze darted around the large foyer, taking in his surroundings with wide-open eyes.

Jake closed the door, and silence filled the air between them. He wasn't quite sure what to do next. He knew he had to get a handle on this mix-up quickly. The kid's family was sure to be worried about him. Before Jake could say anything, Ryder came around the corner from the hall that led to the dining room.

''Ashley sent me to find you. The babies have been fed, and we don't have much quiet time. She said she's not going to hold dinner much longer, that you'd better get your butt in there.'' Ryder was smiling, but then he noticed the young boy standing by the front door. He stopped abruptly and flashed a curious glance at Jake.

''This is Matt,'' Jake said by way of an introduction. ''Matt, this is my brother, Ryder.'' Ryder stuck out his hand, and the boy shook it.

''You come by looking for a job?'' Ryder asked, taking another look at the kid, then watching his brother.

''Not exactly,'' Jake answered for the boy. ''It seems we have some business to discuss. Go ahead and eat. I'll be in, in a little while.'' Ryder's curious gaze flickered from Jake to Matt, but he left without commenting.

''Let's go somewhere more private to talk,'' Jake said, then indicated for Matt to follow him down a hallway. Once inside the large ranch office, Jake extended his hand toward a brown vinyl sofa.

"Have a seat," he told Matt, then walked over to a large walnut desk and leaned his rear against it, bracing his hands against the edge. His gaze followed Matt as he sat down.

"Now, just to be up-front with you, I have to tell you I'm positive I'm not who you're looking for, but why don't you start at the beginning. Where are you from?" he asked, crossing his arms and staring at the youth.

"Lubbock."

Jake nodded and his brows wrinkled. "I went to school there for a while."

"I know."

The two words once again robbed Jake of breath. Jake was stunned by Matt's answer. How much did this kid know about him, and how did he find it out? "You do, huh?"

"Yes, sir." Matt's gaze never left Jake. "You went to Texas Tech, right?"

Jake's eyes widened so slightly it was barely noticeable. He'd attended Texas Tech until his parents were killed. Then he'd returned home to take care of his siblings.

Jake figured that although it was out of the ordinary for Mary Beth to gossip, she must have been the one to mention such information to Matt. Of course, it could have been anyone who lived around Crockett.

Everyone within a hundred miles of their ranch and the town knew Jake and his family. And most of those people knew that he hadn't finished school, that he'd left to come home and take over his parents' ranch when they died in an airplane crash. And that he'd raised his younger siblings. Still, Jake didn't think Matt had come into contact with anyone other than Mary Beth.

Matt was sitting on the edge of his seat. "I found a paper that my mom had in a chest in her bedroom. That's how I found out that you're my father."

Jake felt a little pang every time the boy called him his father. He couldn't deny the yearning and disappointment that pulled at him. A little part of Jake's heart twisted, wishing for something that was unattainable.

He supposed most people would think that after raising three siblings, he'd pretty much raised a family. Jake had told himself that same thing many times and wished he felt that way in his heart. He had been responsible for his brothers and his sister, Lynn, since he was twenty-one, but had never felt that they were a substitute for having a family of his own. Maybe that's why it had been so hard to watch each of them grow and mature. He had nothing to take their place.

It wasn't until Ryder had become a father that Jake realized how much he would miss by not having children. While he was happy for Ryder and Ashley, a little twinge of jealousy simmered in Jake's heart. Ironically, Ryder had been the one who hadn't wanted children, but he'd found the love of his life and had settled down and started raising a family.

Jake knew he would never be able to do the same.

"What kind of paper?" he asked, bringing his thoughts back to the problem at hand. The kid was staring at him as if he had the power to fulfill his dreams.

"A hospital paper."

"Like a certificate—the kind with your footprints?"

Matt nodded, but gave nothing more away.

Jake's lips thinned as he thought about it. "Do you have it with you?"

Matt lifted his pack onto his lap and zipped open an outside pocket. He searched through it for a few moments, then produced a folded piece of paper and handed it to Jake. "It has your address written on it."

As Matt said, Jake's address was written on the back side. For some reason the handwriting looked familiar. Sighing, he opened it and studied what looked like a legitimate hospital certificate, the folded creases worn.

The first thing that Jake searched for was his name on the document. A jolt went through him when he saw it printed neatly beside the word *father.* It was a natural response to look immediately at the line listing the mother's name, and Jake's heart took another blow when he actually recognized it.

Catherine St. John.

Jake's hand shook as he stared at the paper, and he was unprepared for the rush of emotions that assailed him. His chest squeezed painfully. He couldn't seem to get a handle on something as basic as breathing and hated feeling so out of control.

All of his life he'd been the one to shoulder responsibilities, to make decisions, to carry them out and make sure that the ranch ran smoothly and his siblings were well cared for.

How long had it been since he'd thought of Catie? he wondered, letting his mind slide back to his college years. He'd met her at school, had fallen in love with her. They'd even talked about marriage. But they both knew there was school to finish, and Catie's father would have had a fit if he'd known how involved they were.

Catie.

Her face drifted through his thoughts. A beautiful brunette, tall and lithe, she'd touched his soul. But Jake had let go of her and their promise of a future together.

He remembered that the last time he'd seen her, they'd had a fight over something. What about, he couldn't even remember now. That night he'd gotten the call about his parents, and he'd returned home to deal with the responsibilities at the ranch and to care for his siblings.

And somewhere along the way, he'd lost Catie. Jake stared at Matt. This was Catie's son.

His Catie.

No, he corrected himself harshly, not *his* Catie. He'd given up the right to call Catie his a long time ago. He was ashamed that he'd never called her, but he'd arrived home to find the ranch deep in debt, and it had taken all of his time and energy for a while to keep it afloat. Then, there was the accident. In all fairness, Jake told himself, Catie hadn't called him, either.

Jake looked up to find Matt watching him. He took a deep breath and strove to get his emotions under control.

''Catie St. John is your mother?'' he asked, and his voice took on a new huskiness. He cleared his throat, willing away the tightness inside his chest, the grip of emotion that seized him. Instead, it became worse, carving at him like the sharpened blade of a knife.

Matt nodded a little hesitantly. ''I've never heard anyone call her Catie,'' he answered. ''She goes by Catherine.''

Jake digested that information. He'd shortened her name to Catie shortly after they'd met.

''Matt, did your mother *tell* you I was your father?'' There had to be some mistake, some reason Catie had listed his name on her son's certificate. Though it was only seconds, it seemed as if an eternity passed before Matt finally answered.

"No," he admitted, then glanced away momentarily. "I didn't really ask her."

"You didn't ask her?" Jake repeated. Lines indented the skin between his brows as he stared at Matt. "You mean you didn't talk to her about this?" His tone was incredulous.

Matt's head moved from side to side.

"Are you telling me that Catie—your mother," he amended, "doesn't even know that you were curious about your father?" he asked roughly, astonished that the boy wouldn't have discussed something this important with his mother before he took off on his own. What kind of relationship did they share? Had the sweet young woman he'd known changed so much? Was she that unapproachable?

"She doesn't have time for me anymore," Matt stated, a little defiance in his tone. "She's getting married soon. I thought if I found my father, that maybe...maybe I could live with him for a while. I don't have that long until I graduate and then I can be on my own." For the first time he looked worried, as if his plan had flaws that he hadn't even thought about.

Jake laid the paper on the desk, then straightened his shoulders and crossed his arms in front of him. The news that Catie was about to get married shouldn't have bothered him, but his gut tightened a fraction. "Don't you think she might be worried about you?"

Guilt flashed through Matt's eyes. "I guess so," he admitted. His Adam's apple bobbed as he swallowed hard. A sadness stole over his young features. He seemed to want so much to appear grown-up, but Jake saw only a young boy with a need for attention, a need for a father. "I guess you didn't want anything to do with me." He looked right at Jake, staring at him as if his very life depended on his answer.

Jake swore, then murmured an apology to the boy. Jake had let his father's lawyer, Frank Davis, handle all of the correspondence for the ranch. Surely he would have passed any personal letters on to Jake.

"Believe me, Matt, if I'd known about you, I damn sure would have contacted your mother." He stood and paced to the window, looking out at the expanse of the Bar M, his family's ranch. He'd given his life to keep the ranch going, to make sure his family stayed together. Had he given up his son, too?

Turning, he stared at the boy. Yes, now he could see Catie in him and knew that was why Matt had looked so familiar when he'd come to the door. His nose was just like hers and there was something about the way he tilted his head when he talked. Catie used to do that.

Matt was watching him, so Jake walked back over to within a couple of feet of him. "I have to tell you, Matt, that I still believe there's some mistake, but I think we'd better call your mother right away. I'm sure she's very worried about you."

Matt stood, and his stance became rigid. "I don't want to go back to live with her. Can't I stay here? I won't be any trouble, I swear. I do pretty good in school, and I can be a real help on your ranch."

Jake's heart filled with compassion, but he didn't let himself believe that Matt was his son. Jake was sure Catie would provide a reasonable explanation once he got in touch with her.

"I can't make you any promises, Matt. The first thing we have to do is talk to your mother."

Matt looked scared and uneasy. Jake lifted the receiver of the telephone and extended it toward him. When he didn't move immediately to grasp it, Jake shook it gently, encouraging the boy to take it.

Matt put the receiver to his ear. Leaning over the desk, he punched some numbers in, then cast a guarded look at Jake as he waited for it to ring. Moments later his eyes darkened when his mother answered.

"Hey, Mom. It's me, Matt."

Silence stretched as Matt listened to his mother's response. Jake wished now that he'd put the phone on speaker so he could hear what Catie was saying. He was surprised at his anticipation of talking to her, even under these strange and unexpected circumstances.

Matt said, "I'm okay, Mom. I'm sorry I scared you." For a couple of minutes more Matt just listened. Jake watched as the boy turned away to hide the tears in his eyes. "I know, Mom. I'm sorry. I really am." His voice shook enough to betray his emotions, and he took a deep breath.

"I know you're going to be mad, but I came to see my father," Matt whispered into the receiver. "I found the hospital paper with his address. You know, the one in the chest in your room."

Jake watched the boy talk. He was genuinely remorseful, and Jake was impressed. Matt had manners and a conscience, and it seemed as if Catie had raised her son well.

Their son.

Jake's mind wandered automatically. Could it be true? Was Matt his son? He looked again at the boy for some sort of physical sign. Besides his height, all he could see was Catie. Matt had her brown hair color, her dark-green eyes.

Matt couldn't be his son, Jake told himself again. There was no way Catie wouldn't have let him know he'd fathered a child. She wouldn't have kept Matt to herself for all these years. Jake was drawn from his thoughts when Matt held the receiver out to him.

"My mom wants to speak to you," he said, sounding every bit as contrite as he looked.

Jake hesitated a moment before grasping the telephone, taking a breath to prepare himself. Finally he raised the phone to his ear.

"Catie, this is Jake."

There was a long silence on the line, and for a moment or two, Jake thought he'd lost the connection. Then she spoke.

"Jake."

Hearing her say his name touched a vast emptiness inside him. Her voice nearly crumbled, and Jake felt her pain. She must have been out of her mind with worry when she discovered Matt was missing.

"How are you, Catie?" Jake made himself say the words. Emotion choked him, making him feel as if he was locked in a box and suffocating.

"Fine. I'm fine. And it's Catherine," she added, her tone containing none of the warmth that Jake remembered from when they were together. "Look, I'm sorry about this." Again, she faltered, unable, it seemed, to go on.

"He's all right, Catherine." Her name sounded foreign to him even as he said it. He felt as if he was in some kind of time warp.

Through the telephone, Jake could sense Catherine's terror. She sounded desperate and exhausted. He looked at Matt and, for a moment, wanted to strangle the kid. What had he been thinking to run off without talking to his mother?

After an audible gasp of breath, she spoke again. ''I was so worried. I was afraid that something terrible had happened to Matthew. So many bad things can happen to children today. I don't know what got into him.''

''He looks a bit tired, but other than that he's okay. Don't worry about him.''

''Thank you for calling me,'' Catherine whispered through the line.

Jake hesitated, then replied, ''It was no problem.'' Their conversation was stilted, filled with an awkwardness of years gone by, which left Jake wondering how much Catie had changed. When they were together, they'd been able to talk about anything. Now it was as if they were strangers.

Well, they were, he reminded himself. He didn't know this Catherine, and she knew nothing about him. They weren't the same two kids who fell in love in college.

''How on earth did Matthew get there?''

''He said he caught a bus, then hitched a couple of rides,'' Jake told her, repeating what Matt had told him.

''Oh, my— Jake, I'm leaving right away to come and get him.''

Jake glanced at his watch and frowned. ''It's late. Why don't you wait until morning?'' he suggested, thinking it wouldn't be a good idea for her to travel while she was so upset. Then he thought it ridiculous that he was concerned about her. She probably wouldn't be traveling alone.

''I'm coming right now, Jake.'' Catherine's voice held a you-can't-stop-me tone and Jake shuddered. He knew she was worried, but for some reason he thought there was more to it than that. Jake heard the panic in her voice and glanced at Matt who was across the room, leaning against a wall. He looked scared, uneasy and worried.

"Hold on a minute," Jake said into the receiver, then placed his hand over the mouthpiece. "Matt, why don't you wait in the family room while I talk to your mother?" he suggested. "It's the second room as you go out." Matt didn't move and Jake added, "Go on."

After a moment's hesitation, Matt nodded.

Jake waited while Matt went out the door, then put the receiver back to his ear. "I've sent Matt out of the room so we can talk in private," he informed Catherine.

"That really wasn't necessary. The only thing I have to say is that I'm coming to get him. Right now." Her tone was curt, determined.

"Catie, wait." Jake realized he'd reverted to his nickname for her. He frowned, and the thought occurred to him that some habits never change.

He had hoped to wait until he saw her in person, when he could better judge what she was telling him by her expression. But he needed to know the truth. It seemed as if she wanted to come and whisk Matt away without any explanation. Jake wasn't going to let that happen.

He wanted answers.

"Catie, Matt told me why he came here," Jake stated, and the bald statement created a tense strain of silence on the line.

"What…what exactly did he say, Jake?" she asked, her voice once again unsteady.

"He showed me a hospital certificate with my name

on it.'' He let that sit between them for a moment, wanting her to absorb the shock as he'd had to.

When she didn't say anything, Jake took a deep breath. It took every ounce of his courage to ask the question on his mind. ''Is it true, Catie? Am I Matt's father?''

Two

Catherine St. John grasped the telephone receiver tighter, holding on to it like a drowning person would cling to a life preserver after a shipwreck at sea. Her heart stopped, and she squeezed her eyes closed.

Am I Matt's father?

She had been dreading that question for much longer than Jake McCall could possibly imagine. For thirteen years, since the day she'd learned she was pregnant, she'd wondered when this day would come. She'd thought about it, worried about it, feared it. There was rarely a day when she didn't think about Jake or the circumstances that left her pregnant and alone.

"Jake—" Her pleading tone implied stalling and Jake cut her off.

"Catie, I want the truth. *Now. Is Matt my son?*" Jake demanded.

"Yes."

The whispered word was barely audible. The immediate silence it brought was deafening.

Jake was the one who broke it, and his tone wasn't kind. "Why, Catie?" he demanded, sounding incredulous, angry and not at all understanding. "Why in hell didn't you ever tell me?"

Catherine's first thought was to try again to put the conversation off. She was already dealing with one crisis—she couldn't handle another. Not now. Not when she'd been sick with worry for hours, wondering where Matthew was and whether or not he was safe.

"I don't think we should be discussing this over the telephone," she answered quickly, hoping she didn't sound as panicked as she felt. She needed time to think, time to pull herself together. "I'm leaving to come there shortly. We can discuss it then." Her suggestion was met with silence, and she added, "I'll be there as soon as possible."

"Matt's exhausted and probably hungry. I'm sure he can use a night's sleep. You can come in the morning," Jake told her. "Get a flight to San Luis, then rent a car. You could probably be here by early afternoon."

"I want to come now," she insisted, her voice rising just a notch.

"He's not going anywhere, and it seems to me that you both need a few hours to get yourselves together. I'll see to it that he doesn't leave here," Jake promised.

"I'm not concerned with him leaving again."

"Then what are you concerned about?"

Catherine sighed heavily. "Jake, it's complicated. Matt should never have come to you. He's mixed up right now."

"Catie—"

"He's *my* son. I'm sorry that you were brought into

this, that he came all the way there before I had a chance to clear things up with him. But I'm not letting him stay any longer than necessary."

After a moment Jake surprised her by agreeing. "You're right," he replied. "We should discuss this in person." Then his voice lowered to a deep, determined tone. "Tomorrow."

"I don't want to wait until tomorrow," Catherine declared, and her voice cracked a bit. If she waited until morning, it would be afternoon before she got there. She put a hand to her temple and massaged the headache that had started the moment she had heard Jake McCall's voice.

"I'm not giving you a choice." Jake's tone was sharp and to the point. It left little room for arguing.

"That's not—"

"What? Fair? Is that what you were going to say?" he demanded, cutting her off once again.

"Jake—"

"Look," he said roughly as he argued the point. "Matt's upset. It might be best to give him some time to work things out. You can just as easily fly in tomorrow."

Catie stiffened and grasped the telephone tighter, her knuckles turning white. She tried very hard to stay calm, but Jake was making it terribly difficult.

"I don't need you to tell me what's best for my son." How could Jake even know what was best for Matthew? He hadn't even known the boy existed until today.

"Apparently you do," Jake countered. "He ran away from you. That tells me he wasn't happy."

Catherine bristled, and the anger she'd held in check

until now began to seep out. ‘‘It wasn’t like that. You don’t know anything about him, Jake.’’

Jake’s voice took on a hard edge. ‘‘You’re wrong, Catie. I know one thing for damn sure. I know now that he’s my son.’’

Catherine hung up the receiver. In the end she’d given in and agreed to arrive at Jake’s ranch tomorrow. Under the circumstances it seemed the best way to handle the entire situation.

And it wasn’t as if Jake had given her a choice. Oh, she could ignore him and leave immediately. But Jake had already begun sounding hostile, and Catherine didn’t want to make an enemy of Jake McCall. Not now. Not while Matthew was in Jake’s home.

Catherine went to her room and began packing a bag of clothes. After throwing in the necessary items for a day’s stay, she walked to Matthew’s room and retrieved a change of clothing for her son and put them in with her things.

Why hadn’t she seen this coming? she wondered. Had she been so out of tune to Matthew’s needs that she’d missed warning signals that something was terribly wrong in her son’s life?

She’d noticed that he’d been distant and moody over the past few months, but Catherine had just tossed that up to his being an adolescent. All adolescents went through personality changes. As a high school counselor, she knew that well enough. Catherine hadn’t thought there was anything to worry about. Matthew was a good kid. He was respectful and made decent grades. She’d thought that he just needed some time, that he’d come around.

But she’d been wrong. So terribly wrong.

Though Matthew had known about the chest in her

room, she hadn't thought that he'd go into it on his own. She remembered when he was about eight and had come upon Catherine going through some of the contents. When he'd seen a picture of her and Jake together, he'd asked if the man was his father. Catherine had told him the truth, that his father was someone she'd known in college. Matthew hadn't asked about his father since that day.

What had she ever done to make her son feel as if she didn't want him around? Since his birth there had just been the two of them. When Catherine had found out she was pregnant, Jake had already left college and returned home to take care of his younger brothers and sister. Catherine had tried to call him. She'd left a couple of messages, but Jake had never returned her calls.

They'd argued the night before he'd left. Jake's roommate had told her of Jake's parents' death. She'd wanted to go to him, but her father hadn't permitted her to. When weeks passed with no word from him, Catherine had been hurt, assuming that he'd meant to break off their relationship.

Only when she learned she was pregnant did Catherine decide to write him and ask him to contact her. Instead of getting a letter from Jake, she'd received one from his lawyer stating that Jake didn't know her. It was then that she'd decided not to tell him about the baby. She loved him, but she didn't want Jake back because she was pregnant with his child. She'd wanted his love, but he'd shut her out of his life.

Leaning over the table, Catherine held her head against her palms and closed her eyes. She'd felt betrayed and hurt, and she'd held on to that anger for years. It had provided her with the will to take care of herself and her baby. She'd fed on it every time things got rough and she felt like giving up.

How she'd even gotten through the first few weeks after finding out she was pregnant was a blur. She had wanted to stay in school, but without help it was impossible. In desperation, Catherine had turned to her family.

Reverend St. John, her father, had been a rigid disciplinarian. Catherine had feared the fire-and-brimstone preacher for most of her life, so she hadn't expected him to be pleased when she told him of her predicament. She'd known her parents would be upset when they learned of her pregnancy, but she had relied on at least getting some moral support. She had never considered that they would disown her.

Her father had given her a cold, distant stare, then informed Catherine that she was a disgrace to her family. Catherine's mother had watched and said nothing as he belittled his daughter. Her mother had always bowed to her husband's authority, and Catherine couldn't remember one time when her mother had stood up to him.

Catherine cringed as her past came rushing back at her. The hurtful memories caused tears to spring to her eyes. Her father had called her some unforgivable names. That she still felt the pain, after all this time, angered her. She hadn't even been allowed to stay in touch with her two younger sisters. That had hurt the most.

Get yourself together, she mentally admonished herself. She had made it through all of that. She had gotten a job to support herself and had finished college while taking care of a small child. She'd eventually received her master's degree and was working at a rewarding career, was able to provide well for Matthew and herself.

Catherine had been through hell and back, and she was stronger for it. She wasn't going to let Jake McCall bully her. If he thought she was going to roll over and play dead, he was wrong. Catherine St. John was a fighter. Jake McCall had himself to thank for that.

Early the next morning Catherine put her bag in the passenger side of her car. She hesitated only a moment before walking around and getting behind the wheel.

She'd called Douglas last night to tell him that she'd found Matthew. She and Douglas Anders had been dating for a while, long enough to talk about marriage, and Catherine had wanted him to know that Matthew was safe.

He'd been supportive when she had called, had even offered to drive her to the airport, then only seconds later mentioned that he'd have to rearrange an important meeting. Catherine had felt that the offer hadn't really been sincere, but she'd shrugged it off. She was used to Douglas putting his work first.

She'd admired his dedication to his job when she'd first met him and now reminded herself that his job as a stockbroker was demanding. He was a dependable man, someone steady in her life after being alone for so long.

She had told Douglas that she'd probably be back by late evening, and now she hoped it wasn't wishful thinking. She wasn't leaving Matthew at Jake's, no matter what it took. Her son was coming home with her.

Catherine started the engine, then backed out of the driveway. She switched on the air conditioner as she started toward the airport. Since it was early in the morning, the car began to cool instantly. However, it did little to relieve the anxiety Catherine felt building inside her. The last thing she wanted to do was to face Jake after all these years, after all the heartache he'd given her.

She pushed her hand through her hair, brushing it off her shoulder and behind her back. The memories came rushing back at her as if only days had passed instead of thirteen years.

Jake McCall had been her first and only true love. Her father had never allowed her a boyfriend while she was living at home, so she'd had little experience when it came to boys. She hadn't been prepared for her reaction to Jake when she met him. She'd known soon after she met Jake that she had lost her heart to him.

She'd first seen him during her second semester of college. He'd been a couple of years older, and there was something about Jake McCall that attracted her attention. In fact, he drew a lot of attention from girls. He was tall and there was a certain ruggedness about him. She'd heard that he was from a ranching family, which was evident by his muscular arms and trim body. With dark-brown hair and brown eyes, he was rogue handsome.

He'd been so serious about school, not into partying like a lot of the other kids. Even from afar, before she'd even met Jake, Catherine had admired that about him.

She'd never dreamed that Jake McCall would take a second look at her. But he'd approached her after one of her classes, and they'd spent the afternoon walking in a park and chatting. Later they'd gone to a restaurant and talked away the night. They had seen each other every day after that, neither of them wanting to be with anyone else. The more she was with Jake, the more Catherine wanted to be with him.

Trying to shake memories of Jake from her mind, Catherine switched on the radio as she headed down the interstate toward the airport. She'd called and arranged a flight as soon as she'd hung up with Jake last night, then she'd called him back to let him know when to expect her.

After parking her car in the long-term lot, Catherine made her way to the ticket area, then proceeded to the departure gate. She'd timed her arrival well and only had to wait about fifteen minutes before the airline attendant called her flight.

A mixture of relief and trepidation filled Catherine when she arrived in San Luis. All she could think about was driving as fast as she could to Jake's ranch. Though she told herself that she had nothing to worry about, she felt like a bucket of nerves as she stood waiting for her turn to leave her seat.

Catherine retrieved her bag from the overhead compartment and followed the trail of people ahead of her off the airplane, mentally calculating the time it would take to make the drive ahead of her. She'd gotten the directions from Jake earlier and hoped she wouldn't get lost. From what Jake said, it wouldn't take terribly long.

Upon entering the terminal, Catherine's eyes were drawn to the big man leaning nonchalantly against the wall across the small walkway. She started to look past him, then her gaze was pulled back to him of its own will. Her heart shifted and a chill ran down her spine. He had on a black cowboy hat and snug blue jeans that hugged his hips. Small drops of water dripped from his Stetson and dotted his white cotton shirt.

Jake.

As soon as Catherine recognized him, she stopped dead in her tracks. Someone bumped into her, and she barely caught herself, then stepped aside. When she looked up, the full force of Jake's attention staggered her. A freight train would have caused less of an impact.

Jake's gaze traveled lazily over her, from her head to her toes, then back up to her face. He never for one moment gave her a hint of what he was thinking. Catherine wished she looked as calm, but she knew better. She was trembling all over. Surely he could tell.

Catherine still hadn't moved when Jake easily shifted his weight away from the wall and moved toward her. She stood frozen, unable to do anything but watch him slowly make his way in her direction. He stopped in front of her, and she immediately resented the fact that his mere presence robbed her of the ability to breathe.

His granite expression startled her, as did the distant look in his dark-brown eyes—eyes that she remembered being warm and loving. It shocked her to see that he'd changed so much.

He stared at her silently for more than a moment, then tipped his hat up just a bit, leaving his face slightly shadowed.

"Catherine."

On the trip out to pick her up, Jake had worked on how to respond to seeing Catherine after all this time. He told himself to use her given name when referring to her and, as silly as it sounded, he'd even practiced doing so. Anger wasn't something he usually had to work at defusing. Unlike his brother Ryder, Jake wasn't prone to flying off the handle. It took a lot to provoke him.

But, dammit, he was angry with Catherine for keeping his son from him, and he would use any means at his disposal to keep his guard up. He wasn't going to go easy on her now. He had to admit that he was tempted, seeing that she looked scared and overwrought. It would have been easy to comfort her, to tell her everything would be all right.

But Jake couldn't do that. He couldn't be nice to her. He had to keep that edge. His future with his son was at stake, and he wasn't going to give Catherine any leverage over him.

What Catherine had done had basically ruined his easygoing reputation. Ryder and Ashley had tried to get Jake to calm down and give Catherine a chance to explain why she'd kept his son a secret from him.

But secrets could tear a family apart. Jake found that out when he'd taken over the ranch. And he'd kept his father's infidelity a secret to himself, rather than see his brothers and sister hurt. He'd never discussed what he knew with them, even when Ryder had kept insisting that there had to be a good reason for Catherine to keep Matthew a secret from Jake.

In the end Jake had agreed to give Catherine a chance to explain why she hadn't told him about his son, why she had let Jake miss seeing Matthew grow up.

That was before he'd seen her walk off the airplane. Then the anger and frustration settled deeper in his soul.

Jake was pleased that he'd managed not to convey any of the emotions boiling around inside him. He was honest enough to admit to himself that a part of him had been looking forward to seeing Catherine again, but he hadn't *wanted* to feel that way, and he resented the fact that he did.

He wasn't prepared for the sight of her. Dressed in designer jeans and a soft pink shirt, she was still slim, though her body was more womanly, filled out nicely in all the right places. Her hips were gently rounded, her face a bit fuller. She wore her hair shorter, just below her shoulders, its color a rich chocolate-brown. Her features were soft and inviting, her lips sculpted perfectly.

Her breasts, well, damn, Jake thought, they'd filled out as well, and he couldn't stop his gaze from resting on them a moment longer than necessary. Catherine had never been small. Jake could remember how firm her breasts had been when he'd last touched them and found himself wondering how they would feel now.

Before he let himself go farther down that road, he hauled his wayward thoughts back. Jake didn't like the way his body immediately responded to Catherine. The last thing he wanted was to feel any kind of attraction to her. That was dangerous territory, and he knew he had to steer clear of it if he was going to keep his mind sharp. Something told him he'd need every ounce of his mental faculties when dealing with her.

Three

Though last night Catherine had wanted Jake to use her full name, she was taken aback by the aloofness of his tone. The way he said it made her shiver with apprehension. She stared at him and swallowed past the lump in her throat. Tears stung her eyes as she thought of the gentle, loving young man she'd known so many years ago. There was no trace of him in the hard, distant person standing before her.

"Jake," she whispered, an ache in her heart appearing out of nowhere. There was disappointment and sadness in her voice. Too many years had passed since she'd seen Jake. There was so much she wanted to say, so much she wanted to know. She wanted to ask about broken promises, wanted to know why he had discarded her love and broken her heart.

"What…what are you doing here?" was all she managed to get out, and she decided that she should be thankful that she sounded remotely normal. "I thought I told you that I was renting a car. I'd planned on driving out to get Matthew."

"You did," he acknowledged, his clipped tone cutting her no slack. He hooked his arms together across his chest.

Catherine was having a bit of trouble following their conversation. "Then why are you here?" she asked again. Her brows wrinkled.

"I decided to save you the trouble."

He reached toward her, and Catherine braced herself for his touch. Her heart skipped several beats. Jake took her bag from her and easily lifted it. A shock of disappointment rocked through her.

Well, what had she expected? He wasn't likely to embrace her, now, was he? And it was ridiculous for her to even entertain such a notion.

But the memories that had assailed her last night had continued to this very moment. Catherine had wondered if Jake would look anything the way she remembered. While she'd recognized him instantly, there was little about him that reminded her of the young man she'd once loved with all her heart and innocence.

"That isn't necessary." As if he hadn't understood her plans, she explained once again. "I've already made arrangements to rent a car. I'd like to get on the road back to Lubbock as soon as possible." She waited for him to acknowledge her words, but he remained quiet, his gaze boring into her. "I told you that, on the telephone last night," she reminded him when he continued to stare at her without speaking.

Catherine looked at his face and decided the years had been good to Jake. Too good. Though tiny lines creased the corners of his brown eyes and bracketed his mouth, his face was lean and tanned. Irritation swept through her. She would have preferred him to be balding and fat.

Not a chance. Apparently, years of working on his ranch had perfected his physique, giving him muscles and a rock-hard body that Douglas spent hours in a health club trying to achieve.

"I thought if I picked you up we could discuss the situation on the way to the ranch," he said, then nodded his head. "This way." He stood aside and waited.

Catherine didn't move. The last thing she wanted was to give Jake the idea that they were going to discuss what was best for Matthew. It wasn't up for debate. "I'm here to get my son. He should never have come here."

Jake's gaze swung back at her, and his eyes met hers with deadly force. "You're wrong about that," he replied, his tone unnervingly calm. "Matt is my son. *Mine.* And he has every right to be here."

It took every ounce of her courage for Catherine to hold her ground and not back away from Jake. "You don't even know him, Jake," she declared defensively.

Jake's expression turned colder. "And whose fault is that?" he demanded. When Catherine didn't answer, he said, "Look, we can have this out right here for all of San Luis to see, or we can talk in private. It's up to you. Right now I don't really give a damn. But I'll warn you that my temper is at a boiling point. You can continue to push me if you want, but you might not like the end result."

He stared at her, his expression unforgiving, and Catherine thought his heart would be just as hard to reach. If she was going to make any ground with Jake, she was going to have to work for it.

It was in her favor to at least be civil with him. She didn't want a fight for her son on her hands. She wanted her son plain and simple. She was going to do whatever she had to do to bring Matthew back home where he belonged.

Catherine had a bad feeling that no matter what she said, Jake wasn't going to like it. Still she didn't want to let him get the upper hand. "I don't know," she said, looking around them and realizing that they were drawing the attention of some of the people in the small airport. "I prefer to have my own transportation."

She started walking away from him but knew without looking behind her that Jake was following. When they neared the desk for the rental agency, she heard him call her name.

Catherine stopped and swung back toward him. For a brief moment he sounded like the young man she'd once known and loved, and the years dropped away as if they'd never happened. Yet, all she had to do was to meet his intense gaze and she realized again how much he had changed.

There was a hard edge to him now that hadn't been there years ago. His demeanor was remote, his eyes distrustful. Catherine's heart softened. What had his life been like? she wondered.

Catherine immediately put a damper on those thoughts. She couldn't afford to let down her guard where Jake was concerned.

"You really don't need a car. I'll bring you back as soon as you're ready to leave."

He looked as if he meant it, but Catherine was still filled with apprehension. She didn't know Jake now. He was nothing like the young man she'd fallen in love with. He'd hurt her once before. Nothing had changed. She had no reason to trust him.

Maybe he's thinking the same thing about you.

The thought jarred her. Was that what Jake was thinking about her? That she couldn't be trusted? Did she even care? After she retrieved her son, there would be no more contact between her and Jake. Perhaps the best thing was for them both to start over. Maybe she should make the first effort by accepting his offer to drive her, she thought. After all, he *had* made the trip to pick her up. The least she could do was to accept graciously.

"I'll ride to your ranch to pick up Matthew if you promise to bring me back to the airport without an argument," she stated, then waited for his reply.

Jake hesitated a moment, then nodded. "You have my word."

Catherine wanted to believe Jake. She told herself that she had nothing to worry about. The ride from San Luis to Crockett, where Jake's ranch was located, wouldn't take that long. She could stand being alone with him for the time it would take to pick up her son. The quick return trip to the airport would be worth it. With luck she and Matthew would be home before midnight.

As they stepped outside they were showered with pellets of water. It was a heavy downpour, and wind and rain whipped at their faces.

"Wait inside," Jake instructed, then pushed her back through the door.

Catherine watched him make his way to a white Suburban. He tossed her bag in the back, then got in behind the wheel. A minute later he pulled up to the curb. Before she'd gotten out of the door, he was at her side and ushering her to the truck, blocking as much of the rain as he could with his big body.

Catherine was relieved when he closed the door behind her. She hadn't had time to think about having Jake so close to her, and she didn't like the way her heart hammered when he'd touched her back.

He slipped behind the wheel before she had a chance to take a deep breath. His nearness was having an unwelcome effect on her body. Catherine hoped the ride wouldn't take long. When she'd agreed to let him drive her, she hadn't thought about being alone in such close quarters.

He turned the key, and the engine roared to life. With deft movements he pulled out of his parking spot and they left the airport in silence.

''Whew,'' Catherine sighed, running her fingers through her damp hair. ''I should have thought to bring a raincoat.'' The pointless statement served to cut the tension in the air.

''It rained all the way here. The weatherman says we're in for a few days of it.''

Jake turned onto the highway in the direction of the ranch, sloshing through standing water on the road. It had started raining during the night. He hadn't wanted to admit to Catherine that he'd picked her up from the airport because he'd been worried about her driving through the downpour.

That was a part of Jake's character that he couldn't change. He was used to handling things. Regardless of his feelings of betrayal and resentment, he would have been worried, knowing that Catherine was making her way to his ranch through poor weather on her own.

Jake told himself to keep his concentration on his driving. Unwillingly his thoughts shifted to the woman riding beside him. He hadn't figured on it being so hard to see Catherine again. He'd told himself that a lot of time had passed, that she wouldn't look like the young woman he'd fallen in love with.

And she didn't. That was a fact. If anything, she was more beautiful. He hadn't expected that, hadn't wanted to admit even to himself that he'd wondered about her since last night, but he had.

Jake stole a glance at Catherine, then quickly looked back at the highway, and his heart pumped just a little faster. The soft, musky scent of her perfume filled the inside of the truck.

Jake shook his head to dispel thoughts of how good Catherine looked to him, how good she smelled. She wasn't here to see him. She was here only because of Matthew.

Their son.

A tight coil of irritation swept through Jake every time he thought about the fact that he had a twelve-year-old son. He had to take a deep breath to quell the anger simmering inside him.

He'd never thought that Catherine had the power to hurt him, but he'd been wrong. Hadn't Maxine taught him a hard lesson? This time he wouldn't be so gullible. He would think with his head instead of his libido.

They traveled for a few more minutes when Jake spoke. His deep voice cut through the stark silence.

"The ranch is west of Crockett, which is a little farther down the road. It shouldn't take too long to get there."

Catherine nodded.

Obviously she was worried, if the way she was twisting her hands together was an indication. Jake told himself that he didn't care. Catherine wasn't his problem. She had no one to blame for this mess but herself. No, he wasn't about to feel sorry for her. Or attracted to her, he reminded himself.

"Did you tell Matthew that I was coming for him?" she asked. Her gaze landed on Jake and stayed there.

"He knows," Jake answered, not revealing that he and Matthew had discussed his mother's arrival in detail. Catherine was in for a surprise. Jake was torn between warning her and letting her face her son's determination on her own. He decided to say nothing. He didn't owe her a thing. She was the one who'd betrayed him. She was the one who hadn't told him he had a son.

"He's never done anything like this before." Catherine's voice quavered, and she gripped her upper arms with her hands. "I want you to know that he's a good boy."

Jake nodded slightly, but said nothing. He could think of a hundred things he wanted to say to Catherine, none of them particularly kind at the moment. He figured he was better off holding his tongue, at least until he came to grips with her deceit.

Catherine turned to look in Jake's direction, studying his profile as he stared straight ahead at the road. Her heart twisted painfully. The resemblance between father and son was striking, so much so that she couldn't have denied the truth if she'd wanted to. He had his father's height and build. No doubt her son would grow to look even more like Jake as the years passed.

Curiosity made her gaze drift to his strong hands gripping the steering wheel. He wasn't wearing a wedding ring. She had no idea of whether he was married or if he had other children. The fact that a ring was missing from his finger meant nothing. She supposed ranch work was hard and even sometimes dangerous. It was possible that he was married and didn't wear a ring. Catherine couldn't help but wonder.

"He's a good student in school," she said when he didn't reply.

Jake glanced at her briefly, seeming unwilling to make small talk. Finally he offered, "He seems to be a nice kid."

It was meant as a passing comment, rather than a compliment of her parenting skills. Catherine's carriage stiffened. Jake's hostility rankled her. It was *his* fault that he didn't know his son. *He* was the one who had left and never contacted her. "Look, I know this is an awkward situation."

That afforded her a hard look before he once again turned his attention to his driving and the rain pelting the windshield.

"That's putting it mildly."

Jake couldn't begin to tell Catherine how hard this was. Finding out he had a son had floored him. Learning that Catherine was Matt's mother was another huge shock. He hadn't thought he would ever see her again, or that she'd be so beautiful when he did. Or that he'd be so tempted to touch her.

He didn't like the way she affected him. He didn't like the familiar tug on his heart every time he looked at her. He opted to try to find out as much about her as he could, information that could prove to be useful to him in the future.

"Do you have other children?"

The personal question startled her. "No. I've never married. Matthew is my only child," she admitted.

Jake nodded casually, but her answer surprised him. Catherine was a lovely woman. He couldn't believe that some man hadn't snatched her up. Then he remembered that Matthew had mentioned his mother was getting married and that was the reason he'd run away from home. The boy had felt in the way. Jake wondered why.

"Matthew tells me that you're getting married, though," he commented, unable to stifle his curiosity.

"Matthew has been quite talkative," Catherine answered, neither confirming nor denying her relationship with Douglas. They'd talked about marriage, but she wasn't going to discuss her personal life with Jake.

"He said he didn't want to be in your way."

Catherine drew in a quick breath as her fingers touched her lips. "What?"

Jake glanced at her and saw raw pain register in her eyes. "He's upset and unhappy." It sounded like an accusation.

"He hasn't said a word to me. Until a month or so ago, I thought everything was fine." Catherine knew that Matthew didn't adore Douglas, but she'd thought they'd gotten along fine. She was surprised that her son had shared his innermost feelings with a stranger, be it his long-lost father or not.

"What happened then?" Jake questioned, wanting to know exactly where Matt was coming from. If Catherine had been a bad mother, it wasn't apparent.

Jake made the admission to himself grudgingly. No, he couldn't find fault with Matt's upbringing, except for the fact that he'd been able to slip away from his home unnoticed and travel miles away on his own.

Catherine shrugged her shoulders. "It's really nothing I can put my finger on. We didn't have a big argument or anything like that." She wished she could go back and relive the past, search for signs in her son that would have warned her of Matthew's rash decision to find his father.

"Matthew's always been a little quiet, so I didn't really notice a big change in his behavior."

"Something must have happened to upset him," Jake commented.

Catherine thought about it a moment. Suddenly a sinking feeling pulled at her chest and her heart ached. How could she not have realized? That was about the time she'd told Matthew that she and Douglas had discussed getting married.

When she'd brought the subject up, she hadn't thought the news would be a surprise to Matthew or that he would have this kind of reaction to it. She'd dated Douglas for almost a year. Matthew seemed to like him. When she'd asked how he felt about her getting married, Matthew had shrugged and said it was okay with him. To Catherine it had been a typical adolescent response.

"I talked with him about the possibility of my marrying Douglas," she finally said, hating to make the admission to Jake.

"Douglas?" Jake repeated, and his brow arched curiously.

Catherine flashed Jake a look, then glanced away, noticing that the rain had slackened a bit. "We've been friends for about a year, and I thought Matthew liked him. He's never given me any reason to suspect that he didn't," she assured Jake. Actually Matthew and Douglas *seemed* to get along. Catherine wondered if that had been planned on her son's part for her sake.

Though she did care for Douglas, she knew she wasn't wildly in love with him. But love had hurt her terribly once, and she had held back from giving her heart to another man. It didn't bother her that Douglas wasn't a particularly affectionate man. He had his interests, and Catherine had her own. She'd wanted Matthew to have a father figure to look up to.

How could she have been so wrong? she wondered now.

"Except by running away." The words sounded like an accusation. Jake didn't apologize.

Hurt etched Catherine's expression. "You're right," she admitted. Tears stung her eyes. "I should have seen that Matthew wasn't happy. I don't know how I missed it."

Jake hadn't meant to make her cry, and he didn't like feeling sorry for her. He had needed to distance himself from thinking about her feelings and he'd struck out automatically. "What do you plan to do now?" he asked, his voice gruff.

"I have to talk to Matthew before I decide anything," Catherine said, knowing there was no way she could marry Douglas. Her son was the most important thing in her life.

"What about you?" she asked, letting her gaze rest on Jake's ring-free hand as she sniffed back tears. He raised a dark-brown eyebrow. "Are you married?"

"No," Jake admitted, then added, "The timing was never right." He thought again of Maxine, how she'd reacted to his inability to father a child. She'd taught him a hard lesson. Bitterness swept through him. Over the years he'd had his share of women, but he hadn't been tempted to offer any of them more than a few months of his time and attention.

He glanced at Catie. Despite what she'd done, he did feel a sense of gratitude that he'd fathered Matthew before the accident. Still, he couldn't bring himself to admit to her that he had nothing to offer a woman, that he was unable to give a woman a child.

"Did you ever go back to school?" Catherine asked, pondering his answer. He was handsome, apparently successful and probably pleasant when he wasn't around her. The fact that he'd never married seemed strange to her.

Jake shook his head. "No. I had my hands full. First I had to be sure that my family had a roof over their heads and food to eat. Then there was the ranch to contend with. It was heavily mortgaged. I briefly thought of selling it and getting a job, but I couldn't. The ranch has been in the family for more years than I can count."

It sounded as if he'd sacrificed everything for his brothers and sister. A touch of sorrow filled Catherine's heart as she thought of such heavy responsibilities given to such a young man. Unfortunately, she told herself, she was one of the things that he'd sacrificed.

She'd thought she was over what had happened between them years ago. Matthew's recent actions, however, had dredged up old, painful memories. Memories that Catherine would have preferred not facing again.

"This is Crockett," Jake informed Catherine as they passed through a small town. "It's grown a lot in the last year." He indicated the new Wal-Mart, as well as a modern motel and a small shopping center. The rain let up slightly as Jake took a turn and headed up a paved road. "We'll be at the ranch in a few minutes."

Catherine nodded and tried to get a grip on her emotions. She didn't want Matthew to see her upset. Right now all she wanted was to put her arms around him and hug him tight.

"I'll warn you that we have a houseful. My brother

Ryder is married and lives at the ranch with his wife and twin daughters. His wife, Ashley, is expecting another baby in six months.''

Catherine noticed Jake's eyes soften when he spoke of his family and felt envious. Her father and mother had turned her away. She had hoped that over the years she would have heard from her younger sisters, but they hadn't answered any of her letters. Eventually she'd quit trying to contact them. She could only take a certain amount of rejection.

Jake watched Catherine's expression. She was quiet, listening to him without comment. He wondered what her life had been like. Had she had help with Matthew? He remembered her father was a preacher. Though he'd never met the man, Catie had said he was a rigid disciplinarian. Jake figured it must have been hard for her to tell her parents about her pregnancy. He was sorry about that. If he'd have known, he would have been there for her. He wondered if she knew that.

''I remember that you often talked about your brothers,'' she answered. ''You have a younger sister, too, don't you?''

Jake nodded his head. ''Yeah. Deke, my youngest brother, is away right now on the rodeo circuit. My little sister, Lynn, lives here also,'' he informed her.

''How little is she?'' Catherine asked. Thinking back, Lynn had been a little girl when Catherine and Jake were in college.

A wry expression crossed Jake's features. ''Not so little anymore. She's nineteen.''

''That is quite a houseful,'' Catherine commented, wondering where all the years had gone. Jake seemed happy when talking about his siblings. ''You're lucky to be so close to your family.''

"I've always thought so." Jake didn't look at her as the car passed under the large wood-and-iron sign indicating they were on the Bar M ranch and nearing his house.

Catherine's teeth sank into her bottom lip. Now that they had arrived, she was even more anxious to see Matthew. Jake pulled up in front of a large ranch-style house and turned off the motor. He kept his hands on the wheel a moment longer, then turned in his seat.

"Family is the most important thing to me," he stated.

Something in the way he said the words made Catherine wince. Worry etched her brow.

Jake gave her an accusatory look. "Now I have a son that I knew nothing about. He's part of my family."

His words shook her to her very core. He was telling her that now that he knew about Matthew, he wasn't going to just forget that his son existed.

Oh, Matthew, Catherine thought. What kind of Pandora's box did you open?

Four

They'd arrived at the ranch at an opportune moment. The rain had almost stopped, Catherine noticed, but thick gray clouds in the overcast sky threatened more of a downpour. Jake got out of the vehicle and opened the back door to retrieve her bag. By the time he was around the opposite side of the car, she had her door open. Catherine got out and stepped away from him. As Jake turned to close the door, she ran a hand through her hair to smooth it, then surveyed her surroundings.

The McCall ranch was expansive, impressive to even one of novice knowledge of ranch life and all it entailed. There were several outbuildings—a large structure that housed ranch vehicles and equipment, and what she assumed were lodgings for employees.

As they drove in, she'd seen hundreds of cows in pastures and horses grazing in several fenced areas.

Catherine turned back toward Jake, who was watching her. She just as quickly looked away. "This is quite an operation," she commented, sounding impressed. "I can imagine why it takes your whole family to keep it going."

"There's always something to be done," he agreed, his tone matter-of-fact and not necessarily inviting further conversation.

Catherine looked around her, rubbing her hand against her thigh. Where was Matthew? she wondered, wanting to see her son.

"Let's go inside," Jake suggested, apparently reading her expression. "Watch your step," he said, indicating the rain-soft mud beside her. She'd already started to move, and Jake grabbed hold of her arm to save her from stepping right into a mud hole.

The action brought her back toward him, and Catherine found herself pressed against his body. His arm slipped around her to steady her. She lifted her face automatically and suddenly couldn't breathe. Jake's gaze raked her face, and in that moment Catherine wanted to press herself closer, to soak up his strength and warmth.

Jake didn't seem too pleased by their predicament. After a moment he moved away from her yet still held her arm. Catherine regained her footing, but her equilibrium had taken a beating. She felt a little dizzy and shook her head, trying to get her bearings.

"Thank you," she muttered. The brief contact between them had shaken her, and she didn't like it a bit. Without seeming ungracious, she pulled free of his grasp and stepped around the mud.

Jake walked beside her, and she noticed that he kept his distance. She wondered if he'd felt the same sense of longing that had attacked her in those few moments their bodies had touched.

The steps led to what looked like a newly constructed wooden porch. It was wide and wrapped around the expansive house. A large swing was suspended from hinges attached to the roof.

Jake glanced her way and said, "Ashley loves the outdoors. She was raised in the city, but I've never seen anyone take to country living the way she has. We had the porch constructed so she and Ryder could swing the twins. Sometimes it's the only thing that will calm them when they're fussy."

Catherine managed a smile. Jake had told her his twin nieces were adorable and warned her that they had the ability to steal hearts. She tried to imagine Jake holding an infant and comforting it. She couldn't bring a gentle image of him to mind. To her he was abrasive and distant.

But she could have sworn a moment ago that something akin to awareness had passed through his eyes when he'd caught her to him. He had an exceptional ability to hide his emotions. Something inside her wanted to break through his aloofness.

No, she reminded herself, that wouldn't do. She couldn't afford to let down her guard around Jake. She needed to remain focused. She needed to get her son and leave as soon as possible. She couldn't let old feelings for Jake blur her main objective.

Jake opened a screened door and motioned Catherine ahead of him without touching her. She walked inside and drew a deep breath as he followed her and removed his hat. He held it loosely in his hand.

From the foyer she could see that the house was

immaculate, well cared for and beautifully decorated with antiques.

"Your home is lovely," she said, and her tone implied that the compliment was genuine.

"Ashley usually takes care of it. However, now that she's pregnant again, we're looking to hire a housekeeper to come in daily."

"And I'm still not happy about that," a young woman said, smiling as she entered the foyer from a long hallway. She was very pretty, with long black hair and big brown eyes. She didn't look pregnant. Catherine would never have known if Jake hadn't mentioned it. "Hi. I'm Ashley, Ryder's wife. I see Jake brought you home safely."

Catherine smiled, for it was impossible not to. Jake's sister-in-law looked the picture of health and contentment.

"This is Catherine St. John," Jake said. "Matt's mother," he added as if it was an afterthought.

His tone was impersonal, not at all implying that there'd ever been an intimate relationship between them. Well, that was fine with her. She didn't want any reminders, either. She couldn't help wondering, though, how much Jake's family knew about their past.

"It's nice to meet you," Catherine offered. "I hope Matthew hasn't been a bother."

"Are you kidding?" Ashley asked. "He's been having the time of his life. Ryder took him when he rode out a while ago. They should be back any minute."

Concern crossed Catherine's expression. "Matthew doesn't know how to ride," she informed them, then looked at Jake. "I mean, not really. He's been horseback riding a few times with friends, but not very often."

"Take it easy," Jake said gruffly. "He's perfectly safe with Ryder. He'll take good care of him," he assured Catherine.

"Of course he will," Ashley chimed in. "I didn't mean to alarm you. Ryder gave him one of the gentler horses, and he didn't let Matthew hold the reins. I wish I'd had a camera," she continued. "Matthew was really excited."

That declaration brought a new concern to Catherine's mind, as if she didn't already have enough to worry about. She hadn't expected Matthew to be at Jake's long enough to sample any kind of ranch life. And the last thing she needed was for Matthew to actually like it here.

"Thank you for taking care of him," Catherine said, remembering her manners.

Ashley nodded. "It was our pleasure," she assured Catherine.

"Maybe you'd like a cup of coffee or something while you wait," Jake suggested, placing his hand against Catherine's back and urging her forward.

"Well—"

"Yes, of course," Ashley agreed. "Come on into the kitchen."

Catherine followed Ashley, feeling a bit bewildered. Once again Jake's touch had stirred long-buried emotions within her. She didn't want to feel any connection to him. Things weren't exactly going as she had planned.

"We've already had lunch," Ashley went on. "But I can quickly fix you something to eat if you'd like. Jake?" she inquired, looking his way.

"Nothing for me." Jake shook his head, but he flashed Ashley a brief smile.

Catherine was momentarily stunned. His smile had transformed Jake's detached expression, and she couldn't believe how much so. His gorgeous brown eyes sparkled at Ashley with love and admiration. Before Catherine could adjust to the sudden change that came over Jake, the stoic look that had accompanied him from San Luis had returned.

"Catherine?"

"Um, no, thank you. Maybe just some coffee."

Ashley nodded and poured them each a cup. She offered one to Catherine, then indicated for her to take a seat at the kitchen table. Catherine slid onto a seat, then wrapped her hands around the warm mug just to give them something to do.

Jake remained standing, and Catherine couldn't keep from watching him as Ashley passed him a cup. It was obvious that she held a warm place in his heart.

Ashley slid into a chair and breathed deeply. "How were the roads?" she asked, looking at Jake.

"Slick." Jake set his cup on the counter.

Catherine nodded. "We saw several accidents on the way here," she commented. "I hope it won't be too long before we can start back."

Jake flashed her a questionable look. "I doubt if that will be possible."

Catherine's gaze darted to his. "What?"

"I don't think we'll be driving back this evening."

Was he kidding? she wondered. "But you said you'd take us back right away."

Jake shook his head. "What I said was, if you wanted to return right away, I'd take you back. I didn't plan on the rain preventing us from driving back."

"The rain?" she repeated. "Why would it?" Catherine asked, confused.

"The Styron bridge for one thing," Jake stated, glancing at Ashley, then back at Catherine. "Didn't you notice that the river was running high on both sides as we crossed over it on the way?"

Catherine looked surprised. She'd been so worried about Matthew that she hadn't paid much attention. "Actually, no, I didn't."

"We've had a lot of rain over the past few days. It could be dangerous crossing back over the bridge. We made it here okay, but that doesn't mean that by the time we drive back it'll be safe."

Before anyone spoke again, they heard a deafening crack of thunder. The screened door banged open, then a door slammed. Anticipation kept Catherine's next breath captive. Moments later Matthew walked into the kitchen ahead of Jake's brother. They were both damp from the rain.

"Hi, Mom," Matthew said, then tentatively stepped toward his mother. Catherine was already out of her seat and met her son in the middle of the kitchen. She threw her arms around his neck and hugged him to her.

Then she cried.

Catherine couldn't help it. Relief swept through her. Matthew hugged her briefly, then, looking embarrassed, stepped back away from her. Catherine ran her hand over his head and across his cheek, letting her palm rest there a moment.

"I was so worried about you." She wanted to hold him to her, but was wise enough to realize that Matthew didn't want to be treated like a child. Sheer willpower kept her from hugging him to her again.

"I'm okay," Matthew insisted. "Ryder took me riding." He said it with a big grin as he glanced at Jake's brother, whom it was apparent he already idolized.

Jake introduced them, and Ryder nodded. He didn't look like Jake at all. He was only a tad taller, but his hair was blond and he had gorgeous blue eyes. His smile, accompanied by his blond mustache, immediately charmed her.

"Matt's a natural," he informed Catherine, as he stood behind Ashley with his hands on her shoulders.

Catherine nodded and forced a smile. Silence filled the room.

Ashley started to get up, and Ryder helped her to her feet. "I think I hear the girls." She looked at Ryder, then back to Catherine. "Excuse us, please." Taking his cue, Ryder followed his wife out of the room.

A bolt of lightning flashed outside the kitchen window, followed closely by the roar of thunder. It briefly vibrated the walls around them. Catherine turned worried eyes toward her son. "Matthew, get your things. We need to head back right away."

Matthew didn't move. He took a step away from her, closer to Jake. "I don't want to go back," he declared.

Stunned, Catherine's hand went to her chest as the agony of his words hit her. "Matthew—"

"You can't make me!" He looked at the floor instead of at his mother, reminding her of the troubled teens she often dealt with at school.

Catherine reached toward her son. "Matthew, of course you're going home with me." What was he talking about? For heaven's sake, he was only twelve years old. He wasn't old enough to know what was best for him.

"I like it here," Matthew said.

"That's ridiculous," Catherine blurted out, then wished she'd held back the words. She didn't want to put Matthew on the defensive. This wasn't the time or place to discipline him for his behavior. ''You've only been here twenty-four hours. You don't know anything about living on a ranch.''

Matthew stuck out his chin. ''I can learn.''

Catherine tried desperately to remain calm. She glanced at Jake, who stood nearby, taking in their conversation. Something in his expression disturbed her. She turned her attention to her son. ''Look, I know we have some things to talk about, but we can work this out at home.''

''Please, Mom, let me stay,'' Matthew said, and his gaze pleaded with her.

Catherine closed her eyes for a moment and wished for this nightmare to end. She opened her eyes and pinned her gaze on her son. ''I'm not going to argue with you about this. Go and get your things.'' Even as she said the words, she knew she'd made a mistake.

Matthew's carriage stiffened. ''If you take me back, I'll just run away again.''

''Matt, that's enough,'' Jake broke in as he took in Catherine's shocked expression. Tears gathered at the corners of her eyes. ''Why don't you go watch television or something and let your mother and I talk?'' he suggested.

Without having to be convinced, Matthew left before Catherine could prevent him. She was amazed that Jake had such control over her son after only one night in his home. Suddenly she was very worried.

''I don't know what's come over him,'' Catherine whispered. ''He's never been defiant before.''

''There's a lot going on in his life right now,'' Jake reasoned. ''He's confused. Give him some time.''

Catherine's gaze met Jake's. ''You're not suggesting that I leave him here?'' She searched his face. ''You *knew* he was going to give me a hard time,'' she accused. Jake didn't deny it. ''You could have warned me.''

''Like you warned me that I had a son? Be honest, Catherine. You didn't really think you could just show up here, whisk Matt away and pretend that none of this had happened, did you?'' Jake leaned against the edge of the sink, looking at her with an accusing stare.

Catherine folded her arms about her and looked away. Jake *knew* that's exactly what she'd planned. ''I expected Matthew to talk to me.'' Her gaze went back to Jake. ''What have you said to him?'' she questioned.

''Only that we'd discuss the situation and work something reasonable out,'' Jake told her.

''There's nothing to work out,'' she insisted, resolving not to cry. ''I'm taking my son home.'' Her voice rose a notch.

''Let's finish this conversation in the office,'' Jake suggested. Jake wanted to be sure Matthew wasn't within hearing distance of their discussion. He turned and walked out, leaving Catherine behind. She had no choice but to follow.

They went down the hallway, then into a large room. The office was filled with modern-day devices. One wall was completely taken up with a computer, table, a printer and a fax machine. In the middle of the room was a massive walnut desk. Jake motioned for Catherine to sit down. She chose a seat on the large brown sofa.

Jake leaned against the edge of the desk, and Catherine couldn't help thinking he did so to put her at a disadvantage. She had to look up at him.

''I think we need to get a few things out in the

open.'' Jake's tone left no doubt as to what he was talking about.

Catherine had to agree. She nodded and waited. Jake owed her an explanation. Not that anything he said would excuse the letter his attorney had sent her.

For a few moments silence reigned between them. Finally Catherine said, ''Well?'' If he was going to apologize, he wasn't making any headway in that direction.

Jake's face wrinkled a bit. ''Well what?'' he countered. ''I think you're the one who has something to say.''

''Me?'' Catherine almost laughed. ''I'm waiting for *your* explanation,'' she insisted. ''You're the one who never called me back.''

Jake stared at her. ''I don't know what you're talking about.''

Catherine looked aghast. ''I called you, Jake. Several times. I left messages, but you never returned my calls. Why not?'' she asked. Despite her resolve to remain aloof, her emotions betrayed her. She remembered how alone and desperate she'd felt when she hadn't heard from him.

''I didn't get any messages,'' Jake insisted, standing and approaching her.

He sounded as if he didn't believe her. Catherine stood as he came nearer and stopped in front of her. ''I can't help that. I called,'' she insisted. Regardless of whether he'd received her messages, there was the letter she'd written. He'd dismissed her as if she never really mattered to him.

Jake didn't give an inch. ''A couple of phone calls hardly excuses the fact that you kept Matt's birth a secret all these years.''

Catherine's mouth gaped open. Finally she said, "You've got a nerve, Jake McCall." Fuming, she balled her hands beside her, trying very hard to keep her temper intact.

Jake's expression hardened. "Me?"

"Yes, you!" The anger and disappointment of twelve long years filled her. "I sent you a letter."

"I never received a letter from you."

Dismissing his answer, Catherine said, "I asked you to contact me. I didn't want to tell you about my being pregnant in a letter, for heaven's sake! If you'd bothered to call me, you would have known about Matthew, wouldn't you?" she accused. She wanted, needed to know why he hadn't contacted her.

Jake's jaw tightened. "And the fact that I didn't call you excuses your actions," he answered. He leaned forward, causing Catherine to retreat a step. It put her against the sofa.

"I don't need an excuse for my actions," she stated tightly. His breath fanned her face and she could smell his aftershave. Suddenly she very much needed some space between them. Scooting around him, she walked over to the desk and touched it briefly. Then she faced him.

"I sent you a letter, Jake," she said again, and her voice became low and filled with years of sadness. She shivered and closed her arms around herself. "You wrote back that I was never to contact you again."

Jake raked a hand through his hair, frustration driving the movement. "That's crazy. I never sent you a letter like that." When he looked at her, his expression changed. "I would never had done that. Hell, Catie, you knew me better than anyone."

Catherine only looked at him with disappointment.

"I thought I did." Suddenly she wanted to cry. But she didn't.

Jake put his hands in his back pockets to keep them from reaching toward her. "Do you still have this letter?" he asked, patience lacking in his tone.

Defiantly Catherine's gaze locked with his. "You don't believe me." Her laugh was forced. "Well, that's just dandy. You think you'd remember having your lawyer send me a letter."

"My lawyer?" Jake stopped speaking to think a moment. Back then, the only lawyer he knew was his parents' lawyer. "You got a letter from Frank Davis?"

"As if you didn't know," she replied.

"Catherine, I don't know anything about a letter. I swear it. Frank Davis was my parents' lawyer. Shortly after I came home, he had all the mail sent to his office. He handled all the correspondence and bills while I learned everything I needed to know to keep the ranch afloat."

The ranch hadn't been in the best of conditions when Jake had taken over. He had always admired his father, but he never really knew how much the man struggled until he died. There'd been a drought that year, and cattle prices had dropped drastically. His father had worked hard for years, only to end up in debt and struggling to hang on to their land.

Jake's admiration of his father had taken a nosedive when he'd learned that he'd been the result of his father's adulterous affair. Jake stiffened as he thought about when he'd first learned the truth. Then he pushed the bad feelings to the back of his mind. He refused to let it haunt him today.

His gaze fell on Catherine, who had walked across the room to stare out at the rain beating against the window. She jumped when lightning flashed across the sky. He called to her and she turned toward him. ‘‘If Frank wrote you, I didn’t know about it,’’ he said again. Jake looked closer and saw tears fall down her cheeks.

‘‘The letter said you didn’t know me.’’

Jake expression changed to one of shock and disbelief. ‘‘Why would Frank do something like that?’’ Jake wondered aloud. Jake wasn’t used to having his word questioned. ‘‘Does that even sound like something I’d do?’’ he asked, walking toward her.

Catherine didn’t think before she answered, ‘‘Yes.’’

Her words stopped Jake dead in his tracks. ‘‘You believe I would deny knowing you?’’ he asked, anger in his voice.

‘‘We’d argued right before you left to go home, so I believed you didn’t want anything to do with me.’’ And if he hadn’t wanted her, he wouldn’t have wanted their baby. She hadn’t wanted Jake to come back to her out of a sense of responsibility. She’d wanted his love. She glared at him, then said, ‘‘Look, this is getting us nowhere. I don’t see why we have to hash out the past. I came here to get my son and I intend to leave with him.’’

‘‘We need to get to the bottom of this. Frank Davis died, but we can probably get access to his files.’’ Before Catherine could answer, there was a knock at the door. It cracked open, and Ashley’s head appeared.

‘‘I’m sorry for interrupting.’’ She stepped farther into the room. ‘‘Matthew’s missing. Ryder’s gone outside to look for him.’’

Jake had only a moment to register Catherine’s distressed look before he bolted for the door. ‘‘Damn,’’ he swore, then looked at Ashley. ‘‘Did you call the men?'' he asked, referring to the hands who stayed on the ranch.

''I wanted you to know first.''

Jake brushed past her and headed for the back door. ''I'll take care of it,'' he said over his shoulder.

''Jake, wait,'' Catherine called. ''I'm going with you.'' She caught up with him as he was putting his arms though the sleeves of his raincoat.

''No, you're not,'' Jake stated firmly. ''You don't know the ranch well enough to go off on your own, and I don't have time to keep an eye on you.''

Insulted, Catherine bristled. ''I'm an adult. You don't have to watch out for me. But I'm going out to find Matthew,'' she insisted.

''Catherine, just wait here.''

''He's right,'' Ashley said softly, putting her hand on the other woman's shoulder. ''Matthew might come back. One of you should be here.''

Catherine couldn't argue with Ashley's reasoning. ''All right,'' she said, relenting.

Jake headed out the back door. ''I'll let you know as soon as we find him.''

Pushing against the wind, Ashley closed the door. ''Don't worry,'' she said. ''Matthew couldn't have gone far. They'll find him.'' She led Catherine back to the kitchen and ushered her to a chair.

Ashley poured them both coffee. Catherine accepted a cup, then Ashley sank onto a chair across from her. ''Try not to worry. I'm sure they'll find him.''

Catherine shook her head back and forth. ''I don't know what's come over Matthew. He's never acted like this before.''

''Sometimes children, like adults, have trouble expressing their feelings. Matthew's just mixed up right now.''

For such a young woman, Catherine thought, Ashley was very wise. ''You'd make a great counselor,'' she told her.

''Is that what you do?'' Ashley asked.

Catherine nodded. ''I'm a counselor at a high school.'' She brought her hand up and wiped tears from her eyes. ''You'd think I'd do a better job of understanding my own child.''

Ashley's expression filled with sympathy. ''I'm sure you're a wonderful mother. Matthew's a very polite young man. You should be proud of the job you've done.''

Catherine managed a small smile. She wanted to think that she was a good mother, but she'd been having a lot of doubts over the past twenty-four hours.

Seeing how Matthew responded to Jake hadn't helped. Her son had quickly implanted himself in this home, with his father. Catherine wasn't sure what was going to happen next, but she didn't like the feeling of foreboding that hung over her.

The back door opened and Catherine turned to see Matthew, Jake and Ryder enter. She was on her feet and standing, by the time they walked into the kitchen. Matthew was soaking wet, dripping on the vinyl floor.

''Matthew, what on earth has gotten into you?'' she demanded. Realizing she probably sounded hysterical, she took a deep breath and stepped back, her gaze running over him.

Jake spoke instead of Matthew. ''The good news is we found Matt. He was in the barn.'' Taking off his coat and shaking the water from it, he added, "The bad news is that we just heard over the radio that the Styron bridge is impassable." Looking directly at Catherine, he told her, "You're stuck here."

Five

Stuck, Catherine learned, meant that she and Matthew weren't getting back to Lubbock anytime in the immediate future. She stood in the bedroom she'd been shown to and took stock of her situation. Jake told her that once it quit raining, it could be a few days before the water receded enough for them to cross the bridge.

Catherine was glad she'd had the foresight to bring a change of clothing with her and something to sleep in.

She supposed she would be able to wear the same two sets of clothing for a few days, until they were ready to leave. She'd rinse out her underwear and hang them in the bathroom to dry.

Jake's sister, Lynn, had brought Catherine to Ryder's old bedroom so she could have an adjoining bath. Matthew had been moved to Deke's room, since he wasn't home.

Lynn looked a lot like her brother Ryder. Her blond hair was cropped short, and she had the same beautiful blue eyes. She was pretty and petite and very outgoing and friendly.

Nothing at all like Jake, who gave Catherine cold stares and frustrated looks most of the time. He thought she was at fault for the current crisis in his life, and from what she could gather, Jake wasn't used to being the center of attention. Neither was he used to not having everything under control.

Well, Jake was going to learn he couldn't control her. As soon as the weather allowed, she and Matthew were leaving—if she had to steal a car to drive to the airport!

Catherine glanced at her watch and realized she should be getting ready for dinner. Lynn had refused her offer of help, insisting that she and Ashley were used to working together in the kitchen, but Catherine was welcome to come in and talk with them.

She headed for the bathroom to wash up, then she would accept Lynn's offer. Though part of her wanted to, she couldn't just hide here in the bedroom until the weather let up and she could go home.

Catherine reached for the handle of the bathroom door and swung it open, then caught her breath at the sight of Jake standing at the sink, naked to his waist. His jeans rested low on his hips, exposing his navel. Lather partially covered his face, and he held a razor in his hand.

"Oh!" she exclaimed, her gaze taking in his hard-muscled shoulders and chest. For a man in his thirties, he was in excellent condition. Catherine glanced at the open door behind him, then back at Jake. Apparently the bathroom serviced both bedrooms. "I didn't know…um…"

Jake raised an eyebrow. "That we were sharing a bath?" he furnished, his voice a bit husky. His dark gaze slipped over her as he set down the razor and grabbed a towel off the rack on the wall. He looked at her as he cleaned off what remained of the lather from his face.

"It's just as much my fault. I'm not used to anyone being in that room, and I don't usually check the door," he admitted gruffly.

"I'll just wait," Catherine said, her breathing constricted. She started to close the door.

"No, that's all right," Jake said, stalling her movements. "I'm about finished." He dried his hands on the towel and tossed it on the counter. "There are fresh linens in here," he said, opening a small closet door and removing a clean towel and washcloth. His shirt was hanging on the doorknob to his room, and he picked it up and shrugged into it.

Catherine watched his muscles ripple as he moved, her heartbeat speeding. Jake was nothing at all like Douglas: his body was hard and tanned; his chest lightly covered with soft brown hair that about disappeared across his flat belly.

What would it feel like to touch him there? she wondered, remembering the days when she could freely do so. As he buttoned his shirt, Catherine looked away, her gaze resting on the mirror. His reflection shared the details as he slipped each button through its matching hole. His gaze connected with hers as she watched him, and Catherine could have died at that moment. She blushed furiously.

"I think we need to finish our conversation," he said, leaning against the small counter.

"Um, yes, of course," Catherine said, agreeing. There was so much more she wanted to say to him. But the tight, intimate confines of the bathroom was definitely not the place.

He reached around her for a small bottle, bringing his body in close contact with hers. He smelled of soap and shaving cream, amazingly male, and to Catherine it was an awesome mix. She watched him dump a small amount of cologne in his hands, then pat his face.

"Maybe after dinner?" she suggested. "I was just going to go down and see if I could help."

Jake nodded, watching her a moment longer before turning away. "Fine." He stood and walked out of the bathroom, then closed the connecting door.

Behind it, he heard Catherine moving about. He ignored the sound of running water, but a vision of her filled his mind. He wished he could ignore how his body responded when he was around her. He'd thought that all he would have to do was keep her at arm's length.

Their brief contact upon their arrival had told Jake to be leery of Catherine. In the flash of a few moments her body had pressed close to his and he'd wanted to pull her tighter against him. He'd had to steel himself not to.

Now he was sharing a bathroom with her. Close quarters for someone who wanted to keep his distance. He reminded himself that she wasn't the vulnerable, innocent young woman he'd made love to years ago. But somehow, his body wasn't accepting his explanation.

She was able to bring out many emotions that he'd

managed to keep to himself for most of his life. Since she'd arrived, he'd wanted to both comfort her, kiss her and strangle her within a single conversation.

They still needed to come to some kind of agreement where his son was concerned. Whether the lady knew it or not, Jake had already decided exactly what was best for all of them. At the very least, Matthew was going to spend his summer here at the ranch.

Catherine didn't have to like it. She just had to agree to it. The weather had given him an advantage. Keeping Catherine and Matthew here for a day or so was exactly what he needed. A little time and he'd be able to convince her that it was in Matt's best interest to let him stay.

Jake wasn't beyond demanding that his son live with him permanently. First, he had to get Matt settled here on the ranch. Then he'd have more leverage.

Having Catherine here for a few days could prove a test to his patience, though, and his libido. He'd fallen for her so easily when he'd first met her. He wasn't going to make the same mistake again.

So what if he still felt an attraction toward her. It had been quite a while since he'd been with a woman. That his body was suddenly responding sexually to an attractive woman wasn't unusual. It could have been any woman and he'd have had the same reaction, he told himself.

Catherine looked as if she spent time keeping herself in shape, no doubt for this man she was planning to marry. Jake just had to keep reminding himself that he could be around Catherine, even be attracted to her, and it wouldn't have to lead anywhere.

By keeping Matthew a secret she'd hurt Jake, and he couldn't forget or forgive that. Just as he couldn't forget his father's indiscretion. Every time he looked at his siblings, he knew how hurt they'd be if they found out. Jake couldn't share what he knew with them.

Catherine went in search of Matthew and found him in the den watching a sports event on television. She talked with him about what he'd done and how dangerous it was for him to travel on his own. There were so many things that could have happened to him. Matthew listened, and it was apparent that he was sorry for his actions and that he'd worried her so much.

He asked her again to let him stay at the ranch. Catherine tried to reason with him, to make him understand that his life was in Lubbock, not here on this ranch. Matthew was having none of it. By the time she left him alone, he'd become sullen and withdrawn. She was right back where she'd started.

Catherine walked into the kitchen after her talk with Matthew, and a smile crossed her features. Earlier, she hadn't noticed the playpen cluttered with toys. At the moment, two little dark-headed babies shared what room was left. Ashley and Lynn were moving about the room.

Both little faces looked in her direction as she walked over to the playpen, their angelic smiles welcoming the stranger entering their world.

"Oh my, they're adorable," Catherine exclaimed, her gaze running over them. Each one was standing and holding on to the side of the pen.

Ashley smiled. "That they are," she agreed. "They're also quite a handful. They look perfectly innocent," she went on, "but don't believe it."

Lynn grinned and said, ''They're angels with minds of their own.''

''Just like every true McCall,'' Ashley commented.

''Can't disagree with that,'' Lynn answered.

Catherine ran her hand over each baby's head and was rewarded with smiles and gurgles from them. ''What are their names?'' she asked.

Ashley pointed at one of them. ''That's Michelle with her hand in Melissa's hair.''

Catherine helped free Melissa's hair from the baby's grasp. ''Can I hold one of them?'' she asked. It had been a long time since she'd held a baby. Ashley grinned and nodded, and Catherine picked up Melissa. She hugged the baby to her, and Melissa rested her head on Catherine's shoulder.

Jake picked that moment to walk into the room. He took stock of everyone, his gaze finally coming to rest on Catherine. His heart thudded. He wasn't prepared for the sight of her holding one of the babies.

She was cradling Melissa in her arms, and he had a sudden image of her holding his son as a baby. Jake walked over and scooped Michelle up in his arms. Giving her a quick kiss, he patted her back. Michelle giggled and drew a smile from him.

Catherine watched the byplay between Jake and the baby and was sorry about how much of Matthew's life Jake had missed. Of course, she reminded herself, it was his own fault. Still, she felt a sadness for him. Those years were gone now, never to be regained.

''Dinner will be ready shortly,'' Ashley announced. She looked at Jake and Catherine. ''Would you mind putting them in their cribs for me? If we're lucky, they'll settle down right about the time we eat.''

Jake nodded. Dinners, which used to be around six,

had been moved to seven and sometimes later to accommodate the babies' schedules. Most of the time they went to sleep about the time the adults ate and remained quiet for the night. The trade-off was that they were early risers. Ashley and Ryder usually went to bed early also, anticipating the morning when they'd be busy with the babies.

Jake motioned Catherine to follow him, and led her to a bedroom filled with baby items. There were two of everything, as if items could only be purchased that way.

"How many bedrooms does this house have?" she asked, surprised that this was another one she hadn't seen.

"Not enough if Ryder doesn't stop reproducing," Jake said, cracking a quick smile. It was gone after only a moment. "When the new baby arrives, it'll stay in Ryder and Ashley's bedroom for a while. We may have to put an addition on."

They put the babies in their cribs. Jake kissed each one, then walked toward the door. Michelle fretted, wanting to be picked up, but Melissa lay quietly in the middle of the crib looking at them with big, expressive eyes.

"Give your mom a break and go to sleep," Jake gently ordered the two little ones. He walked out of the room, then waited for Catherine.

By the time they arrived back in the kitchen, Ryder was helping Ashley and Lynn set the dining room table. Even Matthew was lending a hand. He barely looked at his mother, and Catherine felt hurt surge through her.

Dinner conversation went smoothly enough, considering the fact that Catherine avoided eye contact with

Jake. Though he answered questions when spoken to, Matthew was quiet and noncommunicative. After they finished eating, everyone carried their dishes into the kitchen. Lynn shooed everyone out, insisting that it didn't take all of them to stack the dishwasher. Ryder and Matthew went to the den to watch television. Ashley confessed she'd been looking forward to a long, hot bath.

That left Jake and Catherine alone to finish their conversation from earlier in the day. Once again Catherine followed him to the ranch office. He closed the door for privacy.

Jake sat on the sofa, then waited for Catherine to take a seat. She joined him, surprising him by sitting on the other end instead of one of the chairs. She folded her hands together tightly, looking as tense as a person being robbed at gunpoint.

"Sit back," Jake said, leaning forward and closer to her. "I'm not going to eat you."

She didn't seem amused by his words. He was trying to put her at ease. He figured they'd get along better if she didn't think she was under attack.

"I don't want to rehash what we went through this afternoon," Catherine stated, starting the conversation. "Obviously we both have different views of what happened between us years ago."

Her words conjured up images in Jake's mind of making love to her. It wasn't hard for Jake to recall how good they'd been together. His body reacted in kind, and he shifted a little in his seat. He couldn't afford to let his mind wander so easily.

"Obviously," he agreed. He still had trouble with her story.

"And it has little bearing on the current problem we're facing with Matthew," Catherine reasoned.

"I agree." Jake wasn't ready to let the past go. He still blamed Catie for keeping his son from him. But the most important thing for them to talk about now was what was best for Matthew.

Catherine sighed heavily, and her gaze met Jake's. "Please don't fight me on this, Jake," she pleaded. "I think the best thing for Matthew is for us to go home and pick up where we left off."

"I don't think so," Jake stated, then rested his arm along the back of the sofa. "That's what's best for you. You're not even thinking about what's best for Matthew or me."

Catherine licked her lips, and Jake's gaze followed the movement of her tongue. He remembered kissing her, touching her skin, and had a sudden urge to see if she still tasted the way he remembered.

"I'm not saying that you can't see him," she told him. "But I don't want Matthew to get the idea that he can call this ranch his home."

"This *is* his home. Matthew's my son. That makes him part of this family. Someday he'll own his share of the ranch." He sat forward, leaning closer to her. "What's more important, I have a son that I've never had the opportunity to know. We need time together to bond, time to enjoy each other. Are you going to deny us that?"

"Of course not," Catherine assured him.

"Then, what better place to do it than here," Jake said, his gaze pinning hers.

Silence filled the room for a moment. Then Jake told her what he really wanted. "I want Matthew to spend the summer with me."

"The summer?" Catherine looked stunned.

"School's out," Jake reminded her. "There's no reason why he can't stay here for the summer. That would solve this problem of him threatening to run away."

"No," Catherine replied, after absorbing Jake's suggestion. "Absolutely not. I'm not leaving Matthew here for the entire summer. That's out of the question."

Jake gritted his teeth, clamping down on the spark of anger that flared within him. He tried to reason with her. "Think about it, Catie," he told her, realizing that he'd slipped back to using her nickname. "He's already fighting you about going back. What could it hurt?"

Losing control, Catherine's eyes welled with tears. "Oh, Jake." Her breath caught and she bit her lip.

Automatically Jake reached over and touched her hand, cupping his around it. His thumb stroked back and forth. "What?" he asked.

His gaze searched her face, and he forgot they were talking about their son. For a moment, just seconds, he had the sudden urge to pull her into his arms. Jake shook his head, clearing the uninvited thought away.

Catherine ran a hand through her hair, getting it out of her way. "I'm afraid," she confessed. "What if he loves it here?" she asked. "What if he never wants to come home?" There was so much at the ranch to entertain him, so much to entice a young boy.

"Why don't we worry about that when the time comes."

Catherine snatched her hand back. "That's easy for you to say!" She stared back at him defiantly. "You've got nothing to lose!"

Jake's shoulders squared. "I've already lost twelve

years,'' he retorted, beginning to lose his temper. ''I'm not losing another day,'' he told her, his voice rising. He got to his feet. ''Now, you can agree to this and save us all a lot of trouble, or I'll have my lawyer take you to court,'' he challenged.

Catherine was on her feet in barely a second. ''Don't threaten me, Jake!''

''Don't make me,'' he countered, leaning closer to her. His hand grasped the back of her neck, pulling her toward him. ''I won't lose, I can promise you.''

''Damn you,'' she stated hotly, glaring back at him.

Jake stared into her eyes. The fire in them fueled his desire to taste her. Jake was reminded of a couple of heated arguments they'd had when they were together—after they'd made up, they'd made love.

''Damn you,'' he grated, then covered her mouth with his.

It was a fool thing to do, he told himself, even as he tugged her closer to prevent her from breaking away. She fought him for a moment, her body stiff and resistant, her hands against his chest. Jake felt the heat of her palms as she pushed against him.

His tongue seared hers and she groaned low in her throat. It was all the encouragement he needed to drag her body against his and close his arms around her.

She tasted sweet, like honey. He remembered the first time he'd made love to her. She'd been a virgin and unsure of what to expect. But she'd also been eager to learn and just as eager to please him.

And one of the times they'd made love, she'd conceived his son.

The thought flitted through Jake's mind, clearing the way for rational thinking. He lifted his head and stared at Catherine's face. Her lids slowly slid open, and her eyes were glazed. She licked at her lips, and the action made his knees want to buckle.

With a slight movement, Jake pushed her away from him. "This doesn't change anything," he grated, angry at himself for touching her. Angry, also, because he wanted to kiss her again.

Catherine glared back at him, looking confused, as if she'd been in a coma and was just waking up.

"Think about what I said," he warned her, then he stalked out of the room.

Catherine stared after him, still shell-shocked. He'd taken her by surprise when he'd kissed her. And like a complete fool, she kissed him back.

Idiot! she berated herself.

How could she have let him touch her? How could she have succumbed so easily to his embrace? Did he think he could seduce her, then talk her into his plan?

No, she thought, he didn't seem any too happy with the kiss they'd shared than she was. It was the heat of the moment, she decided. First they were yelling at each other, then he was kissing her. It just happened. That didn't mean that it would happen again.

She wouldn't let it, she decided. So he kissed her. So the memory of how good they'd been together haunted her. So what?

By the time Catherine got her bearings, Jake was long gone. She left the office and headed for her room to think. She wasn't going to give that kiss another moment of thought.

Jake had meant what he said. Now she was trapped in this house with him, with his ultimatum. Not only did she have Matthew begging her to let him stay, now his father was telling her she had no choice.

Catherine went in search of Matthew. Despite his

distant attitude, she hugged him good-night and told him she'd talk to him tomorrow. Right now she couldn't even think of what to say. She had to deal with Jake first. It would do no good to bring her son into it.

She made her way to her room and closed the door, exhausted and ready for bed. She wasn't sure where Jake was, so she leaned her head against the door to the bathroom to see if he was there. No sound came from behind the door. She opened it and was relieved to find it empty.

Catherine rushed in. She locked both doors, then washed her face and patted it dry. Then she unlocked Jake's door and returned to her room.

She crawled into bed with a heavy heart. Whether she wanted to admit it or not, Jake held all the cards. She had no idea what a judge would say if she tried to fight him and they ended up in court. Most times, judges still favored mothers. But the fact that Jake hadn't known about his son, and that Matthew wanted to live here, would probably work against her.

Not to mention that Jake had the monetary resources to tie her up in court. She'd end up losing everything trying to hold on to her son. To Catherine, nothing was more important than Matthew.

Catherine sighed and rubbed her temples with her fingers. The last day and a half had taken its toll on her. She no longer heard the rain and prayed that it had stopped. Maybe she could hold Jake off, pretend to consider his suggestion, then take Matthew and leave when he wasn't looking.

That was her best plan, she thought. Pathetically, it was her only plan. Catherine sank deeper into the mattress and stretched, trying to ease the tenseness in her body. She closed her eyes and took a breath in an effort to relax. It was an hour before she was able to fall asleep.

The next morning Catherine awoke early, something unexplainable tugging at her consciousness. Quiet surrounded her and she lay still, trying to figure out what was different.

It wasn't raining, she realized. She jumped from the bed and ran to the window. Luck was on her side. The sun was just beginning to shine, and the sky was clear and blue.

Thank God, she thought, for lousy weather predictions. She knew it didn't mean that she could leave with Matthew today, of course, but she could within a day or so.

She listened at the bathroom door again to be sure Jake wasn't there, then opened the door. After locking the door to his bedroom, Catherine stripped off her nightgown and turned on the water for a shower.

She rushed through her bath, dried her hair, applied light makeup, then unlocked Jake's door before returning to her room to dress. After pulling on a pair of jeans, she slipped on a T-shirt and sneakers, then went down the hallway toward the kitchen.

The house was deserted, except for Ashley and the babies. Catherine found them in the den, both babies on the floor. One was rolling over and the other was inching toward the door. Catherine caught her as she was about to escape. She scooped the baby up and into her arms, then greeted Ashley.

"Good morning," she said, laughing at the cherub in her arms.

Ashley looked relieved. ''Thanks for detaining Michelle,'' she answered, smiling.

''You're welcome. How do you tell them apart?''

Chuckling, Ashley explained, ''Mainly by their personalities. Michelle's more demanding than her sister. Also, we think Michelle is right-handed and Melissa's left-handed.''

''Really?''

''It isn't unusual for twins to exhibit mirror-image features. Can I get you some breakfast?''

Catherine declined. ''I'll just have coffee or some juice.''

''There's coffee ready to pour,'' Ashley informed her. She got up and reached for Michelle, relieving Catherine of her rambunctious daughter.

''Thanks. Where is everyone?'' Catherine asked, wanting to know where Matthew was.

''Ranch life starts early. Everyone's eaten and gone out. Lynn's working with the foreman. They're in charge of the horses—or rather, to Lynn's dismay, Russ Logan, the foreman is. Jake and Ryder have gone out, too, doing whatever needs their attention.'' She smiled. ''And in answer to your next question, Matthew is down at the corral, watching Lynn and Russ.''

''Oh. Well, I guess I'll get that coffee. Can I pour you some?''

Ashley shook her head. ''No, thanks, but I'll join you for conversation if it's okay.''

Catherine nodded. ''Sure. Can I bring one of the babies?''

''I've got Michelle, if you can get Melissa.''

They went into the kitchen and deposited the babies in the playpen. Both girls attacked their toys as if it was the first time they'd seen them.

Catherine followed Ashley's directions to locate a cup, then poured herself some hot coffee. She joined Ashley at the table.

"When do you think the bridge will be passable?" Catherine asked the younger woman.

Ashley shrugged. "One or two days if the weather is nice and the sun keeps shining. I guess you're anxious to go home?"

"Yes," Catherine acknowledged.

"I don't mean to be nosy, but have you and Jake agreed on what to do about Matthew?" Ashley asked. "Jake told me what he proposed," she confessed.

"He did?" Catherine was sure Jake didn't tell Ashley he'd actually demanded that she leave Matthew for the summer.

Ashley put her cup down. "He mentioned it before going out this morning, but not in front of Matthew," she said. "He seemed so quiet this morning. I wondered if the two of you had a fight."

Catherine frowned. "We did, sort of."

"Jake's taking all this rather badly," Ashley furnished. "He's usually very agreeable and easygoing."

"I have a hard time believing that," Catherine admitted.

"You know, Jake hasn't had an easy life." She smiled and her voice softened. "Don't get me wrong. I don't know what happened between the two of you years ago, and I'm sure it wasn't easy for you. But Jake came home and kept his family together. I think before he found out about Matthew, he was sorry that he'd never had a family of his own."

"Why hasn't he?" Catherine asked.

Ashley lips flattened to a thin line. "It's personal,

so you'll have to ask him. Then maybe you'll understand why he wants so badly to be with Matthew.''

Catherine pondered Ashley's evasive answer. Was there some secret she didn't know about Jake, something that would make him desperate to have possession of his son? Something that would make him threaten to take Matthew from her?

After she finished her coffee, Catherine decided to go outside for a while. She walked over to the corral and stood beside Matthew. She put her arm around him for a hug, then hovered nearby, just wanting a few moments of peace with her son.

Matthew acknowledged his mother with a look that told Catherine he wasn't ready to listen if she was going to try to persuade him to her way of thinking. Catherine kept her distance. In a day or two he wouldn't have a choice. She was going to leave, and no one was going to stop her from taking Matthew with her.

The next day the sun was shining again, and Catherine decided it was now or never. She and Jake had barely spoken the previous day. He'd gone out of his way to avoid her, Catherine thought, which was fine with her. She didn't like the way he made her feel when he looked at her with his brooding expression.

She packed her things in her small bag, then went to look out the window, trying to spot anyone who could thwart her plans. Someone knocked on her door, and Catherine made a beeline for her bag. The door opened about the time that Catherine tossed it to the floor. Guilt tinged her face pink, and she nervously cleared her throat.

''Planning on going somewhere?'' Jake leaned against the doorjamb as his gaze met hers.

Six

Standing beside the bed with the bag at her feet, Catherine paled. "Um, not really. I was going to ask you if you thought the bridge was passable today, though."

"Possibly," he answered, looking as if he didn't believe her. He took a step inside, then was quiet for a few moments. It was obvious that he had something on his mind. Catherine waited nervously for him to speak.

"I guess I was kinda rough on you the other night," he offered, seeming as if he was uncomfortable with admitting as much.

Catherine didn't answer him. She wondered where this was leading. Surely Jake wanted something from her.

"For what it's worth, I'm sorry." He sounded sincere. That didn't mean that he was, she told herself.

She flashed him a curious look, wanting to rattle him as he'd rattled her when he'd come through her door and caught her planning her escape. ''For threatening me or for kissing me?''

Jake put a hand on his hip. ''Well, for starters, for yelling at you,'' he replied gruffly. He didn't admit that he shouldn't have kissed her. And he wasn't going to admit that he'd enjoyed it. ''I've been thinking, and there's something else I want you to consider.'' Jake figured if he could avoid taking Catherine to court, it would be better for Matthew. He didn't want to put his son in the middle of a tug-of-war.

The entire situation was difficult for all of them. But the adjustment for Matthew was the most important thing to consider. Catherine had to know that, and Jake was banking on her love for her son to get her to agree to his offer.

''Go on,'' she encouraged.

''I want Matthew to stay with me for the summer. And you seem to be afraid that if he does, he won't want to come home. Right?''

She nodded at him, her green eyes wary. ''Yes.''

''I think you should stay at the ranch for the summer, also,'' Jake suggested. ''Then you'd be here with Matthew, and you wouldn't have to worry about what I was telling him or that I was turning him against you.''

''For the summer?'' Catherine repeated, startled by his proposal. ''I couldn't do that. No, that wouldn't work,'' she said hurriedly, shaking her head.

It hadn't been easy for Jake to offer Catherine this option. Having her live with him was going to be difficult, to say the least. Jake was man enough to admit that he still found her attractive. She was a beautiful woman. Even if he hadn't known her before he would be attracted to her.

He didn't like the feelings she provoked in him, and

having her around to tempt him twenty-four hours a day was going to test his control. But he wanted his son for the summer. This solution was far from perfect, but it would satisfy all concerned.

"It makes sense," he said convincingly. "You'd be right here with Matt. He wouldn't be growing apart from you."

"I understand that part, and I'm not trying to be difficult. It's just that I couldn't possibly leave my home that long," she insisted.

Jake frowned. "Because of this man you're involved with? Shouldn't you put your son first?"

Catherine squared her shoulders. "Douglas has nothing to do with this." It was more the truth than she wanted to admit to Jake. She hadn't given a thought to Douglas the past couple of days, hadn't even called him. All along, in her heart, she'd known that she didn't love him. She'd been foolish to even consider marrying him for Matthew's sake.

"He has a lot to do with this if you're putting him before Matthew."

"I wouldn't do that," she stated firmly.

That statement told Jake a lot about Catherine's relationship with the man. If she was truly in love with him, she would be torn between him and her son. To Jake's knowledge, she hadn't even called the man since she'd been at the ranch.

"What other problem is there?" Jake inquired. "Are you required to work summers with your job?"

"No," Catherine answered honestly. "I could, but I like to have the summers off so I can be with Matthew." Until now she'd looked forward to the end of the school year. She'd hoped to take a summer vacation with her son. There wasn't much chance of that now.

"Then what's stopping you?"

"I don't know, Jake. The whole idea, well, it would be awkward," she stated, shrugging her shoulders.

Jake took a step toward her. "You mean because of the kiss we shared?"

"You kissed me," she reminded him.

"You kissed me back," he returned levelly. "And you enjoyed it."

Catherine didn't deny it. And she knew he knew it was true, even if she didn't admit to it. She flushed to her roots remembering how he'd captured her and held her to him.

"That doesn't mean I wanted you to."

Jake frowned. "If it'll make you feel better, I promise to keep my hands off you while you're here."

Catherine should have drawn comfort from that, but she didn't. That he could turn his feelings on and off so easily disturbed her. She was finding it increasingly hard to keep her distance from Jake. He was an attractive man. He'd been easy to fall in love with.

But he'd hurt her once before. She wasn't going to let him hurt her again. She'd trusted him then, and he'd broken her heart.

"I'd like to talk to Matthew about this." She didn't want to do anything, make any decisions, without first discussing them with her son. "If I say yes, and that's a big if, when do you think you could take us to the airport?"

"I've got some work here at the ranch that's going to keep me busy most of the morning," Jake explained. "I'll be free this afternoon."

"Will we be able to get across the bridge?"

"The bridge won't be a problem," he told her, then

shifted his gaze to the window. "I have a small airplane. I'll fly you home."

Catherine's mouth dropped open. "What?" Irritation swept through her, and she advanced on him. "You mean to tell me that you could have taken me and Matthew home before now?" she demanded.

Jake had the decency to flush just a bit. He put his hands up in defense, as if he thought she was going to hit him.

"No, I'm not saying that—"

"Are you going to stand there and tell me you couldn't have?" Her cheeks were red, her face hot. At that moment, Catherine very much wanted to smack him. To keep from doing so, she rested her hands on her hips. Anger radiated from her.

"It's not as if I knew what the weather was going to do," Jake said in his own defense. "Just because the storms cleared here didn't mean it was okay to fly. I called for a weather report and flying conditions just a few minutes ago."

Catherine made a sound of disgust. "Like you couldn't have done that yesterday," she accused. "Get out of here, Jake."

"Catie—"

"Out!" Her temper simmering, Catherine pointed toward the door.

Jake, apparently not realizing what a mistake he was making, cracked the bare resemblance of a smile. "I'm going." He backed away quickly, then paused at the door. "Let me know when you're ready to go."

"Out!" Catherine shouted, fuming. She put her hands on his back and gave him a shove as he was moving toward the door. Then she slammed it behind him, closing herself in the room.

She couldn't get over how easily she'd accepted the news that she was stuck on the ranch. She'd believed Jake when he said they wouldn't be able to cross the bridge, and all along he had a way to take her and Matthew home.

She had a mind to grab Matthew and go back to her original plan to escape on her own. Damn Jake McCall. He certainly had proved to her that he couldn't be trusted.

And that pretty much meant that she *was* going to have to stay on the ranch for the summer if she allowed Matthew to stay. She wasn't going to trust Jake not to turn her son against her.

Catherine couldn't believe she was in this mess. She had herself to blame, of course. She wished she'd been in tune with Matthew. She should have realized that he was unhappy. And she should have told him the truth about his father a long time ago. Maybe she should have tried a couple of times over the years to contact Jake.

No, this situation was not her fault. It was Jake's, and she was going to keep reminding herself of that. She was going to keep it bottled inside, feed on it and use it as a weapon to keep her wits about her when dealing with Jake.

He'd just proved to her again that he couldn't be trusted.

After a heart-to-heart talk with Matthew, Catherine finally agreed to let him stay on the ranch for the summer, on the condition that she remain there also.

Matthew was ecstatic. He'd even insisted that he didn't want to go home and pack his things. He'd begged Catherine to do it for him, and she'd finally relented and agreed, because it was such an easy thing to do to please her son.

She hadn't, however, thought about the fact that it would mean traveling alone with Jake. She also hadn't thought that it would mean spending a couple of days alone with Jake as she packed.

And most of all, she hadn't realized that she and Jake would be sharing her small condo together.

Alone.

"It really isn't necessary for you to stay," she told Jake as he extended his hand to her. They'd arrived in Lubbock in the afternoon, and Jake had pulled the plane up to a hangar.

Jake sent her an exasperated look. They'd had this conversation before, of course, but she was determined to give it one more try as he opened the door to the plane.

"You're not going to be able to move everything on your own." She'd finally agreed to live on the ranch for the summer. Which meant that for now, Matthew was living with Jake. It appeared to her that Jake didn't want her to get cold feet once she got back home, and the only way he could be sure she wouldn't was to go with her and stay while she packed.

"I can rent a van or something," she said once again, for what seemed like the hundredth time. She was learning that Jake was a very determined man.

Catherine shivered as Jake helped her step down.

"Cold?" he asked.

"A bit," Catherine admitted, her feet finally on firm ground. The recent rain had brought with it a cold front, the temperature dropping lower than normal for this time of year.

Jake shrugged out of his jacket and put it around her, then told her to put her arms in the sleeves. Catherine obeyed and was enveloped by his scent. The coat was still warm from the heat of his body, and a feeling of longing slipped over her.

"Thanks," she mumbled, trying not to respond to his nearness or the sensation of desire that pulled at her every time she was close to him.

"No problem."

Jake got her bag from inside the plane, as well as one of his own. He started them toward the terminal of the airport.

"It'll take me a few minutes to rent a truck," he told her, carrying both of their bags.

"My car is already parked here. We can use it," she informed him.

"What kind of car do you drive?"

She told him the make and model of her compact car, and he gave a little laugh. "We'll need something bigger to transport the boxes back to the airport. I figure I'll have to make a few trips. I'm not going to try and fit everything in a small foreign-model car."

"Are you deliberately trying to bait me?" Catherine asked, stopping and staring at him.

Jake stared back at her, determined not to smile. He *did* like getting a rise out of her, he realized. "Not at all. I've just never seen a woman who didn't pack more than she needed," he replied, then took her by the arm and steered her in the direction he was heading.

Catherine shook free of his grasp, which earned her a slight grin from Jake. That look, sexy and inviting, fueled her annoyance even as it tripped her heart. She wasn't going to let him push her around.

After Jake rented a large sport utility vehicle, Catherine led the way to her home in her car. Twenty minutes later they both pulled in the driveway, Jake stopping right behind her.

At that moment Catherine would have given anything if she could have avoided going inside. Just thinking about being alone with Jake was enough to unnerve her. Unable to avoid it, she stepped out of her car.

Jake followed her to the door. Catherine lived in a neat neighborhood, with a number of condos matching her own. They were well kept, with shrubs and small flower gardens adorning them.

Catherine used her key to let herself in, then turned to admit Jake before closing the door. She switched a light on, illuminating the small foyer, as well as the living room and small dining area.

It felt strange allowing him into her world, to share her personal space with him. Funny that, after all the years of thinking about him and wondering if she'd ever see him again, she never once imagined him standing in her home.

He was so big that he seemed to fill the room, closing it in, making it seem even smaller than it truly was. Wanting to distance herself, Catherine moved away, then switched on a couple more lights.

"Should I make some coffee?" she asked, doing her best not to look at him. She glanced at her watch, then added, "I imagine you're hungry. I don't have any idea what there is here to eat." She moved about her small kitchen, opening the refrigerator door and examining its contents.

"How about if I go get some hamburgers? While I'm out, I'll try to pick up a few boxes," Jake said. He dropped their bags to the floor, then followed her into the kitchen.

"That's a great idea," Catherine agreed as she continued to study the contents of the refrigerator, thinking it would be a relief to have him out of her home, even if it was for a short while.

Jake hadn't been back to Lubbock since the day he left, and old memories were taunting him. At his home he'd been able to distance himself somewhat from Catie and the feelings she evoked in him.

He was still plenty upset with her, and there was no forgiveness in his heart for her keeping his son from him. There was still the matter of the letter that needed to be cleared up.

The trouble was, Jake hadn't expected to be so attracted to Catie after all these years. He was annoyed at himself for the way he couldn't take his eyes off her backside as she bent over looking in the refrigerator. He resisted the urge to put his hands on her and pull her against him.

She turned around and looked at him then, her eyes connecting with his. Looking uneasy, she walked across the room and brushed by him. "Let me show you where you can sleep tonight."

She started to grab her bag, but Jake got there first and picked them both up. Catherine led the way up the narrow staircase to the second floor. Each room had a separate bath, which she was very thankful for. At least in her home she wouldn't have to share a bathroom with him.

She opened the door to the right, which led to her room. There were beige Priscilla curtains on the windows, and the room was decorated in soft colors of mauve and teal.

"I think it would be best if you slept in here. The bed is bigger, and you'll be more comfortable." Heavens, Catherine thought, Jake sleeping in her bed. Just the thought made her heart turn over with a little thump.

"This is your room," Jake surmised.

"Yes," Catherine answered, turning to look at Jake.

"I'm not sleeping in your bed," he said abruptly. The thought crossed his mind that sleeping with her in her bed would be quite an adventure. He hadn't been with her in nearly thirteen years, hadn't fallen asleep with her in his arms in what felt like a lifetime. He wondered if she still awakened slowly, the way dawn breaks into a new day.

The implications of his words hung between them. Catherine shifted her feet, wondering what he was thinking. Was he remembering the nights they'd slept in each other's arms?

"Oh, but—"

"Matt's bed will be fine," Jake told her, noticing her slight flush and how her green eyes widened. He set her bag on the floor just inside the room.

Catherine started to argue, then changed her mind. She turned around and opened Matthew's door across the hall, not knowing what to expect. His room was fairly neat for an adolescent, his bed unmade, though, and a few of his clothes were strewn across the floor.

Catherine quickly began straightening up, flitting about the room, moving from one place to another to avoid having to turn and face Jake.

"The bed's a double." She indicated the obvious with a toss of her hand.

"It'll be fine," Jake assured her. He came into the room, then dropped his bag on a chair.

"All right, then." Catherine opened the door on the left. "The bathroom is here. There's also one downstairs, just outside the kitchen. I'll get you some clean sheets." She rushed out of the room, then returned with a stack of folded linens in her arms.

She started to strip the bed. As she leaned over, Jake's gaze once again rested on her rear. Her hips moved and swayed as she struggled to get the sheet off one corner of the mattress. Jake nearly groaned watching the process, then damned himself for it.

"I can do that," Jake said curtly, moving beside her and freeing the sheet with one hand. Catherine stepped back as he gathered the sheets up in his hands.

She took them from him. "Um, I'll just go freshen up, then meet you downstairs," she said, backing away. Then she turned and rushed into her own room. She deposited the laundry in the hamper, then ran a brush through her hair. Downstairs a door slammed, and she drew a breath of relief, ready to enjoy a few minutes without Jake's presence.

This was going to be difficult, she told herself. Catherine hadn't expected to feel a sexual attraction to Jake once she saw him again. He'd hurt her, shown he couldn't be trusted. But those things were at complete odds with the feelings he evoked in her.

Catherine turned off her bedroom light, then went downstairs. She decided to use the time she had alone to call Douglas. She played the messages left in her absence. There was one from a co-worker and one from her neighbor, but Douglas hadn't called.

Catherine wasn't really surprised. She dialed his number, wondering if he'd be home. She prayed he was. She didn't want to have this discussion in front of Jake. Douglas surprised her by answering on the first ring.

"It's Catherine," she said, noticing that he seemed rushed.

"Catherine, hi. I was wondering when you'd get back. You just caught me. I was on my way out."

"I arrived home a few minutes ago," she told him. "I'm sorry I didn't call you while I was gone." She hesitated, hating what she had to say over the telephone, but seeing no way out of it. "Do you have a few minutes? I need to talk to you. I'm sorry to do this now, but I'm not going to have time to see you."

Catherine explained about the last two days and what had occurred as briefly as possible. "This is a terrible way to do this, Douglas, but I won't be seeing you anymore. I'm going to be away for the summer. With Matthew. I have to put my son first." She spoke quietly, but her voice was determined. "I'm really sorry to tell you like this."

They talked a little longer, and though Douglas asked a few questions, he didn't seem too disturbed by her declaration or explanation. Catherine was surprised by the relief she felt. Apparently they'd both been willing to settle for less than love. She'd wanted something for herself and her son, so much so that she'd been willing to think that marriage with Douglas would work. She'd foolishly let a comfortable friendship progress too far.

Jake cleared his throat, and Catherine spun around, startled. She hadn't heard him come in. Catherine hurried to end the conversation. She kept her voice quiet but had a feeling that Jake had heard at least part of her conversation. Still, she said nothing to him and ignored the way he glared at her.

They ate the food Jake brought back while packing. She suggested that he should use his judgment on what to bring for Matthew, while she spent time packing her own things. By the end of the night Catherine was exhausted. Jake had come to find her a half dozen times, asking her questions. Together they decided that Matthew would probably want his stereo and computer. Anything else, he would have to live without.

Close to midnight Catherine decided she'd done enough. She'd practically broken her neck to get everything done in one afternoon and evening, trying her best to shorten her stay at her house with Jake. If there was anything else she and Matthew needed, they could buy it. She went downstairs, and Jake was sitting comfortably on her sofa, his long legs stretched out in front of him.

She raised her eyebrows, and he gave her a small grin. Catherine's heart somersaulted. Turning away, she went into the kitchen. "Would you like something to drink?" she asked. "I have sodas and some wine coolers, or if you'd like, I can make some coffee."

"A wine cooler's fine," Jake answered. The last thing he needed was caffeine to keep him awake. What he needed was a cold shower, he decided. Jake had watched Catie all evening as she fretted over what to pack and what to leave. He'd tried to keep his distance as much as possible, but it seemed fate had been working against him. Every time he turned around he'd needed to ask her something.

When he was near her, he wanted to touch her, wanted to kiss her again. She was driving him crazy. He'd promised her he would keep his hands off her, but was having a hard time living up to his word.

He glanced at Catie as she handed him a bottle, then

he diverted his eyes and opened the cool drink. ''How long have you lived here?'' he asked, curious now to know more about her and his son's past.

Catherine sat in a wooden rocker and sipped her own drink, then set it on the table. ''Two years. It took me a while to save up enough money to buy a home.'' She was proud of what she'd accomplished. It hadn't been easy, but she'd worked hard for everything she had.

Jake frowned, then glanced at the large photo album under one side of the coffee table. He leaned over and picked it up. ''Are there pictures of Matthew in here?'' He opened it and began scanning the first page.

''Yes.'' Automatically Catherine got up and moved to sit next to Jake, then smiled as she pointed to a picture of Matthew as a baby. It was natural for Jake to want to see the pictures, and at that moment it felt just as natural for Catherine to share them with him. He was, after all, the father of her child.

Jake flipped the pages slowly, and they shared the memories of their child's life, Catherine talking softly about each picture. Unconsciously she scooted closer to Jake, her bare arm touching his as she pointed to a picture of Matthew as a toddler, taking a bath in bubbles.

Jake was having a difficult time concentrating on the photo album. He was suddenly very aware of Catherine's scent and the warmth of her body gently pressing against his. She leaned closer to reach across the album and talk about a snapshot of Matthew learning to walk. Her hair softly brushed his face, and he could feel her breath on his cheek.

The fact that Jake was determined not to let Catie get under his skin again made little difference as he listened to her talk, her voice sultry and enticing. The sudden urge he had to kiss her was irrational, yet very real and too strong to resist.

Jake turned to ask her a question, and the words died before he could speak. Her mouth was only inches away from his own. His gaze met hers, then dropped to her mouth with silent invitation. Catie didn't move as Jake slowly lowered his mouth onto hers.

He kissed her gently at first, nipping at her lips, tasting her, waiting for her to stop him, to tell him he'd lost his mind. When she didn't, he slipped his tongue farther into her mouth as he cupped her neck and held her lips to his. Fire exploded throughout him as he touched the tip of her tongue.

Catherine tilted her head, angling closer to him, and her hand caressed the back of his head. Jake put his arm around her and pulled her to him, pressing his body against hers.

His mouth left hers, trailing kisses to her ear and down her neck, inflaming the emotions rocketing through him.

''Oh, Jake,'' Catherine whispered softly, and she pressed a soft kiss beneath his ear. ''This shouldn't be happening.'' Her breathing was labored, her eyes closed.

''No,'' Jake agreed gravely. His lips nipped hers again, then settled on her mouth, taking it fully beneath his, tasting her again, deeply, a little desperately.

She gave herself in that moment, in that one staggering kiss, and the tangible fire between them became an inferno. Jake cupped her head and chin with both hands, fusing their mouths together, drinking her in. His tongue seared hers, and she moaned, then pressed herself closer to him, her hands gliding along his back.

Jake wanted nothing more at that moment than to be inside her sweet warmth.

"I want you, Catie. Right here, right now," he declared, breathing heavily.

Jake's words exploded in Catherine's mind as he touched her breast, lightly at first, stroking her in a soft, circular rhythm that made her pulse race. Then he filled his hand with her and ran his thumb across her nipple. Aching, it puckered beneath the fabric of her shirt.

Catherine put her hands against Jake's chest, thinking she should stop this insanity. She could feel the heavy thud of his heart beating beneath her palm. Somewhere in the back of her mind the thought that this shouldn't be happening between them disappeared, gone in a moment, replaced by a rapid quickening of need in the deepest core of her.

She clung to him, her hands sliding over his hard muscular shoulders and resting on the corded muscles of his neck. She was unaware of the time or place, oblivious to right or wrong, or if she would regret her actions later. This was Jake, the man she'd loved so deeply once. There was a natural awareness between them that wasn't to be denied.

His hands slid down her body, stroking her, touching her thighs, then returning with sweet torture to her breasts. She reveled in his embrace and the pleasurable memories it provoked.

His mouth devoured hers as he began to unbutton her shirt. Then his hand was inside her blouse, touching her skin, and she arched against it and moaned into his mouth.

Catherine kissed him back hungrily. It had been forever since she'd felt this kind of emotional release, this closeness to another human being.

She'd loved this man once, deeply, and she let herself relive her feelings for him. Touching him, stroking his chest and reaching for the buttons of his shirt. She undid them one by one, then ran her hand over his bare skin.

"Ah, Catie," Jake whispered, then closed his mouth over hers again. In seconds he had her blouse and bra off, then reached for the button to her pants. He slid his hands inside, grasping her buttocks, stroking her, sending a scorching heat racing through her.

"Jake." His lips found her nipple and closed over it, sucking her. She lifted her hips, and his hands slid her pants down.

In a flurry of action, Catherine had his shirt off, and her palms stroked the soft hair on his chest, then slid down his rib cage. He sucked in a hard breath when her hands went to his belt.

"Jeez, Catie, you'd better let me do that," he rasped, then quickly unfastened his belt and slid the zipper of his jeans down.

Catherine felt a moment of hesitation when he moved away to remove his pants and boots, but Jake came to her so quickly, pressing his mouth against hers, touching her breasts, then stroking her intimately as he lowered her to the soft carpet.

He was on top of her then, pressing his body seductively against hers. She could feel him hard and ready as he positioned himself between her thighs. His body began probing hers, gently demanding entry. Then he was inside her. Catherine caught her breath as he invaded her softness.

"Catie…ah, you're so soft, so hot." Jake groaned, a deep growl coming from deep inside his chest. Then he stilled. Panting, he slipped out of her, then lifted himself above her, his gaze seeking hers. ‘‘Are you using protection?’’ he asked, barely able to take a full breath.

Catherine nodded, assuring him she was.

Jake sighed with masculine pleasure as he entered her again, then rocked deeper, his hips provoking hers.

Catherine slid her arms around him, running her hands along his back, her nails sinking into his flesh as she felt her body begin to quiver and tighten.

‘‘Jake, oh, Jake,’’ she murmured, and it sounded like a plea. Molten fire melted her bones, and she felt a huge surge of ecstasy enveloping her. Then Jake was sinking deeper into her, pushing harder and harder. Jake’s muscles tightened, and his hands cupped her buttocks as his hips rocked against hers.

And her world exploded.

Seven

Jake's entire body felt as if it weighed a thousand pounds. Making love to Catie had taken everything out of him. All of the pent-up feelings he'd been using as a shield against her and her ability to hurt him disintegrated the moment he'd felt himself inside her. He was sure he must be crushing Catie, but he didn't want to move away from her at that moment. She was soft and warm and pliant beneath him, and with a desperation he wasn't able to understand, he wanted to keep her there.

Then he opened his eyes and saw the photo album. It was open to a page with a picture of Catie standing beside a man. Matthew was in the picture with them. It had been taken at a park. Matt looked to be about eight and wore a baseball uniform. Catie was handing him a bat, and the man was squatting beside Matt, talking to him. That one picture brought it all back home to Jake.

Because of Catie, he'd missed his son's entire childhood. Jake had never had the opportunity to hear Matt's first word, see him crawl or walk, or watch him go off to his first day at school.

How could he have forgotten that Catie had lied to him, that she'd kept his son from him for twelve years? Seeing his son with Catie and this man ripped at his insides. Jake refused to let himself think about how it made him feel to see Catie with another man.

Annoyed with Catie and with his own lack of control, Jake stiffened and rolled away from her. He got to his feet and pulled on his underwear, then his jeans. He should have been the one to teach his son how to bat, how to field a baseball. He should have been there watching his son walk and grow and learn. Seeing his son and Catie together with this *stranger* irritated the hell out of him.

He couldn't bring himself to look at Catie at that moment, but in his peripheral vision he saw her jerky motions as she hurried to dress. She pulled on her flowered blouse and snatched her bra from the floor.

The silence between them was palpable. Jake figured he should say something. He just didn't know *what* to say to her. He shouldn't have let things get so far out of hand, he thought. He shouldn't have kissed her, should never have made love to her. But he hadn't been able to stop himself, and that knowledge left him feeling even more irritated—with his own lack of control as well as with Catie.

He'd asked her about protection because he couldn't admit to her that he was incapable of making her pregnant. His personal life was none of her concern, and he wasn't one to share his innermost feelings. He was glad now that he hadn't slipped up and mentioned it to her. He still didn't trust her, and he wasn't going to give her a weapon to use against him.

Finally, unable to put the uncomfortable conversation off a moment longer, he turned toward her, a frown deepening his brows. ''Look, I'm sorry—''

''Stop,'' she blurted out, interrupting him, her voice eerily calm. She didn't quite meet his gaze. ''We're two consenting adults. These things happen. Let's just put this behind us.''

Already she was sounding as if she regretted what had happened between them. Jake knew he did. He hadn't meant to complicate matters like this. He wondered if she would back out of coming back to the ranch. If she did, it would be his fault.

Jake didn't know why, but it bothered him that she could so easily explain away their intimacy. He should have felt relieved, but he didn't. He wanted to take her again. Just thinking about her writhing beneath him made him hard.

''Yeah, that's what we'll do,'' he replied, his tone even as he shrugged into his shirt. He left it unbuttoned. ''I guess we should call it a night. We'll be leaving early in the morning, unless you have more packing to do.''

Catie shook her head, and still she didn't meet his gaze. ''No…no, I'm finished.''

A tidal wave of relief washed over Jake. At least she was still planning to come with him to the ranch. He had jeopardized the time he'd been anxiously wanting to spend with his son. Now he was being given another chance. He would have to be more careful around Catie.

"I'll turn in, then."

Catie made no comment, so Jake walked toward the staircase. He hesitated, then climbed the stairs.

Catherine watched Jake's back as he ascended the staircase. There was no way she would let him know how much he'd hurt her. The tension in her body coiled as he disappeared and she heard the door to her son's room open. It wasn't until he closed the door behind him that she dropped onto the sofa. She wrapped her arms around herself and rocked back and forth.

She was *not* going to let herself fall in love with Jake again. He'd hurt her terribly once. She'd be a fool to let him hurt her like that again.

She couldn't believe that she'd so easily succumbed to Jake's sexual advances. Of course when they'd been together years ago their bodies had been very attuned to each other. Catherine figured that for a few moments she'd allowed herself to go back in time.

What had happened between her and Jake wasn't real. They'd both been carried away with memories of a period when they'd laughed and loved.

Her gaze fell to the photo album spread open on the floor and the pictures of Matthew playing Little League. So that was it, she thought. That was all it took for Jake to pull away from her and withdraw within himself.

He still blamed her, when it was his own fault for not knowing about his son. Whether he believed it or not, she'd tried several times to contact him. In the morning she'd show him the letter.

She took a deep breath, gathered herself together, then stood and switched off the lights in the room. Slowly she walked up the stairs to her bedroom. Her body was slightly sore, and would probably be more so in the morning.

Trying to ease the tension pulling at her, she took a hot bath. Long afterward she lay between cool sheets, alone in her room with thoughts of Jake sleeping nearby. It was well into the night before she fell asleep.

The ride to the airport was filled with tension, and Catherine knew Jake felt it, too. During their preparations to leave, they had barely spoken to each other. Jake had refused breakfast and made a trip to load packages on the plane. Catherine had used the time to toss perishables in the trash and ready her condo for her absence.

Jake loaded the truck with the last of the boxes while Catie made arrangements with a neighbor to keep an eye on things for her. She'd mentioned driving her car to Jake's, but he'd insisted she wouldn't need it. He explained that there were several ranch vehicles, and she could have free use of any of them whenever she needed.

Catherine had been relieved just to get on the road and out of her home. Every time she looked at the living room floor, she remembered Jake making love to her there. Was she never going to learn?

Once at the airport Jake transferred the last of the boxes to the airplane. After returning the truck he'd rented, he did a final check on the plane before they took off.

Catherine had waited by the plane for him to finish. She hesitated only a fraction of a moment when Jake offered her his hand to help her on board. Her heartbeat quickened as she felt his big hand grasp hers. With his other hand he touched the small of her back, giving her support, and Catherine felt her knees go weak.

She silently admonished herself for her reaction to him as she took a seat in the plane and Jake climbed in and started it.

She needed to physically and emotionally distance herself from Jake, but that was going to be hard to accomplish, since they were now on their way to his ranch where she'd agreed to live for the entire summer. She would have backed out if she hadn't already made promises to her son.

Surely Jake had a lot of responsibilities at the ranch, and they wouldn't be tripping over each other. Of course there were going to be times when they'd be together. At least then there would be other people around them.

Catherine would give staying at the ranch a fair chance since it was so important to Matthew. She wasn't doing it for Jake, although she knew he had the power to make life miserable for her by trying to get custody of Matthew.

Catherine couldn't let it come to that. After spending the summer with Matthew she hoped Jake would be reasonable about working out visitation arrangements. And if it did come down to a court battle, it would look good on her part that she'd agreed to let father and son have the summer together.

Catherine was relieved when they finally approached the ranch. She and Jake hadn't made much conversation on the trip. Obviously he was regretting their intimacy as much as she was. Well, that was okay with her. It let her know where he stood. She was all for being polite and distant with Jake. She just hoped her heart was going to follow the rules.

Jake radioed ahead and let Ryder know they were near arrival. Matthew was with Ryder when he drove out to meet them, and it was evident that her son had already established a kinship with his uncle.

Matthew ran to greet her and Jake, his eyes brilliant with excitement as he chatted on and on about his activities since they'd been gone. Catherine doubted that her son had even missed her. She was amazed by the change in his disposition. He acted as if feeding cattle was as interesting and fun as the games on his computer.

''Hey, son,'' Jake said, smiling as he ruffled the young boy's hair. ''Sounds like you've been learning a lot about the ranch while we were gone.'' Catherine felt her heart turn over at the way Matthew grinned up at him, he looked so happy. It was obvious he was already taking to the ranch and his new family.

''Uncle Ryder let me ride some more today,'' he told them, his voice high-pitched with excitement.

Jake began unloading the cargo. He handed Matthew a box to carry. With everyone helping, it wasn't too long before everything they'd brought was transferred to the house and into the two bedrooms Catherine and Matthew would use for the summer.

Finally left alone, Catherine stood in the middle of her room, listening to the sounds coming from the adjoining bathroom. Good heavens, how could she have forgotten that she was going to be sharing a bathroom with Jake? So much for keeping her distance, she thought.

She surveyed the boxes of clothing she'd brought. Since Ryder no longer used the room, there was plenty of space for her things. She'd given Matthew orders to unpack his belongings before he could go outside again. She thought she might as well get hers done also.

As she began to fill the dresser drawers, the commitment she'd made to stay the summer with Jake and his family hit her. It had been a long time since Catherine had felt part of a family. She hadn't talked to her parents or sisters since she'd left school. Catherine had accepted the fact that she'd let her parents down and they didn't want anything to do with her.

Deep down inside, though, she still felt an enormous emptiness when she thought about her two younger sisters. They would be adults now. For years after she'd left, she'd hoped to see them again one day.

Now she was here with this big, happy family. Matthew was settling in nicely, enjoying the attention and affection of new aunts, uncle and cousins. But Catherine couldn't help feeling out of place. The strain between her and Jake wasn't going to help things.

She finished unpacking the last box, then tossed it aside. Glancing at the clock, she realized it was nearly time to prepare dinner. Perhaps she could offer to help.

Catherine had been tossing an idea around in her head since she'd agreed to stay for the summer. She wasn't about to sit around for weeks and not contribute in some way for her keep.

She headed out of her room and went looking for Ashley. Ryder's wife was really nice and Catherine liked her a lot already. She found her in the den, playing with her twins.

''Hi,'' Catherine said, walking into the room.

Ashley looked up from where she was sitting on the floor with the two toddlers. ''Catherine, hi.'' She smiled, then grabbed Michelle's hand just before she could throw a small wooden block at her sister.

"I was wondering if I could talk to you—sometime when you're not too busy," she added, then realized how ridiculous that sounded. What expectant mother with twins wouldn't be busy all the time?

"Sure." Ashley quickly got to her feet, though she leaned backward a moment and stretched. Michelle and Melissa both crawled over and tugged on her legs. "I was just about to feed these two. Wanna help?"

Catherine gave her an answering smile. "I'd love to," she replied.

"Great!" Ashley scooped up Michelle. "Grab Melissa, will you?" she asked, starting from the room.

"You don't breast-feed?" Catherine followed Ashley to the kitchen.

Ashley shook her head. "I did for a while, but I stopped after I became pregnant. I was just so exhausted. Still am, for that matter."

Catherine smiled. "You'd never know it," she commented as she took a seat.

"By the end of the day I can barely hold my eyes open," Ashley confessed. She prepared the bottles for the babies, then handed one to Catherine before sitting with Michelle still in her arms. "But I'm lucky. Ryder's a great father, and his family has practically adopted me."

Ashley gave Catherine a curious look and went on. "You know it was really hard for me at first. I wasn't sure about living here. I didn't know anyone, and I felt really insecure. But the McCalls are unbelievably close, and they welcomed me into their fold without hesitation."

Catherine held the bottle to Melissa's tiny mouth. She grabbed hold of the nipple and sucked. "That's sort of how I feel, though my stay isn't permanent."

She looked contrite for a moment. "I'm sorry. I didn't mean that you or anyone else has made me uncomfortable."

Ashley gave Catherine a warm smile. "No offense taken. I can see why we'd be a bit overwhelming."

After a few minutes Catherine propped Melissa on her shoulder and patted her back. The baby offered up a small burp. "I don't have any family to speak of, but not living in my home feels strange."

"Are you sure it isn't that you're living so close to Jake now?" Ashley boldly asked. "I get the feeling that all is not quite well between you two. He was awfully quiet when he came through here a little while ago, and when I asked about you, he just grunted something unintelligible."

Ashley was very astute, Catherine thought. "We did have a couple of clashes while we were gone," she confessed without going into details. "I thought about not coming, but it was so important to Matthew. I figured I could at least give it a try."

Melissa finished the last of her bottled milk, and Catherine used a cloth to clean her bow-shaped mouth. "I was thinking, though, that I'll go crazy if I don't have something to do this summer." Her gaze met Ashley's. "I don't want to get in the way or anything, but how would you feel if I helped with the house while I'm here instead of having someone come in?"

Ashley was pleased by the suggestion. "Are you sure you want to?"

Catherine nodded. "I need to do something, and I'd feel as if I was earning my stay, so to speak," she explained.

"Well, I think it's a great idea, because I'd rather not have a stranger come in."

Catherine thought that was an odd statement, since she was virtually a stranger to Ashley.

"I know what you're thinking, and you're no longer a stranger in this house. Matthew is Jake's child. You're Matthew's mother. That makes you part of this family," she explained, as if it was simply that easy to rationalize.

Catherine felt an overwhelming sense of longing. She *wished* at that moment that she was truly a part of this loving family. "That's really nice of you to say."

Ashley grinned. "I mean it." She finished feeding Michelle, then frowned at Catherine. "I'm not sure how Jake will accept this idea, though."

Catherine squared her shoulders. "Jake will have to live with it. I made a concession in coming here. If you have no problem with my help, why should he?"

Ashley grinned. "Why, indeed?" she repeated, thinking Jake had finally met his match. She was going to enjoy seeing him go toe-to-toe with Catherine. "Well, I guess I'd better get these two down for a nap."

"Let me help," Catherine insisted, following Ashley out of the room. She'd gotten over one hurdle talking to Ashley. Now all she had to do was talk to Jake.

Catherine had silently practiced her speech a couple of times as she helped with preparing the meal. She had planned to confront Jake with her idea after dinner. She hadn't figured on Ashley announcing it to everyone while they were eating.

As soon as Ashley had mentioned Catherine's "kind" offer, Jake's gaze shot to Catherine's. "That's not necessary," he stated in that controlling tone of his.

"Actually, it is necessary for you to have someone

come in to help out,'' Catherine informed him. ''Why shouldn't it be me?''

Jake grunted his disapproval. ''Because you're a guest,'' he insisted. ''Guests don't do housework and laundry.'' He stared back at Catherine, his eyes hard and unyielding.

''That's ridiculous, Jake,'' Ashley gently admonished her brother-in-law. ''Catherine's no more a guest than I was when I came here, and you accepted the fact that I wanted to work.''

Her reminder fell on deaf ears. ''That was different.'' His expression softened a bit when he glanced at Ashley.

A small smile played on her lips. ''I don't see how.'' She looked at Ryder, who had been quiet to this point. ''Do you, honey?''

''Nope, darlin', I don't,'' he agreed. He gave his older brother a sharp look, obviously enjoying his disgruntled expression. ''Unless you can explain it to us,'' he added, fighting back a grin.

Catherine wasn't exactly sure what was happening. Obviously, she had the support of Jake's sibling and his wife. She just wasn't sure why.

''I think it's a great idea,'' Lynn said, pointing her fork at Jake as she spoke. ''I can understand why Catherine doesn't want to sit around and twiddle her thumbs.''

Jake could see that he was totally outnumbered and wasn't going to stand a chance of getting out of this. He wasn't sure why he didn't want Catie cleaning the house or doing laundry, except that it seemed like an awfully personal thing to be doing for them.

For him.

"Mom's a cleaning fanatic," Matthew chimed in. "She'll probably drive you all crazy."

"Matthew!" Catherine gasped. Her son gave her a knowing look, and she returned a censuring one.

"You'll get paid, then," Jake said by way of conceding.

"I will not," Catherine stated firmly.

"You will or you won't be doing the work," he returned flatly, the decision already made in his mind.

"You can't make me take money," Catherine replied, her voice just as determined as Jake's.

Jake's jaw tightened. He'd been glad to have work to do away from the house after they'd returned from Lubbock. He'd managed to avoid Catie until dinnertime. Now he was having to look directly at her, and it was driving him crazy. He felt an overwhelming urge to drag her from the table and kiss her senseless. Staying away from Catie was going to be his undoing.

He glanced at his son who was taking in the entire conversation. The last thing he wanted was to upset Matthew.

"Let's discuss this outside," he suggested to Catie, shoving back his chair so abruptly that it squeaked across the floor.

Catherine shot him a hard look. "Let's," she agreed, getting out of her seat and following him out the back door.

The June evening had turned slightly cool, but the sky was clear and lit with stars easily seen without the intrusion of city lights. Catherine couldn't get over how beautiful it was. She rarely had the opportunity to leave the city. She was going to spend a lot of time at night watching the sky.

She turned to face Jake, her heart skipping a beat as

she realized that he was standing close beside her. Barely able to breathe, she took a small step away from him. "I really don't want to argue with you about this, Jake," she insisted, and her voice suddenly sounded husky. "I want something to do this summer."

Jake's gaze fell on Catherine's face, and all he could think about was kissing her. He wondered how he could be so angry with her and still want to make love to her.

"I don't want you keeping house for us," he stated tersely, his emotions in turmoil.

Catherine's gaze connected with his, her eyes fiery. "And everything has to be your way, is that it?" she demanded. Catherine saw his jaw tighten a fraction. Jake was used to making decisions. Well, she was going to get her way this time.

"I've changed my entire summer plans to stay here with Matthew. Whether you believe it or not, I did that for you as well as for him. I can't sit here all summer long with nothing to do. Now, whether you like it or not, I *am* going to help out around here!"

Finished with her diatribe, Catie was breathing heavily. Jake's gaze took in all of her. Her breasts were rising and falling rapidly with every breath she took, straining against the pale-blue blouse she wore. Her eyes flashed hotly, and her hands rested on her slim hips.

Jake had a feeling he was in deep trouble. He wanted nothing more at the moment than to drag her to the ground and strip her clothes off. He had to fight the desire to show her exactly what she was doing to him.

Grating his teeth, he grunted, "Have it your way."

Catherine frowned. "What?"

Frustrated, Jake swore. "You heard me. Do whatever you want."

A smile caught on Catherine's lips. She hadn't expected him to give in without more of a fight. "Hmm," she taunted. "No more arguments?" She was surprised that he'd given in so easily, and she was enjoying her triumph. She couldn't help flaunting her victory just a little.

Jake stared at her. "Don't push me, Catie," he growled, not at all happy that he was giving in to her.

Catherine grinned up at him. "Or what? What's wrong, Jake? Are you not used to losing, or is it that you don't like losing to me?" She licked her lips, and her eyes lit with teasing.

Jake stared at her, and he wanted to take her down a notch or two. He knew the best way to do that and to satisfy his own itch.

"Or this," he grumbled.

He snaked his hand around her neck and pulled her forward with enough force to press her body flat against his. Her startled cry caused her mouth to open, and Jake took full advantage of it. He clamped his mouth over hers and smothered the sound of protest that automatically came from her.

Catherine's hands pressed hard against Jake's chest. His free arm came around her like a band of steel, molding her against him. The onslaught of his kiss stunned her and left her unable to react, other than to moan with pleasure as his tongue found hers.

Never taking his mouth from hers, Jake deepened the kiss, his lips hard and demanding, and Catherine responded without giving thought as to why she shouldn't. All sense of reality slipped away from her when Jake's hand slipped up her rib cage and touched her breast.

Her nipples hardened, aching for his touch, and she moved against him, then was immediately aware of his arousal. Before she could react, Jake broke off the kiss and firmly pushed her away from him.

"Be careful in the future not to push me too far," he warned her, trying to get his own breathing under control. "Next time I may not stop, and believe me, you won't want me to."

He turned abruptly and left Catherine standing there staring at his retreating back. She lifted her hand to her lips, swollen now from his kisses. The memory of the taste of him, of how it felt to be pressed against him, rushed over her.

Catherine knew that she was fighting a losing battle. Her heart was in danger, and there was little she could do to protect it when Jake McCall was around.

Eight

The first order of business the next day, Jake had decided, was to find out what had prompted Frank Davis to send a letter to Catie on Jake's behalf. They'd gone into Crockett, which was why he and Catie were waiting in the law offices of Rand Jensen. He'd bought Frank's practice and assumed responsibility for Frank's clientele, and Jake had used Rand's services often enough to be on a first-name basis with his paralegal.

Jake glanced at Catie, who was seated across from him. She'd shown him Frank Davis's letter the morning they were leaving Lubbock to return to the ranch. At that time they'd been barely speaking, so Jake hadn't discussed it with her. But he'd thought about it a lot since then.

It had been brief and to the point, only a couple of sentences to inform the recipient that she'd contacted the wrong person. Jake understood why Catie had been so hurt, but it wasn't as if it was *his* fault. He hadn't known a thing about it. To Jake's way of thinking it didn't excuse what she'd done.

"Come on in, Jake."

Jake looked up and nodded at Peggy Lewis. "Thanks, Peg," Jake said, then waited for Catie to precede him. Peggy led them to a conference room where a stack of folders was sitting neatly on a small, rectangular conference table.

"Make yourselves at home. The files you wanted to see are right there," she said, pointing to the stack. She smiled pleasantly, then promptly left them alone.

Jake grimaced as he and Catie took a seat. He wasn't sure what they would find. He reached for the folders and glanced over them, then chose one to look at. It was labeled Correspondence, and contained a thick stack of papers. Jake moved the folder so Catie could see it, also, which brought him close enough to her to smell her perfume. He had to resist the urge to touch her. Steeling himself, he turned his attention to the letters.

It took a few minutes because the file was in disarray. Frank's wife had been his secretary, and she'd only worked half a day. Jake grunted when he realized they would have to search through the entire file, and even then there was a chance that they wouldn't find any answers.

About halfway through, Jake came upon a copy of the letter that was sent to Catie, with her letter attached. He flipped the pages, then reread the words Catie had written him all those years ago. The anguish she'd felt was apparent. Though she hadn't mentioned the baby, she had practically pleaded with Jake to call her.

"I don't understand," Jake murmured, shaking his

head. Why hadn't Frank asked him about this before he'd answered Catie?

"What?"

"Why would Frank send you that letter?" he asked aloud. He turned the pages over, searching for some kind of answer, but there wasn't even a clue. Frustrated, Jake continued going through the stack. Just as he was about to give up, he spotted a small note written on a scrap of pink paper.

"Damn." Jake studied it, and a distant memory tugged at his mind.

"What?" Catherine asked.

Jake leaned closer to her. "Look at this." He handed her the paper. The date on it was a week after Catie's letter had arrived at Frank's office, and there was a notation that he'd talked with Jake.

"It says, 'Kathleen.'"

Jake swore again, and his lips thinned. "I vaguely remember one day when Frank came out to the ranch on some business. He'd been in a hurry. Just as he was leaving, he asked me if I knew a Kathleen. He said that he'd gotten a letter from someone named Kathleen, but at the time he couldn't recall a last name." Jake sighed heavily. "He never mentioned it again after that, and I never gave it any more thought."

"Oh, Jake." Catie touched his arm.

"Frank must have thought he'd asked me about the right person, then sent a letter to you." He turned and looked into Catherine's green eyes. "I'm sorry, Catie. I never made the connection."

Catherine wanted to cry, and sniffed back the tears threatening to spill from her eyes. So many years. So many hurtful, agonizing years. All because one man made a mistake. Even if she and Jake had never gotten back together, Matthew would have had a chance to know his father. She would have *wanted* him to.

"Don't cry," Jake said, then touched her cheek with the pad of his thumb.

Jake's breath whispered over her mouth, and Catherine's breath caught. She licked her lips, then blinked. A tear slipped from the inner corner of her eye, then slid down her cheek.

"All because of a simple mistake," she murmured sorrowfully.

Jake nodded thoughtfully. "At least the mystery is solved. You know, it's not as if Frank did it on purpose."

Catie moved away, breaking contact with Jake. In essence he was reminding her that she'd purposefully kept Matthew from him. But she didn't apologize. She had thought that Jake didn't want to hear from her. And if he'd loved her the way he'd professed, he would have called her, she silently reasoned. How could he blame her, when he was guilty of the same thing?

Catherine had never been on a horse in all her life. From the looks of things, that probably wasn't going to change. So what if she'd grown up in Texas? Not *everyone* in Texas knew how to ride a horse. She stared at the big gray mare that Ryder had brought out from the barn, watching from a distance as Jake's brother tossed a worn saddle on her back.

Reading her uneasy manner, Ryder patted the horse along her neck. "This is Flo. She's real gentle," he assured Catherine in that charming tone of his.

Looking from Ryder to the horse, Catherine wasn't so sure. She didn't want Ryder to think that she didn't trust his judgment, but something inside her resisted the idea of sitting on the animal. ''I don't know about this,'' she confessed shakily.

''Don't worry, darlin'. Flo will do all the work.'' He gave Catherine a reassuring grin, his mustache turning slightly upward. ''She's done this before, you know. All you have to do is get on, and she'll do the rest.''

When Ryder grinned like that, Catherine knew why Ashley had fallen in love with him. He had a magnetism like no other man Catherine had known. Ashley was a lucky woman.

But no matter what Ryder said, Flo was a big animal and a bit scary, too. ''I don't see why it's so important for me to learn to ride a horse,'' Catherine said, sounding as anxious as she felt.

Ryder gave her a patient look. ''You've been here several weeks and you're already antsy. You've cleaned the house until it's spotless. Ashley told me I'd better get you outside before you go crazy. The best way to deal with excess energy is to get out in the summer sunshine.''

Fluttering her eyes, Catherine replied, ''Shopping works, too.''

Ryder chuckled. ''C'mon. Riding a horse can be fun. Just give it a chance.''

Catherine wasn't so sure about that. Ryder had insisted that Flo was gentle, easy on beginners. He didn't seem the type to lie, but she had a distrustful nature. She put her foot inside the stirrup and jumped. Flo did a little sidestep, then whinnied.

Exasperated, Catherine stepped back and took a breath. ''Maybe I should try another time.''

''Catherine, you can do this,'' Ryder encouraged. ''C'mon, I'll help you.'' He instructed her to put her foot in the stirrup, then when she jumped, he put his hand under her backside and gave her a push upward. Catherine landed in the saddle, her hands grasping the saddle horn as she bent over.

"Don't you have something else to do?" a hard voice questioned, interrupting them. Jake stared at Ryder, his hands on his hips.

Ryder's palm rested along Catherine's backside. He held the reins in his other hand. He'd seen his brother approaching out of the corner of his eye. Ignoring the harsh tone of Jake's voice, Ryder turned his back to him.

"I thought it was about time Catherine learned to ride," he offered, giving Catherine a smile and a wink.

"I thought *you* were going out to the south pasture to check the fencing today," Jake reminded his younger brother. He glanced at Ryder's hand again and didn't think it was appropriate for him to be touching Catie so intimately.

Very slowly Ryder turned to face his brother. "The last time I checked, I was pretty much my own boss."

"I didn't say you weren't," Jake replied stiffly.

"Look," Catherine said, interrupting them, "I'm not too fond of this idea, anyway. Why don't I just—"

Ryder touched Catherine's thigh, then took note of the way Jake chewed at the inside of his mouth. "Stay put, darlin'," he said when she made as if to dismount. Without a fraction of hesitation, he confronted his brother with a sharp look.

"Catherine's been working hard for the past few weeks. She cleans the house, does tons of laundry and is one of the best damn cooks Texas can claim. She deserves some time off to relax."

"No one's sayin' she doesn't," Jake countered, glaring at them both.

"Well, she admitted at dinner last night that she didn't know anything about riding, and you didn't exactly jump up and volunteer to teach her." There was an accusation in his tone.

That was true enough, Jake thought. He'd been working with Matthew daily, wanting his son to learn how to handle a horse on his own. He was proud of Matt's progress, too, though he hadn't yet allowed him to ride alone.

"I'll take over now," Jake stated, and he sounded as if it was going to kill him to do so.

Jake had tried his best to stay away from Catie because he was all too aware of his attraction to her. He hadn't *wanted* to teach her to ride until he walked up and saw his brother instructing her. They looked just a little too friendly. Not that Jake thought Ryder would ever betray Ashley, but Catie was a beautiful woman who could turn any man's head.

Ryder gave Jake a sharp look. "With that kind of attitude, Catherine might not want your help," he commented.

"I don't have an *attitude,*" Jake countered.

Ryder's hand went to his hip. "Sure could've fooled me."

Catherine was sure she looked as uncomfortable as she felt. The last thing she wanted was to make Jake feel as if he was being forced to teach her to ride. And she sure didn't want to be alone with him. "Let's not worry about it right now," she insisted, squirming in her seat. "I'm not really ready for this, anyway."

Ryder patted her thigh again, then handed the reins to Jake. "Don't be silly, darlin'. You're goin' to have a ball." Grinning, he stepped back. "She's all yours," he said to his brother. Giving Catherine one of his warmest smiles, he added, ''You're in good hands.''

Catherine didn't doubt that. Jake's hands, as she well knew, were all too capable in more ways than one. He checked the saddle and adjusted it a bit, her heart thumping a little harder as he nudged her leg with his arm.

''Jake, we don't have to do this,'' she insisted, self-conscious from being turned over to him.

He frowned at her. ''Do you think I can't teach you to ride?'' he demanded, giving her that patently challenging look of his.

''I'm not saying that at all!'' Catherine gritted her teeth, trying to think of some way to get out of this.

''Maybe you're afraid to be alone with me.''

His blunt statement silenced Catherine. She swallowed hard, trying to find her voice. ''That's ridiculous. Why would I be?'' she finally replied, bravely leveling him with a stare.

Jake didn't answer. He just turned away from her, and Catherine had no idea what he was thinking. ''Hold on,'' he instructed, then moved forward, leading the horse with the reins.

Catherine fell forward and grabbed at anything to keep from falling. Flo did another little sidestep and lifted her head, shaking her thick mane. Jake almost laughed at Catherine's expression of fear, but appeared to check himself at the last minute.

''Loosen up a little,'' he instructed, giving the horse a reassuring pat. ''You're scaring Flo and making her nervous.''

''*I'm* making *her* nervous?'' Catherine countered, breathless. ''She's the one making me nervous.''

Jake studied the situation. ''Well, she wouldn't if

you'd stop hanging on to the saddle horn as if you were glued to it.''

The tension along Catherine's spine mounted as she contemplated Jake's words. There was no way she was loosening her grip. She tried to straighten her back so it would appear that she was more at ease.

Apparently she didn't fool Flo or Jake a bit. The horse that Ryder insisted was *gentle* seemed uneasy and not at all worthy of Catherine's trust. Jake just glared at her.

''Here,'' Jake said. He brought the horse to a halt, then turned around and stood beside her. ''Scoot up in the saddle.''

Before she knew what he meant to do, he moved her foot out of the stirrup. Then he swiftly mounted the horse and slid behind Catherine, which molded her bottom intimately against him.

His arms came around her, and he pried her fingers from the saddle. ''I've got you,'' he said, holding her tight about the waist. ''You need to loosen up a bit. Flo won't have any problem with you riding her as long as she thinks you know what you're doing.''

''Well, I *don't* know what I'm doing,'' Catherine reminded him tightly. ''And I don't think your being up here with me is going to fool her.''

Jake chuckled, then clicked his tongue and jabbed the horse lightly with his heels. Flo responded immediately and moved forward. Instinct made Catherine squeal, but Jake whispered in her ear to take a breath.

Catherine wished she *could* get a deep breath. This was so much more than she'd bargained for when she'd confessed at dinner that she'd never learned to ride a horse. Her breath dammed up inside her, and she knew it didn't have anything to do with riding Flo.

Jake took her hands in his, then gave her the reins, instructing her on how to guide the horse. They rode around in big circles.

"You're still too uptight," Jake commented. "Relax."

Catherine wondered how she was supposed to accomplish that with Jake whispering in her ear, his breath fanning her cheek. Her heart constricted, and the air she'd sucked in got trapped somewhere inside her lungs.

Jake's warm body was wrapped around hers, and Catherine felt as if she was going to melt against him if she relaxed even a fraction. What she wanted more than anything was to be off the horse and out of Jake's arms. But there was no way she was going to let Jake know how he made her feel.

Since the night after dinner when he'd kissed her, he'd done his best to steer clear of her. For the most part Catherine saw him only at meals. He might be physically attracted to her, but he seemed to not want to explore his feelings.

Well, Catherine wasn't stupid. If Jake felt regretful about the night they'd made love, then so did she. It *had* been stupid of her to let it happen. The trouble was, she admitted to herself, she couldn't seem to forget how easily she'd come apart when he kissed her…or how much she still wanted him to.

"Hey, Mom!" Matthew came running up to them, his green eyes big and round. "Wow, you're learning to ride, too!" he exclaimed.

Catherine tried to give her son a confident grin as Jake slowly brought the horse to a stop. She'd been about to let Jake know that she'd changed her mind, that she wasn't really interested in learning to ride.

Now, with the way Matthew was gazing up at her, his eyes aglow, she had to rethink her decision. She didn't want to disappoint him. Forcing a smile, she said, "I'm giving it a try."

Matthew grinned. "Dad says anyone can learn to ride."

Catherine's stomach somersaulted. Matthew had called Jake *Dad.* Twisting around, she looked at Jake, and his gaze collided with hers.

"He asked me this morning if he could call me Dad," Jake told her, his tone thick with emotion.

"Oh, Jake," Catherine said on a whisper, her voice cracking. Tears stung her eyes. Clearly, Matthew's request had taken his father by surprise. She could see how much it meant to him, and her insides melted a little. A tearful smile wavered on her lips.

Jake's gaze fell to her mouth, then traveled back up to her eyes. All of his good intentions about not getting involved with Catie disappeared as he remembered the way she tasted when they'd made love. Everything and everyone around them ceased to exist.

Without even thinking about it, Jake bent his head in her direction. Flo chose that moment to whinny and move, breaking Jake's gaze with Catherine's. Jake grabbed the reins and gentled the horse.

What an idiot, he admonished himself. Wanting Catie was driving him crazy. Without preamble, he dismounted.

"That's enough for today," he stated gruffly. He slid Catherine's foot into the stirrup, then motioned for her to get off the horse. Catherine swung her leg over the side of Flo and slid down, aware of Jake's strong hands on her waist. When she had sure footing, he let her go. She didn't look at him.

"It's getting late. I'd better go see about helping with dinner," she said, looking down and dusting her jeans with her hands. She couldn't bring herself to look at Jake, couldn't bear to let him see how he affected her. "Thanks," she offered, then called to Matthew. "Come on in and wash up."

Jake watched Catherine walk away, admiring the gentle sway of her hips. He thought about having made love to her after all the years they'd been apart, and his body tightened with consuming lust. He wanted to slide into her again, to feel her heat, to see her come apart in his arms.

He'd been with his share of women over the years, but after Maxine he'd never been tempted to form a permanent, lasting relationship with any of them. Only once had he felt like that—a long time ago with Catie.

And she'd lied to you, his mind taunted. *She kept your son a secret, kept him from you.*

Secrets.

Jake couldn't seem to let her deceit go. Everyone important to him had hurt him. His father. Maxine.

Now Catie. Regardless of the letter his lawyer had sent, she should have tried to contact Jake again.

He couldn't allow himself the luxury of trusting Catie. He had too much to lose. Desiring her was one thing. He could handle wanting her. But he couldn't take a chance on getting his heart broken.

Despite his reasoning, Jake watched her disappear into the house, and all he could think about was how much he wanted her.

Damn, he was a fool.

Nine

Catherine wasn't prepared for what was coming. She'd tried and said everything she could think of to get out of it. After that first day, she had assumed that Jake wouldn't continue trying to teach her to ride.

She'd been dead wrong. Ryder had brought it up at dinner the very evening of her first lesson, asking how it went, egging his brother on by declaring that he could teach Catherine to ride if Jake couldn't.

Jake seemed determined not to let Ryder get the best of him. He stated that he was expecting to continue with her lessons each day, just as he was with Matthew's.

After a few weeks Catherine felt as if she was beginning to get the hang of riding. Flo didn't seem nearly as nervous, which made Catherine more at ease, and the two of them appeared to be less leery of each other.

Today was supposedly Catherine's big moment. She groaned as she left the safety of her room and headed toward the front door. Okay, so maybe she was dreading being alone with Jake more than she was reluctant about riding Flo. After all, she and the horse had apparently made peace with each other.

Not Catherine and Jake. There was an unspoken awareness between them that seemed to spark every moment they came into contact with each other. Catherine had endured being alone with Jake without giving him any hints that she was in danger of falling in love with him again.

She wasn't sure how much longer she could go on being near him. She didn't think the attraction she felt was one-sided. The smoldering looks Jake gave her now and then made her shiver with need. He'd almost kissed her the day he'd started teaching her to ride. Catherine had started wondering *when* he would kiss her again.

She crossed the yard and went into the barn. The acrid smells of hay and horses hit her as she walked inside, and she let her eyes adjust to the shadows of the structure. Jake had taught her to saddle Flo, though Catherine still had trouble lifting the heavy saddle on her own.

Russ Logan was in the barn, and she greeted him as she approached Flo's stall. As Catherine led the horse outside, he offered to get the saddle for her, and for that Catherine was grateful. He was a quiet man who kept to himself most of the time, though from comments she'd heard, he was well liked by most everyone who lived on the ranch. And heavens, he was handsome in a rugged, cowboy-of-the-West sort of way.

His eyes seemed to miss nothing. He didn't talk very

much, which didn't exactly encourage idle conversation. Catherine sensed there was a lot to this man, only he wasn't letting anyone close enough to discover much about him.

As Russ lifted the saddle to Flo's back, Catherine raised her hand to shade her eyes from the hot sun so she could study him. Though he seemed nice enough, she was all too aware of his fiery altercations with Lynn. Catherine shook her head thoughtfully. As far as Jake's sister was concerned, Russ Logan was pig-headed and cantankerous. Catherine could see none of those traits in the good-looking, quiet man standing before her.

He turned toward her, and Catherine smiled. "Thanks, Russ."

"No problem, ma'am." Russ nodded, his gaze locking briefly with hers before breaking contact.

Catherine went about the task of securing the saddle, patting Flo and talking quietly to her. She put her hand in her pocket and pulled out a piece of carrot to offer the horse.

"Okay, you can do this," Catherine whispered to herself when Russ was out of hearing distance. Jake was expecting her to ride out with him today. He would be showing up at any moment, and she was determined to appear calm and sure of herself, despite the reservations attacking her at the moment.

Actually she and Flo had gotten along quite well over the past few weeks that Catherine's lessons had taken place. Jake had even complimented her several times.

Catherine put her foot in the stirrup and took a deep breath. She mounted Flo without difficulty, then let out a puff of air. She had wanted to show Jake that she was capable of mastering riding, and she'd worked hard to keep up with Matthew. Leaning forward, she patted Flo affectionately. As she sat up, she caught sight of Jake riding into the yard on his brown roan.

Her heart skipped a beat. She sat straighter, wishing he didn't have the power to make her heart ache so.

He purposefully kept her at a distance, and it annoyed her that Jake still blamed her for not telling him about Matthew. He'd seen the letter the lawyer had written her, had proof that it was *his* lawyer's mistake. Apparently, Jake still needed to accept the fact that she'd believed he hadn't wanted anything to do with her, and to Catherine that had meant her son, as well.

"I see you're ready," Jake commented, his intense, dark gaze sliding over her.

Catherine glanced briefly at him, avoiding his eyes and his piercing stare. "Ready as I'll ever be, I guess."

He nodded, then turned his horse around. They rode out of the yard and around the outside of the fenced pasture toward a patch of trees.

"There's a trail through there," he said, pointing to a barely discernible opening.

Catherine glanced over at him. "You want me to ride through there?" she asked, her tone questioning his sanity. The grove of trees he'd pointed to left a lot to Catherine's imagination. She couldn't even see the trail he was pointing at.

"It'll open up more as we go through," he assured her. "Go on," he encouraged. "You won't be sorry."

Catherine wasn't too sure about that, but she did as she was told and started her horse through the trees.

"Watch out for low branches," Jake warned, calling to her.

Catherine nodded. The small path did open up after

a bit, and she had more room to negotiate the trees. She and Flo seemed to be getting along fine, which was a relief. ''You promise not to throw me,'' she whispered to the horse, ''and I promise I'll give you a nice treat.''

It was dark under the canopy of the trees, and Catherine wondered what wild animals made this their home. She reminded herself to warn Matthew not to come out here on his own.

Even though she had on a sleeveless blouse, she felt a trickle of sweat slide between her breasts. She had to admit that the shade of the trees was a welcome respite from the blazing Texas sun, and she was glad that she'd pulled her hair up into a ponytail and off her neck.

They'd been riding for about fifteen minutes when she saw a clearing up ahead. She turned in her seat a bit to look back at Jake just about the time he called a warning to her. Catherine realized she should have been watching where she was going when she turned back around and was slapped by a tree branch.

''Ouch!'' she cried, then put her hand to her neck. Holding it there, she leaned a little forward, trying to catch her breath. She maneuvered Flo into the clearing and managed to bring the horse to a halt.

Despite the pain from the scrape, Catherine couldn't believe the beautiful sight before her. There was a small meadow and beyond it a large lake surrounded by trees and wildflowers.

Jake rode out of the woods and stopped beside her.

''Are you all right?'' he asked, and his gaze roamed over her face.

''I'm fine,'' she insisted, her hand covering the wound. Tears had gathered in her eyes from the stinging sensation, but Catherine wasn't about to mention it.

Jake shook his head impatiently. "Let me see," he demanded.

"It's nothing," Catherine told him, but she didn't move her hand.

"If it's nothing, you'll let me see it," he reasoned. Leaning over, he reached for her hand.

With the little bit of skill she'd acquired, Catherine urged Flo to start walking again. "I'm okay," she called over her shoulder. She was aware of Jake following her, and she led the way over to the lake. She stopped just short of it.

"Is it okay to let them drink?" she asked, looking in his direction.

He nodded sharply as he dismounted. He took the reins from Catherine and held Flo still while she got down from her horse, then turned the animals loose. With a determined expression he faced her.

"Let me see."

"Jake—"

He ignored her protest and stepped closer, grasping her wrist before she had a chance to move away from him. Catherine caught her breath as Jake removed her hand from her neck.

A string of curse words flowed from Jake's mouth as fluidly as hot lava out of a volcano. Several deep, red welts were striped across the side of her neck, and blood had begun to ooze from the worst one. "What in hell did you do to yourself?" He tilted her chin up and to the side, examining her without really expecting an answer.

"It's nothing," Catherine said again, but she winced when he touched her neck with the tip of his finger.

"Dammit," Jake bit out, "I told you to watch out for the branches."

"I was watching out for them—"

"Not very well," Jake barked. "If you'd been paying attention to where you were going, this wouldn't have happened."

Catherine tried to shake his hand free from hers, but Jake didn't let it go. "I only turned around for a moment," she replied, justifying her actions. "I was going to ask you something."

"Well, you should have been watching where you were going." Jake began dragging her under the shade of the trees and Catherine tried to dig in her heels. Her strength proved no match for his.

"What are you doing?" she demanded, struggling to free his hold on her.

"You're bleeding. The cuts need to be cleaned," Jake told her, his tone stern. With his free hand he retrieved a canteen of water from his saddle.

"Here, give it to me. I can do it," Catherine told him. At the moment she was more concerned about Jake's hands on her than how much the cuts hurt.

Jake ignored her. At the edge of the lake he let her go. "Sit down," he said, pointing to the base of a tree.

Catherine refused, and the look she gave him could have melted a snowman on a freezing winter's day. "Jake—"

"Sit," he ordered again.

Catherine shrugged her shoulders and gave up. She watched as Jake pulled a handkerchief from his pocket. He opened the canteen and poured water over the cloth, then twisted out the excess water. He dropped to his knees in front of her.

"Tilt your head up," he instructed, then helped her with a finger under her chin.

To avoid a clash of minds, Catherine obeyed. However, as soon as the cold, wet cloth touched her neck, she yelped.

"It's okay," Jake said soothingly as he gently dabbed at Catherine's neck, wiping away the traces of blood that had collected along the cut. He slid his other hand behind her head to hold her still. "It's just cold."

Catherine nodded. "It startled me," she admitted, and she hoped he didn't notice the huskiness of her tone. His nearness was disturbing enough without his hands on her. She held her breath, both wishing the moment over and wanting him to keep on touching her.

Jake leaned forward to get a closer look at the scrapes. "We're going to have to clean this better when we get back and put some antiseptic on it," he told her, then looked up. Their gazes collided. Heat radiated between them.

Catherine swallowed hard. She'd been dreading, yet anticipating this moment for weeks. There was no way she could pull away from Jake now. If he didn't want her, it would be up to him to back off. She no longer had the strength to keep him at bay.

"Catie."

His message was clear. Nothing more needed to be said. He wanted her and he let her know it, let her see the desire raging inside him. Yet he waited for what seemed like an eternity before he pressed closer.

He didn't kiss her. Instead he lowered his mouth and touched his lips to the tender area of her neck, soothing it with his mouth in a way that a healing cream and a bandage could never do.

"Oh, Jake," Catherine whispered, and the sensations

he made her feel stole her breath. ''Jake.'' She put her hand against his cheek as his tongue slid out and caressed the sensitive area.

Without even thinking about it, Catherine went up on her knees and pressed her body against Jake's. She wanted to guide his mouth to hers, but Jake made slow work of easing the pain from her cut and the result of his ministrations started a burning sensation in the deepest part of her.

Catherine had known it would come to this. She should have been strong enough to resist temptation. But she knew she and Jake shared something special. The years that had passed hadn't changed that.

''Please.''

Jake answered her plea by covering her mouth with his. Pleasure soared through her, piercing every nerve along her spine, making her ache for so much more.

Catherine knew that being with Jake like this wasn't in her best interest. A voice was whispering to her to stop things before they went too far, not to let Jake back into her heart. She was taking a chance on getting hurt by this man once again.

Jake drew Catherine against him, and she felt his hardness against her belly. All reasonable thought left her at that moment. He groaned low in his throat as their bodies touched intimately, her breasts grazing his chest. Catherine grasped his shoulders and held on to him as if she were in danger of falling off a cliff. His tongue slid into her mouth, searching, desperately seeking hers.

Catherine couldn't breathe. Jake's kisses seemed to overpower her. She pressed even closer, wanting to feel him against her, to feel the heat of his body seep into her.

Jake tugged at her shirt, yanking it up until he could slide his hand beneath it. He covered her breast, then molded it in his palm, stroking her, sending shafts of heat racing through her.

He pulled away from her, his gaze heavy-lidded with desire. He lowered his hands and locked them around her waist. "I want to see you," he rasped. "Take off your shirt."

His demand didn't shock her. Catherine complied, wanting the same thing. She needed Jake's touch, needed to feel his mouth on her breast. Her gaze remained fixed with his as she slowly unbuttoned her blouse, tantalizing him, enjoying the power she had over him. She slipped the last button free, then prolonged the moment of exposing herself to him by reaching behind her back and unsnapping her bra.

Her breasts were aching now, swelling, yearning to be stroked. Catherine slid her blouse off, then her bra. She put her hands beneath her breasts, lifting them, and Jake lowered his mouth to her, first touching each nipple briefly with a kiss, then grazing them with his teeth.

Catherine hissed as Jake finally settled his attention on one of her breasts. He licked her with his tongue, then sucked her into his mouth. She moaned deeply as his hand covered her other breast, massaging it, then swirling her nipple between his fingers.

"Jake."

It was a cry for more, and Jake's hands slid to her bottom, then intimately pressed her closer. "This is how much I want you, Catie," he admitted. "Tell me you want the same thing," he demanded.

"Yes," she confessed.

Jake eased her down to the soft patch of grass beneath them and covered her body with his own. Catherine's arms slid around his shoulders to the back of his head, holding his mouth to hers.

She trembled in his arms as his hands searched and discovered the softness of her body. Catherine gave herself to the moment, to the ecstasy of being touched by Jake, being intimate with him. Maybe she couldn't have him forever, maybe that wasn't to be, but she was with him now, and she was reveling in his lovemaking.

Jake slipped open the button of her jeans and slid the zipper down, exposing her white silk panties. Catherine lifted her hips as he tugged her pants from beneath her. With ease, Jake removed her shoes, then the remainder of her clothing.

Catherine lay exposed before him, and Jake made quick work of shedding his clothes before lying beside her in the grass. He couldn't believe she was there with him. He ran a finger across her cheek to the base of her throat. She lifted her head, her eyes searching his as he lowered his hand to cup her breast.

Her eyes closed momentarily, then opened again as his hand slid lower, across her abdomen, then lower still. Her hips arched when he touched the core of her, and Jake took his time learning every inch of her body once again.

"Oh, Jake." She whispered his name between her teeth. Her hand slid behind his neck, drawing his mouth to hers. "Kiss me, Jake."

He lowered his head and gently touched her lips, then his mouth rested on hers, feasted on hers, until they were both breathing heavily.

Jake slid over her, his body hard and ready, aching to feel her warmth, to be inside her. Catie opened her legs for him, and Jake slid into her.

"Ah, Catie," he whispered, sinking deeper as the

words left his mouth. ''You feel so good.'' His lips nudged hers as his hips rocked against her. Catherine moaned low in her throat as she returned his kisses.

She spread her legs wider, and Jake gave her more of himself, pushing against her hips. His hands grasped her buttocks, lifting her to him, giving him deeper access.

''Yes,'' Jake grated, his teeth clenched. ''Take all of me, Catie.'' His hips rocked faster, and he was rewarded by the glazed look in her eyes as her pleasure came to her.

''Oh, Jake...Jake.''

Jake lost control, pumping his hips harder and faster until he couldn't think, couldn't comprehend anything except the gratification of being with Catie, of loving her body. He felt himself slipping into a void, and a low growl came from deep inside him as he slipped over the brink of reality into a world of wonder and fulfillment.

In the aftermath, as he lay naked with Catie, Jake could remember many times when he'd made love to this woman. His heart seemed heavy, constricted by the thoughts rushing at him.

What was he thinking, letting things go this far with Catie? He closed his eyes and admonished himself with a few silent words.

''We always were good together, weren't we, Jake?'' Catherine whispered.

Jake pulled away and looked down at her. ''Catie—''

''Don't you dare apologize, Jake McCall,'' she warned him, her tone suddenly curt. ''Neither of us planned on this, but I'm perfectly capable of handling an affair—''

His sharp look stopped her words. *An affair.* Jake should have been pleased that she was looking at the situation so pragmatically. Apparently she wasn't looking for a commitment. Well, neither was he, so he should have felt relief instead of this odd sense of irritation.

Hell, she was right. They'd always been good in bed.

"I don't know what it is about you, Catie. I take one look at you and my sanity disappears."

He said it grudgingly, already regretting letting Catherine a little closer to his heart. Turning his back to her, he gathered their clothing and handed Catherine hers. He dressed, then watched as Catie finished, her fingers fumbling with the buttons on her blouse.

She was beautiful, bewitching, and Jake knew he was in trouble. His heart thudded heavily in his chest, an ache he couldn't quite identify. He had a gut feeling this was going to end badly…for both of them. Nothing good could come out of them having an affair. Jake had nothing to offer Catie.

That they were still physically attracted to each other didn't mean anything. They only had Matthew in common. They lived different lives in different cities. In a few weeks, Jake reminded himself, Catie would be leaving to go home.

Catherine finished dressing and turned toward him, brushing her hair away from her face with her fingertips. "What did happen, Jake?" she asked quietly.

Jake knew what she was asking. He didn't have an answer for her now, any more than he had the first time they talked. "You know what happened." He said it more brusquely than he intended. He hadn't thought about compromising the situation between them. He should have been thinking about Matthew instead of his mother.

Catie didn't know everything about him, and to Jake's way of thinking she didn't need to. She was still young, still had the chance to find someone to love, get married and have more children. Something Jake couldn't give her.

"You never called me."

Jake buckled his belt, then rested his hands on his hips. "I meant to. I swear I did. There was just so much to do when I got home." He shook his head. "Catie, if I had known about Matthew, I'd have found some way to be there for you." He briefly thought of mentioning the accident, then stopped himself. He just couldn't talk about it with her.

She looked as if she wanted to believe him, but still had doubts. Jake didn't know what to say to convince her. Apparently, she wanted to believe the worst about him. He didn't pretend to know what it had been like for her, raising Matthew on her own.

"How did your parents take it?" he asked, raising a brow in question. "Were they upset when you told them?"

"What do you think?" Catherine answered, her defensive tone giving clue as to her parents' reaction. She tucked her blouse into her pants, then walked to the edge of the lake, away from him.

Jake followed her. "Tell me what happened," he said.

"Oh, you don't want to know." Catherine kept her back to him.

Jake reached out to touch her shoulder, then stopped himself. Just the thought of touching her made him hard, made him want to strip her clothes off and make love to her again. She'd said she could handle an affair. It crossed Jake's mind to wonder if he could.

"Tell me, Catie."

She turned to confront him, and all the sorrow of the past was in her haunted green eyes. "They disowned me."

It took a moment before he absorbed the shock of her words. "What?" Jake grated, anger pulling at him.

She twisted her hands back and forth, locking her fingers together, then separating them again. "I worried for days about how to tell them. I knew they'd be upset, that they'd be disappointed." She took a deep breath, as if she needed it to go on.

"What did they say?" Jake prompted when she stopped speaking.

"I waited as long as I could before telling them. Finally, when I got the letter from your attorney, I realized that you weren't going to call me." She sniffed, then ran a hand through her hair. "As much as I hated to admit it, I wanted their support. I needed someone to listen, to reassure me that everything was going to work out."

She trembled violently, her body visibly shaking. She held her arms in an effort to control herself. "My father called me a slut. He said I had no morals and that God was punishing me for being weak."

"Oh, Catie, I'm sorry." Jake reached toward her, but before he could touch her, she shrank away from him.

"I wanted so much for them to be there for me." Tears came to her eyes and still she held them back. "Of course I expected them to be upset. I knew my pregnancy would be shocking, but in my heart I'd hoped and prayed that my parents would love me, that they would want to help me.'' She sobbed then, the tears finally breaking through. Her shoulders slumped as she raised her hand to her face, covering it.

''Catie, come here.'' Jake reached for her again, and this time she didn't resist. He pulled her into his embrace and wrapped his arms around her, holding her against him, rubbing her back with his palm. ''I'm so sorry you had to go through that on your own.''

''Jake, they wouldn't even let me see my sisters,'' she told him on a ragged breath. ''They said I was a bad influence, that I didn't deserve to ever talk to them again.'' The tears in her throat stopped her from speaking.

Jake had never met Catie's parents, but from what she'd told him, they were strict, especially her father. He remembered being in the room when Catie talked with her father on the phone, and the times she'd cried afterward.

''Hush, Catie. They can't hurt you now.''

Catherine cried harder as she stood in his arms. All of the years of hurt and pain came rushing at her. She allowed herself the luxury of being held by Jake, of feeling his powerful arms surround her with warmth and strength, something she'd needed for so long.

Finally she sniffed and looked up at him, her eyes swollen with tears. ''Bethany and Sarah would be in their twenties now,'' she commented, her tone filled with sadness. ''I wanted so much to talk to them, to tell them that I loved them, but my father made me leave that day before they came home from school.''

Jake tightened his arms around her. ''I know that must have hurt you.''

Catherine shook her head. ''I never saw them again. I've written them letters, but they've never answered them. I don't know if they don't want to see me or if my father never let them have my letters. After a while the envelopes started coming back unopened. My parents must have moved away.''

Jake ran his hand up to the back of her neck, then his palm cupped her chin, lifting it so he could see her face. ''I'd give anything to be able to go back and change things for you. I want you to believe I would never have let you go through that on your own.''

''It doesn't matter anymore,'' she said, then abruptly pushed out of his arms and away from him. ''I don't know why I told you all that, except that you caught me at a bad moment,'' she insisted. ''I've learned to live with it.''

Jake figured it must have been tough for Catie, but he wasn't ready to let his heart soften toward her. She still hadn't explained why she'd kept Matthew a secret from him.

''Twelve years is a long time, Catie. Don't you think you could have found time to tell me about Matthew during that time?'' She shot him a look then, full of guilt or remorse, he wasn't sure which.

''You know I tried to contact you. I even left messages at your house.''

Jake nodded. ''That was when you first found out?'' he asked pointedly. She nodded. ''What about later? What stopped you from calling me sometime during the twelve years my son was growing up?''

Catherine bit at her bottom lip as she contemplated her thoughts. ''When I got the letter from you—''

''You know I didn't send that letter,'' Jake interrupted, his tone insistent as he began to rebuild his defenses toward her.

''Regardless, Jake, I *thought* you did. You need to

try and understand how I felt. I believed you didn't want anything to do with me. I wasn't going to force myself or my son on you."

Jake looked over at the lake, his expression solemn. "I wish I'd known. I would have been a part of his life. I've missed so much, so many years that I can never get back." Inside, he couldn't seem to let it go.

"I know." Catherine started to touch him, then instinct stopped her.

"Matthew is the most important thing in my life now. I'm not going to let you keep him from me any longer." It sounded like a warning. Jake intended it to. Regardless of the fact that they were attracted to each other, that they'd made love, Jake wasn't going to let anything, or anyone, not even Catie, come between him and his son.

"Oh, Jake, I know that," she whispered. "Whatever happens, I want you and Matthew to spend time together."

Whatever happens. Jake took that statement for what it was worth. If a summer fling was what Catie wanted, he was going to oblige her.

He leaned down and brushed his mouth over hers. The kiss, which began as a light meeting of their lips quickly became much more. Jake had to pull away. Kissing Catie wasn't the only thing he wanted to do with her at that moment.

"I guess we'd better get back before someone comes looking for us."

She licked her lips, then nodded. Together they walked toward the horses who were grazing nearby. Jake made sure Catie had no trouble mounting Flo, then he whistled. His horse obediently trotted over to him, and he swiftly climbed up on him.

Catherine let Jake lead the way, following closely behind him. She'd told Jake that she could handle an affair. Now she just had to prove it. Making love with him had only reassured her of how much she loved him. Was it wrong to relish every moment she could have with him, knowing that in a few weeks she'd be going back home and leaving her heart here?

Catherine sighed deeply. Her heart had been terribly bruised once by this man. She had never expected to fall in love with Jake again.

When they arrived at the barn, Jake dismounted, then held Catie's horse for her. "Let's get you inside," he said. Before they took a step, Matthew came running up to them.

"Hey Mom, Dad, guess what—" He stopped speaking and his eyes widened. "Mom, what happened?" he asked, then darted a questioning look at Jake.

"It's nothing," Catherine said in a rush to reassure her son. "Jake and I were riding through some trees, and a branch hit me. That's all. It needs a little cleaning."

Matthew didn't look quite convinced. "Does it hurt?" he asked, and he looked worried.

Jake was proud of his son at that moment. When Matt had first come to the ranch, he'd been so afraid that Catie would take him home that he was angry with her for a while. Since he learned he could stay for the summer, he'd gradually let down his guard. He was genuinely concerned about his mother.

"We're on our way up to the house to do just that, Matt. How about taking care of the horses for us?"

"Sure." Matt smiled and eagerly took the reins.

Jake and Catherine started for the house. As soon as

they entered, they ran into Lynn. She took one look at Jake and stated, "I swear that man is the most disagreeable, ill-tempered man I've ever had the displeasure of knowing." She yanked off her gloves and slapped them against her thigh.

Jake's gaze darted to Catherine. "Russ."

Catherine's brows lifted as Lynn continued her tirade.

"He thinks he knows everything. *And* he thinks I'm incapable of learning the smallest of tasks. I don't know how much longer I can put up with him. He's so—" Her gaze went to Catherine's neck. "What on earth happened to you?" she cried, her own problem temporarily forgotten.

"I had a run-in with a tree branch while Jake and I were out riding," Catherine stated.

Lynn moved nearer to get a better look. "I'll say you did. That must really hurt."

Catherine nodded, remembering how much it had hurt until Jake had started kissing her and licking it with his tongue. The pain from her cut had been easily forgotten as he'd awakened every sensual nerve ending in her body. She tried not to blush, but her cheeks reddened slightly. "It does," she admitted.

"What's going on?" Ashley asked, coming from the hallway and stopping beside them. She had a baby on each hip.

"Catherine got hurt while riding," Lynn told her, taking one of the babies and cuddling her. She kissed the top of Melissa's head.

Ashley saw the red welts. "Oh, my goodness! Catherine, come into the bathroom, and I'll help you clean that."

Jake grabbed Catherine by the arm. "You look busy.

I'll do it,'' he told the two women. Before they could answer, he dragged Catherine from the room, leaving Lynn and Ashley standing in the foyer with surprised looks on their faces.

''Whoa,'' Lynn commented, raising her blond eyebrows and rolling her eyes. ''Did you get a whiff of that testosterone?'' She grinned.

''Sure did,'' Ashley agreed, smiling. Her gaze met Lynn's. ''The next few weeks should prove to be quite interesting.''

Lynn nodded, and the two women shared a knowing look.

Ten

Catherine heard the shower running in the bathroom between her room and Jake's. It had been over a week since they'd made love, and her body seemed to be craving his. Jake and Ryder had been out with some of the ranch hands hunting a wild animal that had attacked cattle grazing in the north pasture.

Instead of returning home every day, they'd camped out until they'd tracked the animal down. Finally, this evening, they'd rode in, and Catherine had been so relieved to see Jake. Only she hadn't been able to throw her arms around him as Ashley had with Ryder.

Catherine had been worried about Jake, but she'd limited herself to discussing his safety along with that of Ryder's when talking about how dangerous it was to be out with rifles in the dark wilderness.

Ashley and Lynn had assured her that the men were fine, that this was a part of ranch life, but to Catherine's way of thinking, that didn't matter. She'd wanted Jake to come home safely.

Now he was naked in the shower, and she wondered if she was brave enough to do what she was thinking. She quickly unbuttoned her blouse and slipped it off. The rest of her clothes were shed in a hurry, before she lost her nerve.

She'd told Jake she could handle an affair. It didn't matter now whether she could or not. She wanted to be with him, even though they only had a short while before she had to leave. Jake hadn't *seemed* opposed to the idea. If he was, she was going to make a big fool of herself.

With her hand shaking, she tried the bathroom door. Relief washed over her when she realized he hadn't locked it. As she stepped in, steam engulfed her. She took a deep breath, then moved the shower curtain aside.

"Jake?"

"Catie." Jake stepped from beneath the spray, his expression momentarily one of surprise. Shock quickly gave way to desire. His eyes widened appreciatively as he stared at her naked body. He didn't say a word as he held his hand out to her.

Catherine hesitated a moment, her gaze sliding over his hard-muscled chest, down his flat belly, but before she could look further, he reached for her, drawing her into the shower and against him. Water ran freely over them. He was hard against her, making her feel powerful and seductive.

"Ah, Catie," he whispered, then his mouth lowered to hers. Catherine lost her breath as he kissed her deeply. She clung to him as his tongue caressed hers. Erotic thoughts raced through her mind as his hands glided along her back. She sighed with pleasure as he grasped her buttocks and pressed her intimately against him.

"I guess it's okay that I surprised you, huh?" she asked when his mouth finally released hers.

"You can surprise me like this anytime," Jake answered, his voice raw with desire as his gaze met hers. His hand slid up and down her back, sending her nerve endings into a frenzy. "You feel wonderful."

"You do, too." She slipped her hands over his broad shoulders and around his neck as she lifted her lips and placed kisses along his mouth and neck. "I was worried about you," she confessed.

Jake grunted as her tongue grazed his. "It took a lot longer than we thought it would," he told her, capturing her mouth beneath his for a moment, nipping her bottom lip with his teeth. His hand found her breast, and he grazed the hard peak of her nipple with his thumb. "I thought about doing this to you the whole time I was away."

"You did, huh?" she asked, then she moaned when he lowered his mouth and captured her breast with his lips. He sucked on her hungrily.

"Yeah," he answered. "I wanted to touch you like this." He ran his finger down her middle and between her legs. "And like this." He slipped his finger into her and she arched her body against his hand.

"Oh, Jake." Catie felt her world slip a little. Jake had the power to make her wish she could have him for a lifetime. "Mmm, Jake, that feels so good."

"What about this?" he asked. He kissed her other breast, sucking her nipple greedily, then ran his tongue along her belly. He dropped to his knees and looked up at her.

Catie felt her legs go weak. "I think we'd better get out of here before I can't move at all."

"In a minute," he promised. His warm tongue touched her, and Catherine's head fell back as her world exploded right then and there.

"Jake."

After a moment he stood and faced her. "Turn around," he commanded, then helped her with his hands on her shoulders. He kissed her neck as he ran his hands along her rib cage, then cupped her breasts. Catherine pushed against him and he grunted with gratification.

"You're killing me," he whispered in her ear, his tongue slipping out to trace the pink shell. His teeth nibbled her lobe. Her hips rocked back against him and he groaned. "Mmm, Catie, I think you're right." He leaned over and turned the faucet off. "I can't wait much longer. I want to be inside you."

Catherine started to grab a towel, but Jake prevented her. "Let me," he whispered, wrapping a towel around his waist. She stood docilely as he gently rubbed the soft fabric over her body. Never before in her life had Catherine believed that something as simple as drying her body could be so sensually awakening. Her entire being felt as if it was on fire.

Jake dried her hair, then ran the towel down her back. He watched her as he moved it between her legs. Ripples of pleasure shot through her, and Catherine had to brace herself by putting her hands on his shoulders. "Jake, please."

He rose to stand beside her, his gaze locked with hers as he dried the remaining water from his body. He threw the towel to the floor, then pulled her toward him. Before she could say anything, he swept her into his arms and carried her to his bedroom. Together they fell on the bed. Jake rolled over on his back and pulled Catherine on top of him.

Spreading her body over his, Catherine writhed against his manhood, and he hardened even more. She kissed his chest as she raised herself above him. Then he was inside her, and her whole world seem to shatter. There was no buildup of desire, just fireworks rocketing through her body.

Catherine moved her hips, and Jake pushed deeper into her. She sighed as a million lights burst into a display of colors in her mind. Unable to remain upright, she fell across him and his arms surrounded her.

She found his mouth, and their tongues intertwined as Jake grasped her buttocks, his touch urgent as he sought his own release. She shuddered, her body quivering with erotic pleasure as his muscles tensed.

She loved this man with all of her heart. And in a couple of weeks she was going to have to leave him.

''Are you going to take a break all day or do you plan on doing any work?'' Jake demanded, his gaze raking his brother Ryder as he leaned casually against the fence post. They'd been repairing the roof on one of the barns for the past two days. At the rate they were going, they'd be at it all day tomorrow unless, as Jake saw it, Ryder got off his butt and started working.

''What the hell is your problem, big brother?'' Ryder demanded, casting Jake a sharp, observant look. ''You've been as cantankerous as a rodeo bull all morning.'' He swigged down cold water from a thermos, then capped it.

''Nothing's the matter,'' Jake denied, his tone biting.

Ryder eyed his brother speculatively. ''This

wouldn't have anything to do with Catherine and Matthew leaving in a few days, would it?''

Jake's gaze met Ryder's. ''No, it wouldn't.'' His denial came too quickly, and his brother arched one brow.

''Yeah, right.'' Ryder shoved away from the fence and approached Jake. ''What are you going to do?''

''About what?'' Jake asked, not willing to get into a personal conversation about Catie. The fact that she was leaving soon had been eating at him for the past week. He'd gotten too used to having her around—too used to having her in his bed. They'd managed to make love together every night since that day in the shower. In a houseful of people, that was quite an accomplishment to keep secret.

Exasperated, Ryder took a deep breath. ''About Matthew. Are you going to let Catherine take him back to Lubbock?''

''What choice do I have?'' Jake said, leaning an arm against the fence. ''I asked Catherine to let him stay the summer and she did. I can't ask her to let him live here.''

Actually, he'd wrestled with the thought of doing just that. He wanted his son on his ranch. He didn't want another day to pass, when his son would grow and change, without being close enough to enjoy it. Watching Catherine leave was going to be hard enough. He didn't want to lose Matthew, too.

''You could ask Catherine to stay,'' Ryder commented, then slanted a look in his brother's direction.

''That's not going to happen,'' Jake stated firmly.

''So you haven't gotten over the fact that she didn't tell you about Matthew?'' Ryder asked pointedly.

Jake grunted. ''You think I should forget that she kept my son a secret from me for twelve years?''

Sleeping with Catherine, making love to her, hadn't softened Jake's stance on how he felt about her keeping Matthew from him for so long. Jake had tried, really tried, but he couldn't seem to let it go. Just as he couldn't forget about what his father had done.

"What purpose does it serve to continue to be angry about it?" Ryder asked.

Jake glared at his brother. "You don't have any idea what it feels like to have someone lie to you like that."

Ryder tugged at his mustache with his fingers. "Ashley kept her pregnancy a secret from me. I seemed to have learned to live with that," he reminded Jake.

"That isn't the same thing," Jake told him, wondering what Ryder would think, how he'd feel, if he knew the truth about their father. If he did, maybe he would understand why Jake wasn't able to forget, or forgive, what Catie had done.

Ryder frowned. "As I see it, it's exactly the same thing." There was something in his brother's eyes, a deep sadness that Ryder didn't think had anything to do with Catherine. "What aren't you telling me?" he asked.

Jake turned his back and started to pick up a piece of plywood. "Lay off. You don't want to know."

Without meaning to, Jake had piqued Ryder's curiosity. "What the hell is eating at you? It's more than what Catherine did, isn't it?" he pressed. Jake didn't say anything, and Ryder swore. "Dammit, Jake, talk to me."

Jake swung around and faced Ryder. "I'm not your brother—only your half brother," he stated harshly. All the hurt and anguish Jake had been feeling for years was revealed in his dejected tone.

Ryder shook his head, confusion forming his expression. His eyes questioned Jake's statement. "Now I know you're losing it, big brother."

Jake murmured, "It's the truth, Ryder. I didn't mean for you to find out this way."

Ryder looked at Jake as if he had two heads. "What in the devil are you talking about?"

Jake was quiet for a minute, then he said, "I didn't want you to know. I still don't want you to—" He hesitated, then gave in to Ryder's determined expression. There wasn't any way to get out of this now. "I know this is going to hurt, and I don't mean to do that." He waited a moment, then stated, "Dad had an affair with a woman who lived in San Antonio while he was married to Mom. Apparently, the woman got pregnant with me."

"You're crazy. Where did you hear that?" Ryder demanded. His hands coiled into fists.

"It's true," Jake said, aware that his brother was seething. Jake knew how he felt. He'd experienced the same kind of rage when he'd found out. It would be even harder for Ryder to understand. He had shared a special bond with their mother.

"Mom wouldn't have stood for that."

"Apparently Mom did."

Ryder swung at him then, and Jake dodged his blow, blocking it with his arm. He shoved Ryder away, hard enough to knock him into the fence. "It's the truth. I found it out when I took over the ranch. There were papers explaining everything, and a legal adoption by Mom," he explained, his voice rising. "I didn't want to believe it, either," he confessed.

Ryder looked stunned as he straightened and faced Jake. He didn't say anything.

"It makes sense, Ryder, when you think about it. I

don't look like you or Deke or Lynn. You've all got blond hair, and mine's brown. Your eyes are blue, mine are dark-brown. Think about it,'' he stated defensively. ''It's true. I guess they never intended to tell us.''

''Who else knows about this?'' Ryder demanded.

''Just me, now that Frank Davis is dead. And my biological mother, whoever and wherever she is.'' He bit his lip, then said, ''I don't want Lynn or Deke to know.''

Ryder swore, then took a deep breath. ''If it's true,'' he began slowly, as if he still doubted it, ''what difference does it make? You're our brother and you always will be.''

Jake just looked at him, his jaw tight.

''Damn, Jake, did you think this would matter to me or Lynn or Deke?'' he asked. From his brother's expression, it was apparent that Jake had worried about exactly that. ''We have the same McCall blood running through our veins. You're our brother, for heaven's sake!''

Jake said nothing, and Ryder swore again. ''Even knowing about this, you took care of us. If you loved us enough to do that, how can you even *think* that we'd feel differently about you?''

''I don't know.'' Jake shook his head. ''It was a hell of a thing to learn after Mom and Dad died.''

''I guess that's so, but it doesn't change anything. I mean it.'' He put his hand on his brother's shoulder. ''You've been carrying this around for years,'' he commented. ''Is that why you've been so hard on Catherine?'' Ryder asked.

Jake didn't say anything. He knew Ryder was right—he just couldn't admit as much.

''So you're punishing her for Dad's indiscretion?''

"That's not what I'm doing," Jake told him. "But I can't let myself trust her again."

Ryder glared at Jake. "You're going to just let her walk out of your life?"

Jake favored his brother with a hard look. "I'm not *letting* her do anything. She doesn't live here. She doesn't want to live here."

"Are you sure about that?"

Jake grunted. "She's going back to Lubbock. I'm not going to stand in her way."

"Even if it means that she'll be taking Matthew with her?" Ryder persisted.

Jake looked over the fence at his son, who was out riding in the pasture. "Damn, I'm going to miss him." His voice was strained.

"Then don't let him go," Ryder told his brother. When Jake said nothing, Ryder continued, "Look, I'm no idiot. I've seen the way you look at Catherine and the way she looks at you."

Jake glared at him. "Mind your own business."

"You're going to tell me you don't care if she leaves?"

"I'm not going to tell you anything. Let's get back to work."

Ryder swore. "You're dumber than you look."

Jake sat at the desk in the office and tried to think about anything except the fact that Catie was leaving tomorrow. It wasn't as simple as Ryder made it out to be. Catie was ready to go home. She'd mentioned that she was leaving several days ago. She had a job, a life in Lubbock.

Jake had no right to ask her to stay. As Jake saw it, he had two choices. He could fight Catie for Matthew, or he could accept a custody agreement that would allow him to see his son on school breaks and during the summers.

Jake didn't want to let Matthew go. They'd become close over the summer. It did a little something to Jake's heart every time his son called him Dad. Matthew was the only child Jake would ever have. He couldn't contain the pride that made his chest swell when Matthew looked at him as if he could move mountains.

Catie was the problem. Jake wandered over to the window and looked out. He was immediately aware of the ache in his chest as he watched her talking to Russ. Ryder was wrong. It was lust, not love, he felt for Catie. He couldn't love her. He couldn't *afford* to love any woman.

He had nothing to offer Catie. She was young and vibrant and still had a yearning for life and all it entailed. Over the summer Jake had watched her change. While living on the ranch had come easily to Ashley, Catie had had to work at accepting things moving at a slower pace. She'd seemed happy enough, though, living on the ranch for the summer. Probably because she knew it was temporary.

Jake moved away from the window when he saw Catie heading toward the house. He walked over and stopped in the doorway of the office. His chest grew heavy as she stepped into the hallway.

"Catie."

Catherine smiled when she saw Jake. "Hi." Her heart sped into high gear just at the sight of him.

Jake frowned. "I'd like to speak with you for a minute."

"Sure." For a reason she couldn't state, that one

sentence sounded ominous to her. Catherine tried very hard to keep her breathing steady. This past week had been the hardest in her life. She'd let herself hope that Jake had come to terms with why she'd kept Matthew a secret from him. She'd even let herself dream of them making a life together.

She and Matthew could be happy living on Jake's ranch with all of his family. Though it still hurt that she'd been rejected and disowned by her parents and sisters, Catherine felt so much love and acceptance from the McCall clan. In her heart she secretly harbored the wish that Jake loved her as much as she loved him. The foreboding look on his face, the stern expression in his eyes, warned her that she was living in a dreamworld.

Jake nodded. "Come on in."

Catherine walked through the door, and he slowly closed it. With trepidation, she watched him circle the desk and stand behind it, as if to put distance between them.

"What's the matter, Jake?" she asked, trying very hard to keep herself calm. She moved closer to the desk. Something was about to happen that Catherine felt she wasn't going to like. She could sense it from Jake's distant manner.

He stood quietly looking at her, his expression determined. Then, without blinking, he stated, "I want to keep Matthew here on the ranch with me."

"What?" Catherine didn't exactly understand. Then she figured that he meant until school started. "I wish he could stay a while longer, really I do, but there's a lot to do to get him ready for the beginning of the school year. We have to go back now or else I'd never get everything done."

Even though over the past few weeks they'd become lovers, Jake hadn't made any reference to their relationship becoming permanent. Though Catherine loved Jake, she had her pride. She wasn't going to make a fool of herself and confess her love for him. She had to accept that he didn't love her. Sure, they were still good together in bed, but apparently to Jake that was all she meant to him.

Jake put his hands on his hips. "You don't understand. I want to keep him here permanently."

Catherine swayed, his words knocking her off balance. Her mouth fell open as she stared at him with disbelief. "Oh my, oh, no—" she squared her shoulders "—you want to take him from me." The realization hit her like a heat wave. "I let him come here for the summer so you could get to know each other. I never dreamed—" Her eyes clouded with pain. "This is how you repay me?"

Jake didn't say anything. It was exactly what he'd intended when she'd agreed to let Matthew stay at the ranch for the summer.

"What have you told Matthew?" she demanded. "Did you tell him you were going to keep him here?"

"I haven't said anything to Matthew yet. I wanted to talk it out with you first."

"Talk it out? Well, you can't have him, Jake. How's that for talking it out?" Her eyes darkened, her pupils becoming as black as thunderclouds.

"I'd hoped it wouldn't come to a fight between us," Jake returned roughly.

He'd caught her off guard. She'd never expected him to betray her trust like this. She'd done her part by agreeing to spend the summer on the ranch. This wasn't fair! Her jaw locked as she clamped her teeth together. Finally she took a deep breath, then spoke.

"What? You thought I'd just give up my son without a fight?" Then a horrible thought dawned on her. She'd been such a fool! "Is that what sleeping with me was all about?" she demanded, remembering the way she'd so easily given herself to him. "Was it your plan all along to get me into bed? Did you think that it would be that simple—that for a summer fling I'd let you have my son?"

She began trembling, her body shaking with fury. Her eyes filled with fire. She opened her mouth to speak, clamped it shut again, then turned her back on him and marched toward the door.

Jake started after her. "Catie, wait!"

She stopped, then whirled around to face him. "Leave me alone, Jake." She hated the tears that came then. And she hated the tremor in her voice. She'd have given anything to have appeared strong, instead of on the edge of breaking down.

He frowned at her, and she turned her back to him again. Jake grabbed her arm and made her face him, and she tried to jerk away. She was so angry, so hurt. She looked pointedly at his hand on her arm.

"Take your hand off me."

Jake did, but he didn't move away from her. "I didn't want to do it this way. I never meant to hurt you," he claimed.

"Well, you failed miserably!" she retorted. "If you think I'm giving up my son without a fight, you're mistaken," she cried, her voice vibrating, her throat aching. "I'll fight you with everything I own," she promised. "I swear to you, Jake McCall, in the long run you may win, but I'll die trying to keep Matthew."

Catherine jerked open the door and hurriedly left the office. As she was going down the hallway, she brushed past Ashley without speaking. She couldn't talk to anyone at the moment. She was likely to break down and cry. Jake had hurt her more than she'd ever dreamed possible. She'd trusted him when he'd said he only wanted Matthew to come to the ranch for the summer. All along he'd had other motives—plans to take Matthew from her.

Catherine entered her room in a flurry and rushed to pack her clothes. She was leaving this ranch. Now, before Jake or anyone tried to stop her. And she was taking her son.

Fuming, she threw what she'd brought with her in her suitcase without thought or reason. She would ask Ryder to drive her and Matthew to the airport. If he refused, she'd take one of their damned cars!

What a complete fool she'd been to trust Jake. She had to get away, to distance herself from Jake mentally as well as physically. She'd found it so easy to talk to him, to lean on him, to let him close. Then, without warning, he'd walked on her heart.

Any hope that Jake had feelings for her died the moment he'd told her that he was planning to fight her for Matthew. He couldn't care for her and hurt her like that.

She'd told Jake that she could handle an affair. Well, that's what it had been, no matter how she tried to sugarcoat it. Foolishly she'd let her heart get in the way of her good sense. Now she was going to pay for it.

Jake hadn't really wanted her. He'd wanted Matthew.

"What's going on?" Ashley asked, bewildered. Jake was standing in the doorway, staring after Catherine as she disappeared down another hallway. ''Is Catherine all right?'' She took one look at Jake, and asked, ''What did you say to her?''

''I told her I want to keep Matthew.'' Jake went back into the office. Ashley followed him.

''You didn't!''

''I've missed the first twelve years of his life. I want him here on the ranch with me. He likes it here. He'll want to stay,'' Jake insisted.

''Maybe for a while, because this is all so new to him. But eventually he'll miss his mother, Jake.''

''We'll work out some kind of custody agreement.''

''It didn't sound to me as if you're going to work out anything,'' Ashley commented. ''Catherine was really upset.''

Jake looked away. ''I can't help that.''

''Oh, please.'' Ashley gave him one of her knowing looks. ''Well, did you bother to tell Catherine how you feel about her?''

Jake's gaze swung back to Ashley, but he didn't answer. He sat behind the desk busying himself, making an effort to not give away his thoughts. His sister-in-law didn't give him the opportunity to ignore her. She marched over to him and stood in front of the desk.

''Jake.''

''Ashley—''

She put her hands on her slightly rounded hips. ''You love her, don't you?''

That brought Jake's gaze to hers again. He didn't deny it, but he didn't admit to it, either. Apparently, that didn't matter to Ashley.

''Jake McCall, have you lost what good sense God gave you?'' she demanded.

Jake returned her stare, his brows drawn together. ''You seem to think so,'' he returned flatly.

Letting out a frustrated groan, Ashley leaned over the desk and placed her hands flat on it. ''Are you telling me that you don't love Catherine?'' she asked, lowering her voice in a way that made Jake feel like a trapped animal. ''Jake, anyone with eyes could tell what was going on with you two over the summer.''

Jake had thought that he and Catherine had been very discreet. It was disconcerting to find out differently, first from Ryder, now from Ashley. ''It's complicated,'' he said defensively. How he felt about Catie wasn't the issue. She was better off without him.

Ashley didn't let him off the hook. ''Well, suppose you explain it to me.''

Jake looked away and shuffled some papers in front of him. ''You know I have nothing to offer her.'' Jake wasn't used to discussing personal matters about himself. And he damn sure didn't like where this conversation was going. Ashley, it seemed, wasn't going to give up.

''That's the most pathetic excuse—'' she began, then caught herself before continuing. ''Oh, Jake,'' she whispered on a sigh. Ashley's gaze softened as she lowered her voice. ''This is about your sterility, isn't it? Did you even discuss it with Catherine?''

Jake's chest tightened. ''It's not up for discussion,'' he returned, his voice hardening a fraction.

Ashley straightened and put her hand on her back. ''It's why you're letting her leave.''

''Catherine's still very young. She can have other children if she wants. I won't trap her in a relationship she'll likely regret.''

"How do you know she wants more children? Did you talk with her about it?"

"No, I didn't," Jake answered irritably. "And I'm not going to. And I'm not talking about this any longer." He stood and reached for his hat. "I've got some things to do. I'll be back later."

"Jake—"

"End of discussion, Ashley," he stated, his tone sharp. He gave her a half-apologetic look. "I mean it."

He stalked to the door and walked out.

Eleven

Jake walked outside the house just in time to see Matthew disappear inside the barn. Stepping off the porch, he headed in the same direction, thinking about asking his son if he wanted to go riding. Matt would jump at the chance. He loved riding that much, seemed to love living at the ranch.

"Hey, son." Matthew looked in his direction as Jake walked inside the barn.

"Dad!" Matthew smiled happily.

"Wanna go for a ride?" Jake asked, already knowing the answer.

"Sure," Matthew agreed quickly. "Can we ask Mom, too?"

The pressure in Jake's chest tightened, causing it to ache. He wasn't surprised by Matt's request. The three of them had gone riding several times lately. "Not this time. How about if it's just us guys?" he suggested.

"Great."

Together they saddled the horses, then a short while later they rode around the corral and toward an open pasture. Jake's heart ached with devotion. He'd never known how much a man could love a child until he'd had a chance to know his son.

They chatted as they rode, but that didn't keep Jake's mind from returning to his argument with Catie. He hadn't meant to hurt her. His motives had been selfish, he knew. But he wanted nothing more than to have Matthew with him all the time, to be an integral part of his son's life.

That Jake wanted Catie also wasn't debatable. He would be a fool if he tried to convince himself otherwise. Somehow, to his way of thinking, Jake had hoped that he could keep his son and still not hurt Catie.

He told himself that he was doing the right thing letting Catie go. She deserved so much more than what he could offer her. She'd had a hard life, and she didn't deserve more heartache.

Many years ago they'd been in love and probably would have married. Jake had never dreamed that he would have thc chancc, temporarily, to be with Catie again.

And he'd never meant to fall in love with her again.

He glanced at his son. Matthew was happy living here. He would probably want to stay, if given the choice of remaining at the ranch or returning to Lubbock. The boy hardly mentioned his friends or his life in the city. He loved his new baby cousins.

What Ashley said flitted through Jake's mind. Would Matthew want to lose his mother in the bargain? Would his son grow to hate him because Jake had hurt Catie? Jake had learned that his son was very protective of her. That was natural, since it had been just the two of them for a long time.

Jake could have his son, but at what cost? Though he wasn't able to tell Catie how much she meant to him, Jake couldn't deny his feelings for her.

And he couldn't take Matthew from her. Admitting to himself that he was in love with Catie, Jake knew he would sacrifice his own wants, his own desires, for her.

After a while Jake said, "I guess we'd better be getting back."

Matthew nodded and turned in the direction of the house. Jake watched his son, who seemed as comfortable on a horse as if he'd been riding all his life. He had McCall blood.

"I'm going to miss you," Jake said, knowing what he had to do. He would have to be the one to take the heat from Matthew. Jake felt the need to protect Catie. It was the last thing he could do for her.

Matthew looked at his father, his brows angled, his expression confused. Jake had known this would be hard, but he wasn't prepared for the way his own heart ached at the thought of letting his son go. "You know you have to leave with your mom."

"Can't we stay here?" Matthew asked, and there was the blind hope of a child's wishes in his green eyes.

"I'm afraid not," Jake answered. "Your mom has a job in Lubbock. You knew that your visit here was just for the summer," he reminded him.

Matthew shook his head. "But I don't want to go. You could ask Mom to stay here," he said hopefully. "Then we could live together like a family."

Jake's heart ached for his son. He didn't want to hurt

him. ''We're not a family, Matthew,'' he said. ''Your Mom's leaving and it's time for you to go, too. But I want you to know how much I love you, and I want you to come here whenever you're not in school. Your mom and I will work out a schedule.''

Matthew's eyes teared. ''Don't you want me to stay?'' he asked.

''That's not possible,'' Jake told his son. ''You have to leave with your mom.''

''Then you don't care about me!'' Matthew shouted. ''I thought you loved me, but you don't!''

''Matthew—'' Before Jake could say anything, Matthew kicked his heels against his horse and the animal took off. Knowing his son was in control of the horse, Jake watched him ride back toward the barn. Slowly he headed in the same direction.

''You're leaving now?'' Jake asked when he saw Catie's bags packed and sitting on the edge of the bed. He stepped into the room. He took his hat off and held it in his hands.

Catherine stiffened when she heard Jake's voice, and her heart tripped over itself. She wanted so much to tell him that she loved him, but she held back, reminding herself of this man's power to hurt her. She couldn't bear to be rejected by him again.

''I called the airline and booked a flight for late this afternoon. Ryder said he would drive us to the airport.'' She looked away and fingered the handle of her suitcase. ''Ashley and Lynn offered to pack Matthew's computer and things and send them to us.'' Moments passed as she waited for Jake to speak.

''Catie, I won't fight you for Matt,'' he finally said. ''I talked with him a while ago. He's pretty upset.''

"I know. He came in crying." Tears sprang to Catherine's eyes. She knew what it cost Jake to make that decision. He was giving in, letting her have Matthew. Her son had come in from riding, angry at his father. Catherine had talked to him, had tried to make him understand that they couldn't stay here. He blamed his father. That had to hurt Jake.

"I don't know what to say, except thank you from the bottom of my heart. Matthew will be all right after a few days. Give him time to come around." She sniffed, then touched a finger to her eyes.

"I want him to come here as often as possible—that is, if he still wants to see me."

She nodded, her throat constricted from holding back a sob. She drew a deep breath and managed to choke out, "Oh, Jake, of course he will." She ran her fingers through her hair, pushing it away from her face.

Jake slapped his hat against his thigh. "I guess that's it, then." He turned to leave.

Catherine watched him walk toward the door. She loved Jake so much, more than she'd ever dreamed possible. In her heart she felt he had to care for her. Was he really going to let her go?

Please tell me you love me.

But he didn't stop when her heart called out to him. She had to stifle a cry of anguish as he walked out of her life.

"We're going to miss you so much," Ashley said, then hugged Catherine, holding her tight for a moment.

"I can't believe you're leaving," Lynn added. "You're going to come back, aren't you?" she asked, giving Catherine a hug, also.

Catherine drew a breath, then blinked back tears. "I

don't know, but I'm going to miss you all.'' She patted Ashley's rounded belly. ''You'll let me know?'' She smiled tearfully.

''I'll call you. I promise,'' Ashley assured her.

Catherine glanced over her shoulder. Ryder and Matthew were waiting at the car. ''I'd better go.'' Unable to stop herself, she looked down the hallway. Her heart was at war with itself. She wanted to leave before she saw Jake again, but she also wished for one last look at him.

Reluctantly Catherine turned and went outside and got in the car, shutting the door behind her. She didn't look back, couldn't bear to. She was leaving her heart with Jake.

''All set, darlin'?'' Ryder asked.

Catherine nodded. She looked at her son. He was slumped down in the back seat, a sullen expression on his face. Well, she knew how Matthew felt. She loved Jake, as well. It was too bad that he didn't care for her in the same way.

Most of the ride to San Luis was made in silence. She and Ryder made quiet conversation, but to Catherine it felt forced. All of her thoughts were on Jake.

Ryder was nice enough to check her baggage through, then walked to the departure gate with her. They waited in silence for about an hour, until Catherine and Matthew's flight was called. Before saying goodbye, Ryder gave Catherine a reassuring look.

''You hang in there, darlin','' he told her, putting his arm around her shoulders. ''My brother's pretty stubborn. All of the McCalls are, and that's a fact.'' He grimaced at the fresh tears that came to her eyes. ''Don't give up on him.''

Catherine nodded, but she'd already given up any

hope of Jake loving her. If he cared for her, if he loved her, he wouldn't have let her leave. She watched as Ryder ruffled his nephew's hair. Matthew threw his arms around his uncle and clung to him until Catherine told her son it was time to go.

''Thank you for everything,'' Catherine told Ryder, hugging him again. ''I wish—'' She stopped herself before speaking what was in her heart.

''Be careful what you wish for, darlin',' ' Ryder told her, then he winked.

Catherine forced herself to return his smile, then she and Matthew boarded the aircraft.

In the time it took to take the flight from San Luis to Lubbock, Catherine tried not to think about Jake or how much she missed him. She'd been unsuccessful. The memories of being with Jake, lying in his arms, making love with him, taunted her. If only...no, she wasn't going to go down that road.

Jake didn't love her. Catherine had to accept that, and she would have to find a way to put her life back together. She was going to be seeing Jake occasionally when he came for Matthew. Somehow she would have to get past the hurt and go on living.

She'd done it once before when he'd left her pregnant and alone. She was stronger now, she told herself. She would find a way to get over the pain of Jake's rejection. She'd have to for Matthew.

When the plane landed, Catherine and Matthew walked off and entered the terminal. She was looking down at Matthew, talking to him, when he suddenly screamed, ''Dad!''

Catherine's gaze swung up and her steps froze.

Jake!

He was standing across the small corridor, leaning casually against the wall, much like the time he'd come to the airport in San Luis months ago to pick her up. Her breath caught in her throat, and the air in her lungs expanded.

What was he doing here?

Matthew darted over to his father, and Catherine was aware that her son's anger with Jake seemed to be no longer an issue. He was so happy to see him. He threw his arms around Jake and hugged his waist. Jake dipped his head and looked at his son, his hat preventing her from seeing his expression. Catherine's heart ached for them both as she watched them embrace. She was so glad that Matthew wasn't going to stay angry with Jake, but she hadn't realized how hard it was to see him again so unexpectedly.

Somehow she found the strength to approach them. As she came closer, Jake looked at her, and their gazes collided.

"Catie."

"Jake."

Jake studied Catie's expression, looking for any sign that she was glad to see him. Instead, her eyes questioned his presence. Well, he deserved that, he supposed. He'd let her leave the ranch. Now he was here to beg her to come back.

He'd thought that once she and Matthew were gone, he would be able to go back to being the man he was before. That wasn't possible any longer, because that man no longer existed. Catie hadn't been gone very long before Jake had realized that letting her go wasn't an option.

He'd gone to her room, and memories of them together surrounded him. Her perfume had lingered in the air, taunting him, reminding him of her. She'd left a few items of clothing on the bed. Jake hadn't sat there long before deciding to go after her in his plane.

He hoped he wasn't too late.

Jake took his eyes off Catie long enough to ask Matthew to go and watch for their luggage to be unloaded. "Go on," he said, "we'll be there in a few minutes." Matthew was eager to please his father and agreed.

"Don't go anywhere else," Catherine called after him.

Matthew frowned at his mother. "I won't, Mom," he answered in a tone that said he was old enough to handle the task given to him.

Jake turned to look at Catie. She was regarding him with a wariness that he felt was deserved. He put his hand on her shoulder and ushered her to a quiet area, out of the path of other passengers.

"Jake, what are you doing here?" Catherine asked, looking shocked and wary.

"I wanted to talk to you," he said quietly, and he watched her expression for any sign that she hadn't given up on him.

"You could have done that back at the ranch," she returned, stating the obvious.

"I know." Jake was feeling a little foolish now. Catie didn't act happy or relieved to see him. He might have come to see her for nothing. He cleared his throat, looked away, then turned his gaze on her face. His stomach began to churn.

Catherine cocked her head and looked at him, her expression guarded. "Well?"

"I know I hurt you. I didn't mean to, but I did."

"Yes, you did," she agreed, her heart aching.

"I'm sorry."

Catherine nodded. ''Thank you for saying so,'' she answered coolly.

Jake grimaced, his jaw tightening. This was harder than he'd ever imagined. ''Are you sorry about the time we spent together?'' he asked.

''We never made each other any promises,'' she said quietly, watching him.

Her lips trembled slightly. It was the first sign that she wasn't as calm and collected as she appeared. Jake tossed his hat in his hands like a big round Frisbee. ''Maybe we should have,'' he told her, and his heart stopped beating.

Her eyes widened slightly. ''What?''

Jake reached out and ran his palm along Catie's cheek. ''I tried to do the right thing. I thought I could let you go, but I can't.'' He waited a moment, then whispered, ''I love you, Catie.''

''Jake—''

He forestalled what sounded to him like a protest with his finger to her lips. ''Wait. Don't say anything yet. Please, just listen to me.'' She nodded and waited, her eyes watching him. ''I was angry with you for a long time for keeping Matthew from me. But I held on to that anger because I knew right here,'' he touched his chest where his heart was beating hard, ''that I was falling in love with you.''

''You were?'' Catherine's gaze softened.

''I thought I could settle for having you beneath me in bed for a while,'' he admitted, then shrugged. ''It was easier to let myself believe that sex with you was enough. That way I could have you, and it didn't matter that you were leaving at the end of the summer.''

Catherine swallowed and licked her lips. She stared at him silently.

"I was a fool, Catie. I'm so in love with you that I couldn't stand to be without you when you left."

"Do you mean that?" she asked, sounding as though she didn't quite believe him. "Really, Jake?"

He nodded, then caressed her face with his fingers.

"Oh, Jake, I love you, too. So much." She smiled at him, excited and breathless. She moved into his arms, and Jake pulled her tight against him.

Jake lowered his lips, then settled his mouth on hers. He kissed her with all the passion pent up inside him. Her arms went around him, and her hands, warm and gentle, settled on his neck. Lifting his head, Jake looked into her eyes.

"There's a lot you don't know, a lot we need to talk about," he told her. Unaware that they were getting curious stares from other passengers, Jake kissed her again, not wanting to let her go.

"Nothing matters except that we love each other," Catherine whispered, sighing with happiness.

"This is important. You have to know everything." Jake stiffened and set her away from him. He hesitated, glancing away. Then he took a deep breath and turned his gaze on her. "I can't give you any more children," he grated.

"Jake—"

"No. Listen. There was an accident years ago. When I returned to the ranch after my parents died. I can't have children."

Catie stared at him. "You can't?" she asked.

"No." Jake swallowed hard.

"And you thought that would make a difference to me?" she asked.

"Of course. You're young enough to have more

children. You work with them, so you obviously love kids.''

''Oh, Jake, the only thing that truly matters is that you love me. I've never given thought to having more children. I never thought I'd fall in love again.''

''Are you sure?'' Jake asked, wanting to believe her.

''I'm sure.'' She looked into his eyes. ''I love you, Jake McCall, with all my heart. I always will.''

Jake kissed her lips lightly, then gazed into her eyes. ''In that case, will you marry me?''

Catherine cocked her head at him, then grinned with delight. ''I thought you'd never ask.''

Epilogue

"You look beautiful," Lynn told Catherine, admiring her ivory satin dress and matching lace veil. "I'm so happy for you and Jake."

Catherine smiled dreamily. "I've loved your brother with all my heart for so long. I can't believe we're finally getting married." They'd planned an intimate family wedding, which included anyone who lived or worked on the Bar M. Both she and Jake hadn't wanted to wait to plan a big wedding.

"*I* can't believe Jake is getting married!" Lynn stated, then grinned. "Maybe now that he's going to have a family of his own, he'll stop trying to run my life."

"He cares about you, Lynn. He wants what's best for you. You know, when your parents died, he didn't even think about himself or his education or what he was giving up to raise you and your brothers. He knew it was his responsibility to make sure his siblings were taken care of.'' Jake had told her of his father's secret, though he'd yet to share it with Lynn or Deke.

Lynn nodded. ''And we love him for it. But we're really happy that he found you and Matthew. He deserves to be happy, too.''

A knock sounded at the door, and they both turned in unison. ''Yes?'' Catherine called as Lynn went to crack it open.

Ryder poked his head around the edge of the door. ''It's time, darlin'.''

Catherine couldn't control the butterflies flitting around in her stomach. She'd waited for this moment forever. ''I'm ready.''

Lynn checked Catherine's dress one last time before leading the way out the door. She'd agreed to be Catherine's maid of honor. Catherine had pleaded with Ashley to be in the wedding, as well, but she'd patted her growing belly and insisted there was no way she would parade around six months pregnant in a formal dress.

Ryder held out his arm to Catherine, and they slowly walked down the hall, then stopped at the doorway to the family room. It had been decorated with an abundance of white ribbons and an array of flowers and greenery. Though it was lovely, to Catherine it really didn't matter where she was married. She'd have been thrilled to marry Jake anywhere, just so long as she could be with him the rest of her life.

Her gaze swept the room, and her heart swelled when she spotted her sister, Bethany. As a wedding gift, Jake had secretly hired an investigator to search for Catherine's siblings, then had flown her sister to the ranch for the wedding. Their youngest sister, Sarah, hadn't been able to come, but Catherine had chatted with her on the telephone, and they were both looking forward to a reunion.

After a long, heart-wrenching talk with Bethany, Catherine had learned that her sisters had never received any of her letters, that their father had told his younger daughters that Catherine had moved and left no way to contact her. Neither sister had known how much Catherine had longed to see them.

As she waited for the wedding march to begin, Catherine's heartbeat quickened. In a corner of the room, Michelle and Melissa babbled with each other in their playpen, oblivious to the ceremony. Ashley had wanted to have the wedding when the girls were asleep, but Catherine wouldn't hear of it. She wanted the entire McCall family present, for they were her family now.

There were quite a few of the ranch hands and their families present, also. Catherine spotted Russ Logan over in a corner, watching from a distance, as if he didn't belong or didn't want to be there, she wasn't sure which.

Ryder had taken his place beside Ashley, and Matthew stood proudly between his father and Deke. Her son had been thrilled to learn that his parents were going to marry and they'd be living at the ranch. Jake had his son's name changed, and Matt had already been registered for the upcoming school year as Matthew McCall.

The music began, and tears of joy formed in Catherine's eyes as her gaze met Jake's. In his dark suit he was so handsome. Just looking at him stole her breath. His gaze remained steadfastly on her as she stopped beside him, and Catherine felt his love flow through her. He reached for her hand and enclosed it in his, and she moved closer, wanting to feel his warmth. ''I love you,'' she whispered.

Jake's heart felt as if it was going to burst. Catie's eyes shone with love as she stood beside him, and he was happier than he'd been in his entire life.

A hush fell over the room as the minister began the ceremony, but Jake was only aware of Catie's presence next to him. He steadfastly repeated his vows to love, honor and cherish her. For Jake, those vows were sacred.

Catie's voice was sure and strong as she spoke. Jake waited until the minister said, ''I now pronounce you man and wife,'' then claimed Catie as his wife with a passionate kiss.

Lifting his mouth, he whispered, ''I love you,'' then he slipped his arm around Catie and drew her tightly against him.

''I love you.'' Catie smiled at him.

Together they gestured for Matt to join them, and Jake gathered his son close to his side, his heart swelling with pride.

This was his family.

* * * * *

SILHOUETTE® DESIRE™

AVAILABLE FROM 20TH SEPTEMBER 2002

EVEN BETTER THAN BEFORE

THE REDEMPTION OF JEFFERSON CADE BJ James
Men of Belle Terre
For Jefferson Cade protecting his only love, Marissa, from danger was easier than living without her had been. But now he was determined to rekindle their passion...and this time he'd never let her go.

A COWBOY'S PROMISE Anne McAllister
Charlie had left Cait Blasingame because settling down wasn't his style. But getting shot had changed his perspective. Now all he had to do was convince Cait they belonged together—forever.

UNDER SUSPICION

THE SECRET LIFE OF CONNOR MONAHAN
Elizabeth Bevarly
Undercover cop Connor Monahan knew he had to bring in suspected madam Winona Thornbury. But it was hard to keep his mind on the case—and his hands off the lady...

ADDICTED TO NICK Bronwyn Jameson
Wealthy, gorgeous Nick Corelli didn't need a new business partner like sexy, spirited Tamara Cole! He thought she must be after his money, but he couldn't resist her...

THE NANNY AND THE BOSS

WYOMING CINDERELLA Cathleen Galitz
Gorgeous multi-millionaire William Hawk was captivated by tantalising nanny Ella McBride. A massive primal desire hammered at his resistance—so for how long could he avoid her bedroom eyes?

TAMING THE BEAST Amy J Fetzer
Loner Richard Blackthorne had hired lovely Laura Cambridge as a nanny for his only child. He certainly didn't want to be attracted to her, but found all he could think about was Laura—as his wife!

0902/51a

THE STANISLASKI
Sisters
NORA
ROBERTS
From the bestselling author of the Stanislaski Brothers, Nora Roberts brings you the spirited, sexy Stanislaksi Sisters.
Bestselling author of Night Tales

On Sale
16th August 2002
Beloved Wolf *by Kasey Michaels*

20th September 2002
The Virgin Mistress *by Linda Turner*

I Married a Sheikh *by Sharon De Vita*

18th October 2002
The Doctor Delivers *by Judy Christenberry*

From Boss to Bridegroom *by Victoria Pade*

15th November 2002
Passion's Law *by Ruth Langan*

The Housekeeper's Daughter *by Laurie Paige*

20th December 2002
Taking on Twins *by Carolyn Zane*

Wed to the Witness *by Karen Hughes*

17th January 2003
The Trophy Wife *by Sandra Steffen*

Pregnant in Prosperino *by Carla Cassidy*

21st February 2003
The Hopechest Bride *by Kasey Michaels*

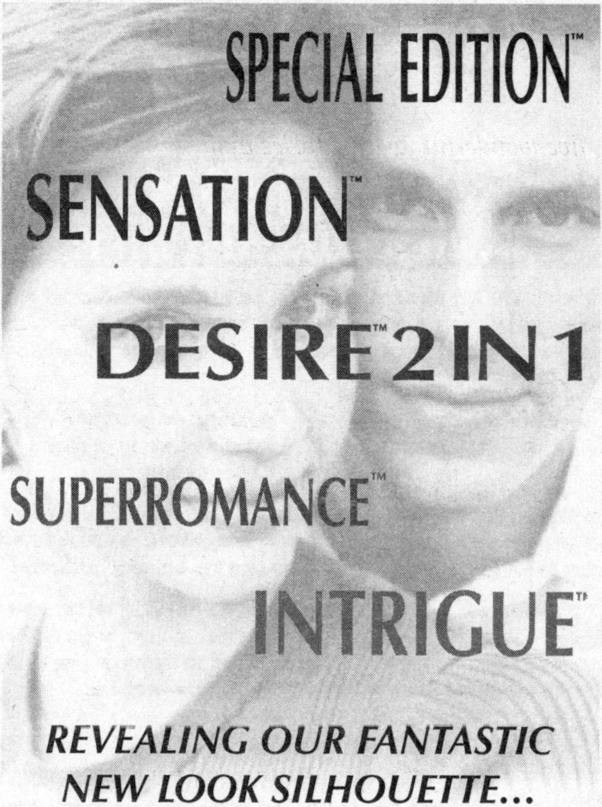
SPECIAL EDITION™
SENSATION™
DESIRE™ 2 IN 1
SUPERROMANCE™
INTRIGUE™
REVEALING OUR FANTASTIC
NEW LOOK SILHOUETTE...